Born in London in 1874, M a scion of a family long pr(
the British Empire. The sc
director of the Bank of Engl
Bros.), he was educated at E
the diplomatic service in 189   ̲ ̲ame a journalist
and reported the Russo–Japa.̲.̲⌐⌐e War in Manchuria; later he
was a correspondent in Russia and Constantinople. He is
credited with having discovered Chekhov's work in Moscow
and helping to introduce it to the West. Baring is remembered
as a versatile, prolific and highly successful writer, who
produced articles, plays, biographies, criticism, poetry,
translations, stories and novels. He is regarded as a
representative of the social culture that flourished in England
before World War I, his work highly regarded to this day for the
acute and intimate portraits of the time.

MAURICE
Baring

Tinker's Leave

HOUSE OF
STRATUS

This edition published in 2001 by House of Stratus, an imprint of
Stratus Holdings plc, 24c Old Burlington Street, London, W1X 1RL, UK.

www.houseofstratus.com

Typeset, printed and bound by House of Stratus.

A catalogue record for this book is available from the British Library.

ISBN 0-7551-0110-3

Allegro molto.

Paris China Menders' Tune.

> But shall I go mourn for that, my dear?
>   The pale moon shines by night:
> And when I wander here and there,
>   I then do most go right.
>
> If tinkers may have leave to live,
>   And bear the sow-skin budget,
> Then my account I well may give,
>   And in the stocks avouch it.

SHAKESPEARE

DEDICATION

TO ADM

MY DEAR M,

In former days a Preface was considered to be indispensable to a book. Stevenson said that to write a book without a Preface was like going out without a hat. Now it is seldom done. People go out without a hat, and so does this book. But I dedicate this book to you, because without your help it could not have been written. Indeed, the correspondence that has passed between us about it would make a book in itself; and if this correspondence were printed as an Appendix, the Appendix would be longer than the book.

The two together would make the kind of novel some people aim at writing now: not the comparatively old idea of a novel within a novel; but a story and *no* story, a story and the story in the making: the work, and scenes from the workshop; peeps behind the scenes; the carpenter's conversation, his hesitations; what he sketches, and what he rejects as well as what he finally selects; the plans, the chips, the shavings.

Books, in my experience, start out by being one thing; they start in one direction, and they take the bit into their teeth and go somewhere else. That is what happened to this book. It is difficult to remember where and when the seed of a book is sown; but I think the seed of *this* book fell into the ground in a railway carriage, somewhere between Kharbin and Lake Baikal, in the year 1905.

What has it turned out to be? What is it? A novel? A book of travel? An argument? A picture of manners?

I think it is perhaps a record of impressions received in Russia and Manchuria, in war time, and transposed into a phantasy. I have tried to collect these impressions, to sort them, and to string them like beads on a slight thread of story.

Or to change the metaphor: the story in this book is a thread which I present to the reader to guide him through a labyrinth in Limbo; it is not the *"fil fatal;"* of Ariadne for in this maze there is no Minotaur to kill or to avoid; but there is a definite starting place, and there is an appointed goal.

The labyrinth is no Cyclopean maze hewn out in the Cretan rock, but rather a vague, winding corridor, full of faded mirrors, muffled doors, and dim windows.

The corridor is tortuous; the reader will need a thread to guide him; and he will find, as he walks along unwinding it, that it may catch in the fastenings of doors and windows, which will spring open at a touch. He will then, perhaps, pause and look and listen.

These doors and windows open on to scenes, episodes, and moments in the lives and minds of other people and the reader, if he has the patience to linger, will have glimpses of their comedy, sometimes of their tragedy, and of the problems – 'the hopes, fears, belief, and disbelieving' – which face and perplex them.

As I wrote it, I remembered the conversations we used to have in the Trans-Siberian express; the interminable waits at Chinese railway-sidings; the noise and colour of the streets of Mukden, and its solemn walls; the sun-baked villages, the granite stepping stones, the indigo-clad husbandmen, the smell of fried beans, the green *gowliang*; the lemon-coloured dawns, the mauve twilights; the sunlight and the spice; or later on, the plains of Southern Russia; the sleepy little town of Kuznetsk in the autumn weather, during those damp and grey days when we were held up for nearly a week at the station.

The roads were soft and muddy, and there was a smell of rotting leaves in the air; in the market place (do you remember?) we watched a man trying to sell geese, and saying to them, as he drove them home unsold in the evening, as one might say to a dog, "Cheer up, we shall soon be home."

If some of the chapters in this book remind you of these sounds and sights, it will have served its purpose.

If you approve, I need fear no other criticism. For you know, at first hand, not only the landscapes and atmosphere, but the events, situations, problems, and moods which I have attempted to stage in these *Ombres Chinoises*.

"Va, petit livre, et choisis ton monde."

MAURICE BARING.

3 GRAY'S INN SQUARE, LONDON,
February 1927.

CHAPTER I

Although Miles Consterdine was twenty-seven, he had never been to Paris till this Easter. He had lived with his Aunt Fanny, in Regent's Park, for half the year, with the exception of the Easter, summer and Christmas holidays, which were spent at the Manor House, Wheatham, in Norfolk.

His Aunt Fanny thought that Paris was a dangerous place for boys, and she still regarded Miles as a child.

Miles' father, John Consterdine, had been a wine merchant. He used to spend the greater part of the year in Madeira, where he had considerable business interests. He visited a younger brother, Joseph, in England, every year in the summer, and stayed until the partridge-shooting was over. Joseph was his partner in the wine business.

John Consterdine was the embodiment of everything that is English and conservative: in politics a Liberal, a Free-Trader, and the rigid upholder of the traditions of many generations of Consterdines, who had carried on the wine business and handed it down from father to son from the eighteenth century.

He was a well-known figure in Madeira, and used to be pointed out to tourists as the leading English citizen. You noticed him at once, dressed in a grey frock-coat, a buff Holland waistcoat, and a Panama hat. There was something reassuring about his steady grey eyes, his white whiskers, his cool, firm hand, and his massive walking-stick.

He could speak with authority on timber, flowers (roses especially), claret, and Trafalgar sherry (pronounced by him *Trafflegar*). He quoted Horace. He never smoked; he was afraid of blunting his palate.

He had married the only daughter of a Norfolk squire. By this marriage the Consterdines, who were already prosperous, became still more so, as Euphemia Dene (called Effie for short) was an heiress. She was not beautiful, except on horseback, but she had a vague, detached fascination that nobody could account for.

She was killed in a hunting accident when Miles was four years old. Miles was the only son. He spent the first years of his childhood in Madeira; afterwards he retained the haziest memories of the place. When he went to school, he stayed in England for good, with his Uncle Joseph and his Aunt Fanny, and spent his holidays at his uncle's comfortable Queen Anne country house.

As soon as Miles was born, it was settled that he should go into the business, which he would eventually become the head of. His Uncle Joseph had no children; even if he had had sons, they would not have preceded Miles in the Consterdine business hierarchy.

John Consterdine died while Miles was still at a private school (at Worthing), and Joseph Consterdine became the head of the firm. Joseph was a more subdued edition of his elder brother. He had not needed the climate of Madeira to attenuate him and to increase his distaste for making a decision.

Fanny Consterdine (*née* Summerfield) was one of a large family. She came from Dorsetshire. She had fresh, healthy looks. She was sensible, practical, and full of energy. She held strong opinions on all subjects, and had no patience with people who disagreed with her. She was a Conservative, and she admitted a particular shade of High Church opinion, which was not ritualistic. She had patience with ritualists; but she would not speak to a Nonconformist. She went to church on Saints' Days as well as on Sundays. She allowed no card-playing nor theatre-going on Ascension Day and other festivals of the Church. In Lent she indulged in an orgy of extra services and sermons. She was fond of the country. She was an admirable housekeeper, and she made excellent jam. She had a breezy sense of humour. She was devoted to Miles, and she determined to manage his life for him and to see that he came to no harm. It was thought necessary that he should go to a public school. His uncle wanted to send him to Harrow, but Aunt Fanny thought the Headmaster's views on Church matters were too broad. Eton was considered too sophisticated; Winchester too "rough." "Miles," Aunt Fanny said, "must learn French and German, as he will one day be head of the firm. He ought to go somewhere where there is a Modern side." Aunt Fanny decided it should be Westminster. There was a Modern side there, but only the duffers belonged to it. He could thus live at home, and home influence would be maintained, while he would still enjoy all the advantages of school life.

Miles had been taught a little French in Madeira; his mother's maid was Swiss; but he soon forgot it at school, although French was, of course, taught there. When he was eighteen, it was clear that he knew no French; and Aunt Fanny said that something must be done about it. It was one of the traditions of the Consterdine family that French, and if possible German, even Spanish, should be learnt in the interests not only of culture, but of business. There was a tradition in the family that Miles' father could speak Portuguese, but he had never been heard to say a Portuguese word, even in Madeira, except once by accident, and that was Spanish, and would perhaps have been better unsaid.

Miles had just reached his eighteenth year when his uncle and aunt thought it necessary to migrate to Madeira for the winter. Aunt Fanny was concerned about Joseph's bronchial catarrh. They went there, and the London branch of the firm was left in charge of Ernest Saxby, Joseph Consterdine's junior partner.

Miles was the problem. He had to live in London. Saxby was married, and had a large family and a small house at Wimbledon. There was no room for Miles. Miles was a day-boarder at Westminster, and his aunt and uncle now wished to find a home for him in London, and to improve his French. The problem seemed likely to prove insoluble. Mrs Consterdine thought she would consult Mr Spark, the crammer who had passed generations of young men into the Foreign Office and the Diplomatic Service. Several of her cousins had passed through his hands.

Mr Spark received Mrs Consterdine with respect, and was relieved to find that she did not expect him to find an appointment for her nephew at one of the European Embassies, without further ado. He thought for a moment, and then he said he knew of something which would meet the case. His French lecturer – one of his French lecturers – M. Mourieux, lived with his wife permanently in London. They had a house in Delamere Terrace, and they took in one or two boarders, pupils who attended Mr Spark's establishment; candidates either for the Foreign Office or the Diplomatic Service, who wished to practise colloquial French, and have an opportunity for talking it at meals. M. Mourieux was a charming and cultivated man. The pupils liked him, and Madame Mourieux was a sensible woman who "looked after the boys." Mr Spark looked knowingly at Aunt Fanny as he said this.

M. Mourieux was in the building at the time, and Mr Spark sent for him and introduced him to Mrs Consterdine. Mrs Consterdine's French was untainted by any affectation about accent; it was – when you got used to it – intelligible. She was delighted with M. Mourieux, who was a frail, distinguished, bearded Frenchman, with a certain mouselike look, an elegant phraseology, and manners which soothed Mrs Consterdine. Her accentuation distressed him; he couldn't help – not a wince, but the shadow of a shiver, whenever she dealt with the diphthong "*oi.*"

M. Mourieux happened to have a vacancy. He had already two pupils in the house, but there was room for a third. He would be delighted to take in young M. Consterdine. The matter was settled, and Miles moved to Delamere Terrace as soon as his uncle and aunt went back to Madeira.

As soon as they reached Madeira, Joseph Consterdine found the climate suited him so well that he became disinclined to move, and he stayed in Madeira all through the summer. He seemed to be spellbound by the place, and he lost all desire, not only of returning to England, but of doing anything at all, except entertaining visitors in the charming house that had belonged to his brother.

So Miles, during his eighteenth year, lived at M. Mourieux' house and learnt a certain amount of French.

M. Mourieux shed rather than imparted the language; it was for you to pick it up or not, as you liked.

Besides Miles, there were in the house other pupils who were being coached for the Foreign Office and the Diplomatic Service examinations. They all went to Spark's chambers in Gower Street every day, and they were engrossed in the life of that place. They looked upon Miles as stupid, and he, being shy, withdrew into his shell and led his own life. M. Mourieux was pleased with his work, which he said showed signs of promise.

When Miles was nineteen it was settled that he should not go to a University, but straight into the "House," as all the other Consterdines had done before him. He was to begin in the London house as a clerk, at the lowest rung of the ladder. His commercial career had only lasted a year, and he was only just twenty, when his uncle Joseph died in Madeira. His Aunt Fanny came home, and Miles moved from the Mourieux' to Regent's Park. During these two years Miles had lived *en pension* at the

Mourieux'. Pupils had come and pupils had gone, all of them from Spark's; some of them had passed into the Diplomatic Service or the Foreign Office; others had left London and gone to families in France or Germany. Miles had lived with them, met them most nights at dinner; but during this epoch he had only made one friend, a certain Geoffrey Haseltine, who was working for the Civil Service, and ultimately became a clerk in one of the Government offices. He walked every day to Spark's, either alone or with Haseltine, and walked back every evening. On Sunday mornings he went to church with his Aunt Fanny, and did the acrostic in Saturday's *Vanity Fair*.

His City life was no different. He did his work conscientiously. But he made no friends, although his fellow clerks and his seniors were all of them prepared to like him. He was civil and considerate, and obviously without of shadow of pretension.

With the death of his uncle he became the head of the firm, but it was arranged that Saxby should have control until Miles came of age. Except that he lived with his Aunt Fanny, this made little difference to the tenour of Miles' life. He went to the City every day by bus, and came back every evening by Underground. His only friends were M. and Madame Mourieux, whom he would occasionally visit, and Haseltine, whom he saw on Sundays.

It was suggested more than once by Saxby, his partner, that Miles should go to Madeira. Miles assented to the proposal, but nothing came of it, and life went on as before.

His affairs were managed entirely by his Aunt Fanny, who still treated him as a child.

Miles grew up to be tall. By the time he came of age – an event which made no difference in his mode of life – he looked slightly overgrown. He had inherited his father's grey eyes – but in Miles they were softer and bluer, his mother's delicate pink-and-white skin and her fair hair. He was bashful, and never spoke unless he was spoken to. He would blush scarlet if suddenly addressed. The society of girls made him speechless, and especially that of his cousins, who were invited every year by Aunt Fanny to spend Christmas at Wheatham. This would have been a period of misery for Miles, had he not somewhat ingeniously made for himself avenues of escape. He was fond of riding, and he had inherited his mother's competent hands and easy horsemanship. He spent all his days in the saddle, and when he was not hunting, he would go out for long solitary rides. He thus managed to avoid, to a certain extent, the boisterous society of his numerous cousins. He had a den, too, at Wheatham, a sitting room of his own, to which he would retire and read books. He was, in the matter of literature, entirely self-educated. By going on the Modern side at school, much against the advice of the headmaster, who in vain had tried to turn Aunt Fanny from her purpose, he had not learnt Greek, and he had not learnt German. He had picked up a considerable amount of French from M. Mourieux, and he had read a great many books, without system or plan, so that his education had bright spots of intensity and large gaps.

He read what he came across, and made no effort to search for new fields, to improve his mind or to widen his views. He took literature as he took life, as it came. Reading and books had played up to the present only a small part in his life. But he had one engrossing and all-absorbing hobby – photography. He had, so his Aunt Fanny said, a real talent for photography. And besides the pleasure it gave him to experiment, he thoroughly enjoyed the hours he would spend in the darkroom; for this was, too, an avenue of escape, and perhaps the best of all.

He was fond of his Aunt Fanny, and relied on her opinion absolutely. He took her views on people as gospel; he accepted her religion and her philosophy without inquiring into them – and, moreover, she amused him. She was sane, sensible, and shrewd; brisk too, and gay.

She, on her part, had determined eventually to steer Miles into the safe harbour of matrimony. But he was not, she

7

decided, to marry until he was thirty. She would find him a wife. So their lives had passed uneventfully, regularly, pleasantly, and calmly. Miles had met several eligible girls at Wheatham and at Regent's Park, but, although not unsusceptible, he had remained fancy-free. The only romantic dreams he had so far had centred round figures far removed from Aunt Fanny's ken – stars of the stage, and stray brief encounters with lesser luminaries. But nothing permanent had come of such dreams or encounters.

Aunt Fanny was easy on that score. Nothing unexpected had marred the perfect smoothness of life at Regent's Park and at Wheatham until Miles' twenty-seventh birthday was about to be celebrated. It was then that Miles threw a bombshell into his Aunt Fanny's life by announcing to her one morning at breakfast, without any preparation, just as he might have said he was going for a walk in the Zoological Gardens on Sunday, that he intended this year to spend his Easter holidays in Paris.

"By yourself?" asked Aunt Fanny, when she had recovered her breath.

"Yes," said Miles, "by myself."

CHAPTER II

Aunt Fanny was defeated, and, being a sensible woman, she acknowledged the fact at once. There was no possible reason why Miles should not go to Paris if he wished to, nor any reason why he should not go by himself.

Thus it happened that Miles started for Paris shortly before his twenty-seventh birthday.

He stayed at an hotel which had been recommended to him by M. Mourieux. It was on the other side of the river. Aunt Fanny had also recommended him an hotel. Hers was not far from the *Avenue de l'Opéra*, where you could live reasonably *en pension*; but Miles preferred M. Mourieux' choice, an old-fashioned hotel where no meals were served.

Never was there a less adventurous tourist than Miles Consterdine in Paris. He wanted to go to one of the well-known restaurants, but he never could muster up courage to pass through the doors. He took refuge in a *Duval*, and went over and over again to the same one, till the night before he was to leave Paris. He wanted to go to the *Théatre Français*, to see a modern play, but he made a mistake in reading the yellow *affiche*, and instead of seeing, as he had expected, a play by Dumas *fils*, he found himself watching a tragedy in five acts in verse, the action of which took place in the thirteenth century. He found it tedious. His seat, too, was uncomfortable; he had wanted a stall, but instead of saying "*Fauteuil d'orchestre*," he had said "*Parterre*," which turned out to be a different affair.

Miles had dined early. The play was long. When it was over, Miles felt hungry – so hungry that he was determined to go to a restaurant. He walked up the Boulevard. He was not dressed, so he dared not go into several places where he saw men in white ties feasting at bright tables with elegant ladies; but at last he found a place which he thought would do. Here were people sitting at small tables in the street, drinking beer; and inside, supper was going on. Nobody was dressed, but everybody was talking. Miles chose a table against the wall,

He ordered some cold meat and a whisky and soda. He had hardly begun his supper when the table next to him was suddenly occupied by a family who, although they were talking loudly, and in French and English alternately, did not seem to Miles to be French, and were certainly not English.

There was a tall man with short grey whiskers, an oblong, distinguished face, and rather pale-blue vague eyes, dressed in a long black frock-coat; there was a rather large middle-aged lady, dressed in black, with her hair parted in the middle, and a comb in the back of it – voluble, brisk, and full of gesture, talking torrential English, interlarded with French sentences and German words, and not without parentheses in another strange language which Miles did not understand.

With them was a girl, who might have been thirty. She, too, was dressed in black; she was neat and serene. There was another girl, possibly a sister – more likely, thought Miles, a cousin – who was smaller, with regular features, rather rebellious hair, and mischievous eyes. There were two other men. One, Miles concluded, was an Englishman, as all the others spoke English to him, although he, too, had something foreign about him – something slightly Teutonic; but that was perhaps because he wore a pince-nez, and because his fair hair was rather long at the back. The other man was certainly a foreigner, nor could Miles make a guess at his age. Nor did he know whether he belonged to the others, or whether he was just a friend. There was a distinct likeness between him and the smaller girl. He was certainly over forty; his face, or rather his expression, had the stamp of manifold experience. His shoulders were wide and square. He was one of those people whose backs have been made stiff and straight in their teens, and cannot afterwards unbend. You would have called him ugly at first sight. There was a permanent frown; his hair was thick, black, and unkempt; his cheekbones high, his face full of little wrinkles – not wrinkles of age – his skin yellow and tanned; his nose was short and turned up; but his eyes arrested you; and the moment he smiled – and he always smiled before he spoke – his face lit up, and then he seemed almost good-looking.

He was the least talkative. He sat with his head rested on his hands, looking out in front of him, as if he were unaware of his surroundings. He was the most interesting member of the party. You looked at him, and the others receded into the background.

He and the younger girl, thought Miles, must be brother and sister. They, too, had been to a play, to an Opera which Miles had never heard of. It was called *Pelléas et Mélisande*. The older gentleman, who had a whiff of 1830 about him, and made you think of Guizot, Lamartine, and the Reform Bill, said: "*Ce n'est pas de la musique, c'est de la cacophonie.*"

"No, no, papa; you are too unjust," said the elder girl.

"It is interesting, an interesting experiment," said the elderly lady decisively. "I will try and get them to mount it *à Petersbourg; j'écrirai à Dubkin demain; c'est une honte de ne pas donner cela*. It is something new. One must remember that people thought Wagner a bad joke when it was first done – *malo tovo*, Wagner – Gluck; and Mr Lawrence," she pointed to the man Miles had thought to be an Englishman, "who is *un musicien sérieux, une autorité*, agrees with me that it is something, and something new and *trés remarquable*."

11

"I wonder whether M. Lawrence really admires him," the old man said in slow, deliberate English, "or whether it is only *sa politesse*?"

"Mr Lawrence is the only person who so far has said nothing, and he is the only one of us who has the right to speak. What do you think, Mr Lawrence?" asked the lady. "Now let him speak, please, and don't interrupt, Pierre."

Pierre, Miles supposed, was the older man, and so far he had shown no wish to interrupt.

"The first time I heard it," said the Englishman in quiet, low tones, "I enjoyed the music so much that I thought it was perhaps over-obtrusive; but the second and third time I heard it I thought, on the contrary, the music so appropriate, you hardly noticed it. It never says too much; it is simply right; and in itself I think it absolutely on the first line; the beginning of a new tradition. You saw how the audience appreciated it?"

"But I speak of the libretto, cher Monsieur; it is the words that I find so idiotical," said the older man.

But, papa," said the elder girl, "Mr Lawrence is *un vrai musicien*; he has studied at the *Hochschule*, and he knows."

"I know, I know; I do not wish to be wanting in respect to Mr Lawrence's knowledge, nor to pretend I know anything about music – *mais j'affirme que cet opéra n'a pas le sens commun*. It is the libretto that I find *infecte*."

"But you must admit," said the older lady, "Mr Lawrence, that Wagner is greater than all that... Think of *Tristan*, and the *Meistersinger* – "

"I think – " said the Englishman. He was not allowed to finish his sentence because the younger of the girls, who had been talking to the tall man, and paying no attention to the others, broke into the conversation and said: "You will bear me witness, Mary, that I *never, never* said such a thing! Alyosha has the face to say that I used to say that Wagner was ridiculous; I never said such a thing. Did I, Mr Lawrence? You know how I always admired Wagner from the first – ever since the first time I ever heard an Opera."

"Never again will I go with you to the Opera," said the old man. *"Cela finit toujours par une dispute.* If you had only gone, as I wished, to the *Théatre Français*, we should not have had all this unpleasantness."

"It is all Alyosha's fault," said the younger girl. "Never will I go anywhere with him again."

At that moment the waiter brought the wrangling party their food, and as they had all apparently ordered different things, there was some dispute as to who had ordered what. In the first place, the old gentleman had been given a glass of beer, and the elder girl at once interposed and said: "No, no, papa; you must not drink that beer; you know it disagrees with you; you must have your *camomille.* I ordered it – *garçon, apportez à monsieur la camomille que j'ai commandée."* And handing the beer to the dark man, she said, "You can drink that, Alyosha."

Alyosha said nothing, but handed the glass to the younger girl, and said wearily to the waiter: *"Un grog Américain."*

"Tu sais que je déteste la biére," said the younger girl violently; "besides which I have ordered some tea."

"Je vous en supplie, mes enfants; teesche, teesche," said the old man, and Miles wondered what *teesche* might mean.

The whole conversation of all the company, with the exception of the Englishman, was from that moment suddenly carried on in a tongue which was unintelligible to Miles, but which he guessed to be Russian. His guess was confirmed by the old man saying to the company: "It is very rude of you all to talk Russian before Mr Lawrence."

That is what I am always telling Alyosha," said the young girl. "I am always telling him he never talks Russian except when there are people there who don't understand it. *Il choisit ce moment. On dirait qu'il fait cela exprès, pour le plaisir!"*

Never had Miles felt so lonely. The effect of this intimate, animated conversation going on next to him, so near and yet, as he thought, so infinitely remote, so impossibly out of reach, made him homesick and almost inclined to cry.

At that moment a waiter brought him the whisky and the syphon. Miles stretched out his hand to press the metal lever.

CHAPTER III

…There! I knew he reminded me of someone. *Comme le monde est petit! Pierre, chéri,* don't you remember *ce charmant Monsieur* Consterdine whom we knew *à Madére, en soixante-treize*? The old gentleman living on the hill, and his villa all covered with red flowers – what are they called in English – pointers-and-setters? And the dinner we had at his house, *et ce merveilleux coucher de soleil*! Mr Consterdine, this is my husband, Mr Dashkov, and my name is Elizaveta Sergeevna, only that is too difficult – so just call me Mrs Dashkov, *tout court.*"

The old gentleman was once more on his feet, and shook hands with Miles, saying how glad he was to make his acquaintance. There was a mutual buzz of phrases, during which Miles made a mental note that he would never be able to call the old lady "Mrs Dashkov" comfortably. It seemed to him like a joke.

"These," the old lady went on, "are my daughter and my niece, Princess Kouragine. And this is her brother. We all call him Alyosha, and so does everybody else, for we are all very fond of him."

A trifle had done it. Miles, in pressing the lever of the syphon, had spurted soda water all over the old gentleman's knees and frock-coat. Apologies had been offered and received, and the incident smothered in conversation. The elderly lady went on: "This, Mr Consterdine, is Mr Lawrence, whom you certainly must have heard of. His *suite* was performed at the *Palais de Cristal* last winter. Mr Lawrence is the best connoisseur of German music abroad. He has been studying at the *Hochschule* in Berlin, and he understands *everything*. Lamoureux never gives anything without asking his advice."

Miles shook hands with everyone.

They all sat down again, and instead of leaving the matter at that, went on with the conversation, and roped Miles into their talk, making him sit at their table. They asked him whether he had been to the Opera, and when he said he had been to the *Théatre Français*, the old man at once ejaculated: "There is a sensible man! What were they giving?"

Miles blushed scarlet, for he had forgotten, or rather he had never known the name of the play. He had not bought a programme, and he had looked at the wrong posters in the theatre. He couldn't explain all that.

"It was historical," he stammered.

The older lady, seeing his embarrassment, helped him out of the difficulty by saying: "Yes, Pierre, of course; you know quite well. It was Hernani."

The old man said "*Hernani*," and nodded his head with quiet approval, and added that the revival in '79 – or was it '80? – was "unforgettable."

"How long did you say you were staying?" asked Madame Dashkov. "Only till tomorrow? That is impossible; you must stay at least till Monday…because on Sunday afternoon there is a beautiful concert at the *Cirque d'Été*, and it would be a pity for someone so fond of music as you are," (she seemed to take it for granted, as if he had been to the Opera with them that night) "should miss such a treat. We are all going; perhaps you would like to come with us; we have room in our box."

"The concert is not at the *Cirque d'Été, maman,*" the elder girl said.

"Well, at the *Châtelet*; it is almost the same, and I always mix them. But Mr Constantine will come to *déjeuner* with us first."

Miles stammered, blushed, and said he thought he ought to go home.

"But why?" asked the girl.

"It would mean staying three more days here," said Miles.

"Why not?" said the younger girl.

"Why not?" thought Miles. There was indeed no possible reason why he should not stay a day, or even a week, longer in Paris if he wished to.

He said something about having to go back to his business.

"But you have holidays at Easter?" said the elder lady.

"Yes," said Miles; "I do go away, as a rule, for a fortnight."

"And how long did you say you had been away?"

"So far, only ten days," said Miles.

"There, you see! Well, of course you must stay till Monday, or perhaps longer," said the elder lady decisively. "It would be a crime for you to go just as we have made friends, and to miss that concert, wouldn't it, Mr Lawrence? They are playing the *Charfreitag* music and the *Liebestod*, a real treat, and Lamoureux is conducting. We have a large box. How strange and fortunate that I should have met your father in Madeira! He was very musical too, *n'est-ce pas, Pierre? Tu te souviens de ce charmant Monsieur?* And you shall have *déjeuner* with us before. We are staying at the Bristol. We are used to it. I wonder what your *Imya* and *Otchestvo* can be, because I find your name a bother. I mix it up with Constantine. I mean your Christian name and your father's Christian name?"

"My Christian name is Miles, and my father's Christian name was John," said Miles; and before he was able to get any further, and as far as his surname, the lady interrupted him and said: "That is perfect; we will call you Mihal Ivanytch."

They then sent for the bill, and after saying goodnight to Miles, they left the restaurant, leaving him gasping with astonishment.

CHAPTER IV

Miles went to *déjeuner* with his new friends the next day. They occupied the whole of the small *entresol* of the Hotel Bristol.

He arrived punctually at the hotel at half past twelve, the appointed hour, and was told that if he would kindly wait, "they" would be down directly.

He waited over half an hour, reading the *New York Herald*, which had been given him by the maid, and a little after one Madame Dashkov burst into the room, with her hat on, saying: "I am so dreadfully distressed to have kept you waiting so long, but the children have been trying on, and I had to go with them, and they kept us – and Alyosha is only just up." She rang the bell. " But we will have breakfast at once – "

She called through the bedroom door something in Russian, and from the next room came a small voice answering, "*Seychass, seychass,*" and presently the old gentleman walked into the room, stately and tidy in his frock-coat, with his spectacles on, and the *Revue des deux Mondes* in one hand.

"I thought we would miss the *Tannhäuser*," Madame Dashkov said. "The concert begins with the overture to *Tannhäuser*, which I'm sure you think vulgar," she explained to Miles. "Then there is the *Feuerzauber*, then the *Tristan*, the *Vorspiel* and *Liebestod* in one, then the *Charfreitag*, and, I think, the *Waldweben* and the Funeral March."

Miles was just beginning to explain that he had never heard *Tannhäuser*, when the rest of the family burst into the room, all voluble with explanation and counter-explanation, and Madame Dashkov led them into the little dining room, which was next door.

This breakfast seemed to Miles like the continuation of the last night's supper. The same conversation seemed to be going on in the same headlong polyglot manner. No statement made by any one member of the family was allowed to pass by any other member of the family; the old man assisted patiently at the wordy combats, and every now and then made an ineffectual attempt to smooth matters.

They arrived at the concert in time for the second item. Miles had never heard a note of Wagner in his life. Wagner was a composer whom Aunt Fanny disapproved of. She said he was noisy, and that his operas were "tiresome."

Miles, who had absolute confidence in her taste and authority, had never thought it worthwhile to check her opinion himself. So the music he heard that afternoon at the Concert Larnoureux startled him out of his wits. He was not particularly musical, and he had no musical knowledge or training, but he was sensitive to new impressions, and the effect of this music on him was, from the first, overwhelming, and probably far greater than it would have been on a more musical man. All he had heard in the way of opera was *Faust, Carmen,* and on one occasion *Don Giovanni.*

The second item of the programme, which happened to be the Fire Music from the *Walküre,* not only went to Miles' head like wine, but it filled the cup of his aesthetic sensibility, of all that in his nature was capable of receiving a musical impression, to the brim.

The rest of the concert made no impression on him at all. He sat through it as one in a trance. The prelude and finale of *Tristan,* the forest whispers of *Siegfried,* the streaming sunshine of the Good Friday music, the tremendous grief of

Siegfried's funeral, brushed past him like shadows, without reaching him. He was like one possessed or obsessed. The house of his soul was occupied and closed. He was in a whirl – in fact, he did not know where he was, nor what had happened to him. He had never received such impressions before, never known that one could receive such impressions...

The comments of his friends – the applause of the audience – the arguments between mother, daughter and niece and the others about the interpretation of one of the pieces, all passed by him without his noticing, as if either they or he were in a dream world.

He was suddenly aware that the concert had come to an end. He would not have been surprised if the world itself had come to an end.

Madame Dashkov asked him to go back to the hotel with them and have tea. He followed obediently, in a cab with the nephew, the daughter (Alexandra), and the niece (Mary), who throughout the drive continued an argument which had begun while the concert was still going on, as to how the interpretation compared with that of Nikisch.

If you had asked Miles to hum a single phrase of what he had heard that afternoon, he would not have been able to do so, not even of the music which he had listened to. Yet, in a sense, it was all there, inside him; and in spite of not being able to recollect or to formulate or reconstruct any of the magic that he knew had touched him, he was aware, intensely aware, that something catastrophic had happened to him – nothing would ever be the same as it had been before; something was either broken inside him, or had been added to him, he was not sure which; he felt as if he had been taken out of space, turned inside out, and put back again... He could not account for nor analyse the process; he only knew that he felt "upset"; as though he had been through a mental shipwreck, rescued from drowning and restored to life, and had "suffered a sea-change."

All this was going on inside him. Outwardly he seemed to be the same as ever. He answered civilly, although in reality mechanically, the questions that were put to him; he was able to take part in the conversation without anybody noticing that anything odd had happened to him.

The two cabs in which they drove back from the concert arrived together at the hotel, and Madame Dashkov at once ordered tea and offered Miles a cigarette. She was smoking hard.

The musical argument proceeded, and Madame Dashkov silenced her rebellious daughter and revolutionary niece by invoking the authority of Liszt himself, whom she had known.

"But Mihal Ivanytch is tired of hearing about music," she said, when the tea was brought, "and so am I. After a concert like that, after such a treat, I do not wish to argue. I only want to remember and be thankful. You enjoyed it, Mihal Ivanytch, I could see. Mihal Ivanytch," she explained to the rest of the family, "*est très musicien.*"

" Yes," said Miles, "I enjoyed it very much."

"And to think you will not have the chance of hearing another. Next Sunday there is a still more beautiful concert. But in London you have beautiful concerts. What are they called? I remember the Saturday to Monday Pops, at the St James's Hall."

"I'm afraid they don't exist any more," said Miles, "but there are concerts. I'm afraid I have seldom been…my aunt – "

"But you will now that you are initiated. Fancy, Pierre, Mihal Ivanytch had never heard any Wagner before, not a note; it was his *baptême de Feuerzauber!*"

"It is a pity," the old man said, "it was not classical music. I would have given all that we heard today for one song from *Don Juan* or *Le Barbier de Séville.*"

"I always say that *l'un n'empêche pas l'autre,*" said Madame Dashkov. "But it is a pity, for every reason, that you must leave

Paris so soon," she said, turning to Miles. " Is it really necessary that you should go? Are you in such a slap-bang hurry?"

"I must get back to my business."

"But who is the head of your business?"

Miles blushed.

"There isn't one; at least I suppose I am. I am the head in a way, although my partner is older than I am."

"Then you can surely take a holiday when you like, for as long as you like?"

"This is the first time I have ever been abroad, except, that is to say, to Madeira, as I told you."

"Just fancy," said Mary, with sparkling eyes, "you have never travelled? You have never seen Rome, nor the Mediterranean, nor Switzerland, nor Florence, nor the Alps, nor the Midi, nor the Coliseum, nor the *Citronen*, nor the Sistine Madonna? never been to Germany? never been to the *Philharmonie* and heard the music?"

"No; this is my first trip abroad. I'm afraid I'm very ignorant and backward." Miles blushed again.

"But, if you go away," Mary asked eagerly, "is there no one whom you could leave in charge of the business for a time?"

"Oh yes, my partner. His name is Saxby. He knows far more about it all than I do."

"And would you like to travel and see the world, and see pictures, and hear music, and go to the south or the east or the north?"

"There is nothing I should like to do more," said Miles, with calm conviction, realising, as he thought of Aunt Fanny, how impossible the project appeared to be.

"Have you ever been to Russia?" asked Alyosha.

"No, never. I have been *nowhere*. I should like to go to Russia," Miles added, "and to China."

"Then why don't you take a year's holiday," said Alyosha, "and go there now?"

"But the war –"

"And leave your business," added his sister, taking no notice of Alyosha, "in the hands of the competent M. Saxon – I am sure that M. Saxon is very competent – *très raisonnable* – and go and see the world."

"Yes," went on Madame Dashkov, "and develop yourself. You are like someone who has been in prison; you need setting free. I am sure you have great possibilities and capabilities. *J'ai vu cela tout de suite, n'est-ce pas, Pierre*? What you want is *Erlösung* and *Anregung*. You must see the world for yourself; it is no life to go every day to the same office. *Ce n'est pas une vie*. Not a life – "

"I agree," said Miles; "it is monotonous. I should like to travel, but – "

"But then why not?" asked the younger members of the family in chorus.

"I cannot see why he shouldn't," said Madame Dashkov. "*N'est-ce pas que j'ai raison, Pierre*?"

"*Parfaitement raison*," the old man said. "It is natural that Mihal Ivanytch should travel…the 'grand tour' *pour se former*. One only lives once, one should try and see what one can."

Miles was not in the least astonished at the younger members of the family urging him to such a course, but to hear their opinions endorsed by the father and mother, by people so much older than himself, took his breath away. That they – grown-up, experienced, respectable people, as old as his Aunt Fanny – should encourage what seemed to him so reckless an act, so fantastic an adventure, seemed almost incredible. Nevertheless, he could not but be affected by the fact.

"But I have relations," he said.

"How many?" asked Alexandra.

"Well, there is my aunt. I live with her."

"Is she very old?"

"Oh no."

"She doesn't want taking care of?"

"Oh no." He laughed. The idea of anybody wanting to take care of Aunt Fanny tickled him. "She can take care of herself very well, and she has a house in the country and – "

"And plenty of friends?"

"Yes, and relations."

"Ah, I knew it!"

"But do you like your business?" asked Mary.

"I don't mind it."

"You just go to a counter every day, and sign letters?"

"Not exactly a counter, but that's more or less what happens."

"And you have done that for how long?"

"About seven years."

"And never had a holiday?" asked Madame Dashkov.

"I have always had holidays at Christmas and Easter, and in the summer. We go to the country."

"*Cela ne compte pas.* You must certainly take a very long holiday *at once*," said Madame Dashkov. "You must see the world, especially Italy and Germany – Italy for pictures and Germany for music. *N'est-ce pas, Pierre?*"

" If I were Mihal Ivanytch," said the older man, "I would certainly travel, and perhaps leave the business in the meanwhile to the partner. One only lives once," he added sadly.

"Yes," said Alyosha, who had been silent up to that moment, "and it's no use travelling when one's old."

"But I don't care for travelling alone," said Miles.

"You can come with me the day after tomorrow. I am going to Russia, to Petersburg," said Alyosha.

"*C'est une excellente idée,*" said Madame Dashkov. "It will do you both good."

"But I'm afraid," said Miles, "that if I gave up the business for a year, I should have to give it up altogether. I should never be able to go back, if once I lost the habit of going to the City now."

"And supposing you never *did* go back, would you be on the pavement?" asked Mary. "Would you starve?"

25

"Mary, Mary, *ne soyez pas si indiscrète,*" said her uncle.

"No, I should not starve," said Miles, blushing. "I do not think it would make any difference to me at all. I have more money than I can spend, anyhow."

"Then what is to prevent you giving up the business altogether?" asked Mary, with the greatest eagerness.

"Nothing…except…except – "

"*Le qu'en dira-t-on,*" said Madame Dashkov.

"And your relations?" said Mary.

"My aunt would think it odd."

"My dear boy," said Madame Dashkov, "it's you who are going to live your life, and not your aunt. You cannot sacrifice your life to an aunt, however estimable she may be. You must take a long holiday; and if you do not care to go back, you must not go back; and I tell you, you will not care to go back. There are plenty of other more interesting things to do in the world, or not to do. To sit in an office all day when you need not is, for a young man like you, with possibilities, not *une vie.* You must have leave – *leave to live.*"

"Yes," said Mary, with decision, "it is a crime, a waste; you only live once; you are not old, and it is only old men who need to stagnate. Why not give up your business at once?"

"Why not?" said Madame Dashkov.

"There is no reason why he should not," echoed Alyosha, and the old man nodded.

"*Après tout, pourquoi pas?*" he murmured.

This was just a question that Miles had never been put, and had never put to himself before. Until that day he would have answered it by saying that it was out of the question. He would not have reasoned; but today it was different. He was different. Something had happened to him. Was it the effect of the music, or the company of these strange, friendly people, who seemed to say such unreasonable things so reasonably, and to make them sound so plausible? He did not know. He only felt now that there was indeed no reason why he should go to the office in the City every day for the rest of his life, and play the part of a figurehead. For it was Saxby who did all the work. Miles merely signed letters, read the *Bradshaw* during office hours, and would pass the time of day with clients, bandying civilities. It was, as Madame Dashkov said, not a life. Well, then – why not?

CHAPTER V

The conversation was at this moment interrupted by the arrival of some acquaintances of Miles' new friends.

Miles took leave of his hostess, and he thought the adventure would be put away in the limbo in which so many projected dreams, journeys, castles in the air or in Spain, are stored.

But as he left the *appartement*, Madame Dashkov said to him once more: "We will expect you to *déjeuner* to-morrow. And we will go on with the discussion."

Alyosha followed him to the door and said: "Think it over. I am serious. Tomorrow morning, at ten, we will arrange everything. I have to go to Petersburg. I have just come back from America. I went there on business for my Government, to buy machines for them. Anyhow, *la nuit porte conseil*. I want a companion, and it would interest you to see Russia."

"Very well," said Miles; "I will think it over."

He wondered at his own words. He wondered that he could even pretend for a moment to consider so wild a scheme,

Miles dined as usual at his Duval restaurant. He was glad to be by himself. He sat on after dinner, smoking cigarettes. It was, of course, out of the question – this fantastic journey. But why? – why not? What was to prevent him? It was true it wasn't a life to go every day to the office and sign letters…it was not as if he were leaving responsible work...he was merely a machine – not even a machine, just a figurehead. There was Aunt Fanny...but he would not even have to face an interview with her; and then he might say it was good for his business to get into touch with some Russians. At any rate, it would give him experience, and experience could never do any one any harm. Well, he would think it over in the night. He intended to ponder over the question for several hours, and to consider it from every angle, and in every detail; but as soon as he was in bed he fell asleep, and he was surprised to find when he woke up that it was half-past nine.

After he had dressed and drunk his *café au lait*, as he looked at the bright April sun shining on the quays and on the Seine, he felt that the conversation of yesterday had been a dream...he was now back in real life once more. He would go for a brisk walk, on his way to the Bristol. He would tell Alyosha Kouragine that the matter was out of the question; he would then make his arrangements for going back to London.

It was a lovely spring morning. The sky was of the palest, cleanest blue. Most of the trees in the *Champs Elysées* were still bare, but here and there there was a touch of green. There were buds everywhere, and the boughs were red with sap.

As Miles crossed the *Place de la Concorde*, he paused and wondered at the elegance of Paris. The city seemed to have put on her spring apparel. He looked up the *Champs Elysées* towards the *Arc de Triomphe*, and that monument seemed to be unreal as a bubble, a part of the sky, a bit of watercolour flung lightly on the canvas by an artist in a moment of careless inspiration. He looked up the *Rue Royale*; the buildings with their graceful colonnades to the right and the left of the street, and the *Madeleine* at the end of it, looked as clean and as clear as those of a coloured print in perfect condition. And then the *Louvre* and the gardens of the *Tuileries* and the bridges and the Chamber of Deputies: they were all of them notes in the spring symphony...there was no smoke in the air. Cabs drove by, and the sun glinted on the shiny white hats of the cabmen; here and there a red *taxi-auto*; a boy passed him, carrying a basket on his head, whistling; a man in the *Tuileries* gardens was calling to the birds, who seemed to know him and came to him tame and in flocks; an old priest passed by in a shabby *soutane* reading in a little book; nurses, children, soldiers, neatly dressed women, lounging *voyous*, all of them seemed today to be part of the spring landscape. The scene, thought Miles, had been staged especially for him.

He walked on past the gardens of the *Tuileries*, down the *Rue de Rivoli*, and when he reached the *Rue Castiglione*, instead of turning up it, he walked further on, wishing to prolong his walk. At last he turned up a side street into the *Rue St Honoré*, which was full of bustle, and then suddenly he was aware of a sound in the distance: four or five notes played on a reedy pipe.

What was it? Who was it?

Had he known, it was only one of the street cries of Paris, a mender of china or umbrellas advertising his trade…but to Miles on that April morning the notes had an intoxicating lilt and magical gaiety about them. It was as though the Spring itself were calling. Miles thought of a fairy tale; he could not remember which.

The music got into his blood; a spirit of intoxicating irresponsibility seized him, and he said to himself: "Yes, why not? Why not? Why shouldn't I go away?…travel…travel…over the hills and far away, and seek adventure…live?… Why should I go back to London? Must I?" It was no doubt the sensible thing. But was it really? And why? And what did that matter?

When he arrived at the hotel, Alyosha hardly kept him waiting a moment.

"I asked you to come early because there are several things to be done. You must go to the Embassy and get a passport. Have you a passport?"

"No," said Miles, "but – "

"And then you must get it *viséd*, and we must go to the Russian Embassy, and then we will take you to the *wagonlits* and get you a ticket." Alyosha seemed to take it for granted that Miles had made up his mind to go. He did not even ask him whether he had thought over the matter. "In the way of clothes," he went on, "I expect you have got what you want. But I would advise you to buy a kettle – what you call a tea basket. I think they are always useful when one wants to make tea for oneself on long journeys."

"But I really think," said Miles, and he knew he was only saying this for the sake of form, "that before taking such a decision, it would be only fair for me to consult my partner." He would have been miserable if Alyosha had agreed.

"Why?" asked Alyosha. "What difference will it make to him? If you stop to consult him, it will be too late. I thought we had settled all that. My uncle and my aunt say it's absurd that you should waste your life in this manner. Let us get a *fiacre*."

Miles and Alyosha walked downstairs, and Miles felt that he was in the hands of a delightful familiar; that he had no more will of his own, but that he was being borne away like Faust in the cloak of a reliable Mephistopheles. After all, Alyosha was right. It would not make the slightest difference to Saxby whether he was in London or not. Saxby treated him as a piece of furniture.

"Well, I must send him a telegram."

"We will do that presently."

They drove to the sleeping-car office. Alyosha had his seat already. They booked one for Miles. They went to the British Embassy, where Miles interviewed one of the secretaries, and obtained a passport without difficulty. They then went to the Russian Embassy, where other formalities were accomplished. Alyosha quietly took charge of the proceedings, although he never put himself forward. He seemed to do nothing except be there, but nevertheless he suggested each step, and saw that it was carried out. He managed Miles as a skilful conductor

31

manages an orchestra – not a single dot or quaver escaped his notice, and yet he seemed to be doing nothing.

Their business lasted the whole morning. It included the dispatch of two telegrams – one to Saxby and the other to Aunt Fanny, announcing Miles' departure for St Petersburg; and the purchase of a convenient suitcase and a tea basket for the journey. Alyosha had known at what shops to procure these articles.

They had been so busily engaged in practical details that it struck Miles, as they got into a *fiacre* to drive back to the hotel, that he had as yet no idea what Alyosha was going to do in Russia – whether he lived there and was going home, or whether he meant to go for a short visit.

"Are you going to Russia for good?" he asked him suddenly.

Alyosha had just been explaining to Miles that he always slept in loose blankets, and could not bear a Jaeger sleeping bag.

"I am on my way from America. I was sent there by my Government when the war began… I was in the Far East; they sent me to British Columbia to buy things. I was an officer before, long ago, when I was young, but 'that's another story,' and I can't tell it to you now, it is too long; perhaps I will never tell it to you at all. But for reasons which you would understand if I told you, it is not possible for me to get a job as an officer in the Army at present… I am a kind of freelance. I have to get what jobs I can. They may be many and different. I have had some already: I have bought cattle in Mongolia and I have been on an embassy to a *Hun-Hu-se* general…you know what the *Hun-Hu-ses* are, not red-bearded brigands but cultivated outlaws – a sort of independent Chinese Foreign Legion or militant Freemasons – a state within a state – who live on blackmail. I went to arrange with them that they should annoy the Japanese if war broke out. I didn't know Chinese, but we got on very well all the same. Then the war broke out. As I was in British Columbia, I was caught and so I had to come back this way and not by sea. I hope to get the same job when I come back… It depends."

"Then you are going back to the war?"

"Of course."

"At once? Then I shall be left to myself. I shouldn't, I suppose, be able to go with you?"

"Would you like to go?"

" Yes," said Miles.

He had never thought of such a thing before, but he knew that nothing was more true.

"Well, we should have to arrange that," said Alyosha.

They arrived back at the hotel in time for luncheon. Madame Dashkov and her husband took the arrangements they had made as a matter of course. They seemed to think it an excellent as well as a natural thing that Miles should be starting for St Petersburg.

So much so, that Miles was infected by their mood, and began to think that it was a natural thing himself. They all dined together that night and went, to please Dashkov, to the *Théatre Français*, where there was a performance of Victor Hugo's *Ruy Blas*. Alyosha excused himself at the last moment, saying he had too many letters to write.

Madame Dashkov criticised the play and Monsieur Dashkov criticised the acting, but Miles was moved to tears. He had never in his life seen anything so touching or so romantic.

The next morning he started for St Petersburg with Alyosha. The Dashkov family came to see them off at the station. That evening Mrs Consterdine arrived in Paris. But she was too late to stop Miles. He had gone, so they said at the hotel, that morning, and he had left no direction.

CHAPTER VI

The journey to St Petersburg, although uneventful, was full of excitement for Miles.

Every sight, each new face in Germany, and still more at the frontier and beyond it, was an event to him.

Alyosha was a curiously easy travelling companion. Sometimes he would talk incessantly for half an hour or so; sometimes he would remain silent for hours at a time. He smoked cigarettes all day, but never opened a book. Whether he talked or whether he remained silent, Miles felt equally at his ease with him. He arranged all that needed arrangement with an effortless efficiency. He spoke German as fluently as English, and had a knack of getting his way.

They arrived at St Petersburg in the evening. There was no snow in the streets. The cabs were on wheels. Alyosha took Miles to a small shabby hotel, where he seemed to be at home and to have a number of acquaintances of all nationalities. There was a young American who greeted him warmly. Alyosha asked Miles to wait for him a moment in the hall while he talked to the American. He then came back after a while and fetched Miles, and took him upstairs, where they washed and unpacked.

"We shall only have a day here," he explained. "We shall start tomorrow night if possible…if we can get everything settled by then."

"But do you mean me to come with you?"

"Of course, if you still want to."

"I want to, but I don't see how it is to be done."

"There is only one way," said Alyosha; "you must go out as a newspaper correspondent."

"But I can't write, and I have no connection with any newspaper."

"Can you draw?"

"No, I can't draw, but I can take photographs. It is my hobby. I got the first prize at the Norwich amateur competition last year."

"That will do," said Alyosha; "that is just the very thing; you will go as a photographer for a magazine."

"But what magazine? I don't know any magazines."

"No, but I do. I think – I think I have already struck the very thing we shall see. Have you any of your photographies" (pronounced phŏtōgrăphiĕs) "with you?"

"Only three: a view of London, a meet of foxhounds, and" – he blushed – "a portrait."

"Let me see them."

Miles searched his bag and brought out a small copybook, in which he made notes, wrote fragments of a diary sometimes, and had even occasionally copied out verses and stuck in cuttings from newspapers which had pleased him. Loose in this book were a few letters and three unmounted photographs. One was a view of the Thames taken on Waterloo Bridge at dawn, the second a snapshot of a meet of foxhounds at Wheatham, the third was a portrait of a girl who came on in a turn at the Hammersmith Music Hall. One of the pupils at Mourieux's had introduced Miles to her, and he had been to tea with her several times. She lived with her mother and an aged grandfather in Ladbroke Road. Miles thought her celestially beautiful, and had begged her to let him photograph her. She had consented with alacrity. But to her great disappointment, he had insisted on taking her with her hair down and against the light, and not, as she wished, with her new hat on, sitting on a chair next to a bowl of roses and holding a roll of music in her hands.

He did the photograph, and she cried from mortification when she saw it. A few days later she left for Manchester. She was on tour.

Alyosha looked at the photographs critically.

"Yes, they will do," he said. "You have talent. The river effect is good, and you have got the Gretchen effect from that vulgar little town sparrow."

Miles blushed again.

They finished unpacking. "There is an American," Alyosha said, "I know him – he is going out for *Skreibners'*. I will see him after dinner, I think – "

They dined together downstairs at the restaurant of the hotel. Alyosha seemed absent-minded; he spoke little during the meal. He seemed to be thinking something out. Directly they had finished dinner, and Alyosha had lit his cigarette, he said to Miles: "I have got an appointment. I must go out at once. I will come back and fetch you about twelve o'clock, and we will have supper."

"Ought I to dress?" asked Miles.

"Oh dear, no."

"It is no use your going to the theatre," Alyosha said as he went; "is it?"

"No; I shall be quite happy here, reading a book."

Miles was, in fact, engrossed in a book he had never heard of before, and which he had bought at one of the stations they had stopped at, in the Tauchnitz edition. It was called *Tom Jones*. Alyosha reappeared sooner than Miles had expected him. He was back by eleven o'clock.

"I am going to take you," he said, as he came into the room, "to the house of another aunt of mine – to stay, I mean; we will be more comfortable there. She wishes you to come just now; but I must warn you that she detests all Englishmen – not personally, but politically, now that they are the allies of Japan."

"Then surely I had better stay here?"

"Oh no. I have told her all about you, and she thinks that it is such a good thing that an impartial Englishman should go to the war, and tell the truth, and take truthful photographs. You see Reuter tells such lies, and our Government has quarrelled with the *Times*."

"But am I going?"

"I think it will be easy. There is an American, I saw him after dinner – I mean I caught sight of him directly we arrived, but I spoke to him after dinner. His name is Paul something Haslam, and he comes from the west. He has got a contract with *Skreibners*', the American magazine, to write a monthly article, with war pictures from the front; but they want real pictures, something artistic, and he has never taken a photography in his life. He pretends he has – he lies; he doesn't mean to go near the front, unless he is made to. What I have said to him is this. He can stay where he likes – say Mukden. You can take the photographies, and he can 'write them up,' as he calls it. You can go out as his partner; the magazine will pay. It can be arranged tomorrow with *Skreibners*' agent – it will make it easier – they have got an office here. Then you will have to see your Ambassador, and get a letter from him, and I will take you to the War Office and do the rest. Of course the photography business from the point of view of the magazine is all nonsense, because, if they let you take any photographies of any interest, they won't let you send them off till it is too late. But you will be able to do views of China. The streets at Mukden."

"Do you think they will let me go?"

"Yes; I will answer for you," he laughed; "they know me."

"Who?"

"Oh, the kind of authorities that matter. I mean those that really matter, the people who get things done."

"Now we must pack up all those things again. You had better pack mine, you pack better than I; no Russian can pack."

Miles got through the packing of their few belongings quickly enough.

They went downstairs and paid their bill, took back their passports, and Alyosha ordered a cab.

"Tell me," said Miles, "about your aunt; is she the sister of your aunt in Paris?"

"Oh no, not at all. Certainly not. She has been the wife of my Uncle Kouragine, who is dead, so she is really what you perhaps call an aunt-in-law. She has no children, and she lives alone in a large house, in the…but what is the use of telling you the name of a street? It is some way off…the distances here are great…her name is Princess Kouragine. She wears her husband's name of course, but there are dozens of Princess Kouragines, and *she* is always called Kitty."

"Does she speak English?"

"Of course; it is the only language she can speak, except French and German."

"But surely she speaks her own language?"

"A little, very badly; just enough to be able to speak to the servants…she learnt it when she was grown up."

They drove across the *Nevski*, along the *Morskaya*, past St Isaac's Cathedral, down along a canal till they came to a Palladian stucco building with a portico and pillars.

They were let in by a hall porter who waved them up a staircase.

"I feel very shy," whispered Miles as they walked upstairs. They were shown into a long, low drawing-room by a footman, but there was no one there. They walked through it to a smaller square room, with faded red silk on the walls, a few French pictures and Empire furniture, where, sitting near a tea table, was a small lady dressed in black, with grey hair, pronounced features, and bright grey eyes, smoking a cigarette. There was a small Irish terrier in the room that barked.

"*Bon soir*, Alyosha," she said. "*Ah! voici votre ami.*"

She walked to meet them. Alyosha kissed her hand and introduced Miles. She gave him a penetrating glance as she shook hands with him.

"Come and sit down, Mr Miles," she said, pointing to a chair. "I believe you have another name, but it is too difficult for me. I shall call you Mr Miles. I am delighted to see you; I like the English as a rule, but not now; they are behaving abominably. Personally I have always got on with them. They are nice, but your Government is detestable. Many years ago I was staying at a large country house, by Lord Stonehenge, in Shropshire. He was a great friend of mine, and I liked him. I lit a cigarette in my bedroom, and I was told that no one may smoke in the house, and that if one wanted to smoke, one must go into the garden – it was winter too – so I went to Lord Stonehenge, and said that I was going to be the exception to his rule, and to smoke when and where I wanted. He laughed and said he would be delighted. He even smoked a cigarette after dinner to give me a *contenance*. The butler was very shocked. But then the English are always easily shocked. Are you easily shocked, Mr Miles?"

Miles got scarlet, and began pulling up his left sock.

"I don't understand," went on the Princess, "why Englishmen's socks are always coming down. Other people's socks don't come down, but Englishmen are always pulling up their socks."

Miles got redder still.

"Well," she said, "you will not be wanting to talk to an old woman like myself, and it is late, and I am sleepy. I suppose Alyosha will take you somewhere. They will show you your rooms. You will have the *appartement* on the ground floor," she said to Alyosha. "It doesn't matter how late you come in. We will meet tomorrow at *déjeuner*. I have ordered some *Bliny*."

Alyosha said something in Russian. She nodded and got up. Alyosha kissed her hand, said "Good-night," and added: "We shall be alone, then?" As she walked out of the room, she said to Alyosha, "*Ton Anglais me plaît*," and then she said a few words in Russian and laughed. She walked through a little door to her apartments, and Alyosha took Miles downstairs. They had two bedrooms and a sitting-room, and a bathroom between them, on the ground floor.

"It is now getting on for midnight," said Alyosha. "Just right for supper." They drove to a restaurant which seemed to Miles a long way off.

"I am going to introduce you to your American, to the man who will be your colleague," said Alyosha. "He has got a little supper here with some ladies... Olga Varina, the famous singer – she sings ballads – she has no voice; Maltzova the dancer, and Maya Komarova. They won't be there yet, not all of them..."

"I shan't be able to understand what they say."

"Haslam doesn't speak a word of Russian. My aunt," he went on, changing the subject, "is very clever. She has no prejudices. You see there are few, really no houses I could go to here at St Petersburg now...owing to, well, a bother I go into some time ago, a long time ago... I will tell you all about it some day...in England it would have been worse,...but even here it would be uncomfortable, only my Aunt Kitty doesn't mind – she wouldn't – she doesn't care. When I had the bother, she did everything she could to help me, although she is not at all sentimental, and not what is called *kind*...but she understood – she has no prejudices at all."

"Except against English people?"

"That is political and temporary. She has disputed and quarrelled with English politicians and diplomatists all her life – but the English, they are really her best friends. She used to write long letters to Kingslake and Kingley, and to Mr Gladstone; she knows your Ambassador, or at least the man in charge, well, and will give you a letter for him. I have asked her to. She is a Slavophile, but at the same time she is very liberal, and is always talking against the Government. She thinks this war is a folly. So it is; but she thinks it is wicked of England to be allies with Japan – wicked and silly. Wicked, well, yes – perhaps she is right – I don't care; but silly it is; and you will regret it when we lose the war, which we probably shall. But she is clever outside of politics, and she has written a book in French on Chopin. She is a great musician."

"Like your other aunt?"

"Aunt Lizzy? Oh no, quite different. They hate each other. They are both energetic, and both do things, but different things. Aunt Lizzy gets up classical and theatrical concerts; Aunt Kitty sees nobody, and never gives parties, and yet knows everyone of any interest in Europe – they are drawn to her as to a magnet. Aunt Kitty is much cleverer."

"But your other aunt is kind to you too, isn't she?"

"Yes, she has to be; she is my mother's sister, *la voix du sang*, and then she is very good-natured – of course she is rather absurd, but Aunt Kitty is *someone* – you must have seen that from talking to her for five minutes. She has read everything – seen everyone – and everything – "

"Yes, I thought she was rather alarming."

"She is frank, and sees everything. You will get used to her soon. She is not at all frightful, and she likes you – that is everything."

After what to Miles seemed an endless drive, they arrived at the restaurant, and left their coats in the cloakroom. Alyosha led Miles through a large hall in which there were a few people having supper at small tables – there was a stage at the end of it – to a private room, which looked out like a box on to the hall. In this box there was a table laid for ten people, and a great many bottles on the table, besides caviare, kippered salmon, and other cold *hors d'oeuvres*. So far the only people there were a tall, dark, thin, slim-looking man, who turned out to be Haslam – he was in day clothes – and another American in evening clothes. He, too, was a journalist, the correspondent

of a New York newspaper. Miles was introduced to both of
them.

"The ladies are late, but we will have a little vodka to keep
us warm," said Haslam.

He looked at Miles in a friendly way. He was good-looking,
with an amused expression and good-humoured, dishonest
eyes.

Haslam poured out some vodka for everyone.

"Wait one moment," said Alyosha; "before the drinking
begins, I have something to do. Have you got a visiting card?"
he said to Miles.

"Yes," said Miles; "but what on earth do you want it for?"

"Give it to me."

Miles handed him a card. It had his London address.

Alyosha wrote something on it, and gave it him back.

"There; I have written your name and address – the address
of the house where we are staying – in English and in Russian,
so that if we get separated and you get lost, you will be able to
find your way, or somebody will be able to find your way
for you."

The other two men laughed.

"But I shan't get separated from you, shall I?" asked Miles
anxiously.

"Not if we can help it, *but one never knows.*"

They all drank a small liqueur glass of vodka, and then Miles
was given some caviare. The dose was doubled and repeated –
a third time for the Trinity, a fourth time for the four corners of
a house, a fifth time for the five cupolas of a church.

Miles felt a warm glow, and soon began to feel pleasantly
exhilarated, but he remained quite clear-headed. They sat down
at the end of the table, and Paul Haslam treated him to a long
and confidential monologue: the story of his life. He had been
a circus-rider, an actor, a stoker, and a banker.

"*Tu sais,*" said Alyosha suddenly, "*il ne faut pas croire un
mot de ce qu'il dit, il ne sait pas dire la vérité.*"

After Miles had drunk his fifth glass of vodka, more guests arrived – three elegant ladies: Olga Varina, Maltzova, and Maya Komarova. They were accompanied by an Englishman and several other men whose nationality Miles could not guess, although he was introduced to them, but he was vaguely aware that they were not Russians. They sat down to supper, and champagne bottles were opened, and toasts were drunk. The ladies treated Miles with great friendliness, as if they had known him all his life. They talked French. The hall of the restaurant was now full, and a variety entertainment was in full swing on the stage. Miles felt himself getting happier and happier; he was not, he thought, in the least intoxicated – and this was odd; perhaps it was the dry air of St Petersburg, perhaps he had a strong head. He had always been used to tasting strong Madeira at his uncle's. When supper was over, and the talk was growing louder and louder, somebody raised a cry of "*Tsygan!*" (gipsies), and no sooner was the word said than Alyosha and the Americans and someone else went to arrange the matter.

Presently they moved into another larger, empty room. It was rather dingy. In one corner of the room there was a battered pianoforte, much the worse for wear. On the walls looking glasses in gilded frames, At one end of the room was a plush sofa. In front of it was a table, with champagne bottles, glasses, and candles – the only illumination. Miles and the other spectators all sat down on the sofa.

In front of them, occupying the whole of the other side of the room, was the chorus of gipsies. They were different from what Miles expected; they were not "raggle-taggle" people in shabby and gorgeous clothes, with tambourines and sequins; they were a chorus of men and women in ordinary dress who, though dark in complexion, looked, he thought, like the audience in the dress circle at a classical concert in London.

They were seated in a semicircle. A man with a guitar, dark – and he, too, in ordinary clothes – stood up and led the chorus;

sometimes he took the solo part. His body and his guitar swayed to the rhythm of the music.

Later a woman took a solo part. The chorus rose into a wail as loud and as fierce, thought Miles, as the howling of a pack of wolves, and then died away into an unsatisfied sigh.

Miles thought the music unpleasant: discordant, monotonous, and exasperating.

Champagne was poured out and toasts were drunk. But on the part of the spectators there was no visible gaiety; no noise, no laughter, and little talk. Yet Miles thought they seemed to be enjoying themselves.

He looked on at the scene as it were from the outside. He felt detached, as if he were a spectator at the play. He said to himself: "It is, I suppose, because I don't understand what they are singing, and because this sort of music is so new to me."

He observed the audience.

Alyosha was lying back on the sofa, sitting next to Olga Varina, the singer. He was not looking at her; he was staring with a fixed expression straight in front of him. Olga Varina had a clever, impertinent face; now her eyes seemed full of tears, but sparkling tears of pleasure. The lady they called Maltzova was short; she had dark hair, fine aquiline features, and a long rope of pearls. Miles saw her profile. She was smoking a cigarette. She looked as calm as a statue, aloof and indifferent – and yet Miles had the impression as of being near a loaded revolver. The third woman, Maya Komarova, had a childish baby face, fair hair, and candid eyes. She looked as if she were utterly absorbed, and enjoying herself like a child that is being told a fairy tale. The men were equally rapt and subdued. But every now and then someone would break the silence and ask for a particular song: "The Blue Bird" (Alyosha interpreted) or "Cold Dawn."

The American in evening clothes was sitting on the floor, his head nodded drowsily. All the spectators seemed to be bound by the same spell, as if they had taken an opiate; they were like lotus-eaters, Miles thought; no, not lotus-eaters, because they seemed to *feel* it all...like people who are taking part in a dream. Miles looked at the gipsies. They seemed to him listless and bored. They were carrying on an irrelevant, intermittent undercurrent of conversation among themselves, like telegraph-girls, Miles thought, at a London post office, behind the wire netting.

One of them had toothache and a swelled face, which was bound up with a handkerchief. "This is to them," thought Miles to himself, "what my office used to be to me. It is their daily work. I wonder what their recreation is, if they have one?"

After the singing had lasted some time, Miles' impressions began to change. He lost his detachment. He was touched by the spell. He ceased to think the noise disagreeable. All at once he found himself trembling all over as from fever, and then he became aware that the fever was pleasant. He did not want it to stop; he wanted it to go on. He wanted it never to stop.

He felt that he had been initiated, and whenever the music stopped, he felt he wanted one more glimpse of that sweet and bitter, that discordant and melodious Limbo; he hoped the hurly-burly would never be done.

"What is it all about?" Miles asked Alyosha.

"Oh," said Alyosha, "the usual things: troikas, snow, spring, birch trees, white dawns, sleepless midnights, famishing morrows, eternal farewells, vows of everlasting love, 'Had we never met,' 'Goodbye for ever,' and the music is really German *waltzers* sung differently. You must be hating it; everyone does at first, but it will grow on you."

"It has grown on me already," said Miles.

Then he reached a new phase. He no longer thought about it as a scene; he was in it, an actor taking a part in the dream. He was made to stand up for the *Charochka*, and the leader of the chorus, guitar in hand, stood in front of him, having first asked his name of Alyosha; he was sung to by name, and told to drain his glass at a given moment, which he did. He did not feel in the least shy or uncomfortable. By this time he was simply enjoying himself. He was looking at everything through a veil, but it was pleasant. He wanted the dream to last for ever, the spell never to be broken.

Miles lost the sense of time. The leader of the chorus seemed to sway with his guitar and with his body to the rhythm of the chorus for an eternity. The howling as of wolves was fiercer, louder, and hoarser; the dying sighs softer and more desperately unsatisfied... The cold dawn was beginning to pierce through the window of the cheerless and gaudy private room. The candles on the table were guttering. There were more solos...people asked for songs all at once. It was oppressively hot. The air was thick with cigarette smoke. There was a pause in the singing. Miles said to himself, "I must get some air." He got up. "I will be back in a moment," he said. Nobody took any notice, and he went out of the room, and walked downstairs. He asked for his hat and coat, and walked out into the street. The air – the sharp, cool air of the cold grey dawn – acted on him like magic. It had the effect of making him dance off into happy, irresponsible unconsciousness, into the dawn and the unknown. Upstairs the singing went on and on, until the gipsies sang their last song, which had for its burden "*Domoi, domoi*" ("Home, home").

It was only when the spectators were leaving the restaurant that the absence of Miles was noticed.

Alyosha asked the attendants where he was, but all that he could find out was that Miles had left the restaurant some time ago, after taking his hat and his coat; he had gone on foot.

"What can we do?" asked Haslam.

"Nothing," said Alyosha. "He has got his name and address in his pocket. They will bring him home. It was lucky I took that precaution. It is, I have found, always safe to do that with strangers in Russia."

"He won't give the police any trouble, I guess, anyway," said Haslam.

"One never knows," said Alyosha calmly. "English people are sometimes so very violent when they are – what do you call it, say, when they have drink-taken."

"That's Irish, and Irishmen are certainly violent; but that boy looks as if butter would not melt in his mouth."

"He is most willing to learn," said Alyosha.

Alyosha did not go home immediately. He went to Haslam's rooms. They had a further discussion of plans. Alyosha pointed out to him that it would be most advantageous for him to take Miles with him. He had everything to gain and nothing to lose by it.

Alyosha did not get home till seven in the morning. He asked the hall porter whether Miles had arrived.

"Yes," said the night porter calmly. "They brought *them*" – he used the third person plural, which in Russian indicates respect – "twice from the police station, and I didn't recognise them, and sent them back. They were 'drink-taken,' they were unconscious, and their coat was torn. Then they took them to the back door, and Petrushka, the *dvornik* (the man who swept the backyard), recognised them and said: 'Yes, that is our *Barin.*'" ("That is our gentleman.') "They are asleep." ("*Oni spiat.*")

CHAPTER VII

When Miles woke up the next morning he was asked by the servant whether he would have some tea. The Russian treated him with sympathetic knowingness. But as Miles did not understand him, and the servant knew no other language but Russian, the effect was wasted. Miles remembered nothing of what had happened after he had left the restaurant. Tea was brought to him in the sitting-room, and after he had got up and was dressed Alyosha appeared and said he was going to have breakfast.

His breakfast consisted of four glasses of vodka and a pickled cucumber. While he ate it he reconstructed to Miles the events of the evening.

"Yes," he said, "you must have been very drunk and what is called disorderly. I expect you resisted the police. They took you to the *Uchastok*."

"How awful!" said Miles. "Will the Princess ever know?" (He wondered whether she could possibly tell Aunt Fanny.)

"She knows already. I have seen her. She had been told, but she doesn't mind; on the contrary, she expected it. She likes you a thousand times the better. The household already respect you immensely."

They had hardly finished dressing when three policemen called. They were shown in by the footman, who was grinning. Alyosha interviewed them.

They said they had found Miles wandering about the streets in a state of exhilaration.

"Drunk?" said Alyosha.

They demurred at that. They were in the habit of appraising accurately, not only as professional critics, but as fellow-artists, and their standard was high. No, they said, not *drunk* – certainly not drunk. "*Wypimshi*," they said, which can be well rendered as "not drunk, but having drink-taken."

They had suggested his going with them to the police station, to find out about him; but he had refused to go with them, doubtless owing, they suggested, to his ignorance of the Russian language. "He understands nothing," they said. When they had tried to take him there, he had fought them all three like a tiger. That is what they had come about. He had torn their clothes; Government property, for which they were responsible. They were poor folk. They would get into trouble. Nobody listened to excuses. Ultimately he had been taken to the police station. He was, they said, very savage – *ochen dikii*. Once there, he had fallen into a quiet sleep which had lasted two hours. The officer in charge had found his address written on a card in his pocket, and when he had attained to semi-consciousness he sent him to Princess Kouragine's house in a cab with a policeman. But there the night porter, or whoever had opened the door, had disowned him. Miles apparently had presented a sorry appearance: his coat was in rags, his shirt dripping, torn, and blood-stained, his hair dishevelled, and he had a cut on his chin.

He was then brought back to the police station and was given a glass of tea. Once more he fell asleep. When he came to the second time, he was sent back, with two policemen this time, to Princess Kouragine's house, and again the hall porter denied him, with an oath this time. He was brought back to the police station, and after another refreshing nap and another glass of tea, he was restored to a state of more advanced consciousness, and he repeated the name of Princess

Kouragine several times quite audibly and intelligibly. The police officer in despair sent him back a third time with another policeman. The policeman had the brilliant idea of going to the back door, where they were let in by Petrushka, the *dvornik*, the man whose duty it was to look after the outer premises, and sweep the yard of snow in winter. He was a peasant, with hair like tow, and he sympathised with the intoxicated, as we have already seen.

Petrushka had claimed him with pride.

"And now," concluded the spokesman of the police, with tears in his eyes, "we ask His Brightness to have pity on us. We are poor folk. Our uniforms are torn, and we shall be made to pay for new ones out of our pay. Ten roubles will be little...a small sum, *Batiushka*..."

Ample, indeed handsome, compensation under Alyosha's directions was paid. The police retired murmuring blessings on everybody concerned, and the episode was closed.

"And now," said Alyosha, "we must be busy, very busy. The first thing for you to do is to go to *Skreibners'*, then to the British Embassy. Here is a letter which my aunt has written for you to her friend, the Chargé d'Affaires. There is at this moment no Ambassador, as the new one has not yet arrived. I will drive you there, and I will wait for you while you are there, but I will not come in; we must go to *Skreibners'* first."

"But what am I to say to them?" said Miles.

"I will explain," said Alyosha. "You must take those photographies you showed me with you."

They took a cab, and on the way to the Embassy they stopped at an office in a large street full of shops, where, surrounded by typists and clerks, sat Mr Silas K Blomberg, the agent for *Skreibners' Magazine*.

"Do you know him?" asked Miles as they stood outside the door.

"Oh yes," said Alyosha. "Haslam introduced me last night."

"Come right in," said Mr Blomberg when they were shown in, "and sit down." Three glasses of tea were brought and Miles was introduced. "Glad to meet you, Mr Consterdine," said Mr Blomberg, offering Miles a cigarette. "You want to go to this darned war with Haslam? Now we want pictures, and Haslam can't take pictures. Haslam'll write up anything you take, but we must have a picture expert. He tried to bluff us into letting him do the pictures... Now the first question is, what is your work like?"

"Show him the photographies," said Alyosha.

Before Mr Blomberg could make a comment, Alyosha began to present the pictures, and to discuss them with a wealth of technical detail and phraseology which made Miles gasp.

It was Greek to him. "You see it's the new process," said Alyosha. "That got the first prize at Munich," he said, pointing to the view of the Thames (Miles gasped); "and that was reproduced in *Country Life*," he said, pointing to the snapshot of the meet at Wheatham; "and that is Eulalie Collins – *the* Eulalie Collins, the famous music-hall star. She made a sensation with that song, 'Kiss me when the moon is new.' They have engaged her here at the Aquarium for the winter. You see the point of Consterdine's pictures is that they are so various: he could take a battlefield as easily as a prima donna, and then he has experience of the new processes, which makes all the difference for reproduction in magazines. He is thinking of doing colour pictures."

"Oh, we couldn't run to that now," said Mr Blomberg, alarmed.

"Of course, Haslam," went on Alyosha, "is a perfect newspaperman and a good writer of long stories; but he cannot take a photography – no, not even of a donkey in a field. He has no sense of grouping, or horizon, or foreground. He told me so himself."

"I know," said Blomberg. "But I guess he could get someone out there to do the pictures for him."

Alyosha chuckled.

"Who," he asked, "will be the unselfish newspaperman who will give away his copy?"

"It wouldn't be a question of giving."

"Who, then, is the editor who will sell his scoops at a loss?"

"Not necessarily at a loss."

"To sell them anyway would be a loss at this moment, in those circumstances. Don't be childlike, Mr Blomberg. If you don't want Consterdine, say so, and I will take him across the road and fix him up with Lautenberg for the *Woche*. They pay good money."

"Don't fly off the handle," said Mr Blomberg. "I don't say the stuff is bad. I don't say they wouldn't get across with Haslam to write them up, but the point is this: it's no use my having the first picture taker in the world unless he can get to the front and take the pictures I want taken. Now will Mr Consterdine be able to hit the front? It's no good my having Haslam at the front writing up pictures which might just as well have been taken in the Chinese quarter at San Francisco. Do you get me?"

"I get you perfectly," said Alyosha, "and I say there is more chance for Consterdine, who is the head of a firm which has had historic relations with Russia" – this was news to Consterdine – "and who will be recommended by General Z and have personal letters to the Viceroy and to the Commander-in-Chief – there is more chance of his getting to the front than anyone else getting there. Besides which, he is pro-Russian – his firm has naturally always been pro-Russian ever since the days of Catherine the Great – and he is giving proof of his sentiments by wishing to go for your paper instead of for the *Times*, or for any of the English papers."

"Well, there's something to that," said Blomberg.

"My aunt, Princess Kouragine," said Alyosha, "is giving him letters to several of the Generals – the British Chargé d'Affaires."

"Well," said Blomberg," as to the terms."

And then another battle began, which was conducted entirely between Mr Blomberg and Alyosha. Miles looked on gaping. An arrangement was arrived at, to which Alyosha reluctantly consented. To Miles it seemed beyond the dreams of avarice. As far as he could make out in English money, it amounted to £100 a month and £200 a month for expenses, for a monthly illustrated article – that is to say, for the illustrations.

When the bargain was struck, Mr Paul Haslam was announced. The coincidence had been arranged by Alyosha. He came, saw, and agreed. Mr Blomberg gave Miles a written certificate that he was the accredited photographer to *Skreibners'*; and after arranging to meet Haslam at the hotel – they were all to start that night if they could get matters arranged – Miles and Alyosha took their leave of Mr Blomberg.

"Do you really know all about photography?" Miles asked as they were driving to the British Embassy.

"Only from what you told me during the journey out, and from once having a Kodak."

"It seems a lot of money to get for a few photographs."

"You will have to give all the pay to Haslam," said Alyosha. "I arranged that with him; but you need not feel the loss unless you like, as he will let you share his food and lodging, and charge it up in his expenses; and as you have the expenses, you will be able to make both ends meet."

"Oh! I don't mind the expense," said Miles, thinking, not without a twinge, of Aunt Fanny. "Now what have I got to do at the Embassy?"

"You have got to see the Chargé d'Affaires – his name is Geoffrey Walter. Give him this letter from my Aunt Kitty. It is telling him who you are, and that her family knows relations of yours, and asking him to help you to take advantage of a great opportunity. I explained everything to her, and that Uncle Pierre knew your father, and that you were a great artist being wasted in the City office, and had this great opportunity of seeing the world and of doing creative work; and just now, when all the world was anti-Russian, what a good thing it would be for you to take pictures and write articles in a pro-Russian American magazine like *Skreibners*, which has a vast circulation. When you have given him the letter, you must tell him you are going out for *Skreibners*, as an artist, and ask him for two letters of introduction – one to General Z, at the War Office here, and an unsealed letter of introduction that you can show to any authorities out there. It had better be addressed to the Viceroy, and perhaps you had better get another addressed to the Commander-in-Chief."

"But will he do all that?"

"Try," said Alyosha. "While you are here I have got a commission to do. I will call for you in twenty minutes. If you are ready first, wait. If I am ready first, I will wait for you down here in the cab. *Au revoir*."

"I shall never be able to ask for all that," said Miles.

"Then I had better come with you," said Alyosha. He asked the hall porter whether he could see Mr Walter, the Chargé d'Affaires, and sent up their cards. They were shown into a waiting room, and presently one of the younger secretaries came to them and asked them in the high, refined, languid idiom of Oxford what it was they wanted. Alyosha said that they must see the Chargé d'Affaires in person, and no one else. They came from Princess Kouragine, and Miles had a letter that he had been asked to deliver in person. The matter was urgent.

The secretary left them, and presently took Miles and Alyosha into the Chargé d'Affaires' room.

Geoffrey Walter was getting on for forty. He was a great friend of Princess Kouragine, one of her few intimate friends; and although they quarrelled over politics, they agreed about literature, of which they were both genuinely fond.

Miles presented his letter. Walter greeted them affably. He had no idea who Miles was, and the Kouragines were legion. He had never seen Alyosha and had no idea who he was. So he asked them to sit down, and put on his spectacles – or rather

54

the gold-edged pince-nez, which hung on a broad black ribbon – and read the letter. The letter was written in French, for Princess Kouragine, although she could speak English fluently, found it impossible to spell.

"MON CHER GEOFFREY" (it ran), – *"Je vous présente un nouvel ami, un grand ami de Pierre Dashkov, le mari de la soeur de ma belle-soeur Lizzy, et de sa famille, que vous connaissez. Il parait que c'est un garçon tout-à-fait remarquable, qui a découvert de nouveaux procédés de photographie en couleur. Jusqu'à présent il a été forcé par sa tante de travailler dans un stupide bureau à Londres ce qui n'est pas du tout nécessaire, le garçon ayant hérité d'une* immense fortune, *et du reste sa maison d'affaires, une vieille maison* respectable, *comme dans Dickens, est dirigée par un associé, un vrai* businessman *qui fait tout, donc il n'a rien à faire sauf de signer des lettres et dire bonjour aux clients. Maintenant un 'magazine' Américain lui a offert l'occasion de prendre des vues photographiques au front en Mantchourie. Ce sera une occasion magnifique pour le développement de son caractère aussi bien que pour son art. Je vous prie donc de lui donner une lettre pour le General Z, au Ministère de la Guerre, pour lui recommander mon protégé, et de faire tout ce que vous pouvez pour l'aider.* Il est nécessaire qu'il soit recommandé par SON AMBASSADE.

"Venez prendre une tasse de thé après-demain soir si vous êtes libre.

"P.S. – *Quel horrible article dans le dernier* Times!"

Walter read the letter and smiled. He was used to Princess Kouragine's sudden enthusiasms, but he was surprised that she wished to send an Englishman to Manchuria.

"What magazine are you going for?" he asked.

"I am Princess Kouragine's nephew," broke in Alyosha, "and she has asked me to come and be Mr Consterdine's spokesman, knowing that he was shy, as all Englishmen. She thought *que je saurais plaider sa cause*, and she said that you would be able to arrange everything. Mr Consterdine is, of course, the senior partner in the historic firm of Consterdine, of London and Madeira."

Walter did not know the firm, but made up his mind that he would get some port wine.

"A firm," Alyosha went on, "that has always had relations with Russia, and whose name is known among the connoisseurs of great wines. Mr Consterdine is taking a holiday. He wants to see the world, the East. He has a talent for photography, and has won prizes at International *Concours*, and has made some discoveries in colour photography. *Skreibners'*, the American magazine, has made him an offer to go out for them. *Skreibners'* is *for* our poor country at this moment, so it would be an advantage for the good relations between England and Russia that a man like Mr Consterdine should give the English and American public impartial *comptes-rendus*."

"Ah, that accounts for it," thought Walter.

Skreibners', he knew, was a wholeheartedly pro-Russian and violently anti-Japanese organ.

"Of course," said Alyosha, "our Government will give you alone the credit for this. They know all you have done to try and settle that foolish *brouille* with the *Times*."

"I wish he could go for the *Times*," said Walter. "It is really too silly that there should be no correspondent for the *Times* there at such a moment."

"Ah," said Alyosha, "it is indeed a pity, but the fault, I am afraid, is on our side."

"The newspapers are always very tiresome," said Walter wearily; "but what is it you want? – a letter to General Z? I don't know the General very well, but I have met him."

"It is necessary," said Alyosha, "that Mr Consterdine should be recommended by his Embassy."

"Of course, your Government," said Walter to Alyosha, "is not over-anxious to have correspondents – what Government is? – and I doubt if they will let you send anything off; but after all, pictures in a magazine, and in *Skreibners'*... I will do what I can."

He began to write a letter.

"It would be still more valuable," said Alyosha, "if you could also give Mr Consterdine a letter, an unsealed letter, that he could show to the authorities out there when necessary."

"What authorities?"

"Well, the Viceroy at Mukden and the Commander-in-Chief," Alyosha said airily.

Walter thought a little. He knew neither of these important people, but he hated admitting that anything was impossible to a man of tact and *savoir-faire*. Also he genuinely liked arranging and settling things for people, especially officially; he liked to show people there was no red tape in his work and that diplomats were not necessarily unbusinesslike. He took pride in it.

"They should be from a Russian," he said. "I am going round to the Foreign Office this morning, in half an hour's time. I will see what I can do. If you could call back just before luncheon, you shall have the letters then if I can get them."

"My Uncle Dashkov is a great friend of Olenev's," said Alyosha, naming one of the higher officials at the Foreign Office.

Walter wrote the letter to General Z. He wrote it in French very quickly, in a clear, bold handwriting, copying Miles' name from the visiting card.

"There," he said to Miles, "is the letter."

"You were at Mourieux', weren't you?" Miles said. "Madame Mourieux used to talk of you so often."

Walter's manner changed. He beamed.

"Yes, indeed! how are they? How is the old man and Madame? I am devoted to them both. They always write to me on New Year's Day. Fancy your having been there! – to learn French?"

"Yes, to learn French."

"You will now see that Mr Walter will arrange everything as by magic," said Alyosha as he took Miles away after saying goodbye. They went straight to the War Office, where Alyosha seemed to be quite at home. After several confabulations with orderlies and other underlings, Walter's letter was sent in to the General, and presently Miles himself was shown into the General's room, alone this time.

The General addressed him in broken French, begged him to be impartial, and gave him a printed form to fill up in ink, which he signed then and there, and which allowed him to proceed to Kharbin and to the seat of war. The General then shook hands with him, wished him luck, and begged him to have his articles forwarded to him.

The interview only lasted a few moments, and it seemed to Miles that it was as simple as ABC to go to Manchuria; so no doubt it was when the problem was tackled in the right way. Alyosha then drove Miles to several shops, and they purchased what to Miles seemed strange equipment – a number of grey sarcenet shirts, some loose high Russian boots, some flannel tunics, and two Caucasian cloaks called *Burkas*.

"Shan't we want saddles?" asked Miles.

"No," he said. "Haslam will have all that. We will travel light; other people will travel heavy for us. There are several correspondents going out who have never been to a war before. They will take the unnecessaries."

Before luncheon they called back at the Embassy and once more they saw Walter. He presented Miles triumphantly with two typewritten letters: one addressed to the Viceroy and one to the Commander-in-Chief, stating that Mr Miles Consterdine, the senior partner of the firm, which had had age-long relations with Russia, and was a celebrated artist, was proceeding to Manchuria, to take special views of the front for the extremely important and Russophile American magazine, *Skreibners'*. It was to be hoped that all possible facilities would be given to Mr Miles Consterdine, who was a man of culture and of importance in the City, as well as in the world of art in London. The letters were signed by the Minister of Foreign Affairs himself.

"That being so, we will start tonight," said Alyosha.

"It is useless for us to waste another day here." They then drove back home. Princess Kouragine was awaiting them upstairs.

The Princess shook hands with Miles, Alyosha kissed her hand; they went into luncheon immediately. The Princess made no allusion to what had occurred the night before. She asked about their plans, and was delighted to hear that everything had gone well.

"I knew Walter would do what I asked him," she said. "One must let him think he is a Providence, *mondain*, a mixture of Talleyrand and the Good Samaritan, and he will do anything. I like him all the same, very much. He is agreeable, and has good taste in literature, and speaks Russian better than I do. You must learn Russian, Mr Miles, especially as you are so musical."

"I – musical? I have heard hardly any music," said Miles, bewildered.

"But you appreciate it very much, especially gipsy music, I think. Alyosha told me that you went to the *Bohémiens* last night," she said, with a twinkle in her eye. Miles blushed. "I am delighted you did," she went on. "I used to be fond of them too, when I was young. It is a pity you are not staying; you could go again tonight. It grows upon one. When I was first married we used to go night after night, and we used to feel so comfortably sad and melancholy, like the lovers and clowns in Shakespeare; later on one is melancholy in a different way – it is no longer 'idle tears' but 'tears of recognition.' That is the poet Patmore.

59

Do you know the poet Patmore? No? He is a great poet, one of the best modern English poets. Don't you know your English poets, Mr Miles?"

"Very little, I am afraid."

"You have not had time. You will have time at the war to read. I will give you one poet. One poet is enough at the war, and you will not have room for two. I will give you my favourite English poet. I will not tell you who he is. You will guess. I delight in your English poets. After Pushkin, I like them best of all; better than the Germans and Italians and French. I am putting aside Shakespeare, Dante and Goethe of course. They are apart. But your English poets. There are so many – Milton and Byron, and Wordsworth and Longfellow, and Browning and Lord Lytton. And Patmore and Tennyson, and Keats and Mrs Hemans. Walter reads to me sometimes. He will read me Swinburne, *c'est joli, mais vide, 'poustoi.'* But I have discovered a new poet for him, or rather a poetess. I found her book by Watkins. She writes such beautiful things. Her name is Ella Wheeler Wilcox. You don't know her?"

"I am afraid not," said Miles.

"Ah, Aunt Kitty, she is like the words of the gipsies' songs," said Alyosha.

"*C'est possible*; but I am old and sentimental, and I like simple poems:

> 'Laugh and the world laughs with you,
> Weep, and you weep alone.'

What could you have better than that? I like simple things I can understand. And also difficult things sometimes that give one to think, *quand ils sont très beaux*, like Browning. He is the lovers' poet. Have you ever been in love, Mr Miles? No, not yet," she answered for him, seeing his blush. "Not really, only small adventures – *cela viendra*. Then you must learn Russian to read Pushkin. He says certain things like no one else. More

simply than anyone else, as I imagine the Greeks did. Oh, how
I wish I knew Greek! Translations are impossible. There is no
war news today, Alyosha, so I feel there must be bad news. *Oh,
ces Japonais!* Walter knows them. He lived in Japan. He liked
their poetry, but he says it is all gone. They are materialised,
Tant pis pour nous et pour vous. They and the Chinese will
conquer us some day. I shall be dead, thank Heaven! So you are
going tonight? You will have a glimpse of Moscow. You must
take him to Testov, Alyosha, and give him *rastigai* and *kalachi*
to eat. He must see the Kremlin and the Tretiakov Gallery."

"We shan't have time," said Alyosha.

"Nonsense; you will have the whole day."

The Princess' monologue, punctuated by questions, went on
thus throughout luncheon. Sometimes the aunt and the
nephew had a short argument. After luncheon they smoked in
the little room. At three o'clock the Princess' carriage was
announced.

"I will take Mr Miles for a drive," she said. "I know you have
things to do, Alyosha. You will have an early dinner here, and
then go to the station." Alyosha left them, and the Princess took
Miles for a drive, during the course of which she drew from him
the whole story of his short and uneventful life. It made her
thoughtful.

As they were nearing home she said to him: "I am satisfied,
Mr Miles; you may go with Alyosha. It is not everyone who
would allow you to go to Manchuria with Alyosha. It is not
everyone I should allow him to take. He has been, you know,
what is called 'unlucky,' and he has made a mess of his life; he
has had *des malheurs*, as I know he has hinted to you. But he
is not bad *au fond, malgré tous ses défauts*, and he will do you
no harm. I can let you go safely, and you may not see much of
him. After all, one has to face life some time or other. You will
do him good."

They had a hurried meal later without the Princess, who was
dining out, but she came to say goodbye to them. She gave

Alyosha and Miles each a little holy medal, and to Miles a parcel as well.

She followed them out on to the landing. There she stopped, and Alyosha bade her a last goodbye. He kissed her hand. She kissed his forehead, and gave him her blessing. Miles felt impelled to kiss her hand too, and she blessed him too.

"Take care of yourself, Alyosha, and *surtout* you are to take care of Mr Miles. Goodbye, Alyosha. You will never see me again."

CHAPTER VIII

Miles and Alyosha were settled in the first-class carriage of the Trans-Siberian Express; they had two compartments. When they had boarded the train they were given one compartment, with two sleeping berths to share between them. The train was full. There were, besides Miles and Alyosha, several officers going to the front, some officials, some men of business; four Americans besides Paul Haslam – two of them newspapermen, and the others mining engineers; a Norwegian military attaché, a French man of business and his wife, and an Englishman called Walter Troumestre who was going out as the correspondent of an English newspaper.

On the morning after they had started, Alyosha had a short talk with the train conductor; and at the first station at which a passenger alighted, his compartment, which contained two berths, was given to Alyosha and Miles, so they now had one compartment each, and they opened the door between them.

They were somewhere between Samara and Pensa, and steaming through the brown rolling plains. There was as yet no sign of Spring. They passed village after village of squat brown log-built houses thatched with straw. The weather was warm and grey.

Miles was writing a letter to his friend Haseltine. He had written to his Aunt Fanny. After giving his friend a short summary of the events which had taken him to Russia, and a brief sketch of his adventures in St Petersburg, he got as far as his arrival at Moscow.

"We arrived in the morning about half-past nine. Everything was unlike what I expected; the houses are low and square, and all coloured, green and red roofs. It is very noisy – cobblestones – and everybody shouts. The coachmen wear a blue dressing gown, and some of them are stuffed. They wear a sort of clothes basket under the blue cloth dressing gown, which is swelled out tight. It makes them look like giants. They drive very fast, in a one-horse carriage. Kouragine took me directly we arrived to a small church called *Our Lady of Unexpected Joy*. We went there from the station. He put up a candle there, and one for me. I asked him if he expected anything; he said 'No' – that was the point. We then drove to a rather shabby hotel called the *Dresden*, in a large red square. The basins in the bedrooms had no water jugs, but a sort of fountain that plays on your hands. We then went and had tea, and some good rolls called *kalachi*, which K told me you could only get properly made here, because of the Moscow water. Only Moscow water produces the right kind of taste. I wanted the recipe for Aunt Fanny, but he says it would be useless to send it, as anywhere else they would turn out differently.

"Even in St Petersburg they cannot make these rolls the same – so much so that one of the Tsars (K says we should never say *Tsar*, but *Emperor*) had Moscow water sent to him every day to St Petersburg, so that he might have his rolls for breakfast.

"Next door to the hotel there is a tailor, and K says that this man had lent him and all his friends a lot of money at one time. Debt, he said, was the cause of all his troubles. I do not know what these troubles are.

"We went to the Kremlin, saw the Cathedral and a twisted church, drove to some shops, and walked about till luncheon time. Then K remembered he had an appointment, and said I must have luncheon by myself. He said he would write down the names of the dishes for me in English and Russian. He tried to teach me how to pronounce them. One was *Ikra*, and meant caviare; the other was *rastigai*, it meant a fish pie. The third I forget. He went with me to the restaurant in a cab. The restaurant was on the first floor of a large building. The waiters were dressed in white. I was bowed to a seat, and felt helpless. I had lost the piece of paper. I remembered the first word, and said '*Ikra*' to the waiter. But all that happened was that he went to a large orchestrophone (one of those closed cupboards that hold all the instruments in the world), and it started to play *William Tell*. I said 'No, no; *ikra, ikra,*' and the waiter then changed the tune and made the instrument play *Carmen*. K said they had probably thought I said another word which means 'play.' I had no better luck with the *rastigai*, so I asked for the menu and chose a dish at random. It was written in Russian, and I did not understand a word of it. The dish, which took a long time in coming, turned out to be an enormous slice of roast pork embedded in brown rice. I could only eat a small piece of it."

When Miles had got as far as this, Alyosha said: "We are just reaching a station; would you like to come out?"

It was a large station. There was a crowd of peasants on the platform, a smell of boot-leather, tobacco, and damp stuff.

Alyosha and Miles walked up and down the platform. There was another train at a siding, a slow train, also full of people; these got down and made a rush for the refreshment room, where they jostled each other to get to the counter, at which hot meat patties were being sold. A little further up the platform there was a small gang of men dressed in dun-coloured clothes with square caps. They asked Alyosha for something. He at once gave them all the cigarettes he had in his pocket and some money besides.

"What are those people?" Miles asked.

"They are what we call *unfortunates* – convicts on their way to Siberia. They were asking for tobacco."

"And you are allowed to give it to them?"

"Of course. You had better give them some too. Nobody understands tobacco as much as prisoners. Did you think we treat the poor like you do?"

"What do you mean? Do you think we treat the poor worse than you do?"

"Of course."

"I thought the poor in Russia had no rights. I thought anyone could be put in prison at any moment for anything, because, after all, you are governed by an autocrat."

"That is just it. Well, take your own case. You were put in prison the other night...we had better get back into the carriage – that is the second bell ringing." They climbed back into the compartment. "You were put in prison," he went on, "the other night for being 'drunk and disorderly and for assaulting the police.'" Miles blushed. "If that had happened in England, what would have been done to you? Would you have been sent home by the police? Would the police have called on you the next morning, and asked you to give them something towards a new uniform, seeing that you had spoilt three Government uniforms, made them 'unserviceable.' I think not. You would have been locked up for the night. You would have had to appear the next morning before the magistrate, and you would have been fined, or put in prison; and it would probably have been written about in the newspapers – most certainly so if you were well known. Here in Russia you are sent home with care, like a precious parcel, and no questions asked."

"I agree that I should have been taken up in London, but once taken up, I should be sure of my rights, sure of the *Habeas Corpus*."

"Exactly; but that cuts both ways. You couldn't be imprisoned illegally, but you couldn't be *let out* illegally either

– and the great thing for a prisoner is to get out. It is impossible to get out in England if it's against the rule…"

"But," said Miles, "there is no *Habeas Corpus* here at all."

"There are dozens, but they are overlooked; and I repeat, this is a thing that cuts both ways. For *you* it was an advantage. If the rules are kept to the letter, one suffers as much, and sometimes more, than when they are laxly kept and elastic – as I showed you in your case."

"But you began by saying the poor. I don't belong to the poor. Your police knew I was staying with a Princess, in a well-to-do house."

"I say the poor are better treated here than in your country. In your country people are put in prison for begging, and they starve in the streets. That would be impossible here, *really* impossible."

"But when they are put in prison here – "

"Even then I don't know if they are not better off here. I once heard a Russian sailor say that there is less liberty at large in your country than in prison in ours."

"Really?" asked Miles.

"Yes," said Alyosha, "and I will tell you a story.

"One of my aunts was married to a rich man, who was a General, and lived in Petersburg. Every summer they used to go to a house they had beyond Moscow and take a few servants with them. The cook always took his holiday in the summer, and they had to hire another. My uncle managed everything always, my aunt never interfered, nor even asked to know about anything. Every summer they went to the country, and they always had the same temporary cook there. He was a kind of peasant, and he cooked extremely well, far better than a French cook; and he could have got a magnificent place, I expect, only he didn't care. One day my aunt asked him where he was going for the winter, and he said 'To prison.' She then asked him questions, and he said that he had no family of his own, and as he was a lonely man, he had been in the habit of committing a small theft every autumn – just a big enough theft to keep him in prison at the Government's expense until the spring came. He had himself arrested, he said, (*arestovalsia*), then in the summer he would be cooking again for His Excellency. He was fond, he said, of company. This happened in the 'sixties or the 'seventies, I don't quite know."

"What an extraordinary story!" said Miles.

"Not extraordinary," said Alyosha, "in this country and I daresay it might happen in England, in the winter; but you see our code *is* really milder. For instance, we have no capital punishment. If I had been an Englishman, I should not be at large at this moment."

"Why?"

"Because I have once murdered someone."

"You murdered someone?"

"Yes; I shot him dead, and was tried and convicted."

Miles got crimson; he felt as if he had committed the murder. "Oh!" was all he said.

"They sentenced me to ten years' *travaux forcés*, and to five years in Siberia as well. It worked out at less because there was an amnesty."

Miles felt dreadfully uncomfortable, as if somehow it were his fault, and he wished that he had never broached the topic of prisons…also he wondered what Aunt Fanny would think if she knew he was travelling with a man who had served a sentence for murder.

Alyosha noticed his embarrassment and laughed.

"Don't be uncomfortable," he said; "I shall convert you in time to a more human view of life. Don't be afraid of me either; I am not dangerous. It was what was called *un crime passionnel*, an impulse. I should have probably been let off the guillotine in France. But in England I should have been hanged, without a doubt. I will tell you the whole story some day, not now." Alyosha buried himself in his novel, and Miles went on writing his letter.

"...I was interrupted, and now I can go on. After luncheon we drove outside the town to a hill where Napoleon looked at Moscow for the first time. The Trans-Siberian train didn't start till the next evening, so we had a night to spend at Moscow. We went to see a play called *The Cherry Orchard*, which is new. It was an extraordinary play. K told me the story as it went on. Nothing happens in it, and it is gloomy; but I thought they acted beautifully. K said that only two of the characters were really like they would have been in real life. It has only been running a short time. The next morning we went to see a picture gallery, and did some more shopping.

"I don't like Moscow, but I daresay one could get fond of it in time. K again left me at luncheon, but this time I succeeded in getting a kind of caviare, but not the sort I wanted. It was pressed, and I couldn't explain I wanted the other sort. We started in the evening. The country, as much as I have seen of it so far, is monotonous. We pass village after village; it is all brown and flat; one village looks just like another; log-built huts thatched with straw, and churches with blue cupolas and small white towers, and sometimes a windmill."

Alyosha, as if he had been following Miles' train of thought, threw down his book and looked out of the window.

"What do you think of the country, the landscape?" he asked.

"I think it is rather monotonous," said Miles.

"Yes, it is, and it will be like that until we reach the Urals, and more or less like that, with the exception of forests and marshes, till we reach Irkutsk. But it is what we would call an 'infectious' country. You can't say that in English, I suppose. Some countries are like that. They tell me Ireland is the same. You will be infected. Once the microbe gets into one's blood – the Russian microbe, I mean – the disease never dies; it is fatal like a love-philtre, and to the end of your life you will say, 'Russia, what is there between you and me?' That is what Gogol, one of our writers – you don't know him in translation, no? – explains. Russia is a country without any obvious attractions and ornaments. There are no show sights: no Niagara, no Vesuvius, no Killarney; and on the other hand, no Parthenon, no Heidelberg Castle. Russia has no elegant make-up, no frills; and yet any one of these villages has more charm for me than all those things put together."

"But surely that is because you are Russian; because it is your home?"

"No, you are wrong. In the first place, I am only half Russian. My grandfather was German and my mother was half German. Secondly, I spent nearly all my childhood in France and in Italy. We lived at Mentone in a villa when I was a child, and we would sometimes go to Florence and to Rome. My father was fond of historical research. But in the summer, when it was too hot to stay in Italy, or was thought too hot – it was never too hot for me – we used to go to South Germany, to the Tyrol, and to a castle where my grandmother lived, my mother's mother. It was in Austria, and on the top of a hill near a little river which ran through a toy village with white houses that had red roofs. There were green meadows and fir-woods and white geese and goose-girls; and the castle had round pointed turrets, and storks used to build there. I used to wake up in the morning to the sound of sheep-bells. Germany, not Russia, was the first source of *Romance* to me. It held all the romance of my childhood, and it still is the home of *Romance* for me.

"I was educated in France first, and then I was sent to a school in North Germany. I lived *en pension* with a family in a small town near the Hartz Mountains; and just as I was beginning to be educated, I left it and went to the Cadet School in St Petersburg. That is why I never learnt Russian properly. I began too late."

"But how did you learn English?"

"My nurse was English, and later my governess; and my father and mother often used to speak English together and teach me. We went to England, too, sometimes. We spent a summer in the Isle of Wight, another in Ireland. I taught myself: the only way to learn anyhow. I read English books; there are amusing books for boys to read in English – amusing grown-up books, I mean. I read *Tom Jones*. My childhood was over, you see, by the time I got to Russia, so it is not a question of early associations. But directly I lived in Russia I caught the microbe, and when, after spending all the years of penal servitude in the Island of Saghalien, and of exile in Siberia, I was amnestied, and I could have gone back to Europe again – I thought of Constantinople and Greece, Athens and Rome. I had once been to Constantinople with my parents. It was in the Spring, and the Judas-trees were out, and the wooden houses were smothered in wistaria, and Stamboul shone like a soap bubble with all the colours of the rainbow. And from there we went to Athens and Taurnina and Naples, Rome... I could go back to Russia if I liked, but I didn't want to. I could no more live in Russia, but I had no desire for Western Europe; and at least there was the Far East, so I settled at Verkhneudinsk, and even there I was homesick. But what could I do? I had to live somewhere, and Verkhneudinsk was just the right place for an ex-convict who is a *déclassé* and has once seen better times. And there I settled and married, and lived ever since, till I was sent to America, and on the way back I saw France and Paris; but I had no desire to stay in Europe, only a longing to be back in Russia...and that is what you will feel one day, more strongly perhaps than I, because Russia will be your romance; what Germany is to me. Russia is my blood relation, like a sister, but Germany is the country I was in love with, and France and Italy my stepmothers. *You* will fall in love with Russia."

Miles looked out of the carriage window. The sun was setting; there was a pink streak under the grey layers of cloud in the west. The air was warm, but the fields and the trees were bare, and there was nothing to relieve the monotony of the brown immensity except now and again the outline of a squat village. There were no signs of Spring anywhere yet, and surely it was high time. Soon the invasion would come, and the Spring, like a young Napoleon, would conquer the country in one sudden, swift, and decisive campaign. But Miles did not know this. He watched the great shadows and the rain clouds, deepening to violet, roll over the plain. He wondered whether it was true, whether there would, as Alyosha had prophesied, ever be anything between him and this grey, monotonous brownness; he thought it improbable. He thought of the woods and marshes and fields of his home, the solid, sane, green English countryside. The birds' nests in April; the autumn tints; the horse chestnut and the flaming creeper; the yellow stubble-fields with the corn in stacks against the finely graduated blues of distant fields and near and far-off elm trees; the mellowness – the softness with which one tint melted imperceptibly into another; the sheep penned in hurdles; the dusty lanes fringed with ripening blackberries; the spider's web on the honeysuckle; the climbing tea roses; the Michaelmas daisies. How beautiful, and how comfortably beautiful, that all seemed compared with what he was looking on now!

"But I suppose," he said, "if you hadn't Russian blood, that wouldn't have happened?"

"No, not at all. It happens to foreigners too. It will happen to you; and perhaps some day in the future you will remember this journey, and it will haunt you like the face of someone you once loved. You will never get rid of the infection, never escape. It was so with me. I remember, when I first came to Russia, after my first journey to the country, I thought I hated it; it was all so ugly and uninteresting; too hot in summer and too cold in winter – then when I went away for the holidays, and came back for the first time, I already remember liking that home-coming better than any I had had before. When I say liking it better, I mean it was different.

"Now, after all these years, I remember the first time I went to the country in Russia. It was at the beginning of the summer holidays, the end of June; it was very hot, there was dust everywhere. I travelled all night, and changed when it was still dark at a station, and watched the dawn – the barns and the ricks, great brown shapes, gradually growing distinct. You are sure to see this one day. I travelled in a slow train, that took hours to get to the station I was bound for; and there I drove through the village...it was the day of the bazaar, the fair. People were driving away cattle and horses...the place was full of creaking carts...there was a great noise of talk, and a strong smell of leather *tulups*, the peasants' coats. They were playing accordions... I think there had been a wedding the day before; children were walking about in small processions, beating tom-toms; and there was a braying of song everywhere, and a great many half-drunk, and some quite drunk, people staggering about, happy... I drove to my Uncle Pierre's house – the uncle you met in Paris... A wooden house with a large garden, like the house in *The Cherry Orchard* play...like that house ought to have been. I was met by the old nurse, who had a scarf on her head, and kept on saying, '*Priyechali*' ('you have come after all')...they were making jam. We had luncheon out of doors, on the verandah, and ate *kasha*, and drank *kvass*, and afterwards some home-made *nalivka* – what you call sloe gin. It was so hot we didn't go out till the evening. Then we drove to the river and bathed. The water was still... I thought there might be a *Russalka* in the reeds... That is what you call a pixie. They have green eyes, and if you make friends with them you go mad... And there was a kingfisher...and we came home late...the green corn was in flower, and it smelt good.

"We drove home through the corn. After dinner we sat out on the terrace, and listened to the people in the village singing... They were still celebrating the wedding...dogs barked, and the drunken people sang and danced. You could hear them stamping...somewhere far away lovers were singing...a very sad song... That, I remember, was my first experience of the country in Russia."

"Yes," said Miles, looking out of the window. It had grown dark; the glow had faded from the low belt in the west, but there was still the remains of a watery gleam; the upper clouds were black; lights twinkled here and there. "Yes," he said, "I wonder. At present – so far, that is to say – it all seems to me brown and monotonous, and there is such a strong smell everywhere of boot leather and tobacco, and a kind of smell like the smell of wet tweed or a dog that's been out in the rain."

"Yes," said Alyosha, "that is part of it."

CHAPTER IX

They arrived at Baikal Station, where you have to cross the lake, at one o'clock in the afternoon. It was still frozen, so they crossed in an ice-breaker.

During the latter part of the journey to Irkutsk, Miles made friends with Troumestre; so Miles, Alyosha, Troumestre, and Haslam now formed a party of four. Troumestre could speak Russian and Turkish and Arabic. He had a Montenegrin servant with him.

The ice-breaker was like a large P&O steamer, with cabins, a restaurant, and comfortable accommodation. It did not start till five o'clock. When Miles and the others had got their luggage on board, they stood on deck, and they were confronted with a marvellous spectacle. It was a brilliant, cold, scintillating day. There was not a cloud in the sky. Before them there was an immense sheet of snow-powdered ice, as far as the eye could see, spotless, except for one brown track right across it, which had been made by the sledges. The sun was setting, huge and fiery, in the frozen sky, and on the line of the horizon there was a low range of mountains mantled by clouds.

The mountains seemed to be made of crystal. They were a deep blue, and they shone in the cold air like sapphires. To the west, the mountains merged into a more distant range that seemed no higher than a coral reef, and the blue here faded away into a delicate green.

They looked at the spectacle in silence.

"It's like the *Ancient Mariner*," said Troumestre.

"Or the mountains of glass one hears of in fairy tales," said Miles.

"Whoever painted that would be called a liar," said Haslam.

"Nobody could," said Troumestre.

"It would make a panorama like the Siege of Paris...not a picture," said Alyosha. "Still better, a magic lantern slide."

A band began to play as the ice-breaker started ploughing through the ice – which was about three feet thick – churning it into fantastic shapes and making a grinding noise. As the sun sank, it grew more fiery, and a pink halo surrounded it and spread over the azure; at last the whole sky was pink. As the sun set, the mountains became grey and ghostly.

"Let's go and have some food," said Haslam.

They went to the cabin and chose a table. At the next table were a Colonel and three officers in grey uniforms; at another table two officials and a Russian man of business.

"That was a wonderful sight," said Walter. "When one sees pictures of such things, one thinks they are exaggerated."

"Nature always manages to get Art beat," said Haslam, "Art and artists are always scared of exaggeration. Ours less than yours. Some of our artists – the best ones – found out you can't exaggerate too much; Mark Twain, for instance. And I guess the British had one who was good at it too."

"Who's that – Turner?' asked Walter Troumestre.

"No; William Shakespeare."

"How do you mean?" asked Walter.

"Well, I mean he doesn't care a cent for veracity or accuracy. If he wants a sea coast in Bohemia, he has one there; and then he piles it on – lays it on thick. Think of that bunch of corpses at the end of *Hamlet* and *King Lear*, and the people who get killed in *Richard the Third*. When Mansfield played it in New York, it was like watching a Punch and Judy show."

"Yes; but he's truthful, all the same," said Troumestre.

"I say that's why he's truthful," said Haslam; "he's holding up the mirror to Nature all the time, and Nature is more exaggerated than anything human fiction can invent."

"Of course," said Alyosha, "but that is no excuse for the artist. The artist's business is not to hold a mirror to Nature, but to make pretty patterns – green, blue, red, yellow, black, white; a patchwork. If the patchwork is to be as dull as life, why make it? It is artists' business to make something more amusing than life. Besides which, it is a failure. You can't render life. Life is too improbable. If I put my life in a book – you simply wouldn't believe it."

"That's because you're a European, and get scared at the truth," said Haslam. "I guess an American artist could get your life story across."

"An American comic writer could," said Alyosha. "But your American serious writers are more timid than all, and more refined – so refined one does not know what is happening at all in their books. Our Russian writers are not scared of exaggerating. They *do* hold a mirror to Nature; at least, Pushkin does, and he reflects life in a beautiful clear crystal."

"Then, according to what you said just now," said Troumestre, "he is not an artist; you said the artist's business was not to reflect life, but to make patterns of his own invention."

"He must make the patterns, but the pattern must give the onlooker the impression that he is looking on at real things, however fantastic they are. He must make the reader believe in what he is reading as long as he is reading. He can make his patterns with anything he chooses – out of everyday life, or, if you like, he can take you to the centre of the earth, like Jules Verne, or for a journey through time, like H G Wells, into other planets and new universes if he likes."

"But what about Dostoyevsky?" asked Troumestre. "Is he a realist? Is he an artist? Does he reflect life? Does he hold up a mirror to Nature, or does he invent a peep-show of his own?"

"Dostoyevsky makes patterns, like all artists…and in them he tells, with fantastic bits of stuff and colour, the adventures of the Russian soul."

"And the man who wrote that play we saw the other night?" asked Miles.

"Chekhov? Chekhov makes patterns, but drab patterns. He has written some funny tales. But he will be famous for having been the first playwright to make plays out of *moods*."

"But in all Russian plays there is very little action, isn't there?" said Troumestre.

"It depends," said Alyosha. "There is not the kind of action there is in Shakespeare, but there is *moral* event. The best plays are, to my mind, those in which nothing happens. *Le Misanthrope*, for instance. *Hamlet* is spoiled by the catastrophe. I wish Hamlet had gone on till he was a middle-aged man – that is how a Russian would have written it…he would have gone on thinking about it and never doing it, thinking out his vengeance, and hesitating and weighing."

"That would make an excellent novel," said Troumestre, "but it wouldn't have made a play."

"Oh yes, it could have made a play – but a Russian, not an English, play."

"I suppose," said Troumestre, "that for *Hamlet* Denmark has the first call. *Hamlet* is a subject made for Ibsen. I can see it – Laertes, a young architect with weak lungs, challenging Hamlet; fighting a duel, wounding him but not killing him."

"Yes," said Alyosha, "and the King, of course, would be an assessor. I think Hamlet would have pushed him into a fjord off the quay in the fog. But what about the Queen?"

"He would have poisoned the Queen," said Troumestre, "with strychnine."

"Yes," said Alyosha. "But the wrong dose. She would have recovered."

"Hamlet, I suppose, would have been a medical student," said Troumestre.

"Yes," said Alyosha. "And Polonius a pastor, or a retired pilot."

"It would have rained all the time."

"Yes," said Alyosha, "and Hamlet would be hearing harps in the air."

"Yes; and crowning himself with vine leaves."

"Yes; every now and then," said Alyosha, "Mrs Hamlet would be arguing and proving to her son that the ghost was only a disease inherited from his father, who was a good-for-nothing; and that his uncle was a good man."

"I suppose," said Troumestre, "it would turn out at the end that the father had committed suicide, and that everything had been hushed up."

"Yes," said Alyosha; "but at the end of the play Harriet would really go mad, and everybody would think he was pretending, till he poisoned his mother by giving her strychnine – the right dose this time – in a glass of champagne. But that would be too dramatic for me."

"How would Chekhov treat it?" asked Troumestre.

"Ah," said Alyosha, "as 'Scenes from Country Life.' "

"Yes," said Troumestre; "I suppose the play would begin after dinner and last all night; all Russian plays seem to me to last all night. And the King – who would he be?"

"What you call a squire," said Alyosha. "A landed proprietor of an estate falling to pieces, somewhere near a provincial town. He also would have married his deceased brother's wife long before the beginning of the play, and his nephew Hamlet – "

"An author, I suppose," said Troumestre.

"Yes," said Alyosha, "with a fondness for play actors, who has been publishing articles in the Reviews. He would have, of course, suspected from the first, because he had been playing with *planchette*."

"Hamlet," said Troumestre, "would of course be a free-thinker?"

"Yes," said Alyosha. "But believing in the Devil, and reading Schopenhauer and Paracelsus. He would be wondering whether it was his duty to kill his uncle. One day, while everybody was playing *planchette* (this would be in the first act), the *planchette* would say, 'Look in the cupboard next to the bookcase,' or something like that. He would look, and find some letters written by his mother to his uncle, which would seem to prove everything...only *not quite*. He would be more puzzled than ever and torn asunder, wondering whether the *planchette* was true, or the Evil One, or Chance. It would prey upon his mind. He would behave all wrong, and give Ophelia her letters back to her. She would be thinking all the while that he loves her. He would be talking a great deal about how he was going to kill his uncle, and say: 'I must remember to kill my uncle tomorrow.'"

"Yes," said Troumestre. "Perhaps he would tie a knot in his pocket handkerchief and say, 'Tomorrow I will really "have it out" with Ophelia.'"

"Yes," said Alyosha; "and when he had very carefully planned a way to murder his uncle, he – the landed proprietor – would come home drunk from a regimental dinner – drunk as an umbrella – and slobber prayers in front of the Ikon, and Hamlet, given just the opportunity, would *transiger*."

"Yes," said Troumestre, "out of charity."

"Of course," said Alyosha, "out of charity. In the third act," Alyosha went on, "he would quite suddenly advise Ophelia to be a nun; and this would annoy her, and she would go quite mad; and there would be more *planchette* or table-turning with his uncle, and Hamlet would cheat, and the *planchette* or the table would tell a story of the murder, and his uncle would be only bored, and Hamlet more puzzled than ever. Was he pretending or not? Then Polonius, the land agent, of course, would give Hamlet much advice about how to farm properly, and how to manage the peasants, and Hamlet would get annoyed and shoot at him with a Browning, but miss him also… Between the acts Polonius would have died."

"From shock?" said Troumestre.

"Yes; and the King, the landed proprietor too, and would have left the estate to Hamlet. But in the next act the lawyers would be there, and would be explaining that Hamlet had been mad, and that the estate must go to Fortinbras, a cousin – a not very nice captain in an infantry regiment, who had lost money at gambling, but who is looking honest. And so Hamlet would become an actor."

"What would happen then?" asked Troumestre.

"Ah," said Alyosha, "the last act would, of course, be at a provincial railway station, in the buffet, when he would be starting for Moscow. Miss Ophelia would be waiting till the last moment for him to make a declaration to her, and the opportunity would be there, and somebody would say to her brother Laertes, 'Has he spoken?' and he would answer 'No,' and weep. Then the first bell would ring…and the second bell…the third bell…and the train would start, and Ophelia would be in it, and Fortinbras' friends would take Hamlet away to a supper with gipsies."

"That is a modern play," said Troumestre. "But suppose it were an ancient one – historical?"

"It would all be the same," said Alyosha. "It would be 'humdrum,' ancient or modern, because you see we Russians go to the play to see *what we see every day.*"

"Quite so. And we like a play with a kick to it," said Haslam.

"All the same," said Troumestre, "all the realistic plays which Ibsen invented, and which have now spread all over the world, have galvanised the stage, and produced something interesting."

"It will not last, all that," said Alyosha. "All that makes sermons and speeches more than plays, and turns the stage into a *clinique*. The real business of the theatre is the show, *le spectacle*. The ideal of the stage ought to be the child's charades. They give you illusion, because they believe in the illusion themselves. They are *de bonne foi*, and if they believe, you believe. They make you have the illusion. Modern stage managers spend millions of money to produce the illusion, with lights and scenes and all that, but they fail."

"Ibsen," said Haslam, "gives me a pain."

"I think there are two things," said Alyosha, "which are ruining the modern theatre – one is scenery and the other is plot."

"I don't quite understand," said Miles.

"I will explain," said Alyosha. "There is everywhere a passion now for what is called *mounting*, especially for Shakespeare. But Shakespeare wrote plays to be acted in theatres that had no scenery. He made scenery with words. So scenery is for such things a waste of time and a waste of money. The same thing in modern plays. They are ruining everything with detail. Modern writers are giving you pages of stage directions. Stage managers give you a real cherry orchard on the stage, which is false. Children know better. They take a chair, and they say, 'This is a train.' So do the Chinese. They take a table, and say, 'That is a barge floating down a river full of water lilies at sunset.' It is enough, because the actors know how to look as if they believed it. It is for the words of the play and for the actors to give you all that."

"Yes," said Troumestre. "Shakespeare does."

"And good actors do it," said Alyosha. "By their mimic. If they cannot do it, no amount of details can."

"I agree about that," said Troumestre; "but you said *plot*. Why does plot spoil the *show*?"

"Plot," said Alyosha. "A too-good plot is ruin. Plot should be an accident; anything to hand. The same plot that someone had taken before; just as the Italians always painted the Madonna and the Child. All playwriters now, except ours, are looking for new plots, as if there were such things. There is no such thing but there are at least a dozen old plots."

"They say," said Haslam, "that there are only forty-six stories in the world."

"Not so many," said Alyosha. "Funny stories are cropping up at the same time all over the world, just as the folk tales cropped up. For instance, you," he said, pointing to Miles, "have been telling me a joke one of your comedians was making. The riddle: 'What is it that has two legs and a beak, and barks?' The answer is, 'A pheasant.' And the guesser then says, 'But a pheasant doesn't bark.' And the other man says. 'I put that in to make it more difficult.' That is being told here in our music halls, and I was hearing it a few months ago at Vladivostok, at a circus, told by an Armenian with an Armenian accent; on our stage the Armenian is the comic character."

"But," said Troumestre, "surely one cannot do without technique on the stage?"

"Certainly not," said Alyosha. "When we say we do not like well-made plays, it is not because they are well made, but because we find them uninteresting. Any good play is well made. It all comes to this: on the stage the plot is of no matter, but every word must be necessary, even if it is only, 'What a fine day!' Every sentence must hold the attention, not of you or me in a chair at home, but of a crowd in a hot theatre, ready to be bored at a moments notice, and wanting to be anywhere else except in that theatre, unless they can be made to want to know what is going to happen next."

"I go to the theatre to be amused," said Haslam, "and plays like Chekhov's give me a hump, and plays like Ibsen's give me a pain, and plays like Shaw's make me mad. Give me, I say, plays like Sardou, Dumas Senior, or Sherlock Holmes. If I want to feel sore and get mad, I can do so without paying for a seat in a theatre. What do you think, Consterdine?"

"Yes," said Alyosha. "What is your favourite play?"

Miles blushed, thought a little, and then said: "Oh, I don't know. I have seen so little...but I did like *Charley's Aunt*."

The argument then melted into reminiscence. The talk drifted from theatrical to more personal topics till they reached their destination. It was quite dark, and in that darkness they had to fight their way to find seats in a third-class carriage.

CHAPTER X

At first there seemed to be no room anywhere. The train was packed full with soldiers, but Alyosha managed to take possession of two compartments: a whole section of the carriage. Alyosha, Miles, Troumestre, and Haslam occupied it. They were joined by another Englishman, called Jameson, who was drawing sketches for the *Illustrated Weekly*. Each section was made to hold six passengers, each passenger having a whole plank berth on which he could lie down at full length. Other passengers were perched at right angles to them over the windows, on transverse berths. Troumestre had a patent cork mattress on his plank and several rugs which he lent to the others.

Both Miles and Troumestre kept diaries. Here is Miles' record of the journey:

"There are in the carriage, besides us, many passengers – some soldiers, a sailor, one man who is called a *feldsher*, who, I am told, is a hospital orderly, three peasants, and some nondescript people.

"At dawn one of the soldiers who had slept over the window got up, made a sign of the Cross, and cut off a large slice of brown bread from a loaf which he had in a canvas bag. We stopped at a station, and the soldier got out, and went to a pump and washed. He stood up as the sun was rising and looked towards the sun; he was wearing a red shirt, and he said his prayers, bowing and swaying with his whole body, and making the sign of the Cross over and over again. Some Chinese who looked like coolies got into our carriage. There was an outcry, and they were rolled out like footballs. A little later we stopped at another station. Everybody got out and got hot water. They made tea in kettles, and the soldier in the red shirt ate his bread with his tea. Our tea basket *is* useful.

"Troumestre reads out of a small book. I have not yet opened Princess Kouragine's parcel. In the evening we arrived at a large station. On the platform a boy was walking up and down with a stuffed duck in a glass case which he was offering for sale. After we had passed him I asked Alyosha to ask him how much it cost. He said he would presently. We went into the refreshment room and had some vodka and pickled cucumbers, and some cabbage soup – good. As we went back to the carriage, we passed the boy with the stuffed duck, and Alyosha asked him how much it was. He said scornfully that it was sold. Who could have bought it? and why?

"*Saturday.* – Some of the passengers have gone. New ones have got in. The *feldsher* is drunk. He walks up and down shaking hands with everyone affectionately. He asked me something, but I did not understand what he meant.

"*Sunday.* – We have arrived at a place called Chita. The country is sandy; more people have got in. Up till now there have been few trees. It is becoming flatter. They say this is the capital of Transbaikalia. There seems to be little difference between one Russian town and another.

"*Monday.* – More fir trees. The country is becoming still flatter. We arrived at Manchuria Station. We got out and we waited in the waiting-room – bare and full of flies. We had to have our papers *viséd*. A business man who had been with us in the train on the way to Irkutsk came and talked to me, while Troumestre, Haslam, and Alyosha had gone to find out what was to be done. I was sitting alone, drinking tea, and he came and sat next to me and asked me questions. I told him who I was, and what I was doing; how I was going to take photographs for an American magazine. He told me I would not be allowed to get to the Front. No correspondents would be allowed at the Front. Many had been sent back already. English correspondents would be allowed least of all, because the English Press was pro-Japanese and hostile to Russia. He had business at Port Arthur, and he always read the *Times* and other daily English newspapers. They always told lies about Russia, and were unfair. Did I know Russian? Were we very uncomfortable in our third-class carriage? I said no, as Troumestre had talked to the soldiers and spoke Russian. He seemed much interested. He seems a pleasant man.

"We got our papers and found places in the train, third-class. Directly the train started, two Cossacks arrived, and Alyosha said we were under arrest. He laughed. He is not allowed to stay with us.

"*Tuesday*. – Country flat and uninteresting, but it is getting warmer. Nothing interesting all day, and in the evening a concert. Soldiers sang.

"*Wednesday*. – Some Chinese are travelling in the train now, and in the morning an old man who travelled for a part of the day in the compartment next to us got under the seat in our carriage. The other passengers crowded together so that he should not be seen, and so that it might look as if the carriage was full. After the ticket-collector had been, the old man got out from under the seat. He left at the next station. Alyosha said this happens often, and that such passengers are called *Hares*. The country is hilly; it is much warmer.

"*Thursday*. – We arrived at Kharbin."

Here is Walter Troumestre's record:

"*Friday*. – Haslam told us about his adventures at Peking. He says he has been there before. I doubt it. He said he had had an interview with the Dowager Empress at the time of the Boxer trouble, that she had made him a Mandarin of the Fourth Class, and allowed him to wear a yellow button, and had given him a pearl of immense value. Kouragine listened to this story and made no comment. I asked him later whether he believed it. He said no, but added, that to an American to do a thing, and to say he had done it, was the same. He said Americans were like children of six; they lived in a land of make-believe. You could not call them liars any more than you called children liars for talking of wizards. He said they were childish in every way except in their religion. I asked him which. He said, 'Business is their religion – and when they talk of religion they become rapt like seraphs.' He said Haslam had no religion. He was as an American what in Russia corresponded to an atheist, because he did not care for *Business*.

"*Saturday*. – One of the soldiers asked me whether Paris was in Turkey, and said the Turks were a nice, a clean people. We talked about Turkey. They were interested. One of them asked whether there was not a place where it was all water. I described Venice as best I could. K said to me that I ought to write stories and sketches about Russia, as Kipling did about India. I told him I had no grasp of technicalities. He said, so much the better. Technical details are only a bore. I said they were not tiresome in Kipling; his detailed variety of observation the principal factor of his genius. He could always grasp a whole subject unfamiliar to him, talk of it in the right way, with the right grasp of detail. K said that is true – 'genius is memory.' Haslam said American storytellers better than all. K said

Americans could not write their own language. Wrote a jargon – spillikins. Quoted Henry James. Could not write the vernacular. Haslam quoted O Henry. K and I had never heard of him. K said the vernacular is the only good writing. All writing not vernacular is jargon.

Reading *Esther Waters*, by George Moore, Tauchnitz. K took it up and read a chapter or more. I said he was one of the very best of English writers and wrote the most beautiful prose. K said he was not English, but Irish. Jameson joined in the conversation, and said what is true, that he has no irony, therefore he cannot write properly about English common life. *Esther Waters* is all about English common life – footmen, bookmakers, etc. Dickens could do it, because he was of it, in it; he reflected that life – with a magnifying glass. Jacobs did too, without a magnifying glass. They both understood irony, the irony of the cabman, bus driver, street boy, Tommy, policeman, bluejacket, nightwatchman; said all the English lower-class humour was irony; always saying what was not: 'I don't think,' Not 'arf'; saying it was a lovely day when it was pouring with rain. He told us that once, during the Lord Mayor's Show, a man in the street said to him: "I am not going to have dinner with the Lord Mayor today, because I think he has got too many guests already; but I will go and have some sprats with him some other evening when he is free.' This was typical. That was why Dickens was so great. Why *Esther Waters* failed – in that respect. *Esther Waters* – a good French novel – more like Zola. Kipling made his characters talk right – pictures of petty officers, stokers – alive. Haslam objected that others said they were not true to life. Said that soldiers and sailors complained that Kipling's soldiers and sailors were all wrong. K said, What did it matter, if they are true to us? He said we have a proverb which says, 'Take the singer's advice about pancakes, and the baker's advice about song.' He went on to say this proverb was his own invention, and really the contrary of the real proverb (Krylov). Long conversation.

"*Sunday*. – Haslam says seen Chinese advertisements offering to teach English language as far as letter E. Talked to Russian soldiers about English alphabet. Soldiers said letters X and W seemed to be useless, and one of them said he would write something in English characters, only did not see the use of X and W; but that it didn't matter, that he would find some letter or other in the Russian alphabet which would do as well.

"Consterdine struck by monotony of landscape. K said Russian country being flat, meant there were no sharp differences between the different parts of the same country, to give rise to separate customs and patois. Cause of differences, valleys and hills. Russia flat. Population was spread like butter thinly over bread. Said Russians were colonists: Siberia, Transbaikalia, colonies. Siberians were to Russians as New Zealand, not as Norfolk, to us.

"Soldiers took little interest in the war. Sailor has been to Ceylon, which he thought was in the Yellow Sea. One man told a fairy tale – peasant, ex-soldier – long story. Fairy tale as in Grimm. He had heard it from his parents. They heard it from theirs. All told in dialogue, every person having special epithet as in Homer and Zola's *Débacle*. Hector with the Bright Helmet, Napoleon the Third with his carriage with bees on it. Story usual one: man with three sons; youngest son fool, gets the best of it. K said all Russian fiction based on this fairy tale of three brothers, of which youngest fool. Ivan the fool, the hero, he said, of all Russian fiction and all Russian history. Asked us whether we had ever heard Mussorgsky's Opera, *Boris Godunov*. All Russian history, he said, summed up in the song the idiot sings in it. Said Homeric poems were handed down from generation to generation just in the same way as these fairy tales by peasants. When people knew neither how to read nor write, the power of memory was immense. Bought popular edition of prose translation of *Paradise Lost* at bookstall. Coloured chromo pictures in it, shiny, (Gustave Doré). K said the book was popular among peasants. Showed it to soldiers later. They said, 'good book,' 'near to the heart,' with a 'sweetness' in it. Consterdine much astonished when told. Haslam too. Haslam scoffed. Nothing strange in it, said K. He said it combined all things for them – amusing fairy tale, devils, paradise, Satan, serpent, beasts, fruits, stars, with authority of Scriptures. They felt it true and not an invention. And then the exalted language. They felt the language was exalted, especially in the Russian translation. It affected them like church music (I quoted old woman and 'Mesopotamia'). K agreed, and said church was to the peasant as picture galleries, pictures, concerts, lectures, theatres, were to us. Also they liked simple-heartedness; they were always looking for it, and found it there.

"*Monday.* – Arrived Manchuria station. Difficulty with business man. He pumped Consterdine and gathered from him I had talked Russian to soldiers. Business man suspicious; did his best to stop our going further. K got matters settled. Business-man told officers whom we had met in train on way to Irkutsk that we were spies – Consterdine first spy, having camera. They no longer talked to us. Got our papers *viséd*, all the same, and were allowed to proceed. Just before we got papers Greek merchant arrived, trafficking sponges; wanted to go Kharbin. Came and talked to me. Businessman sat down next to us and overheard conversation. We talked modern Greek. I told him in Greek that the man with the beard was a great nuisance. Man with beard greatly annoyed. Got places in train; man with beard followed us, watched which was our compartment, and put his hat in it to mark it. Saw him do it, he not knowing. Great mind to throw his hat out of window. Settled in our carriage. K had row with man with beard; bearded man made officers telegraph to authorities at Kharbin saying three Englishmen were in the train and behaving in suspicious manner, undoubtedly spies. Curious that all wars are the same – spy fever, as in South Africa.

"Train started, we apparently under arrest. Two Cossacks told off to sleep in upper berths, chosen because they could not speak proper Russian, so were supposed not to communicate. K not allowed to stay with us. He said all would be right the next day. He had sent telegram to Kharbin.

"*Tuesday*. – Colonel who sent telegram to Kharbin received answer, saying we all right and expected. He told K he was sorry incident had occurred. Knew it was nonsense all the time. If we had been spies, we should not have been given pass by War Office. But man with beard made such a fuss that to satisfy him he sent telegram. When we got out at station, officers civil. Concert in the evening, in the next carriage; sailors and soldiers sang. Consterdine said part-songs, and K said, no, not parts but rough counterpoint. Leader sings melody, other singers imitate that melody roughly and drift away from it. Beautiful voices. Sang a song about Lake Baikal, and convict song:

" 'I remember, I remember
The day my mother bore me…'

"Someone asked for a solo. Sailor said he knew good song. Sentimental: like a music-hall song, or a ballad at a sailors' sing-song. Story of simple village maiden, who left life of honest work for homes of the rich, then, things going badly and being deserted by rich lover, thrown into the street, and dying in the snow of starvation. Tune commonplace, but immensely enjoyed by audience, more than other songs. Asked K why they liked this best, so commonplace after the beautiful folk songs. K said, Why did people prefer music halls to classical concerts, or why did I prefer new book to *Robinson Crusoe*? I said quite understood that, but did not understand how other sort, good folk music, was the rule in Russia among the people, and why that music-hall song the exception. K said, because people not educated. When education prevalent all over Russia, all Russian peasants, artisans, etc., would be *half* educated, *half-baked*. Would no more talk pure Russian as they do now; would talk the jargon of the *intelligentsia*. Would say *'merci'* or *'mercis'* instead of *'Spasibo.'* Would use scientific words and sing modern music-hall tunes. Old music would die out, as it has died out in England. I said English still good at picking up tunes. Haslam agreed, and said we wrote good tunes every now and then. *'Chon Kina,'* out of the *Geisha*. K said that tune was still popular in Far East now. We would hear it everywhere. He said English had sense of rhythm. Populace and composers of light opera: Sullivan and music-hall composers. Certain tunes went round the world: 'Daisy, Daisy,' and 'Oh, Mr Porter.' Said most continental serious composers had lost the gift of rhythmical tune. I asked him who was his favourite composer'. He said Bizet. I asked him about Wagner. He said Wagner to him was like noise you make by rubbing your finger on the rim of a glass, pleasant to some people, intolerable to others, but refused to discuss matter then – too late.

"*Wednesday.* – French lady much bothered by behaviour of Chinese."

CHAPTER XI

When they arrived at Kharbin, Alyosha and Miles were separated. Alyosha went to stay with a friend, and Miles went to the Hotel Oriant with Haslam and Troumestre.

They were introduced to one of the Press Censors, a Colonel Ivanov, who spoke English. They made various friends. Troumestre introduced them to two Cossack colonels, who at once asked them to a luncheon on the following day. Haslam met a French man of business whom he knew. They went to the Russo-Chinese Bank and were entertained by one of the managers.

Miles thought that Kharbin was the most depressing place he had ever seen or imagined. The European town consisted of a few isolated houses embedded in a sea of mud. The roads could hardly be called roads. There was a Chinese town about two miles distant. It was dangerous to drive at night. The population consisted largely of ex-convicts. They all seemed to squint.

Miles had bought a Colt pistol, but as he was unsure of the mechanism Alyosha advised him to give it away.

The first day he spent at Kharbin Miles saw nothing of Alyosha. On the second day he and Troumestre and Haslam were entertained by the Cossack colonels at two o'clock in the afternoon. It was a great meal. There were about a dozen guests: a flow of vodka, and towards the end of the meal, champagne. One of the colonels had difficulty in expressing himself, because he had left his false teeth behind him in the train. They could neither of them speak English; at least, the only words they knew were "Mister" and "Christmas," which they used freely. They both could speak a little French. Miles was aghast at the thought of what the meal must have cost them, as a small supper consisting of fried eggs and beer, which he had shared with Troumestre and Haslam, had cost ninety roubles (nine pounds). Such was the scale of prices at the Hotel Oriant, and this meal began with caviare and had many courses.

It lasted until five, and the hosts and some of the guests were unconscious afterwards; the hosts remained unconscious for thirty-six hours. Soon after it was over the Censor, Colonel Ivanov, called on Miles, and said he was on no account to lend any money to the Cossack colonels. Miles said that nobody had as yet asked him for a loan. "No, but they will," said Colonel Ivanov. Later, the Frenchman told Haslam that one Russian officer had asked him to lend him thirteen roubles, which he had done, as it seemed so curious a sum. Troumestre obtained leave to start for Mukden the day after. Colonel Ivanov said that Miles could not travel with him in the same train as there was not room for him. They must seize the opportunities as they occurred.

In the evening Alyosha came to see Miles, and told him he was invited to drink tea with a lady of his acquaintance, who was the wife of a local official. Her name was Marya Ivanovna.

"You must come with me; there will be no one there, except possibly a few *chinovniks*,who won't matter."

They drove for what seemed to Miles an interminable distance, and they arrived at a small house. In a dining-room, seated at a long table, which had a white, shiny American cloth on it, under a hanging lamp, in front of a samovar, sat the hostess. She was a small woman with long grey eyes, fair hair, and restless movements. She spoke very fast in Russian, but to Miles she spoke French. She wore many rings on each hand, gold rings with corals and brilliants, and one with an opal. Presently a man came into the room, who was presented to Miles as her husband. He wore a uniform, but not a military one. Miles had no idea what it denoted. He was short, dapper, with a sandy beard and honest eyes. He bowed stiffly, said a few words in broken English, and went into the next room. He came back presently with a cigarette. He then asked Miles whether he would like to see his partridge. He spoke English painfully and slowly. "She is," he said, alluding to the partridge, "very peaceful." Miles, thankful for this information, followed him into the next room in which there was a partridge in a cage. His host chuckled and whistled to it, but the bird seemed indifferent. Presently one or two other people arrived – a clerk from the bank, a doctor, a post-office official, and others, and later an officer in blue uniform, who kissed his hostess' hand, shook hands with the others, and then took no notice of them. He was a tall, top-heavy man, rather sallow, with an overgrown moustache.

The only people to whom the hostess paid any attention, Miles noticed, were Alyosha, and the officer. Till he came Marya Ivanovna paid no attention to anyone except to Alyosha. Now that the officer was there, Alyosha seemed put out, and he stopped talking. Marya Ivanovna, on the other hand, never stopped talking for a moment. Tea was drunk, everyone was smoking cigarettes and talking at the same time. A little later a game of *Vindt* was suggested. The four players, among whom was the host, played in the next room. They chalked the score on the table and drank tea as they played. Marya Ivanovna suggested some music. There was a pianoforte in the dining-room. The bank clerk sat down and played some tunes with astonishing facility and hard execution – the kind of playing, thought Miles, that gives absolutely no pleasure. Marya Ivanovna seemed bored. She asked Miles whether he could play or perhaps sing an English song. Miles blushed, and said he was afraid he had no such talents. Then one of the guests played on a three-stringed guitar, the *balalaika*, and hummed a song; other guests joined in, and sang the parts in uncertain tune. Out of civility to Miles, the bank clerk played some tunes from the *Geisha*, and somebody sang "*Vieni sul mar*" (which Miles knew as "Two Lovely Black Eyes") to Russian words, "*Poi, lastochka, poi*" ("Sing, Swallow, Sing ").

Towards midnight Marya Ivanovna suggested that they should have supper. The table was cleared. She bustled about, with the help of a maid and a *mouzhik* dressed in a white shirt not tucked in and a black belt. Presently supper was ready. There were sardines, pressed caviare, some small hot sausages and hot mushrooms (which Miles thought were poisonous), bread and butter, and pickled cucumbers and vodka. Miles' glass was filled and refilled. Then there was a second course: some cold meat and salad, and more vodka. The host drank Miles' health. Everybody talked, everybody got gayer. Cigarettes were smoked; Marya Ivanovna paid attention to the officer and none to Alyosha, who began to look gloomy. She was flirting with the officer, so thought Miles, with some deliberate purpose. She is doing it, he thought, to annoy Alyosha, but things turned out otherwise than he expected. When supper was over, and a great deal of vodka had been drunk, glasses of tea were handed round and more music was suggested. Marya Ivanovna suggested to the bank clerk that he should play. He was a tall, fair young man with curly hair, blue eyes, and thick hands. No sooner had this suggestion been made than he flew into a passion and addressed the officer in a torrent of Russian. The officer got up and looked startled and angry, and began to answer on a high pitch; but Marya Ivanovna, with blazing eyes, interrupted, and answered for him with a whirlwind of words, Miles thought she looked like an angry snake. The argument went on. The others took no notice and seemed indifferent, as if they were used to it. At last the bank clerk left the room, fetched his coat and cap, and banged the front door. He went without having said goodbye either to his hostess or to his host. No sooner had he gone than they heard two revolver shots. Miles was startled.

"That is only Dimitri Ivanovitch," said Marya Ivanovna, "he always threatens to shoot himself."

"Is it all right? Shall I go and see?" asked Miles.

"Oh, please do not bother," she said; "he would never dare shoot himself here."

Nobody else took any notice of the incident or referred to it again.

A little while after this (as it had seemed to Miles) painful incident, Alyosha said he must go home. They said good night, and Miles drove back with Alyosha to the hotel. It was two o'clock in the morning. Miles asked what the fuss had been about. "He didn't shoot himself, or try to, did he?"

"Oh dear no; he does that every night. But one night he may shoot himself...if he is drunk; but he never is drunk – never drunk enough. He is working in the bank. He is a Pole, and is hot-tempered and *chatouilleux*, ticklish about his honour. Marya Ivanovna was being annoying, and teasing him by flirting with that stupid *Esaul*."

"What is an *Esaul*?"

"It is Cossack for captain. He is nothing, *une brute*, and belongs to some Trans-Siberian regiment. Marya Ivanovna has him as a slave."

"Is she thought to be attractive?" asked Miles. "I don't admire her very much."

"You are right; there is nothing to admire; but she is worse – she is like some insidious drug you cannot give up once you have taken a little of it; and she knows her power very well. She is not pretty, she is not beautiful, she is not fine, handsome; she has no senses, no sensibility, no passion; she is not clever, she is not charming, she is not alluring. She has no talents and little conversation except the most shabby gossip. She has no

temperament, she has little education, no culture, no
knowledge, and no taste. She has a vulgar mind; she is ill-bred,
spiteful, vindictive, interested, ambitious, calculating,
treacherous – she would betray anyone and anything – her
dearest friend; and yet I tell you I adore that woman. I love her
selfishly – that is to say, the only way of loving that counts. I
love her and hate her, and that, too, is the only real way of
loving. She knows it, and she knows that I can never get free,
and she just enjoys the sense of power. She has never loved
anyone. She has only loved the pretence of being in love."

"And her husband?"

"She is cruel to him; but he has at least the partridge."

"Has she many admirers?"

"They come to her, she does not go to them. She looks for no
one, she has never taken notice of anyone till they have forced
themselves on her attention – put themselves in her way. If they
do that, she will take notice. They may or may not become her
lovers – it depends what sort they are; and if they do, she soon
tires of that; but they can never forget her, or get free from her.
It is the same if they are only friends, like that old doctor who
was here tonight. He goes to see her every night of his life. He
has a wife and family at Moscow, but he will never go back."

"She seemed to me to be flirting with that officer."

"Yes; he is new. She will ruin him. He will first steal, and then
drink, and then – 'finish'!"

"But if she has such power over people, she must have
something more in her than you say."

"Why, what is the use of qualities, attributes, virtues, talents
– all the things she has *not* got? You do not like or love people
for such things, you love them for themselves."

"Yes but you won't admit that she has either beauty
or charm."

"Great beauties are rarely loved. They are generally
unhappy. As for charm, she has something much worse and
something much more powerful. Charm is like a soft tune that

everyone listens to, a glass of sweet or bitter juice that appeals to everyone. But she has something stronger and more subtle; something which affects men as that plant Valerian affects cats, or as they say the scent of lavender affects lions and tigers. Opium is nasty. It makes you sick at first, but once you like it, you can never give it up. Take my case. I have a wife at home at Verkhneudinsk, in Siberia. She looks after my house and manages our tobacco store, for that is how I live. She is an angel. They say she is pretty. She is good-humoured, gay, practical, natural, good, intelligent – the salt of the earth. Unselfish – as much as possible. Devoted, ready to do anything. She loves me and I adore her. She would do anything for me. And yet if Marya Ivanovna were to say to me tomorrow: ' If you leave your wife for ever, and swear never to see her again, I will be your wife for six months, after which I will think it over,' I would do it without a moment's hesitation. Luckily I am safe. She would never have more to do with me *now* than to let me come to tea."

"Have you known her long?"

"I have known her first at Verkhneudinsk; her husband was employed there. He used to come and buy cigars. She knew my history, and that attracted her. We made friends. Soon after they were transferred to Kharbin. He is a kind of electro-technician. And then I saw her again on my way to Vladivostock. While she was at Verkhneudinsk my wife had a baby, a son – we were very pleased – and then six months afterwards it died, and we were sad; but a week after my child died, when we were at our saddest, I asked Marya Ivanovna to divorce her husband to marry me. But don't think I stopped loving my wife. I loved her as much as ever. And don't think I had more illusions about Marya Ivanovna then than I have now. I had none. I never had any from the first. It was simply that she can play upon me as an instrument: she touched the stop and the sound responded. She knew this, and she did it on purpose.

She did it to hurt my wife; my wife knew. She knew my wife would know."

"She must be a very wicked woman."

"Wicked? I don't know. I hardly think so. She has instincts. She fights and kills her prey, like wild animals or birds of prey do – to live. But she has no moral sense, and so, I suppose, no immoral sense. She is not one who knows what is good and does evil for choice. She does not profess virtue and practise vice – she does not know what is good and what is evil. She has no conscience, and so she can have no remorse. She has the instinct to dominate and to take – but she doesn't go out of the way to seek a prey, as I told you. She asks for no attention, and takes no notice except of those who put themselves in her way; so much the worse for them."

"She is like a spider, waiting in her web?"

"No, not even that; she takes no notice of the flies, unless they positively bother her."

"Is she characteristically Russian?"

"She is not at all Russian. Her mother was French. That is why she speaks French as well as she does – although, of course, she speaks very badly."

"And do other people, when they get to know her, always feel the same about her as you do?"

"At Vladivostock there was a naval officer, a young man with a promising career: he shot himself because of her. And then there was a doctor, who was just married to a charming German wife. She ruined that *ménage*, and the doctor left his wife; and later there was an officer – a colonel, on the verge of being promoted – he, in the midst of a brilliant career, stole money because of her from the Government *Caisse*, and it was found out, and he was disgraced and had to leave the Army…and there was another – an artist: he committed no crime, he did nothing; that was worse – he just did nothing; he might have done a lot; he ran to seed – and there were others, many others. Wherever she has been she has made havoc, and

ruined more happy *ménages* than I can count. It is
extraordinary, for she is, after all, only a vulgar little
bourgeoise. But you see she is *Emma Bovary*."

"Who is *Emma Bovary*?"

"You have never read *Madame Bovary*?"

"Never."

"Well, you will read it some day – as they say to children – or
perhaps you won't. I do not know whether you would like it.
But Madame Bovary is a little French bourgeoise, and the book
is her story. It is told in great detail by Flaubert, and the book
is thought to be a masterpiece. I suppose it is. I have read it
once. I could never read it again. But what is remarkable in it is
the type fixed and created in it. Emma Bovary is every other
woman in fiction. She is all the heroines of fiction and of
drama, and not only that but she is every woman in life as well,
nearly every woman. And in some respects *every* woman. She's
of course sentimental."

"But is Marya Ivanovna sentimental?"

"Oh yes; she has funds and funds of bad sentiment, rotten"
(he pronounced it *'rötten'*) sentiment. And it is only the
sentimental in art or books, or people as to that, that appeals to
her and attracts her – and the bad, wrong sentiment. But I don't
want you to make a mistake. Do not think for a moment that
Marya Ivanovna has been the love of my life, and that my heart
has been broken for her. She is a dangerous poison I met by
chance and became infected with, as with malaria, in such a
way that I can never get rid of it entirely; and whenever I am in
certain moral climates, I will always, till I die, have fits of a
certain malarial fever. Because the microbe is inside me, and
the cure for that microbe – the counter-microbe that can kill it
– has not yet been discovered, not by me. But one must call that
poison, and not passion, still less love. The love of my life was
not my wife either. I will tell you. My wife and I were good
friends from the first, and I was and am still very fond of her,
and would prefer to be married to her than to anyone else. We

understand each other, and she is admirable. Have you ever read Homer?"

"No, never except at school, and that was a long time ago. "

"That is a pity. Homer is wise, he sees all round people. Not only through, but all round. Only Homer, as a writer, does this. But women often do it. My wife is like that. She sees all round me, and doesn't mind. That is why I like her."

"What a lot you have read!" said Miles. "At every moment you pull me up by mentioning or quoting something I have never heard of."

"You are quite wrong," said Alyosha. "I haven't read Homer. Not in Greek at all. And no other way, except in smatterings – and in a German translation. You, too, must have had smatterings of Homer at school."

"Yes," said Miles, "at school. But – "

"That is just the mistake," interrupted Alyosha, "all you English people make. You set the Classics up, as something to be respected or hated at school, but not read. That is a very English idea. You are ashamed of reading what is called 'dry,' and you do not take the trouble to find out whether it really is dry. It is snobbishness upside down. We don't do that. If we read the Classics at all, we read them as an ordinary book."

Miles laughed.

"What are you laughing at?"

"I am laughing at something Troumestre told me the other day. He told me an undergraduate once went to the master of his college, and said: 'Master, I read the Gospels as an ordinary book.' " 'Well?' said Alyosha. "Well," Miles went on, "the master said: 'Really! Mr Jones, you must find it a very *extraordinary* book.' "

"That is just what we do find. Our peasants read *Paradise Lost* as an ordinary book, and find it a very extraordinary book. Well, when I read Homer, in German, in smatterings, as an ordinary book, I found that everything was there – *everything*.

There is no situation in life, so *à plus forte raison* in fiction, Homer doesn't touch.

"For instance, Priam goes to see Achilles, to ransom Hector's body. I feel certain that Homer in that interview tells what any parents of nations who have been at war with one another, and whose sons have been killed in the same war, feel towards each other, about the war, *after* it is over.

"I can't read Greek, but they tell me the language is better than anyone else's. I can guess what it's like; they say it's like Pushkin – a simple outline, saying everything."

"But all that proves," said Miles, "that you have read a great deal, you…"

"You are quite wrong," interrupted Alyosha. "I have read little, but I have a smattering of many things, and so I can understand other things. That is what appeals to us. What your people would call superficial. I am badly educated; and what is unusual for a Russian, I have gaps, many subjects I know nothing of at all. That is not unusual in your countrymen. You have gaps. Perhaps it is your strength. One often meets cultivated Englishmen who know nothing of mathematics or physical science, not even geography, and still less history. That is unusual by us. If we have no smattering, we pretend to have one. We are ashamed not to have one, and we bluff success. My smattering is thin, but it spreads wide… You have gaps, but you know more of what you do know than I do of what I know."

"I don't think so," said Miles. "But go on with what you were beginning to tell me."

"It was when I was quite young, in my regiment at St Petersburg. I was one summer staying in the country with my Aunt Lizzie – you met her in Paris. I met a girl there, not a relation of my cousin, just a friend. She was only seventeen. And although so young, she was the most uncalculating and indifferent person I had ever seen – at least so she seemed to me.

"Calm, like a figure on a Greek vase. But if you looked into her eyes, you could never get to the bottom. It was like gazing into a deep well. I thought the calmness was only on the surface, and perhaps I was right.

"Of course it was Spring, with lilacs in flower, and nightingales singing in all the bushes. We called one of them 'Battistini.'

"The house was full of people – guests and relations, all enjoying themselves…

"Well, on the night when she was about to leave – I see it plainly now – she and I in the verandah. Indoors the old people playing *Préférence*, in a lamplit room – the large open window, the bats, the moths flying round the lamp…

"On that night I proposed to her. She was dressed all in white. The moon was not yet up, and I could only see her eyes shining through the darkness.

I told her that I loved her, and I asked her to marry me. She thought for a moment, and then said: 'Yes, I will marry you, Alexei Nikolayevitch, and I know I shall never love anyone else; but for your own sake you had better not marry me, you had better forget me.'

"I caught her in my arms and covered her with kisses. The next day we were officially engaged. Hence all my trouble."

"Why, what happened?"

"It was broken off later, but I can't tell you now. It would take much too long. And here we are at the hotel. It is too late, and time for us to go to bed. I will tell you some day. By the way, I forgot to tell you that I am starting tomorrow morning for Mukden. You will not be able to come with me, because you have not yet got permission to go any further; but that will come soon, and Ivanov has promised me to see that your journey is arranged. I will see you at Mukden; so goodnight and goodbye," he said, after he had paid the cab.

"At what time do you start? Can't I come and see you off at the station?"

"Oh no," said Alyosha, "that is not at all necessary; I am starting early too, before you will be up."

They walked upstairs.

"Well, good night and goodbye – *au revoir*, that is to say."

CHAPTER XII

Alyosha left for Mukden the next day, and so did Troumestre. Colonel Ivanov promised Miles and Haslam they should be given permission to start soon. Miles spent a whole afternoon with the Colonel, while Haslam was exploring the Chinese quarter with his French friend. The Colonel, he thought, was a curious man. He was middle-aged and inconspicuous, with a straggly moustache, active little quick gestures, and an impulsive delivery. He had travelled far and wide. He had been to more than one war. He spoke English fluently, but with idioms all of his own making. He was abrupt, nervous, quick and interrogative – always asking sudden questions, checking statements others had made or that you had made yourself. At first Miles thought he was being subjected to a test examination, and that the Colonel was perpetually trying to catch him out. At the same time, he felt that he was friendly. It was as if he were doing this from a sense of duty and not because of any personal suspicion. Ivanov asked him a great many questions about Alyosha; how Miles had got to know him, whether Miles had seen any of Alyosha's relations in St Petersburg. He evidently thought Miles' story was fantastic, which it was; but Miles was convinced that he, the Colonel, knew he was telling the truth. The next day he and Haslam again went to the Censor's office to inquire whether they might

107

proceed, and they were told that Haslam could go, but not Miles.

Haslam pointed out that this would be highly inconvenient as they were working together.

"There's only room for one in the train at a time," said the Colonel. "These trains are military trains, you see. Every place is valuable. Haslam will go and prepare things for you, and get a place ready where you can live, and you shall follow as soon as we can arrange it."

So Miles had to wait. He went to the station to see Haslam off, who promised to have everything ready for him by the time he arrived.

The days he spent in Kharbin seemed to Miles like an eternity. He wrote to his friend Haseltine, and a long letter to Aunt Fanny; but he had to show the letters to the Colonel, who read them through carefully. He dined with Ivanov that night. The more he saw of him, the more curious he thought him. He never seemed to dwell on one topic for more than a moment. His conversation was disjointed. He never followed one train of thought for long; he was always going off suddenly at a tangent, and yet there seemed to be an underlying thread in his thoughts which was hidden from one. He seemed absent-minded, and it turned out afterwards that he had heard what you thought he had not listened to. He did not appear to look at anything, yet nothing escaped his notice. Miles, on the whole, liked him. He was, he felt, fundamentally good-natured, superficially cynical, and suspicious more by force of habit than on principle.

Miles asked him whether he would be going to Mukden, and whether he would be the Censor for the war correspondents there.

"No," he said, "not yet. I may come later. I shall be the Censor here. For this reason, I can understand English. There is a Censor at Mukden, but he does not understand English."

"Who will censor what the English correspondents write, then?" asked Miles.

"Nobody, except myself. If they want to send things in English, they will have to come here and get them censored, otherwise they must send them in French."

"Won't that be very roundabout and tiresome?"

"It is meant to be," he said, laughing. "But perhaps later on I shall go south. You see we don't want anything sent off just now, as little as possible. There are at this moment three French, two American, three English, two Germans, an Italian, and a Danish correspondent there, and they are giving already a lot of trouble. We do not send them away, we do not forbid them to write, but we take precautions."

"It will give an advantage to the French correspondents."

"The French are our allies; your allies are the Japanese."

"You want to make it difficult for us?"

"Yes – that is, you see, the system of our Government all along the line – it is the line of least resistance. It works beautifully in a Bureaucracy."

"Will the letters we receive be censored too?"

"Of course," he said; "are you expecting any love letters?"

"No," said Miles, blushing, and he felt the Colonel thought he was telling a lie.

Ivanov asked him again whether the Cossack colonels had borrowed any money from him. Miles said they had not. Ivanov laughed. "They would have, if I had not kept an eye on them. And Kouragine, he has borrowed money from you?"

"Never a penny," said Miles hotly.

Ivanov laughed incredulously.

"If he does, I shall know," he said. "But his aunts give him money. Princess Kouragine is rich."

" Is that the one I saw in St Petersburg?"

"Yes, it is that one: she is rich and eccentric. You know Kouragine's history?"

" No, that is to say – "

Miles was confused and stammered.

"What?"

109

"His aunt told me he had had troubles."

"Which aunt?"

"The one I saw in St Petersburg."

"Ah, and he has not told you his history?"

"No; but he has promised to tell me some day."

"Yes," said Ivanov; "his aunt knew you were going out with him?"

"Oh yes."

"And she approved?"

"Yes; she approved."

"And your aunt?"

"Which aunt?" asked Miles, dumbfounded.

"Your Aunt Fanny...ah! I forgot – there is a letter to you from her; it arrived this morning. It was sent to the Bank."

"And you have read it?"

"Of course... She is angry with you...and with us," he laughed. "And your partner, Mr Saxby, it appears, is angry. But I daresay the business gets on well without you. After the war is over, I will come to London, and you will give me a place in your business?" He laughed. "It is a good thing to have a business like that, but you must be careful here. If it gets known that you are a rich Englishman, people will borrow money from you right and left. The Cossack colonels smelt that out at once."

"How do you know?"

"From the way they ordered that banquet."

"You mean they couldn't afford it?"

"On what? On their pay?"

"How did they pay for it?"

"Well, they didn't; but it was arranged...the prices were cut down. You see the hotel proprietor is an ex-convict, and he has been robbing ever since. This bill was put against some of his recent robberies."

"But supplies are very dear, aren't they, now?"

"Yes; but not as dear as the Hotel *Oriant* makes out."

"But why did the Cossack colonels think I was well off?"

"One has only to look at you. How much does your magazine pay you?"

Miles explained that he was to give the pay to Haslam. Ivanov cross-questioned narrowly as to his income, his financial status, and his business prospects. They sat long over dinner and drank tea and smoked cigarettes. Ivanov suddenly left Miles abruptly and said good night.

When he went to the office the next morning, Ivanov said: "You must be ready to start this evening at five. You are going to travel with General Larichev, in his carriage; you will be comfortable. You will like him. I will take you to the station and introduce you."

At five o'clock, in the crowded station, Miles was introduced to the General. He was an elderly man, with a black beard. He greeted Miles with great courtesy, and said he hoped he would be comfortable in his carriage. He could not speak English except a few words, but he spoke French well.

Never had Miles travelled more comfortably. He had a whole first-class compartment with two berths to himself, next door to the General's. The next morning the General sent his servant to call Miles, and to ask him what time he would like to drink tea. He asked him to come and drink tea in his compartment.

After they had drunk tea, with some fresh rolls, the General begged him to make himself comfortable. He had papers to look through, but he would be pleased to have Miles' company. He did not disturb him in the least.

Miles opened his bag to look for a book. He had finished *Tom Jones*. He had no other book. It was foolish, but then he had not been able to buy anything at Kharbin. There were no bookshops, or at least no shops where European books were on sale. What would he do throughout the long journey? As he was rummaging in the bag he came across a parcel. It was the parcel that Alyosha's aunt had given him, which he had quite forgotten. He opened it, wondering what he would find. He found a pocket edition of the plays of Shakespeare in three small volumes.

Miles had never read the plays of Shakespeare for fun. He had learnt a few stock passages by heart, without understanding them; as a child, he had "done" some of the plays at school and read others; and he had seen a few of them acted, and he had even acted in one himself. But he had never looked upon Shakespeare as a source of pleasure. He began on the first day of his journey to read *Romeo and Juliet*, and before he knew where he was, he was caught by the throat by the poetry and whirled away by the rapidity of the action.

Miles and the General had their midday meal together late, about two, and afterwards they retired to their berths to have a siesta. Miles, who had finished *Romeo and Juliet*, began to read straight on till supper-time, when he ate some cold meat and drank tea with the General. This was more or less the routine of their day. The General was a very different man from Ivanov. He had lived entirely in St Petersburg and in the Far East, and had been at Peking during the Boxer troubles. He had been once or twice to Paris and Nice, but never to England. He was a collector of Oriental china and furs, and fond of shooting tigers. He was suave, polished, and courteous. He spoke French to Miles.

Miles surprised him. He could not understand why he was there. "The English," he said, the second evening of their journey, when they were drinking tea, "like adventures. That is their main characteristic. It is to me, as far as I can judge of it, the characteristic of their literature too. I have read it only in translations; French and German and Russian, for although I can read English a little, it is difficult for me. But I have read Shakespeare in German and Dickens in Russian, and Walter Scott, and some novels by Wells, Mrs Humphrey Ward, and Marie Corelli. There is one advantage of reading books in translation. It is like looking at something through a magnifying glass. It brings out the faults and the qualities, and it gives you a perspective. You look at them as from a distance. I feel this spirit of adventure in your literature. The *Paradise Lost*, for instance, after reading parts of that I feel as if I had been for a long voyage…and your English novels are the only novels that give me the sense of time – of time going on – I feel time going on like a river in your English novels – as in Tolstoi. I cannot judge your poetry."

Miles asked him what his preferences in Russian literature were.

"I am old-fashioned," he said; "I like Tolstoi, Gogol, and Tourgenev, and the poets, Pushkin, Krylov and Lermontov. But I seldom read anything now. I had read almost everything I have ever read in my life when I was twenty. When I read now I prefer an old, comfortable novel by George Sand, or something light which amuses me or makes me laugh, like Jerome K Jerome, for instance. I cannot read the modern Russian books at all. They are too sad. And I do not like the French modern books as much as the old. I am old-fashioned, but it is best to recognise it, and not to pretend one likes what one does not understand, and what is not *de son époque*.

"People now boast that they belong to no epoch, or rather to all the epochs; but do they? When we were young, we considered what had preceded us was ridiculous, and now the young despise what we admire; but soon a new generation will arise, and will find ridiculous just the things that the young admire so much now. But that does not matter. Whatever has merit remains and comes back. It can be now in the shade and now in the sun. It is bound on the wheel of Fame and can never fall off. For Fame is a wheel, just like Fortune; it is not a straight line, as the young like to think… They think that everything progresses in a straight line… That there were first the Egyptians, the Greeks, the Romans, etc., the Middle Ages, all getting a little better – the Renaissance, the Eighteenth century, the Nineteenth century, the Twentieth century – each century thinking it has said the last word; they believe that we are always progressing, and becoming more and more civilised... I am not of that opinion. Take the Chinese, for instance. Look at the Chinese you see around you here. I have lived among them now for many years, and I know them well – well for a European. No European ever knows them really well; or, if he does know them, he becomes so Chinese that no European can any longer understand him; he ends by thinking from right to left... Well, the Chinese foresaw the possibilities of our modern civilisation centuries ago, and all the advantages and resources of modern progress. They foresaw machines and all their consequences; but they chose another road. They discovered the art of printing before anyone, and they kept it. They understood at once that inventions like the telegraph and the locomotive would not make life happier. If you live in China, you will understand very soon that when everybody travels in a rickshaw, it is the same thing as when everybody travels in an automobile. Life is no slower and no faster. You will understand yourself very soon that one can obtain more comforts, and that one can obtain them more quickly, in the most primitive Chinese town than in the expensive hotels of Western peoples."

"But," asked Miles, "won't the Chinese follow the example of the Japanese?"

"No, not unless we force them to... It may happen, of course, if the Westerns make enough trouble in China, with missions, and concessions, and annexation, and company-promoting, and what you call 'peaceful penetration.' Every five hundred years there is a revolution and a kind of *débacle* in Chinese history. One of these *débacles* has been happening now, ever since the Boxer rising. What will be the end of it God only knows. I feel certain of one thing only; that we have none of us ameliorated anything, and that if there are troubles for us in the future in the Far East, it will have been our fault. What is happening now is one of the first results of our interference, and whatever happens the result will be disastrous – disastrous for all Europeans."

"But do you really think it is a good thing for a nation to remain where they were two thousand years ago – to ignore progress?"

"It depends upon where they were two thousand years ago, and it depends upon the nature of the progress. If you compare an educated Chinese mandarin with an educated American politician, there is no doubt who is the more cultivated. You see, at present the Chinese think that war is vulgar, that a soldier is the scum of the earth. If we force them to change their minds, we must not complain when they cease, as Anatole France said, to use *'des obus en porcelaine.'* That, he says, you know, has always been considered by Western people to be *de rigueur* when the Chinese fight to defend themselves against Maxim guns."

"But do you think they are right?" asked Miles.

"Do you think war *is* vulgar, and soldiers the scum of the earth?"

The General laughed.

"Well," he said, "I am an officer, high up in rank (which, from their point of view, makes it worse, of course), but I am sufficiently Oriental to understand their point of view, although I do not agree with it. I was born an Orthodox, if not an Occidental Christian. So Chinese ideals and philosophy seem to me topsy-turvy, although they produce admirable things; that is because those who believe such theories in China put them into practice without shame. They believe in their philosophy and in their code of morality, and they practise it."

"But aren't they very cruel?"

"The machinery of the law is indeed very cruel in China, or seems so to us…firstly, because if the punishment of crime is to be preventive, if Society is to defend herself, punishment must be severe. The police are too few in number and too weak, compared with the quantity of criminals; and as it is difficult to catch a criminal, you must, if you want to make an example, to *encourager les autres*" – the General laughed – "make the punishment severe. That is one reason. Another reason is this: unless the punishment is very severe, the criminal will laugh at it. He is indifferent to death; he is almost without nerves; he has a tough skin. So, in order to make him feel pain at all, the punishment must be, according to our ideas, exaggerated... Then there is their *mise-en-scène* of torture, which is done for the moral effect on the spectators... That is also *pour encourager les autres*. But I do not think the Chinese gloat over scenes of bloodshed. I believe that all violence is foreign to them naturally; and whether the machinery of their law is really more cruel than ours I do not know. The application of the law is cruel everywhere. I am told that the Americans torture witnesses in a refined way, by preventing them from sleeping, and by giving them just enough food to keep them alive under a perpetual rain of questions. Whether it is preferable to be driven mad in this way, or to be done to death by the old-fashioned methods of the Chinese, I do not know."

"But you like them?" asked Miles.

"Yes, I like them," said the General. "I like their landscape painting, it is so delicate. I like their handiwork; I like their porcelain. I like their stuffs, their cooking, and, above all, their manners."

"Can you read Chinese?"

"A little. I know their literature a little. Their theory of poetry seems to me the best. It is to record the impression of one thing, a sound, an effect of light, an incident, a ray of sunlight on some straw in the street, the petal of a flower floating down to the stream – just a note in the *chanson universelle*. To seize it on the wing and record it. And they write such things as briefly as possible. That seems to me the ideal of all poetry. I do not like long poems in any language. I find them tedious."

As the General was talking, the sun was setting on a landscape that was typically Chinese. Out of the window you looked on to a wide plain of millet-fields which were green, but the millet had not nearly reached its full height. The air was soft and golden, and there was a virginal touch in it. In the distance you saw the flat roofs of villages here and there, which were brown and blue in the green plain. Here and there on a road, carts with their large, solid, prehistoric wheels lumbered by, and there were labourers going home.

The country looked rich, inviting, and prosperous.

The General chuckled as he looked out the window. "I am laughing," he said, "at what my soldier servant said to me this morning. He was looking out of the window on to the rich landscape, and he said to me: 'This is a beautiful rich country, sir,' and sighed deeply. 'It would be a good thing,' he added, with a smile, 'to exterminate all that Chinese vermin, and to give the land to Russian people.' Only it was funnier in Russian."

The sun sank in glory of fresh springtide gold. They passed a station where a lot of little brown children were playing on the platform, and some Chinese coolies were looking stolidly in front of them. There was a smell of oil in the air, burnt oil – the indescribable smell of China. They passed the station. The sun sank into a belt of lilac clouds, and a thin silvery crescent moon rose, as appropriate as if it had been carved for the landscape by some "cunning workman in Peking." Nothing could have been more peaceful than the landscape. The twilight, grey and lilac and mauve, with soft pink clouds, deepened. The gold faded from the upper sky, and the last touch of fire died away from the pink fleeces. Every cloud was as delicate as the flowers painted on Chinese white porcelain, as soft as the petals of a rose. The very shapes of the clouds seemed Oriental and exquisite. Miles looked on dreamily, but he was rudely awakened from his daydream by a rattle of bullets which rained like hail on the train.

"It is the *Hun-hu-ses*," said the General. "They often do it."

Nothing further happened, and no damage appeared to have been done. They arrived the next day at Mukden.

CHAPTER XIII

When Miles arrived at Mukden he was met by Haslam, who had already arranged quarters for himself, Troumestre, and Miles. The rooms he had taken were in a Chinese inn called the Dragon Inn. This inn consisted of three one-storied houses, or rather rows of small rooms built round and opening on to a square yard. There was a wall round the whole building, leaving a narrow passage all round the houses, full of rubbish. It seemed to Miles like a cloister, with a farmyard in the middle. Haslam told him that when he had arrived, the rooms were as little fit for habitation as pigsties. There was no floor but mud, and nothing on the walls. But a builder, an upholsterer, and a decorator were sent for, and in two days the rooms were floored with matting and papered and ready. They were perfectly habitable now.

There was a platform in each room about two feet high which occupied three-quarters of the room, covered with matting. This was the *Kang*, and if you were cold you could use it as a stove, and by burning *gowliang* stalks – the stalks of the giant millet – inside it, keep the room warm.

The *Kang* served as a bed at night; you put blankets on it, and in the day you could lie down and read on it. Near you, on the *Kang* itself, was a small table with very short legs – like a Dachshund – for your convenience. In the part of the room unoccupied by this platform there was a table and some chairs; the windowpanes were made of paper. Haslam had engaged a Chinese boy, so had Troumestre; one of them could cook. They had bought ponies, too, and engaged a *mafoo*, a groom.

Miles settled down to a new life. He made the acquaintance of the other war correspondents: the French, the German, the American, the English. All the talk was of when they would be allowed to start for the Front. At present there was nothing to do. The English could not even write descriptive articles without going to Kharbin to have them censored. As for telegraphing, there was nothing to telegraph. So the correspondents were all of them in a state of irascible revolt. Their only occupation was badgering the two Censors and going to the railway station. The railway station was the rendezvous and club of the Mukden world. There was a small refreshment room, full of flies, where the correspondents met to gossip and exchange rumours. Tepid beer was on sale. In the afternoons they would go out for rides, but the area in which they were allowed was limited. Of Alyosha, Miles had no news. He had no idea where he had gone to. The two Censors lived in the train. One was a well-bred, conscientious, rather meticulous military official called Colonel Mirovitch; the other was a rather untidy half-Teutonic landed proprietor who had lived long in the Far East. His name was Von Diettrich. He was intelligent and frankly cynical. One afternoon Miles was sitting with Colonel Mirovitch and with Troumestre, who was trying to get a telegram censored, when Mirovitch announced to them the loss of a Japanese battleship, which had struck a mine.

"It is a terrible calamity," said Mirovitch solemnly.

"A Japanese battleship sunk!" said Diettrich, who had overheard him. "I'm so glad! I'm so glad!" he said in a high piping voice. As Miles was riding back with Troumestre and Maurel, one of the French correspondents, they discussed the Press Censors, and Maurel, talking of Diettrich, said, "*Il a des accès de finesse et des bouffées de choucroute.*"

Their life was civilised. The Chinese boy turned out to be an excellent cook. They got supplies of beer and whisky from Newchwang. They had dinner parties, at which they entertained the other correspondents. The Chinese, Miles became aware, seemed capable of doing anything. Troumestre had a camp bed, and Miles regretted not having one as well.

"That is easy," said Troumestre; "the Chinese will make you one." He sent the boy for a Chinaman from a shop, who came, inspected the bed and took it to pieces, and in three days returned with an exact replica.

They had few books. Troumestre had the works of Robert Browning in one volume, and someone had brought out a new book by a rising author called G K Chesterton, *The Napoleon of Notting Hill.*

The weather was fine, warm and invigorating. Mukden was a blaze of colour, sun, and dust. Miles took several photographs, but Haslam said it was quite useless to write them up. The magazine wanted war stuff. They could get Chinese stuff any day.

Haslam led an indolent life. He would lie for hours on the *Kang*, reading some old numbers of an American magazine; in the evening he would ride. He was a perfect rider. He had once been a cowboy, and he had procured, Heaven knows where from, an American saddle.

He talked little, but sometimes in the evening he would play poker with the other correspondents. He always won.

It was after they had been about a fortnight at Mukden that Alyosha reappeared one day quite suddenly out of the blue. He had been, he said, to Headquarters, had done what he had to do, and now he had got a new job. He did not say what it was. Miles discovered that he had made the acquaintance of the other correspondents – of the Frenchmen; of the two Englishmen, Jameson and Hughes; of Strangeways, the correspondent of a big New York newspaper, who was earnest and a Christian Scientist; and of Bristowe, who came from the

West and who was exuberantly comic; of the two Germans – an affable South German called Herrmann and an ex-Colonel Liebknecht, who looked upon war entirely from a professional point of view, and knew the numbers of all the brigades and regiments. He was disgusted, he said, at the amateurish manner in which the Russian Army was being commanded.

Miles asked Alyosha whether there was any chance of their being allowed to go to the Front.

"For some of you, yes; you are being kept here on probation. The Frenchmen will be allowed to go, of course, some day or other. Americans, too – and the English, there are so few of you; there are only four. As for you, although you are working for an American magazine, you are English – and they suspect you a little. You are too innocent to be true. They think you are Machiavelli in disguise. I have told them it is nonsensical. But in the end it will be all right, and you will find that the Front will come to you quite soon enough."

Every day Haslam went to the Censor, and every day he asked for leave to go to the Front, and every day he was given the same answer: that he must have patience and wait. He explained that his newspaper was getting impatient. He had a long talk with Diettrich, and that evening he told Miles that he had a plan. He would not be allowed to go to the Front, but he would be allowed to go to Peking if he took the Censor Diettrich with him. They would only be there a week, and they might pick up some interesting information. In any case, it was better than waiting here, where there was nothing whatever to do except to go to the station.

"Can I come with you?"

"Sure."

"Well, let's do that. When shall we start?"

"Tomorrow; but you must say nothing about it to the others. You can tell Troumestre just when we are starting; you can say we are going on an expedition with Diettrich, but not to the Front – which is true."

122

They were to start early the next morning, but that night after dinner Alyosha came and the first thing he said to Miles was: "I have heard about your expedition. I am coming too. You cannot be left to your own devices, and I promised my aunt to look after you."

"I am delighted," said Miles.

They started early the next morning on their ponies. They took with them a mule, which carried two small trunks with their necessaries, and Diettrich took his Russian servant. Diettrich spoke English fluently, and when Miles asked him why, as he spoke English so well, he could not censor their English articles, he said: "Because I am not the Censor, only the deputy Censor," and he chuckled.

They started on the Hsin-Min-Tin road. They rode all the morning and halted for food at a rest-house, called in Russian The Etap (*étape*). They passed a continuous stream of Chinamen riding either in carts or on horseback. They were travelling on a road which was highly frequented by travelling Chinese merchants. On either side of them was a sea of green millet. The weather was hot but not oppressive. Every now and then they would ride through a sun-baked village built of mud, yellow and hard, when the blue-clothed women, smoking thin-stemmed pipes, and the little brown, naked children with budding pigtails, would stare at them. Haslam and Diettrich rode on in front, Alyosha and Miles behind.

"This is how all the world travelled," said Alyosha suddenly, "till the nineteenth century. If people want to know what the past was like, they have only to travel in China, inland, or in Russia. If you leave the railways in Russia, you can at once get back to the eighteenth century. And here, in China, we have the same comforts and discomforts as the Greeks and Romans had before the Roman Emperors made everything vulgar. I like better these comforts than those of Western civilisation. Here, if you want a hot bath, they will bring you – or build you, if it's not there – a large tub, big enough to lie in, and fill it with boiling water out of kettles. But you will at least be certain the water is hot. You are never certain in the West, in rich hotels or houses. There may be something wrong with the pipes, or else the servants don't get up to light the fire."

"Would you rather have lived in Greek or Roman times than now?" asked Miles.

"No; I have just told you. If we want antiquity, we can get it *now*, by going to the East. I like better living now, with the chance of going back, than with no chance of seeing what we see now."

"But wouldn't you like to have seen things, like ancient Athens, the Parthenon?"

"I think not at all; it was a mercy for us and for antiquity that it was all destroyed. I don't think we should have admired the temples when they were new, and covered with fresh paint and gold."

"But the Greeks admired their own sculpture. They are thought to be good critics, aren't they?"

"Yes; but it is better to have bits of their art touched by Time, than all of it new and painted."

"But I should like just to see it."

"*We* couldn't see it as it *was*. It would be to you, now, like waxworks, and *Bondieuseries*. We can only see with our modern eyes what is fit for them. A question of mood. *Louis Seize* and his contemporaries found the Gothic horrible."

"But we with our modern eyes admire the Elgin Marbles."

"Yes, as *ruins* they are part of an Englishman's education: a classical quotation. But see how the fashion changes in such things. All that Goethe and Byron admired when they went to Rome is hated by the moderns; and probably in fifty years something different in antiquity will be admired – perhaps something older. Perhaps the wheel will go round the other way, and they will admire once more what Goethe admired, only more, the third manner."

"What do you call the 'third manner'?"

"I call the 'third manner' winter, if you like. There are three manners – spring, summer, winter; or in us, youth, manhood, old age."

"And in Art, too?"

"Yes, always. Three stages – the primitive, spring; the mature, 'middle'; and the third period, 'late' they call it. It is the same in any painter or writer. In Shakespeare, is it not?"

"But you can't call Shakespeare's tragedies a winter. And he wrote *The Tempest* at the end of his life."

"No, not a winter. But didn't Shakespeare die rather young? Wasn't he only fifty-something when he died? I believe the principle runs through everything. Spring, summer, winter – and that everything goes back to the scrap heap."

"But don't some men, and trees, die before they have had time to do anything?"

"No. Someone says somewhere that everybody must go back to the scrap heap as soon as his work has been done. They then are used for something else. It is not a question of age; those who have died young, the Mozarts and Raphaels, had done their work, and it was time for them to go and make room. That is just it; blossom – fruit – refuse; it must be kept going for ever; begin again and go on for ever."

"Rule of three?"

"Yes. I think there is something in the *number* three, and I certainly believe in the Trinity."

"Do you mean as in the Athanasian Creed?"

"Of course."

"I thought that was discarded now. I thought nobody believed in the Athanasian Creed, and that they had settled to leave it out."

"Possibly 'they' can do anything in your Church because, beyond the State, there is no authority, and they hate definition. But they can't in ours, nor in the Roman Church. After all, don't you think the doctrine of the Trinity absurd, only perhaps because you cannot grasp it? You can't grasp the facts that red, blue, and yellow combined make white, and yet all the colours are still there; or, ice, snow, frost, all water. And yet any Oriental child sees that at once, but it does not try to explain it."

"And do you believe in a future life, in personal immortality?"

"Certainly."

"Then how does that fit in with the scrap heap?"

"How do you mean?"

"Well, if you think that man's mission is like that of a tree that blossoms, bears fruit and withers, and then is thrown to the scrap heap, surely his life must be over once and for all?"

"Only in so far as it has been performing on the instrument of the body, in the concert hall of this world – there is no more use for him *here*, on this earth, in this shape; but it is perhaps no more over than, say, a composer's musical life is over when he shuts the piano, and leaves the concert hall. The soul goes on."

"Then your rule of three doesn't apply to the soul? You don't think souls go to the scrap heap, and new souls come out of it?"

"No, I do not."

"But why? Why do you think the soul of an individual is so important?"

"Why should it not be as important as a collective soul? Do you think an individual book is important? Why not then a collective book? I believe the individual soul to be important because it is made in the image of God."

"Then you believe in a personal God?"

"You might just as well ask me if I believed in a personal man. Some people don't. Do you believe the universe is by chance or on purpose? By chance or divine? It must be one or the other. To me there seems a plan. Just as much plan in a spider as in the stars. It seems to me right that Napoleon should finish at St Helena; Goethe live till he was eighty; Achilles be

126

shot in the heel by Paris; the white ant blind, and Pushkin die in a duel…if there is no God, then Chance is a great artist."

"But," said Miles, "if you believe that the universe is like a piece of music, in which each note is played only once, I don't see why you think each note must go on sounding for ever."

"I do not say each note sounds once only – I believe in cycles – the seasons and the weather repeating themselves for ever; but that is different. As to the *note*, it may only once *be heard here in this world, for our ears,* but that is the note heard *through one* instrument; the musical thought in the brain of the composer or the player does not die…you are mixing up the instrument with the player…"

"They say," said Miles, "all the working of the brain is caused by a little grey matter; as soon as that grey matter dies, the brain is dead."

"Yes, and you can get all Beethoven's dreams on four strings of catgut; but if you throw away the fiddle and its strings, you have not destroyed the fiddler; and if you kill the fiddler, you have not destroyed the music."

"Then you think there is something separate from the brain which uses the brain as a keyboard?"

"Most certainly: the soul. Plato thought so; Buddha thought so; and the Christian Churches, which Christians believe have Divine revelation, tell us that it is so, and that the soul *is immortal.*"

"Are you a believer in the Orthodox Russian Church?"

"Not exactly. Not at present. I have not made up my mind – but I am not a disbeliever. I see no reason why one should not believe; at least the objections I see are nothing to do with *dogma.* I see no reason why a reasonable person should not believe the dogmas which are laid down by the first six Councils, and on which the Creeds (with a difference that is no difference) of both the Churches – Eastern and Western – are based. The reasons – besides a want of faith – of positive faith, that is to say – are minor reasons like the political position of the Church in Russia; and then I should have to argue out the point with myself, and settle, if I believe in the Eastern Church, why do I reject the claims of the Western Church? Which is schismatic? One of the two must be, as the Church must be One and must be Oecumenic. But I most certainly believe with my reason in an immortal soul."

"I suppose there may be, but you wouldn't – couldn't, of course – believe in eternal punishments and rewards?"

"Nothing would seem to me more probable – in fact, I could not possibly *not* believe in them. As far as I have observed life, everything that men do has a result; and I see there is a law. I notice if you disobey that law, that you suffer. Each fault revenges itself. The law is irrevocable. Well, if this is true in this world, and if you believe the soul is immortal, there is no reason that the law should stop, no reason that the soul should not suffer, that the fault should not revenge itself beyond the earth just as much as on the earth."

"But isn't that begging the question?"

"Why? How?"

"Saying that *if* you believe the soul is immortal."

"Not at all; you gave me the premise; you said it. There might be a life after death, but that of course I didn't believe in reward and punishment. My answer is, of course I can believe in nothing else, if I believe in the *absolute* justice of God."

"I cannot see how you could reconcile eternal punishment with the idea of a loving God."

"In that case you can't accept the Christian revelation. You want there to be cold water, but no hot. You can't have one without the other."

"I don't see that, and I don't see how you are different from a Pagan, an Oriental, or a Calvinist."

"Calvinists believe you may be damned from the start. We, the Orthodox, believe in the *removal* of sins; that sins are not only forgiven but *removed*."

The sun was setting. The ponies were tired, and at that moment Diettrich and Haslam halted and waved to them and called out, saying the *étape* was not far off.

"But surely," said Miles, "it is impossible for an educated man to be a believing Christian at this time of day, with all the discoveries in Science – and still more impossible to belong to the Greek or Roman Church?"

"You are talking like a half-baked provincial, like those asses of our *intelligentsia* who think they are being above religion, and are really being *below* it. Someone once asked Pasteur how he reconciled his religious faith with his scientific knowledge. He said: 'My faith is like that of a Breton peasant; and if I knew more, it would be like that of a Breton peasant's *wife*.'"

They had now reached the *étape*.

CHAPTER XIV

They stayed the night with the officer in charge of the *étape*, who (Miles thought) was hospitable, but dull. This was no doubt because he spoke no other language than Russian. They started early the next morning, and by midday they had reached a shady place, where they halted for their midday meal.

Just as they were getting ready to eat, under the shade of some trees not far from a stream with stepping stones, a Chinese boy, rather smartly dressed, rode up and delivered a long message to Diettrich in pidgin-Russian.

The message seemed interminable. When at last it came to an end Diettrich said, "We are invited to luncheon by a Chinese General who is encamped not far from here."

"What must we do?" said Miles.

"Why, we must surely go," said Haslam.

"Yes," said Diettrich, "I think we had better go."

Alyosha said nothing. They followed the boy through a sea of *gowliang* till they came to an encampment some miles distant. There were a few deserted mud houses and some tents, on the edge of a small pond. They were ushered into a large tent, where they were received by the General, who was gorgeously dressed in crimson satin. Everything was ready for a meal.

The General spoke Russian, and Diettrich interpreted. They were ushered to the table, on which there were cups of green tea, the saucer inverted over the cup, with green leaves floating in the cup. As soon as they had drunk this, there was a succession of small courses.

The food seemed to Miles excellent.

The talk was of current topics. Every now and then a fragment was translated to Miles. The General was interested to hear that Miles was an Englishman and that Haslam was an American. Course followed course. The meal seemed to Miles to be interminable. A sweet beverage was served. The General used chopsticks, but he had thoughtfully provided knives and forks for his European guests. He asked them about their journey, how long they intended to stay in Peking, how the war was going on, whether the Viceroy and General Kouropatkin were enjoying good health. He asked after the Emperor of Russia and the King of England. Queen Victoria, he said, was still much missed in China. She was a great Queen. When the meal came to an end, the General said he was sure they would be glad of a siesta, and they were taken to a large tent, where they found their bedding carefully laid out, and bowls of water and pipes.

"Tell him," said Haslam, "that we shall have to get a move on in an hour or two."

"I will," said Diettrich, and there was a further long interchange of conversation.

"We shall have to stay a little," Diettrich said.

Their host left them with many bows. They lay down on their couches. Diettrich offered everyone cigarettes.

"You know what has happened," he said to Haslam and Miles.

"I know," said Alyosha.

"What?" said Haslam.

"We are prisoners in the hands of one of the *Hun-hu-ses*," said Diettrich, and gave a high chuckle.

"Well, you had better go and tell him right now," said Haslam, "that I am a citizen of the United States, and that he can't put anything across me. It won't go."

"Yes, yes," said Diettrich; "I will go and tell him presently."

"No; go and tell him right now," said Haslam. "Presently will be too late."

"Very well, very well; I will go."

As he went out of the tent he met a soldier at the door of it. This man could speak no Russian, but Diettrich could speak enough Chinese to make himself understood. He said he wanted to see the General immediately. The soldier came back and said it was not possible at present; the General was resting. Diettrich asked for his servant and for the horses. He was told that the horses were being fed, and that his servant was at present asleep, but he would be fetched the moment his services were needed.

When Diettrich came back and reported the result of his mission, Haslam flew into a passion, and he went and harangued the soldier himself, and demanded to be taken to the General at once. He shouted at the soldier in pidgin-English, interspersed with a few Russian and Chinese words.

"My, American," he kept on saying, "*Moya, Amerikanski. Wa de Ee-hwa zhen.*" He made such a noise that soldiers ran up. He tried to approach the General's tent, but he was at once faced by a large armed escort, who led him civilly but firmly back to the tent, soothing him with sentences which sounded like aphorisms and probably were.

A few moments later the first soldier arrived, and said to Diettrich that the General had been informed, much to his infinite chagrin, that the illustrious American guest was not satisfied with the accommodation that had been afforded him. He was right. The accommodation was indeed unworthy of a citizen of the great Eastern Republic, and if he and the illustrious Colonel – he pointed to Diettrich – "would kindly follow him, he would lead him to new quarters – poor indeed and shameful compared to what accommodation should be if it were to be worthy of such heaven-born guests, but still perhaps not so unworthy as that which they at present occupied."

"I've a good mind to shoot," said Haslam. His hand searched for his "gun," and then for the first time he noticed that it was not there.

"Yes," said Diettrich; "they thought of that a long time ago. We are all of us disarmed. Do nothing foolish or rash. We must go quietly."

The soldiers led Diettrich and Haslam each to a separate tent.

"Why have they done that?" asked Miles.

"Just to show politely that we are in their hands."

"But what is his object?"

"That is just what I do not quite understand."

"You are sure he is a *Hun-hu-se*?"

"Quite certain. I have seen him before, but then he was not so high in rank."

"What will they do to us?"

"No harm. They are on our side for the moment – that is to say, they are on both sides always; but here in Russian occupied territory they are on our side. If the Japanese occupy this territory they will be on their side."

"Do they want a ransom?"

"From the Russian Government? for Diettrich? They would not spend a hundred roubles on him, and on me – nothing. For you and Haslam? It would be difficult. If they *did* anything to you, they would get into difficulties with our authorities... They do not want to do that; besides, they get all the money they want from the Chinese merchants, who pay tribute to them regularly."

"But what is their object?"

"I wonder."

"Haslam was in a great rage. I think he would have shot that man if they hadn't taken away his revolver."

"Yes. Have you ever seen an American in a rage before?"

"No, never."

"Well, I have, and I doubt whether Haslam's rage was real."

"How do you mean, real?"

"I mean I think he was making believe."

"But why?"

"That is just what I want to find out. This expedition was his idea?"

"Yes; he arranged it with Diettrich."

"Well, we shall see. I am going to sleep."

"Are we prisoners?"

"Most certainly; look." Miles looked through the tent and saw that it was guarded by a sentry.

They slept till dinner-time, when they were awakened by one of the soldiers, who asked them if they wanted anything. Hot water was brought them, and the soldier said that the General hoped for their company at supper. Supper turned out to be a short meal. Beyond saying that he hoped that Diettrich and Haslam were comfortable, the General made no allusion to what had happened. He said he ought to have realised at once that the large tent was too small for four people, and that Americans liked having tents to themselves.

"Ask him," said Haslam, "if we can go on with our journey to-morrow morning."

The question was put and answered.

"The General says," said Diettrich, "that of course we can start whenever we like; but that it is so great and rare an honour for him to entertain such illustrious, star-bright guests that he hopes we shall not cut our visit too short. He apologises for having lent to our stay a shadow of confinement. This was but a measure of precaution necessary, because the country-side was infested by robbers."

"Listen to his cheek," said Haslam. "Tell him that I am an American citizen, and that the United States won't stand for having any of their citizens molested or imprisoned without a cause."

Diettrich answered with a flow of Russian, with a Chinese sentence here and there, but whether he translated Haslam's speech it was difficult to tell. The General seemed pleased with the answer. Haslam said that Diettrich had not interpreted for him properly.

This game of cross-purposes went on throughout the meal. Haslam became more and more angry, the General more and more suave, Diettrich more and more voluble.

When dinner was over, the General said he was sure his guests must be tired after so long a journey, and they must be looking forward to a rest. He bade them a very good night.

"Ask him again if we can start tomorrow," said Haslam.

"He says," was Diettrich's answer, after he had put the question, "that we can start whenever we like, provided the road is safe for us. He will have news early tomorrow morning, and if the road is safe, he will escort us himself to the next village."

Once more Miles and Alyosha were taken to one tent, and Haslam and Diettrich to another.

The next day the same routine was observed, except that Miles and Alyosha were unable to have any private conversation with Haslam and Diettrich. And on the third day they were told that Haslam and Diettrich were indisposed, and could not leave their tents. Miles asked Alyosha whether he was uneasy; he said not.

Miles and Alyosha dined that night with the General. He never had been more urbane. He told them of his youthful experiences as a Government official and of his travels. No word was said about their going away. He said Haslam and Diettrich were suffering from the sun, which was always trying in this month, but that it was nothing. Once more they were taken to their tent with great ceremony and obsequiousness, and the General promised them some music: the talk had drifted to music during the course of the meal.

Just as they were going to bed some of the soldiers began to sing outside, to the accompaniment of a one-stringed lute.

"Do tell me what that song means," said Miles, when the song had come to an end.

"I think," answered Alyosha, "that it is a soldiers' song, and I think it means something like this:

"*'The sun rises and sets, but it brings us no release. Why must we be taken from home? To work day and night? The wild foxes come and go at their will, but not we; in front of our window there is a sentinel.'*

"It is a soldiers' lament; a song of exile. It may mean that, but it may mean something different. I judge it to mean that, because it reminds me of Russian prisoners' songs and the recruits' songs in our villages. Possibly it may mean something more like this:

"*'The mountain-ash berry is red, and the garden is full of dead leaves; the swallow has flown long ago. The swallow will come back next year. But my youth has flown away for ever.'*

"I do not know whether this last sentence is correct, whether it is Chinese."

"General Larichev," said Miles, "told me that he thought Chinese poetry was the ideal of what poetry ought to be. Just to catch *one* impression on the wing."

"Yes, he is right. The Chinese call these short poems 'stop-shorts.' Because the sense goes on after the sound has stopped. Chinese poetry is, of course, much the best."

"But if you don't know Chinese?"

"That is not necessary. I know from hearsay and by chance what it is like; one does not have to be a scholar to know such things. I can guess. I can guess at Greek and Latin literature. Shakespeare guessed. I can guess Chinese poetry, though I can't read a Chinese character, and know only about a hundred Chinese words. But I know the kind of thing. Partly from being Russian, partly from having lived in the Far East, and from having seen Chinese life, manners, and pictures. It is the only kind of poetry that appeals to me. The chance sight or sound: a girl carrying a pitcher on her head, a kingfisher darting, a dragonfly on a reed. Faust told the Devil he could have his soul if the Devil ever caught him saying 'Stay,' to the fleeting moment, 'you are so beautiful.' Chinese poetry is a record of *moments*, which happen at any time, anywhere, and stop short; that is so much better than long odes, epics, and dramas."

"What about Shakespeare?"

"The best of Shakespeare is his songs. I would give all the plays for them; but the blank verse is to me difficult and pompous..."

"Since I have been out here I have read all the plays through, and several more than once," said Miles. "And I think they are wonderful."

"Englishmen can't see Shakespeare as he is. They did in the eighteenth century. You see him through a glass of respect – from the cradle."

"But I never read Shakespeare for pleasure till a month ago. I saw his plays acted sometimes, but never by good actors; but it is the poetry I admire, the *sound* of the lines. Perhaps foreigners don't feel this. Troumestre says that some people don't *feel* verse, as others don't have an ear for music, or don't *feel* landscape."

"You are right to listen to Shakespeare as if it were music... To treat it like the Opera... Enjoy the *bravura* passages, and remember the plays were written for an audience who enjoyed the sound; they got the sense from the acting... But even so, I find it crude. I am not an Elizabethan. The villain comes in and tells you how wicked he is. And then the killing, putting out of eyes, murderers, alarms… Too much."

"Then you think it's all nonsense about Shakespeare being a profound poet?"

"Nonsense his being a *German*, if you mean that. Everybody makes Shakespeare in his own image. But when people complain that his thoughts aren't deep, I think they are being foolish, because a child can have the deepest thoughts about all the problems we have ever known of… There are only a certain number of things that can be thought about life, and I think Shakespeare has said them as well as anyone. And then he had marvellous *life*. That is the great thing about him. The *vitality* of the Renaissance! Verse came pouring out of him. And then Shakespeare wrote for the stage, for his audience. You must always remember the public, the footlights, even if they are only tallow candles. When our critics complain of his not being modern, I wonder they do not understand that in fifty years' time all that seems to them modern will seem to new people old-fashioned; and all they complain of as *not* being modern in Shakespeare will still be alive. But that is not what I mind. What bothers me is the emphasis, the noise, the embroidery. I know it is good of its kind; but I am too old for all that. I don't like it. I want something simpler and quieter, and as a poet I get it in Dante, for I know that Shakespeare's business was to write plays; but, as a poet, I like better Dante."

"I have never read him in the original."

"Translations are useless. Dante was a great artist; he paints a landscape in a line."

"Doesn't Shakespeare? I think what you call his emphasis is sometimes like the clank of armour and the champing of bits. For instance, the passage about 'young Harry with his beaver on' – and Miles began to spout:

" '…all furnish'd, all in arms;
All plum'd like estridges that wing the wind;

Baited like eagles that have lately bath'd;
Glittering in golden coats, like images;
All full of spirit as the month of May,
And gorgeous as the sun at midsummer…'"

"Yes, yes; that is good, and it reminds me of my youth, of seeing my regiment trotting in the snow on a fine winter's morning, all the troopers in white, with silver eagles on their helmets, the sun glittering on them. But then Shakespeare needs many lines to do it. Dante does it in one."

"Well, as for landscape, what about this:

" 'Night's candles are burnt out, and jocund day
Stands tiptoe on the misty mountain-tops.'

"Troumestre tells me that he has a friend who says that these lines give him greater pleasure than seeing the actual thing."

"Yes, yes; very good. But Pushkin does it still better, without any adjectives at all. He makes you see the ships sailing through the blue – you feel the wind, you see the foam – all in one line, without an adjective. He does it by the lilt."

"Is Pushkin as great a poet as Shakespeare or Dante?" asked Miles.

"I don't know. He is unique, but to appreciate him you must have the language. You might, of course, say the same about the others; but they are read in translations in spite of it. Partly because they tell amusing stories. The *Odyssey* is the best story in the world, and even *Paradise Lost* is amusing enough, as a story, for our peasants… But to a Russian, Pushkin is the best of writers. You see, he paints all Russia – the character, the landscape – like no one else, simply. As I read some of his poems I see the snow; I hear the horses; I smell the weeds burning in autumn; and it is all so well done; he never uses the pedal; there is no exaggeration. I cannot read him much now; it makes me homesick. Like Troumestre's friend said about

139

Shakespeare, his descriptions of Russian life and landscape affect me more than the real thing."

"But, after the war, won't you go back to Russia?"

"Never. I could – I mean there will be nothing to prevent me, at least I think not; but I will never go, and not because I am *déclassé*, and not because I am married, and not because I am settled at Verkhneudinsk – at least not *only* because of all these things, but because I do not need to. I have all Russia with me, inside of me. It is like the Kingdom of Heaven in the Gospel. I do not care whether I am exiled, or whether there is a revolution, and the whole of Russia and everything Russian is exterminated tomorrow; that would not prevent me, as long as I am alive, being a microcosm of Russia; having it all inside me; being the landscape, the people, the spaces, the fields, the harvests, the songs, the dirt, the smells, the disorder, and the feeling that I am Peter the Great and Ivan *Grozni*, and Tourgenev's Bazarov, and Rudin, and Gogol's liar, Hlestyakov, and Chichikov, the hero of *Dead Souls*; and Ivan the Fool, and Tolstoi's Pierre, and Levin, and Dostoyevsky's Raskolninov, and Myskin, and Rogozhin, and all the brothers Karamazov... I am all that, and the clown in the circus, and the peasant in the field, and the merchant listening to *tzyganye*...and the student moping at the University, and the *chinovnik* cheating, and the political prisoner in prison in Siberia, and the young subaltern in his regiment getting drunk after a regimental dinner, and the monk at his prayers – I am all this, and I am Anna Karenina and Tatiana, Pushkin's heroine, and Evgenie Oniegin, his hero. I am the past, the present, the future, the black soil, the grassy steppes, the harvest, the snows, the spring floods and the sudden spring, the nightingale, the lilac..."

At that moment they heard something moving at the entrance of the tent, and a voice said "Hush!"

Somebody entered the tent, holding a small pocket lantern. It was Haslam. He said: "Be very quiet; I have bribed the guards and we can escape. Diettrich is waiting at the entrance of the camp, and his servant is there with our ponies. You can't pack all that," he said, pointing to such of their personal effects as were lying about. "You must come at once; we have not a moment to lose."

They stole out of the tent. It was a dark night; there was no moon; the camp was asleep; the sentinel was sitting down in front of the tent asleep, or pretending to sleep... They stole after Haslam. They walked on tiptoe, past some more tents, till they reached the outskirts of a field. There they found Diettrich, his servant, their ponies, and a mule.

They got on to their ponies as quietly as they could, and they rode in silence through the *gowliang*.

"We go straight on through these fields," said Haslam, "and after a mile or two we shall reach the road."

They reached the road towards midnight, and rode on till they reached an *étape*, at two o'clock in the morning.

CHAPTER XV

When they woke up the next morning at the *étape*, Haslam said to Miles: "I guess we needn't trouble to go to Peking now."

"Why?" asked Miles.

"Because we shall get our permits to go to Liao-yang, and then south to the Front, in the next few days."

"What do you mean?"

"I fixed up the hold-up. I fixed it through my boy, who is the nephew of one of the Big Noises among the *Hun-hu-ses*: this is the get-away act for Diettrich. I put him wise that I wasn't giving him something for nothing. You see the 'General' didn't care a cent whether we were arrested or not, but I had subscribed handsomely to his old age pension and to his Young *Hun-hu-ses* Pleasant-Sunday-Afternoon-and-Fresh-Air Fund, and *Skreibners'* will find rather a large item on my bill next to the word 'bribery.'"

"But they would never have dared do anything to Diettrich?"

"They could have kept him ever so long. You see I should have said that he had just faked him."

"But you wouldn't have left him alone with those bandits?"

"Sure. He would have felt fine. He mixes with the Chinese. They wouldn't ever have hurt him."

"And now you think he will let us go?"

"Sure."

"But he will have to let the other correspondents go too?"

"They don't care a cuss about that. You see, the game was to have us waiting here so long that our papers would get mad and call us home...some of them have been called home...now I have got it in writing from Diettrich not only that we shall go to Liao-yang in two days' time, and then, after a decent interval, to the Front, but that I am to return home when I am through via Japan, and so far the idea has been to bar that route to newspaper men."

"Had Diettrich no idea that we were going straight into the hands of the *Hun-hu-ses*?"

"None at all; he is always chasing round and having tea drinks with mandarins and chief magistrates. He likes airing his Chinese, which I guess he talks no better than you or I, and he was mighty glad of the chance."

"But I believe that Alyosha suspected."

"Why, Kouragine? He knew."

"But he did nothing."

"Why, he wants us to go."

"Why?"

"Why, he can go off with you and me and not worry any."

"I don't understand."

"Well, it makes his job much easier to shirk."

"But what is his job?"

"Aren't you wise to that?"

"I thought it was something to do with buying horses."

Haslam laughed: "Maybe it has been, but it ain't now."

"Well, what is it?"

"Why, he's a stool pigeon."

"What does that mean?"

"It's what you call a copper's nark."

"What's that?"

"You don't even know your own language. A spy."

"But a spy on what?"

"On us newspapermen – correspondents. He's told off to keep an eye on us, and to see we don't exceed the time limit. If he reports favourably on us, it will be all right; what he says goes. They know he's a judge."

"Why?"

"Well, he's done most things and seen most people from peculiar angles. He's been on the bum."

"But if all that's true, and he was going to report favourably on us – and I don't suppose he'd have dragged me here from Paris if he didn't want me to come…"

"Ah, that was before his job – this job – started."

"I was going to say that if he was going to report favourably on us in any case, what was the use of your getting Diettrich arrested by the *Hun-hu-ses*?"

"Just to hasten things. Alyosha can't get a move on his bosses. He can only report, and what he says goes; but if he says 'Get a move on' to the bosses, that doesn't go."

At noon they started for Mukden. It took two more days to get back. The day after their return Haslam came back one evening at dinner-time, saying that he had interviewed the Censor, and that they would be able to start for Liao-yang in two days' time.

When they got their papers, each correspondent would be appointed to a particular corps; he could stay there as long as he liked.

"Would he be able to send off copy from there?" asked Troumestre.

"No," said Haslam, with a dry smile; "to send off a story he will have to go back to Liao-yang; but they are sending a Censor – Colonel Ivanov – to Liao-yang, who understands English, so he won't have to go away back to Kharbin every time."

The next morning was their last day at Mukden. Haslam, Miles, and Troumestre thought they would like a final ride through the streets, and Alyosha went with them.

The streets were crowded. They rode through the swarming, jostling, many-coloured traffic, so bright in colour, so loud, so pungent in smell. There were carts driven by teams of mules, with a noise of bells, urged on by the hoarse, shrill ejaculations of husbandmen...there were Mandarins trotting by on swift white ponies, followed at a respectful distance by their servants...a General, dressed in crimson satin, holding a fan in one hand and his reins in the other; the orange and dark-blue satin tunics flashed like jewels...and in contrast to these there was the coarse indigo of the humbler folk.

There were carts with prehistoric wheels and round hoods; rickshaws, coolies, cattle, dogs being kicked out of the way, foot-passengers, water-carriers, pedlars, fruit-sellers – every kind of vendor hawking his wares. The temple bells tinkled; the gongs clanged and chimed.

They passed the brilliant, variegated, vociferous shops. In front of each shop, at its door, huge signposts carved and gilded and inlaid with coloured glass and gold stars, and bright with all the colours of the rainbow, were fixed upright in the ground and glinted in the sun. In front of the bootmaker's an enormous boot was hanging, as in a pantomime; and at the fishmonger's a curious fish; they swayed in the wind. Large Chinese characters, gold, red, or black, stood out boldly on the boards. Miles said it was like a Hans Andersen fairy tale. Troumestre said it reminded him of Marco Polo's voyage. Haslam said it beat Peking, and made the Chinese quarter at San Francisco look like thirty cents.

They reached the huge grey walls. These were not ordinary walls. They were enormous, wide, solid ramparts, with huge, grey, monumental towers that stood out immense, deserted, and solemn, like mountains or pyramids among swarming ants.

When they reached the wall, they got off their ponies and left them with their *mafoos*.

It was a hot day.

"Today is the eighteenth of June," said Troumestre, "the anniversary of the Battle of Waterloo. Let's climb to the top of the wall."

They climbed by a narrow staircase to the top of the wall, and found themselves on a wide causeway – so broad that no parapet was necessary – from whence they looked down on the flat roofs of the square town, and the shifting kaleidoscope of the streets.

They had not been long on the top of the wall before Miles and Haslam complained of the heat. They climbed down again, and strolled along under the shade of the rampart.

"People talk of progress," said Troumestre, "but war still goes on."

"War will always go on," said Alyosha, "till all the street boys in the world stop who are quarrelling over an orange, and are ready for arbitration. The Chinese have really got to that point. Watch two Chinamen quarrel. They will snarl, but just stop short of coming to blows... If two people can get thus far without getting to blows, it means that in a country consisting entirely of such people you will have no war. But I am afraid that we Europeans will step in and make this impossible for them. They will have to learn to fight in self-defence."

"Surely," said Troumestre, "a country is the better for the possibility of war...when there is no war, doesn't it mean decadence, the decline and fall of empire?"

"The Roman Empire didn't decay because it abolished war," said Alyosha. " It decayed because it relied on mercenaries."

"That is just my point," said Troumestre. "They forgot how to fight..."

"Yes; but there were the Barbarians... In China they have reached the point of *Romans* and *Barbarians* living together and agreeing not to fight because both sides think it vulgar."

"The Japs," said Haslam, "still think it fine to scrap."

"That is the bore," said Alyosha. "The Japs still think it fine to scrap. How unlike us! We are peaceful. So are the English.

We both go grabbing land, almost by accident, and muddling through. It is all muddle, by us and by you; only you pull through owing to two things."

"What are they?" asked Troumestre.

"One is your political instinct for doing the right thing without knowing you are doing it, and the other is your good luck. We are more unlucky. But then that is our point. It is the *failure* who by us is the greatest success. Ivan the Fool, who gains the kingdom – which is not always of this world. That is what we all of us want to grasp."

"Ivan the Fool grabs a little in this world too, doesn't he?" said Haslam.

"A little," said Alyosha, "but not much. Russia looks large, because it can be stretched like an elastic; but think how little we have made of our resources... Think what you Americans might have done with them. We prefer to plough the fields as Adam and Eve used to do; we don't want to develop, to grow rich; nearly all our rich men are foreigners or Jews...we do not care for money; we treat it like what it is – dirt. There is a proverb which says, 'If you have two loaves, sell one and buy lilies.' "

"Is that a Russian proverb?" asked Troumestre.

"No," said Alyosha. "I have been told it is the saying of a Greek sage."

"I expect," said Troumestre, "the proverb was really ' If you have two loaves, sell one and buy rolls,' because the Greek word for lily, κρίνον, means a kind of loaf as well as a lily."

"That may be," said Alyosha, "but the sense remains the same; and we go further, and sell both loaves, or if we have only one, we sell it – if we want lilies or rolls. That is our theory of life."

"Do you remember what Swift said?" asked Troumestre: " 'One has only to look at the people God has given money to, to see what He thinks of it.' "

"That is true," said Alyosha.

"But surely," said Miles, "one can do a lot of things with money; buy pictures, for instance. If I was very rich I would buy old masters."

"Nonsense," said Alyosha; "rich people never buy good pictures. They buy bad pictures. What you want for buying pictures, or any objects of art, is not money but knowledge and taste; *a* taste, and not just the fashion of the time. The best collections have been made by quite poor people."

"Like *le Cousin Pons*?" said Troumestre.

"Exactly," said Alyosha. "A cousin of mine, who lived in Paris and who was very poor, made all his life a collection of French pictures that the Louvre was proud to accept. Money is a hindrance to everything of that kind. If you have money, you can't have anything else; not even good cooking – that is the tragedy of rich people."

"I think what you say is true," said Troumestre; "but you live to the east of us, and it is much easier for people who live in the East to take no thought for the morrow, and to go barefoot, and give all they have to the poor, than it is in the West, because here, in the East, they are all agriculturists; in the West, we live in towns, and towns produce a *grinding* poverty, a slavery, a destitution in which it is difficult for people to live like the birds of the air."

"Yes," said Alyosha, "unless they wish to be jailbirds."

At that moment they passed a cart in which, behind wooden bars, there were three villainous-looking men. They were dirty and unkempt. They were chained, and round their necks there was a portable pillory, a square board called a *kang*. One of them was smoking a cigarette, and they all of them seemed to be looking at the world with indifferent, callous eyes.

"Who and what are those people?" asked Miles.

"They are criminals," said Alyosha, "who have been condemned to death. They are on their way to be executed. They will have their heads cut off presently."

"They don't seem to mind it," said Miles.

"Why should they?" asked Alyosha. "To a Chinaman death in itself doesn't matter. He has always known it is sure to happen. He has been facing it. It doesn't matter to him *when* he dies nor *how* he dies, but only *where* he dies, or rather where he is buried. It is all-important to him that he should be buried in his own country, for the sake of his family pride."

"I suppose that is religious faith," said Miles. "I suppose that people feel like that whatever their religion is, if they've got a religion. I suppose at the hour of death any religion would be the same, provided you believed in it."

"No," said Troumestre, "that is not religious faith. That is not religion. That is good manners or family pride: to keep it up to the very end; and from the Catholic point of view – and I am a Catholic – I would never admit, firstly, that *that was* religion, nor, in the second place, that any religion was the same as any other religion. It all depends whether the religion is a *true* one."

"But," said Miles, "if people believe in a future life, and in rewards and punishments after death, the effect must be the same whatever the religion is called?"

"No," said Troumestre; "the Greeks had religion, and believed in an afterlife, but it didn't help them to die. On the contrary, Achilles said he would rather have been the meanest serf on earth than king among the dead. Death meant going to an unsubstantial world. At the best, the soul was like a bat in a ghostly tree. The *man* lay rotting in his grave. The Greeks thought old age horrible – because, as you grew old, you could no longer taste what life could give, and you were going to a place where there were no gifts."

"That is true about the Homeric Greek," said Alyosha, "but what about a Greek like Socrates, who believed in God? He died well."

"If Socrates," answered Troumestre, "or anyone else you like to mention, has a faith in God that makes them happy to die, it means that the God they believe in is a loving God. It can't mean anything else. *We* call that true Faith; true religion, part of it. We say Socrates or a Quaker or a Salvation Army man have not got the whole true Faith, but we don't mean that nothing in their faith is true. In so far as Socrates or General Booth believed in a God, and in a rewarding God, and in a loving God, we say their religion is true. Theologians call that *implicit* faith."

"You mean," said Alyosha, "if they knew more, their faith would have more truth in it, but it would not make what truth they have got untrue?"

"Exactly," said Troumestre; "but we believe, too, that a false religion, a religion which is wrong on the vital points – for instance, a religion that presupposes a God like a cat, that will pounce on you the moment you are dead, or that you may be damned to start with – we believe that kind of faith will make life more difficult and death more of a torment the more it is believed to be infallible."

"But," said Haslam, "even in our country people have been known to go to the chair with a joke who hadn't any religion at all…and as for these people, why, look at that bunch which has just passed us in the cart, especially the hobo who was smoking a cigarette. Why, if you're going to be executed here, you can get a guy to be hanged for you for less than thirty cents."

"But surely," said Alyosha, "that shows that in that case religious faith has nothing to do with it. All they mind is where they are going to be buried, and they have been trained ever since the cradle not to show emotion. It is bad manners. It is etiquette not to show any emotion before death."

"Well, what it comes to is this," said Miles. "I suppose that people who have no religion at all behave in practice just as people who have got a religion which they believe to be infallibly right."

"I don't think so," said Troumestre.

"No more do I," said Alyosha.

"The Chinese may have no religion," said Troumestre, "but they have a rigid code, and a strict training and tradition in that code."

"What about the Mahommedans?" said Miles.

"Islam *is* a real religion – a fine one and a firm one," said Troumestre, "but limited. They believe absolutely in a God, in a future life, and in rewards and punishments."

"But what about people with no religion at all?"

"They may be brave," said Troumestre, "when faced with death, or they may not; there are plenty of examples of both. The point is – *my* point is – I say once more, that if you believe in the *true* religion you will find it a help in life and a solace in death; but if you believe in a wrong religion, the more you believe in it the unhappier it will make you both to live and to die. Many wrong religions have fragments of the truth, but the truth remains the truth."

"Isn't the truth relative?" asked Miles.

"We believe not. We believe it is absolute."

"Yes; but you admit that there are pieces of the truth in almost every religion?" said Alyosha.

"Yes; but we believe that Catholic Truth contains all truths."

"I suppose that's why Father Damien was happy," said Miles, "but I can't help thinking that anyone would behave like that if he felt his religion *was* infallibly right."

"Yes," said Troumestre; "but you see his religion *was* infallibly right."

"But surely," said Miles, "the Chinese think whatever they believe in – call it code or etiquette or good manners – is infallibly right *too*...and if they are willing to die for it, and if when they die they are indifferent to death, I don't see the difference."

"There is *all* the difference," said Troumestre. "They may be indifferent, but they are not happy. Stoics were indifferent, but they were not happy. Etiquette may make the Chinese accept death stoically, but it doesn't make them accept death joyfully…the man who passed us just now smoking a cigarette was callous, but not happy."

"I've seen gayer boys," said Haslam. "Rudyard Kipling says somewhere, or at least he has a *babu* Indian say, that it is fortunate that Europeans minded death, because, as they didn't mind being hurt, if they knew what every Oriental knows about the future life, and therefore didn't mind death, there would be no holding them."

"By future life he meant, I suppose, the transmigration of souls?" said Troumestre.

"I guess so."

"Well," said Troumestre, "I can only say in the words of the poet:

" 'I thank my God for this in the least,
I was born in the West and not in the East,
That He made me a human instead of a beast
Whose hide is covered with hair.' "

"I can't see," said Miles, "why they shouldn't be just as right as you."

"We know," said Troumestre, "they are wrong, because God Almighty came down to earth on purpose to tell us so."

"Have a cigarette," said Haslam.

"So you say," Miles went on.

"Yes, so I say," said Troumestre, "but if you believe that it was absolutely untrue, you will have to explain a great many things to yourself, and the explanation is not so easy. If Our Lord never existed, or existed and was an impostor or a liar or a madman…then you have to explain a great deal, and your explanation will be as difficult for a thinking, reasonable sceptic to believe as my creed – more difficult."

By this time they had come back to the place where they had left their ponies. They got on them and settled to ride to the palace, which Miles had never seen. It was close by. It was a dilapidated building, and when they reached it they got off their ponies once more and explored it.

The palace was deserted. The courtyards were green with grass. The walls were wooden and carved, fantastic in shape and colour. They climbed up the rotting stairways that creaked. They inspected treasures, jewels, china, embroidery, and illuminated manuscripts which were locked up in mouldering cupboards behind wooden grating. The walls were eaten with damp.

"Wants repair," said Haslam.

"It will not be repaired," said Alyosha, "and I, for one, am glad. I am content that it should be faded, when its time for fading has come. Repairs are dreadful. They are like trying to make old people young…processes – it can't be done; they do not make younger what is old; they make something wrong and ugly. It is better to make something altogether new. Keep your repairers to make skyscrapers, forty storeys high. They do it well, and the effect is good. But let them never touch this. They would spoil it."

"I'm glad some things are repaired," said Miles. "For instance, if no one had ever repaired Westminster Abbey or the Tower of London, they would have fallen to pieces by now."

"My father said they had spoilt both of them," said Alyosha, "even in his day. But with all the repairs in the world, a cathedral lasts only a little time longer than a sand castle…but still, if it amuses you to repair, repair; only the Chinese would no more repair a palace like this than they would repair a sand castle."

"If building is a game like a children's game, with sand, bucket and spade," said Troumestre, "so is repairing. Men must have toys to play with."

"Yes," said Alyosha, "they must. The difference is that the Chinese know that toys are toys. We take our toys too seriously, and come to believe that our sand castles will last."

They trotted back to tiffin through the bustling, busy town. There was a smell of beans being fried in oil... The city and the world on this June morning were bright – hot, noisy, dusty, busy, bright, gay, and spicy with all the smells of the East.

CHAPTER XVI

The next day Miles and Haslam arrived at Liao-yang. They stayed at the Hotel International. It was a Chinese house, kept by a Greek. The little rooms surrounded a dirty yard. There was a small restaurant, or rather a buffet, with an open hall next to it, covered with an awning of matting during the solstice. The ceiling of the buffet was so black with flies that you could not see the smallest white speck on it.

There was a sensible difference between the atmosphere of the life of Mukden and that of Liao-yang.

Mukden had been like a backwater, a place of peace. Liao-yang was full of bustle. You felt near the war. Miles began to be conscious again, as he had been when they boarded the train at Baikal, of the difference there is between war and peace.

The Commander-in-Chief was at Liao-yang, living in a train. Troops marched through the streets, and streams of two-wheeled green carts called *dvukolkas*. Officers coming from, or going to, the Front crowded the hotel. The angle of vision, perspective, and proportion, Miles felt, began to change. Values had changed altogether. A piece of ice was something strange, rare and precious. Everything to eat was lukewarm; everything to drink was tepid – the hotel was squalidly uncomfortable; but you no longer noticed that, any more than you thought twelve hours was a long time in which to travel fifty miles; any more than you thought two hours long to wait at a siding.

Troumestre and the other correspondents were soon all of them assembled at Liao-yang; Alyosha turned up too; he lived somewhere outside the town.

The Censors remained at Mukden, but Colonel Ivanov arrived at Liao-yang and took up his abode in an office near the station.

The correspondents were not yet allowed to go to the Front, but Haslam told Miles that he need not be uneasy. In the meantime, Miles enlarged the circle of his acquaintance. He made friends with many strange people, especially in the garden of a restaurant which was halfway between the town and the station, where the Russian officers and others used to dine.

Most of the Chinese servants, except Miles' boy, took the opportunity of leaving the service of the Europeans. They had no wish to go nearer the war.

They did not say they were going away; they intimated that they had domestic troubles. One had a sister-in-law who was sick in Peking, another an aunt who was not well at Canton. The weather was hot. It was said that next month the rainy season was due, and that it would rain steadily for a month.

The news from the Front was scanty.

The time passed slowly and quickly. Miles and the others lived in the perpetual expectation of leaving the next day, or the day after tomorrow; and yet it seemed to be, like Alice's jam, always tomorrow, and never today. Yet a whole period of time, a whole week, seemed when it was over, to have gone by like a flash. The correspondents were grumbling for various reasons. They complained that the Russian correspondents were being favoured, and were preventing the foreigners from being sent to the Front. The French simply said they wanted a most-favoured nation treatment. The Germans said they were the only correspondents who understood war. The Americans said they were the only correspondents who understood journalism – that the rest were amateurs. As regards Troumestre and Miles, this was true.

Alyosha said to Miles one day, "All this fuss they are making to go to the Front is foolish. When they get there they won't stay there. How can they? They will have to come back here to get anything they send censored – they won't be allowed to send telegrams straight from the Front, which is the only thing they want to do."

"Then why do they stay?" asked Miles.

"They stay because their newspapers have not recalled them."

Haslam was equally phlegmatic. He played poker every evening, when he could find people to play with him; but as he played better than the others, and always won, this was not so easy. He said he did not care a rap whether he went to the Front or not. Miles could photograph what he liked, he would write up everything. They managed between them to send off a picturesque article about missionary doctors at Liao-yang.

Miles photographed one of them in his garden, and Haslam wrote an imaginative description. They spent hours in talk. Miles wondered whether what Haslam said about Alyosha was true: that he was watching the correspondents. He seemed to take little notice of them as a whole. He never went near the French or the Germans, and only met them when they all met together. He spent his time with the English and the Americans, but he was not often with them. He seemed always to be busy, and there were many Russians whom he was obliged or whom he wanted to see.

One English newspaper, growing impatient at the lack of news, wired to its correspondent to come home at once.

After they had spent ten days at Liao-yang, Miles felt that he had lived there all his life.

He was growing restless, impatient, nervous from the heat, the flies, the squalor, and the aimless waiting.

"You are looking depressed," Alyosha said to him one morning. "I have an amusement for you. I will take you to a picnic. I have been asked to pay a visit to a doctor, who is an old friend of mine. He is with the Red Cross, and lives in a Chinese temple with his staff, about three miles from here. I will take you with me."

They rode out together in the brilliant morning through the tall green millet. They reached the doctor's camp about one o'clock, and found a table spread. There were two doctors: one, a fat bearded man, dressed in a grey sarcenet shirt, the other thin and sallow; some assistants, young for the greater part; a Russian war correspondent who represented one of the more liberal Russian newspapers, and three hospital nurses. They welcomed Miles. None of the men could talk English, but they all spoke German, and one of them French. The nurses talked French, and one of them English.

Alyosha at once introduced Miles to this one. He called her Elena Nikolayevna. She was young – not, Miles thought, more than thirty. She had small well-cut features, large still eyes, and black hair. She was calm in her movements, but Miles thought in her presence of guns looking over the brow of a harmless hill.

Miles was cordially welcomed. They sat down to their meal out of doors, under the shade of some trees. There was a small village hard by. In a little over a month's time this quiet spot was destined to be raked with bullets, to be sacked and devastated.

The guests were given vodka. There was a large supply of tinned *zakouskas*. To Miles, the food seemed strangely civilised. He sat between Elena Nikolayevna and another nurse who spoke French, a blond, cheerful person. It was hot. The *zakouskas* were followed by some solid beef boiled in soup and then by the soup itself. After that there was more tinned cold food. Vodka was drunk unremittingly.

The company, with the exception of Miles' two neighbours, seemed to him listless. It reminded him of something – what was it? What had he seen like this before? Of course – it was the play he had seen at Moscow, *The Cherry Orchard*. These people were like the characters in that play – in their ways, that is to say, as far as he could judge.

Alyosha had mentioned Elena Nikolayevna to Miles on the way, but no one else. She asked Miles several questions, but she did not wait for an answer, nor did she seem to expect one. As for the men, they seemed not to be taking any interest in the proceedings. Perhaps, Miles thought, this was because he did not understand what they were saying. Most of the conversation was carried on in Russian.

"You were never in Russia before?" Elena Nikolayevna asked him.

Miles explained the manner in which he had come to be a correspondent in Manchuria.

The luncheon lasted till three. Towards the end, toasts were drunk, and there were speeches. Miles was obliged to return thanks when his health was drunk, which he did in a few sentences of halting French. When it was all over tea was served, and they all smoked cigarettes.

"Oh, you photograph?" Elena Nikolayevna said suddenly to Miles. "You must photograph us."

Everyone agreed, and Miles arranged them all for a group. They were childishly delighted.

Then they went back to the table; more tea was drunk. The men sighed, the conversation languished.

"*La guerre,*" said one of the doctor's assistants to Miles in slow, singing French, "*est une chose très ennuyeuse.*"

"Do you like war?" Elena Nikolayevna suddenly asked Miles.

"I really don't know. I have experienced it so little so far."

"But war," she said, "is all like this."

"Except, I suppose, when there is fighting going on."

"Yes, and then it is worse. How long do you think it will last, and who will win?"

Miles said civilly that he thought the Russians were bound to win, if the war went on long enough.

"But I suppose you wish, you would rather the Japanese won?"

"I know nothing about the Japanese, and care nothing for them."

"I do not know which will be worse, if we lose or if we win," said Elena Nikolayevna. Others heard what she was saying and this started a heated discussion.

"And do you like being here?" asked Miles.

"I am fond of hospitals, and I don't mind."

"But you are not homesick?"

"Oh no; it is a great bore to live in St Petersburg, especially now."

They sat on till five o'clock, when Alyosha said they must be going, more tea was drunk, and then Miles said goodbye.

Alyosha was silent the whole way home. He asked Miles to dine with him at the open-air restaurant.

They met there later in the evening. It was a serene evening after the breathless day. Just outside the restaurant there was a large Chinese pagoda of complicated design, built before the Manchus by Chinese Buddhists. Alyosha chose a table in the corner of the garden. He ordered dinner and champagne.

"I must have champagne," he said. "I am feeling melancholy."

"I thought all those people who were at the temple were melancholy," said Miles, "or was that just because I don't understand Russian?"

"No," said Alyosha; "it is true. They are all of them bored to death!"

"Because of the war?"

"No, anyhow. They would be more bored at home. They are always like that."

"But why?"

"They have played vindt till they are silly...they have no interests. They will tell you it is because there is no political life, and because the Government is so bad...but I am wondering...that is not the reason of course, but I am wondering now for the first time whether, after all, men can be happy unless they can talk politics."

"And abuse the Government?"

"Oh, they do that as it is. They do nothing else."

"Then what more do they want?"

"I do not know. It cannot be to go into Parliament, because they wouldn't, if they could..."

"But my neighbour didn't seem bored."

"No; she is different."

"You knew her before?"

"Yes, I have known her before. They have all of them heads stuffed with sawdust," said Alyosha, going back to what he had been saying before. "They are so futile. They talk of all that ought to be done, and of all that they would do for the people, for the peasant. They never think of *asking* the peasant what he wants, they tell him what he ought to want. They little know."

"Little know what?"

"Little know how much the peasants are bored with them."

"But why are the peasants bored with them?"

"The peasants think them silly and futile, and also they think they are ungodly, which is quite true. Because they despise the peasants for being backward, and, as they think, superstitious. When the revolution comes, it is *they* who will suffer first and worst."

"Do you think there will be a revolution?"

"There is always revolution of some kind in Russia after every war, but when the real revolution will come I don't know...perhaps never. You see the peasants feel the intellectuals patronise them; they are saying 'Poor peasant!' the whole time, 'we would teach you willingly, if only we were allowed to by the Government.' They do not understand that all you can do for the peasant is to open the door for him on *possibilities*. But if it comes to teaching him *how* to do a thing, he can teach you. He knows by experience."

And here Alyosha explained to Miles his views on the land question in Russia.

When he had finished, Miles said to him: "What it comes to is this: you say the peasant believes that the land should be in the hands of those that till it, and you agree with him?"

"Yes," said Alyosha, "I think the peasant right *in the long run*, and I think *in the long run* the land not only *should* but *will* be his."

They had finished dinner by now, and they were smoking and drinking coffee.

"I told you I have known Elena Nikolayevna before," said Alyosha suddenly; "she is the girl I told you about. I was engaged to her. I had not seen her since – since it was broken off, till I met her the other day at the station. I knew she was married. Her husband is uninteresting. He is an officer, and his name is Ilyin."

"She looks young."

"Yes, she *is* young." He drank up his glass of champagne, and sent for another bottle.

"We were engaged for a year," Alyosha went on. "At first it was impossible. She was too young. I was too young. Then my father and mother both of them died, and an uncle died who had property, mines in Siberia. He was rich. Everything was left to me. I had a big house in St Petersburg, a large estate in the country. I spent it all; I gambled. I borrowed money from a Jew. I borrowed a lot of money. I had mortgaged everything. I was loaded with debts. Then I wanted to marry Elena, and she wanted to marry me. We settled to marry. Everyone was pleased and happy. Nobody knew how bad my situation was. They knew I had gambled. They did not know how much money I owed. The night before we were to be married, the Jew to whom I owed all the money – he was an old man – sent for me. I thought to myself, 'It is Fate knocking at the door. He is going to blackmail me.' I owed him a lot – with interest. I could pay nothing. I had dinner by myself, and I got rather drunk – not very drunk, but just enough to matter. I went to see him after dinner.

"I did not think I was drunk at all; but I was more drunk than I knew. I seemed to myself more calm, more in possession of myself than I had ever been; that is sometimes the effect of drunkenness, if one has drunk a lot of vodka. He received me upstairs in his sitting room. I can see it now: there was a canary in the corner of the room, with a baize cloth half over the cage to prevent its singing. I noticed his hands; his fingers were long and thin, like spiders. He chuckled when I came into the room. He spoke with a German accent. 'Sit down, sit down, Alexei Alexandrovitch,' he said, and he looked at me with a grin.

"I felt something rising in me. It was the Devil, I suppose – at least, I know – and I felt I was ready to do anything. 'Dirty Shylock, dirty Jew, dirty *Svoloch*,' I thought, 'you shall squeeze me no more; you shall squeeze neither me nor anyone else any more. I will make an end of you once and for all; you have made too many people miserable.' I drew my revolver and I shot at him twice. He was dead. Nothing happened. I did nothing. I did not search his papers or burn my I.O.U.'s. An old woman had shown me in, and she was downstairs, and deaf. He had few servants. The canary woke up and began to sing, and I got up and went down the street; and the old woman opened the door and I took a cab and went home. I went home, I wrote a letter to the Police, and sent it by hand; and I wrote to my Colonel. I was, of course, arrested. When they examined the old man's papers, they found out that the reason he had sent for me was to release me from all my debts. It was his wedding present, and also he had left a will making me his heir. I was tried for murder, and condemned to ten years *travaux forcés*. I was sent to Siberia. I never saw Elena again. But she wrote to me, and

163

told me she would wait if I was willing; but I told her I was not willing; and to prevent her waiting – for I knew that if she said she would wait, she would wait – I told her that I did not love her, and that I would marry someone else at the first opportunity. Whether she believed this or not, I have not known. Probably no. She did not marry, as a matter of fact, till a long time afterwards. Then I spent ten years on the island of Saghalien."

"Oh! "said Miles.

"Don't think I was to be pitied for *that*," said Alyosha. "Life goes on, you know. It is about the same everywhere. The convict world is just like any other world; certain people come to the top. I ended by being a king on that island – more than a king, an absolute monarch. I was glad, of course, when it was over. I still had ten more years to spend in Siberia. At the end of five years of my exile there was an amnesty for some reason or other; I benefited. I could have come home, but *à quoi bon*? I was a *déclassé*, and in Siberia, at Verkhneudinsk, I had a situation. I started a tobacco store; and I married. I was as happy as one is... And so I never saw Elena again until the other day. Yes, she looks young. You see, it was only fifteen years ago, and she was hardly seventeen when I first knew her. But directly I saw her I knew she had never loved anyone else, and I, too, have never loved anyone else. Now it is too late. Not that she has prejudices, but our lives are in different ruts. I would never let her marry me, however much she might want to – which she wouldn't want, however fond she was of me."

"But she didn't mind?"

"She didn't mind the result. She didn't mind my being a criminal, a *déclassé*; but she did mind my having killed a man – so she told me..."

"Does she love her husband?"

"No, not at all. He is uninteresting. She married him because she thought it was better to marry someone; she knew she would never care for anyone else. He is harmless and conscientious, so she says. She says he is a good man."

"Has she any children?"

"She had one, and it died. She does not care for people, you see; she cares for ideals."

"I suppose she is a kind of Nihilist?"

"Oh, not at all; she has a horror of politics; but she is fond of knowing things and seeing things, and of seeing people who know things. She is inquisitive."

Alyosha called for the bill, and they went home.

CHAPTER XVII

It was shortly after this, at the beginning of July, that Haslam one morning brought Miles the news that they would be able to start for the Front in two days' time. They had been attached to a cavalry brigade in the First Siberian Army Corps.

The correspondents were moving south to Ta-shi-chiao. The night that this piece of news was received they met at the Hotel International, and a small banquet was improvised.

The Chinese staff, faced with the opportunity of improvisation, excelled themselves. The Chinese enjoy making bricks out of straw.

There were many guests at the dinner, which was given by some of the English correspondents to some of their foreign colleagues: two Germans, two Frenchmen, an Italian, a Dane, the Americans. Alyosha was there as well. There was vodka for dinner, whisky and *Tan San*, and even, towards the end, an inferior champagne, besides various rather dubious liqueurs. Conversation was carried on in several languages. Haslam, who had been to a University in Germany, spoke German. Jameson spoke all the languages in turn. After dinner, some of the guests went away. The others sat on at separate tables under the awning in the hall.

Alyosha, Miles, Troumestre, Hughes (the correspondent of the *Northern Pilot*), and Jameson sat at one table drinking Benedictine.

The Americans (Haslam, Strangeways, and Bristowe), Maurel, Berton, Benelli, and Liebknecht sat at the next table, which was within earshot.

"I wonder," said Hughes, "who won the Ladies' Plate? It's the first time I've missed Henley for ten years." Hughes was an athlete. They called him "The Brushwood Boy."

"I don't mind missing Henley," said Jameson, "but I should like to see the 'Varsity Match."

Jameson was a different type – middle-aged and spectacled; an artist, with a brilliant future that had never materialised, constrained to thirty years' hack work, partly owing to circumstances and partly owing to indolence.

"I hate," said Alyosha – "I might say, *we* hate, we Russians – your idea of games; it is all so pompous. When our people play games, it is play; when your people play games, it is work."

"Yes," said Hughes, "that is the whole point of it. 'They toil at games, and play with books,' an Eton poet said."

"But you spoil your games," said Alyosha. "You make them professional. When our people play games, they only care who wins as long as the game lasts; they don't make a fuss: they don't *organise* games."

"If you really care for games," said Hughes, "you must have organisation. If you really care for music, and you want a symphony to be played, you can't let the orchestra improvise – everyone must play his part, obey the conductor, and follow the beat; if not – well, you know. In our games every man plays up for the sake of the game, and ultimately for the sake of every one's enjoyment, including his own."

"No," said Alyosha, "*excluding* his own enjoyment, and as to musicians, no *musician* will care to play in a symphony unless he is paid. A symphony is either music performed by slaves for the pleasure of rich people, or just a commercial business. I used once to have an orchestra of slaves – musicians, I mean, not serfs – at home."

"Professional players at games have just as much right to exist as amateurs," said Hughes.

"Yes," said Alyosha; "but what I think spoils your English sport is the fuss; writing about games in the newspapers for days before and after they are over."

"If nobody cares who wins the game or not," said Hughes, "and if nobody minds what notes people play in an orchestra, it is much better not to play games, and not to have concerts."

"Concerts!" said Alyosha. "When you go to a concert, you don't have to endure a rehearsal; and for me to look on at a professional game for hours would be the same as listening to a stuffy concert with professional players playing something German; I would find it a bore."

"Yes, if you have no ear," said Hughes. "But your concerts are full, just the same; and a great many English people not only *really* enjoy looking on at games, but *really* enjoy playing them."

"Your books are full of stories of boys at school who hated games," said Alyosha.

"Well," said Hughes, "even if they don't enjoy it, it can do them no harm. It's good training. Besides, what is the alternative? They must be occupied."

"Yes," said Alyosha, "but you are the slaves of sport."

"That is quite true," said Jameson, "but what you don't understand, Alexis, is this: that English people are *really* interested in sport, just as French people are *really* interested in the stage, Germans in music, Spaniards in bull-fighting, Russians in dancing.

"If you go to a prize fight in the East End of London, and watch the audience, you will notice the same spontaneous murmur of applause at a piece of footwork or a feint that you hear in Spain at a bull-fight – not at bloodshed, but at a piece of skill on the part of the matador – something which you won't notice. The same thing at the Russian ballet. You won't understand why the gallery suddenly clap the turn of an ankle, just as a French audience – the gallery – do suddenly when a line of Racine is said in a particular way. The English get just that same thrill, not only at a prize fight, but at a cricket match over a well-bowled ball, or at football over a good pass. And why shouldn't they? Why shouldn't they get their thrill when and where they like? Why not?"

"I don't mind their getting their thrills from sport," said Alyosha; "lots of other people get their thrills from sport too – some of us do – but we do not train for our thrills. You think of nothing *but* training – training and exercise. I don't believe that training is important. I think exercise not important at all. Look at the cat and the boa constrictor. They do not think about keeping themselves in training."

"Cats and boa constrictors are like Jameson," said Hughes; "they are born geniuses for killing, just as he is for drawing; less gifted people *must* train."

"No," said Alyosha, "they ought to give it up. People who have no ear ought not to torture us by practising on the piano. *All* training is useless. You can either play football or the fiddle, or you can't; you are either a gentleman or you are not – and if you are not, no amount of training will make you anything but what you call a self-made man – a cad."

"Training is simply practice," said Hughes; "the footballer must practise, so must the fiddler. Look at your ballet dancers."

"Yes; as I have been telling you," said Alyosha, "if a man has to fiddle or dance for his living. But you *all* practise. You think practice in itself is enough. You are content with it – without a chance of there being ever any proper performance. Professionals must train. It is bad enough to have to be a professional at your business, but why be a professional in your play?"

"I would much rather amateurs did not play at all," said Jameson; "I am all for professionals – artists, singers, dancers, players, footballers, boxers, whatever you like. I want them to train – and it's all nonsense about them doing nothing else. Look at the Rugby football players in private life. They are as busy as possible – bankers and architects. I want them to practise; I want them to compete, because I want to see their art at its best. I like it; I like looking on at professional cricket. I hate amateur music and drawing. If the players didn't train, I would rather not look on at them. And it's all very well for you to talk like that, Alexis, but you know quite well you wouldn't go and listen to a lot of amateurs playing a Brahms symphony."

"But that is exactly what I am saying," said Alyosha; "let professionals train, and not amateurs – and I would never go and hear a Brahms symphony."

Just before he said this, Herrmann, a South German, had strolled up to their table. He overheard the last remark.

"What!" he said; "not like Brahms?"

"No, not at all," said Alyosha.

"Have you ever heard his music?" said Herrmann.

"No," said Alyosha, "and I find I don't want to; I don't like symphonies."

"But," said Herrmann, "he didn't only write symphonies; he wrote some of the most beautiful songs in the world."

"Possibly," said Alyosha.

"You don't believe it?"

"I don't think I should like them."

"Well, listen," said Herrmann. He went up to a broken-down cottage piano, which was in the corner of the buffet. He pulled it right round so that he could face his audience, and struck a few chords on the dilapidated keys. There was little ivory left on them. A faint tinkling noise came from the instrument; and yet, under his magical fingers, for he *was* a musician, music was born and took shape. He sang a song about the Spring. He had a pleasant baritone voice. You heard every word he sang. There was no emphasis and no effort. The accompaniment seemed miraculous on that instrument. When he had stopped, everybody clapped. Jameson was in tears.

"Don't you like that?" asked Hughes.

"He sings very well, of course," said Alyosha, "but I don't like that kind of tune. It is to me too professional, what *you* call classical; and then I find the words so silly: 'My love is like a lilac bush' – whose love is like a lilac bush?"

"But what sort of tunes do you like?" asked Jameson.

"I like *Carmen*," he said, "and Italian Opera. You see, the difference to me is this: anybody can play the tunes I like with one finger on the piano, and, compared to that – to what you call 'good music' – they are like games schoolboys play in a village compared to one of your great games which lasts for days, in which people play what is called 'good cricket.'"

"But surely," said Troumestre, "it is just as difficult to sing the sort of tune you like, say a tune of Mozart, well, as it is to play what you call 'difficult' music."

"Comparisons are always wrong," said Alyosha, "especially when one is half drunk. The tunes I mean anybody can sing or *hum*, but the song Herrmann has just sung would be nothing without the accompaniment, and his singing."

"I can hum that tune," said Jameson.

"Oh, so could I," said Alyosha, "but I don't like it."

Herrmann sang another song by Schubert, called *Der Leiermann* (The Hurdy-gurdy Player).

"Don't you like that?" they said to Alyosha when he had finished.

"Yes," said Alyosha, "because in our village I have heard real *Leiermanns*, and they are just like that. But I do not believe Brahms could make tunes like that."

"He could, he could," shouted Herrmann from the piano; "listen to this – I've forgotten the words" – and he played the accompaniment of a sad song, which he hummed.

"I like better Schubert," said Alyosha, when he had finished; "all that kind of music is to me like watching games."

"Well, I like watching games," said Hughes, "as, I suppose, other people like classical music."

"I have an aunt who does," said Miles.

"English people like watching games," said Alyosha, "because no Englishman can bear to be left alone for any time with himself."

"No one can bear being left alone," said Jameson.

"Except saints," said Troumestre, "and they find it difficult."

In the yard the Chinese were singing a long saga in which the words *Der-gwa, Ee-gwa, In-gwa* were constantly recurring.

"I wonder what all that means," said Miles.

"It is a topical song, about all of us; it is extremely obscene," said Jameson – he had more than a smattering of Chinese.

"Like all the best songs," said Alyosha.

At that moment the Americans present struck up a chorus: "Carry me back to old Virginny."

It sounded doleful.

"Listen to that," said Alyosha; "it sounds like a hymn. The Chinese think it is part of a religious service."

"*Nous vous chanterons quelque chose de plus gai que cela,*" said Berton, an amateur in journalism, but an athlete and a lion-hunter, sitting down at the table, and he immediately struck up a song called *La Marquise.*

His voice rang out true, deep, and resonant, like a bugle. His enunciation hit the nail like a hammer: "*Elle s'en va le long de la rivière,*" he sang, and the rhythm of the song carried every-one away. When he had finished, Alyosha was asked for a song. He, too, sang a gay song about a soldier leaving the square: "*Schol soldat s'uchenia.*"

Between each song a toast was drunk in Benedictine and other liqueurs. Miles began to see everything through a haze. He felt more and more exhilarated.

"You have no more song writers now," said Alyosha; "Byron was your last."

"Oh, Byron!" said Hughes; "nobody reads Byron."

"My aunt does," said Miles.

"Yes, that's it; only aunts do," said Hughes.

"I admire Lord Byron," said Maurel. (Maurel was the correspondent of an important French newspaper. In his youth he had studied medicine and published poems. He knew St Petersburg and spoke Russian.)

"He sounds much better in French prose," said Troumestre; "but do you admire Musset?"

"He is too *relâché*, too careless."

"You admire the Parnassians," asked Troumestre, "*Leconte de Lisle and Heredia?*"

"*Parbleu!* Of course; who could not admire this?" and he recited a sonnet by Heredia about a shipwrecked sailor.

"Very nice," said Alyosha, "but too long, too literary."

"Ah! *Vous voulez le feu sacré?*" said Berton; "well, what about Victor Hugo:

" 'La Marseillaise ailée et volant dans les balles,
  Les tambours, les obus, les bombes, les cymbales,
      Et ton rire, O Kléber!' "

"Oh no," said Alyosha, "I don't like that at all. Kléber's laughter – no, no. I hate that *emphase*. I like better Racine."

"Ah! Racine, *c'est autre chose*," said Maurel, and he murmured to himself:

"Captive, toujours triste, importune à moi-même."

"All that to me," said Hughes, "is indistinguishable from prose."

"That is why I like it; I like poetry to be the same as prose," said Alyosha.

During all this discussion Hermann was playing accompaniments of German songs on the piano, humming the tune, and every now and then singing the words. Liebknecht,

173

the Italian, and Jameson had stolen away from their places and were listening spellbound by the piano.

"French poetry," said Troumestre, "seems to me either rhetoric or prose. I hate rhetoric, and I hate prose in poetry. Poetry must have something mysterious, that sings in the heart and in the head."

The Americans began singing again. Hermann shut the piano with a bang. Jameson rejoined the group.

"You don't appreciate our verse," said Maurel, "because you don't feel the values of our language."

"Well," said Jameson, "do you appreciate this?

>   " 'Four and twenty ponies
>   Trotting through the dark –
>   Brandy for the parson,
>   'Baccy for the clerk,
> Laces for a lady, letters for a spy,
> And watch the wall, my darling, while the gentlemen go by.' "

"That is good," said Aloysha. "Who wrote it?"

"Rudyard Kipling," said Jameson.

"The best of your modern poets," said Berton.

"Hear! hear!" said Haslam and Alyosha.

"The best drum-player," said Troumestre.

"To me, that's a nice jingle, but not poetry," said Hughes. "In poetry I want magic. I want *glamour*. I want music, mystery. I don't care even if it means nothing. The best poet to my mind is Shelley."

"Soap bubbles," said Jameson.

"I like something like this," Hughes went on:

>   " 'My soul is an enchanted boat,
>   Which like a sleeping swan doth float
>   Upon the silver waves of thy sweet singing."

"Well then, why not Edwin Lear?" asked Troumestre:

> " 'The owl and the pussy.cat went to sea
>   In a beautiful pea-green boat,
> They took some honey and plenty of money
>   Wrapped up in a five pound note.' "

"That, to me, *is* poetry," said Jameson. "Who is your favourite poet?" he said to Miles.

Miles thought, stammered, and then said, "I think, Shakespeare."

"I'll show you what's good," said Jameson, and he began to sing at the top of his voice:

> " 'As I was going to Salisbury
>   Upon a summer's day...' "

Some of the others joined in the chorus. When the song came to an end, Jameson said: "Here's health to all good poets – French, English, German, Russian, and Chinese. Here's a health to all the jolly poets that had guts – Byron, Kipling, Heine, Musset; and confound Virgil and Ovid, and Shelley and *Judas* the Obscure. Heinrich Heine, he's the man," and he began chanting to himself:

> " 'They loved each other beyond belief,
>   She was a harlot and he was a thief.'

That's you. *Prosit*, Heine!"

"*Nein, nein.* Goethe, Goethe," said Liebknecht.

"Victor Hugo!" said Berton.

"Goethe!" said Liebknecht.

"Hölderlin!" said Herrmann.

"Baudelaire!" said Maurel.

"Keats!" said Troumestre.

"Shelley!" said Hughes.

"Ella Wheeler!" said Strangeways.

"Kipling!" said Jameson.

"Poe!" said Haslam.

"Pushkin!" said Alyosha.

"Shakespeare!" said Miles.

Then Jameson suddenly began to recite a French poem:

> " 'Il était un pauvre gars
> Qui aimait celle qui ne l'aimait pas,' "

and from that he passed on to Kipling and began singing the "Ford of Cabul River," but he broke off in the middle of it, and intoned an Italian ditty, after which he started improvising a song of his own invention, of which the refrain was:

> " 'So carry my coffin home, sonny,
> So carry my coffin home.' "

The guests had reshuffled themselves; Hughes began another serious discussion with Troumestre about poetry. They still thought they were talking sense. Maurel and Berton were talking to Alyosha and Miles in French, and Liebknecht was expounding to Haslam Kouropatkin's strategy, and showing how mistaken it was. He indicated an alternative and said, "*Napoleon hätte es gewagt.*"

"But, after all, you must admit," Troumestre was saying, "Browning has written some beautiful things."

"I hate it all," said Hughes, "all of it. I hate his attitude. I hate his portly optimism, the way he slaps his chest; I hate his style; I hate his puns and word clippings. He reminds me of an intoxicated dentist – "

"Are you boys roasting the poets now?" said Haslam. "I wonder you can work yourselves up about a lot of four-flushers. Edgar Poe has got them all beat, anyhow."

" 'Prince, poets count for rather more than kings,' "

quoted Troumestre. "Poets are the most important people in the world, because they really create something that endures, longer than marble or bronze. We admire Latin and Greek, although we don't even know how to pronounce them. It's a great mystery, and that's why poets are like God on a small scale."

"Yes," said Maurel, "Balzac talked of *un homme revêtu d'un magnifique sacerdoce, le poète, qui semble ne rien faire et qui néanmoins règne sur l'humanité, quand il a su la peindre!*"

"There's no such thing as God," said Jameson, hiccoughing. "That's all rot."

"St Thomas," said Troumestre, "says 'there is apparently no God,' but he comes to the conclusion there is. Bacon said he would rather believe all the fables in the Talmud than that the universe was without a frame."

"There is no God, all the same," said Jameson, "no God at all; and as for the parsons, they're a lot of... Do you believe in God, Troumestre?"

"I do. I'm a Catholic."

"I know. I thought Catholics didn't have to believe in God. I thought they had only to believe in the Pope – which I should call more sensible. We know there *is* a Pope; but if there is a God, and if He is all-powerful, then why did He allow evil to be? You can't answer that! Nobody can!"

"You know what Dr Johnson said," said Troumestre: " 'Moral evil is caused by free will, which means choice between good and evil.' Man would rather be free to be good or bad than a machine which could only do good; and what is best for an individual must be best for the world. If you would rather be a machine, one can't argue. Would you rather be a machine?"

"I am a machine," said Jameson, "a bloody machine. You call yourself a Catholic, but I bet you are not."

"I most certainly am."

"I bet you are not."

"How?"

"Well, if you are a Catholic, you are bound to believe that whatever you have done, a few mumbled words will put it right at the hour of death; but if you don't mumble the formula, you go to Hell."

"Bad theology," said Troumestre, "the formula has nothing to do with it; you could say all the formulae in the world, and it wouldn't count unless the *soul* made an act of contrition at the same time. It is true that it is enough for the *soul* to make the millionth part of the fraction of an inch of a gesture; – also a *perfect* act of contrition is as good as the Sacraments."

"How can you believe a gesture can make any difference?"

"Falling off a cornice is only a gesture," said Troumestre.

"I don't believe you believe what you've got to believe, all the same," said Jameson.

" 'He didn't believe in Adam and Eve,
　　He put no Faith therein;
　His doubts began with the Fall of man,
　　And he laughed at original sin.
　　　With a tow-ti-row,' "

sang Troumestre. Jameson took up the chorus, and then everybody joined in somehow.

Jameson pointed to the awning: "Do you see that bit of rickshaw up there?" he said. "That's what Troumestre's soul will be like in the next world, falling off a cornice, falling off a c – c – co – ornice – what a di – ffi – cult word that is – c – ornice. Come along, C – C – Consterdine. We will go for a walk…in the moonlight…'and they sang to the light of the moon moon – moon.' "

Miles jumped at the suggestion. He felt inclined for more than a walk. He thought he could run, jump, skip, and fly. He seemed to be treading on air. He thought suddenly he was on board ship. And he stood up and began to recite Clarence's dream from *Richard III* to the company. He had learnt it in the schoolroom, when he was a child; he knew it by heart – but it all seemed to come wrong, like the poems Alice heard in Wonderland:

> "Methought, that I had broken from the Tower,
> And was embark'd to cross to Westminster;
> And in my company my brother Gloucester;
> Who from my cabin tempted me to walk
> Upon the…quarter-deck…"

Here he lurched, and fell upon his chair. "Gloucester stumbled, you see," he explained slowly to the company –

> " '…and I fell overboard…
> Into the tumbling billows of the Thames.
> O Lord! I thought, I don't know how to drown!
> What dreadful noise of water in mine ears!' "

"You see I was at the bottom of the Thames, and couldn't drown, and I saw the sculls, the sculls we had lost, and dead bones…heaps of sculls, all scattered in the bottom of the Thames…" Then he reflected, seemed to search for the lines, and suddenly shouted, "I've got it:

> " 'Clarence is come! false, fleeting, perjured Clarence –
> That stabbed me in the field by – Salisbury,' "

and here he broke into the song they had sung earlier in the evening – "As I was going to Salisbury upon a summer's day." Then all at once he became serious once more and said gravely: "You know my name *is* Jack Rover, and I do come from over the hills, and I am going for a walk with my brother Gloucester, good – ole – G – Gloucester," and he walked unsteadily up to Jameson and took him by the arm, and said: "Come with me, brother Gloucester. We will walk upon the hatches. That's the word, hatches."

"Yes," sang Jameson, "we will go once more a-roving by the light of the moon. *Au clair de la lune, mon ami Pierrot,*" and then he changed to another sadder song: *'La lune langoureuse,'*" he sang, "*'Hélas! J'ai dans le coeur une tristesse affreuse...'*" and he began to cry.

"*Déjà!*" said Berton.

"*Il ne faut pas les laisser seuls,*" said Maurel to Troumestre. Upon which Jameson in perfect French explained that he needed air and exercise. Liebknecht intervened, and told Haslam in authoritative Prussian that they must be taken to bed. Jameson at once retorted in finest German, beginning, *Gnädigster Herr*, and quoted Goethe and Schopenhauer. Benelli intervened, and Jameson began to recite a passage from the *Inferno*. He took Miles' arm, and they swayed into the street. Maurel and the others ran after them; they darted and dodged through the streets of Liao-yang, and the others had great difficulty in keeping up with them. Miles and Jameson were now bosom friends, exchanging confidences, and laughing at the thought that anyone could believe that they were drunk.

"They think we are drunk," said Miles, laughing, "but we're not drunk, are we, brother Gloucester? Old Clarence is dead...good old Clarence!"

"Drunk! No!" said Jameson; "of course not." He was walking arm in arm with Miles, and they were flanked by Maurel, Berton, and Benelli on one side, and by Haslam on the other.

Troumestre and Alyosha followed as the rear guard. Never for one moment did Jameson forget to speak French to Maurel and Berton, German to Liebknecht and Herrmann, Italian to Benelli, and Russian to Alyosha.

Suddenly, Miles and Jameson broke away from their escort, and ran down a side street, and were lost.

For half an hour the others searched for them in vain. At last they were run to earth in a Chinese stable yard. They were lying down fast asleep on a heap of stones, near some mules and ponies. They were carried home unconscious, and put to bed by Miles' Chinese servant, who merely said one word – "*Peen*"; he meant "*Pian*," which is Russian for "drunk."

CHAPTER XVIII

The next day Miles, Haslam, and Troumestre started by train for Ta-shi-chiao. Alyosha did not go with them. He said he would meet them later.

With much difficulty they entrained their ponies, their mules, Troumestre's Montenegrin servant, and another Montenegrin and two Chinamen.

When they arrived at Ta-shi-chiao, which was a small village at some distance from the "town" and station, they stayed with the two Frenchmen at the Presbytery of the Catholic Church.

General Kouropatkin was in his train at Ta-shi-chiao, and at the station there was the usual crowd of nondescripts; still more so than at Liao-yang and Mukden.

On the night of their arrival they all dined in the yard of the Presbytery – Haslam, Maurel, Berton, and Miles. The food was cooked by Troumestre's Montenegrin servant, who was an artist in *risottos*.

Haslam, Maurel, and Berton said that going to live with a Brigade, or indeed with any unit, was sheer folly from a journalist's point of view, as they would see little, hear nothing, and not be able to despatch any news. Haslam said he would wait at Ta-shi-chiao till the fighting began; he would then go back to Liao-yang or possibly Mukden. Miles could do what he pleased.

The Frenchmen agreed.

Troumestre, on the other hand, said he was determined to try life at the Front. It would at least give him copy for a descriptive article; it was better than dawdling at the railway station; they would not get left behind. He wanted to take Miles with him. Miles said he would feel out of it with people who could only speak Russian, but Troumestre said it would be an experience, and he could take some interesting pictures.

They spent a day in idleness at Ta-shi-chiao, where they sat for the greater part of the time at the railway station. Troumestre made the acquaintance of many strange characters, to whom he introduced Miles. Together they drank quantities of bad champagne and spurious vodka. Miles could follow little of the conversation, with the exception of the word "Mister," which recurred with an almost cloying frequency.

When their papers were in order, and they had interviewed the General of the Brigade, who was at that moment sick at Ta-shi-chiao and had been temporarily replaced at the Front by another General, they started on their ponies for the Brigade Headquarters, which were about eight miles distant.

They arrived at midday at a small village and were introduced to the General who was living in a small Chinese *fang-tze* with some of his Staff. The others were encamped in a neighbouring field.

The Staff, as far as Miles and Troumestre were concerned, represented a major, a captain, a lieutenant, a doctor, and an *intendant*. It was only the lieutenant's name that stuck in Miles' mind: Semenov. He was young, well built, and brimful of energy. Unfortunately, he could speak nothing but Russian. He talked to Troumestre without ceasing, chiefly about an invasion of India, his favourite dream. One of the other officers could talk French, and the doctor talked German. But Miles began to be fascinated by the Russian conversations that he could not understand; it began to be an amusement to him to pick out a familiar word here and there.

The weather grew hotter and hotter. They lived on the fringe of an immense sea of *gowliang*. In the distance there was a range of blue hills. The Staff spent most of the time in a field. There was a summer house at one end of it, over which an enormous pumpkin plant trailed. Their day began at sunrise. Washing took place. It was performed as a ritual. Water was poured over your face, shoulders, and hands out of a kettle by a dragoon. Then there was tea. Then conversation began, which lasted with few interruptions till bedtime, at nine. They were, so Miles thought, as far removed from any war as the planet Mars. He seemed to be drifting on a sea of leisureless leisure. It was a picnic without any of the fun. Time seemed to be endless, and discomfort – slight discomfort – permanent. There was for the time being a lull in events. Miles and Troumestre slept in a small Chinese house with the doctor and the *intendant*. They had their meals with the General.

Three days were spent in this fashion. To Miles it seemed as if he had been there for months. One evening they were having supper in the field, and drinking tea with the Staff. Someone had produced some tins of sausages, which they cooked. In one of the tins the sausages were bad. This was pointed out. Semenov said it did not matter. He said that he could eat bad sausages without coming to any harm. The doctor begged him not to be so silly. Semenov took the tin and finished it. The effects were not slow in making themselves felt. He was soon in excruciating pain. The doctor gave him remedies, but the pain went on, and they thought at one moment he would die.

The doctor and the others sat up all night. But towards daybreak he got better and by sunrise he was asleep; by midday he said he felt quite well.

After they had spent three days in this fashion, Troumestre thought they had better ride back to Ta-shi-chiao, to find out what was happening. They rode back to their Presbytery. They rode into the town and the station, but they heard nothing definite. The next morning they awoke to the sound of guns, and they knew that a battle had begun.

Miles and Troumestre got on their ponies and rode in the direction of the firing along a road on each side of which stretched the giant green *gowliang*. It was now so tall that men on horseback could be easily concealed in it. The plain of *gowliang* was flanked on each side by small hills. Due south in the distance there was a range of blue mountains.

On the right – the eastern side of the road – there was a small village which was occupied by a detachment of the Red Cross. Miles and Troumestre got off their ponies, tied them up, and walked towards a mound on which an officer was standing giving orders to his battery. The guns were beneath him at some distance. Miles and Troumestre stood near the mound. "Now we are actually in a battle," said Miles.

"Yes," said Troumestre; "the Russians have retired from their first position, and, this battery is halfway between it and their second position. The Japanese have occupied the position the Russians evacuated."

"It's noisy, isn't it?" said Miles. His head was cracking. Behind them there were Cossacks concealed in the *gowliang*. The heat was scorching, the firing went on, and it was nearing midday.

Miles and Troumstre walked back to the village. They talked to a doctor, who was smoking a cigarette.

"We shall retreat soon," the doctor said to Troumestre, who interpreted.

"I wonder they don't fire on us," said Miles.

"Look," said the doctor, and he pointed to the house where the ponies had been tied up. There was a hole in it.

"It looks like a house in a panorama of war," said Miles. The situation seemed unreal to him, like a dream.

The battery stopped firing, and everyone, Miles and Troumestre included, began to retreat through the *gowliang*.

The Japanese were firing on the retreating troops but without doing damage.

"I used to dream as a child," said Miles, "I was riding through tall green stuff like this. I feel as if I were in that dream now."

Presently they emerged from the *gowliang* and came out on the open road.

"I have been under fire," said Miles, "and I never knew it or noticed it."

"One doesn't at first," said Troumestre, "and then one does and one minds, and then there comes a second stage when one minds less. Look at our village now."

They looked back. It was on fire.

They rode back to the Presbytery, where they found the Montenegrins had canvas baths ready for them in the yard, and a meal. In the afternoon it began to pour: a heavy tropical downpour, and the dusty roads became swamps.

Everybody said there would be a big battle the next day.

In the evening Miles and Troumestre started to find their Brigade.

The rain had stopped. There was a soft sunset, which suffused the sky and the earth with peace. There was a faint blush all over the sky, delicate as the tint of a rose. The effect of this over the green seas of *gowliang* was beautiful. The rain had made the going abominable. Small rivulets had swollen into floods. They had to choose a circuitous route. The sun set; the moon rose; and Miles and Troumestre seemed still far from their destination. The country looked different.

"Do you think we shall ever find the village?" said Miles. "I think we have lost the way."

"I'm sure we have," said Troumestre.

They met a soldier and explained their difficulty. He gave them some vague directions.

"He has no idea where we are," said Troumestre.

And then all at once they came upon a village, and found their friends bivouacking in it. It was the same village in which they had lived before. They had not recognised it at first. They slept on mackintoshes on the roadside under a wall – a sound sleep.

The next day at dawn, while the morning star was still shining in the spacious purity of the morning, Miles and Troumestre awoke, got up, and had breakfast of tea and some eggs given them by one of the Staff.

With the first ray of sunrise, the guns were audible, but not loud. Miles and Troumestre rode towards the Russian second position.

They soon fell in with a detachment of transport in charge of a private, which had settled down by the roadside to make a fire, and boil a kettle, which was hung by a small pole on two large forked sticks. Just as the kettle was on the boil, the private in charge said that there was no time for tea, they must be getting on; and off they trotted, cheerful and philosophic. Miles and Troumestre followed. An artillery duel was proceeding. They did not understand what was happening, but they rode on till they met some gunners, belonging to the artillery of the Reserve. There they found transport and some detached Cossacks.

"You had better stay with us," one of the gunners said to Troumestre; and they did.

The sun grew hotter and hotter. The peace of the morning, which had been ineffable, was broken now by incessant noise. There were puffs of white and brown smoke in the sky, as if someone were blowing cigarette smoke rings.

The morning had had for Miles the peace that only Sunday morning seems to have, and now the noontide was full of noise and dust and squalor.

"What a curious Sunday morning!" Miles said to Troumestre.

"Can you read German?" asked Troumestre.

"Yes, a little," said Miles.

"There is a poem by Uhland which describes it, saying the heavens look just as if they were going to open, and ending, '*Das ist der Tag des Herrn*' ('It is the Lord's Day')."

Just then one of the batteries was relieved; there was a crunching of limbers along the road; much noise and shouting…three men in the battery which had just been relieved were wounded. Others were brought in on stretchers. But these had succumbed to the heat. There was an ambulance and staff of *feldshers* and a doctor, for first aid. At midday the Cossacks gave Miles and Consterdine some food. They gave them soup with rice and meat in it, which was issued to the troops in tins; you could heat them, and the soup was good and satisfying. The Cossacks were friendly, hospitable, and good-natured, and asked Troumestre to tell them who was going to win the war, seeming to look upon him as a wizard. After they had finished their meal, there was a sudden bustle. The men were preparing to go somewhere else.

"You had better not stay here," said the departing gunners. "It's dangerous."

"We had better go and look at the battle from the top of a hill," said Troumestre.

They rode back, dismounted, tied up their ponies, and climbed to the top of a high hill. It was crowded with people. There they found Liebknecht and Jameson and Hughes. Liebknecht said the Russians were doing very well. The Japanese fire was having no effect.

From this eminence they could see the positions plainly. But as for a battle, all they saw were puffs of smoke in the air, sometimes white, sometimes brown, and the sea of *gowliang*; troops disappearing into it and emerging from it. Every now and then the flash of guns; sometimes a shell would burst in the plain. The noise was deafening. Miles and Troumestre remained where they were till the evening. Towards the end of the day the firing of the Japanese batteries diminished. The Russian batteries were intact. Liebknecht said that they had got the best of the artillery duel, and so they had; the trouble was that beyond and on either side of these duelling batteries were the flanks, and the Russians, to avoid being outflanked on their left, were obliged to retreat. But no one knew this yet. Firing went on until nine in the evening, and Miles and Troumestre rode home to the Presbytery. At the Presbytery they found it difficult to believe that a battle had been going on. Their baths were ready for them in the yard, and Troumestre's Montenegrin was cooking a pilaff. The Chinamen were waiting placidly for orders. Two stray Chinamen had just arrived, with ladders and paint pots, to paint and repair the church, and they began serenely to work at the frieze.

A gunner staggered into the yard, hot, grimy, exhausted, pouring with sweat and caked with mud. He asked for something to drink. The Chinamen at once told him peremptorily to get out, but Troumestre gave him some brandy and hot tea. Miles and Troumestre fell into an exhausted sleep directly it grew dark.

Early the next morning they rode into the town of Ta-shi-chiao, to the station; there they were told that a general retreat had been ordered, and that Ta-shi-chiao was to be evacuated. They, too, determined to retreat. Their cavalcade started. It consisted of five ponies, two mules which carried their belongings, two Chinamen, and two Montenegrins.

They rode through the town and past the station, which was deserted and stripped bare. Not a cigarette had been left behind. It was like a market place the day after a fair or a racecourse after a race meeting.

They proceeded further and met the Staff of their Brigade, who were now in the lowest spirits.

"It's always the same thing," one of them said; "one is told everything is going well and then it ends in a retreat."

They passed lines of carts and transport, but no officers and no infantry. They halted at midday under the shade of two or three trees for rest and a meal. The two Montenegrins at once began to quarrel. One of them called the other a mule, and they threw things at each other, and finally each refused to proceed any further in company with the other.

Miles and Troumestre did not know what to do. They could not deal with the five ponies, two Chinamen, and two mules between them, and they were in despair. At that moment Alyosha appeared as out of the blue, and with one word he quelled the quarrel of the two Montenegrins. He took charge of the situation, and they obeyed him immediately.

"That is what being a man of action means," said Troumestre.

At three o'clock they started once more. Alyosha said that he had not been able to join them sooner, as he has only arrived at Ta-shi-chiao on the eve of the retreat.

"Nobody knows what will happen," he said; "some say there will be a battle at Hai-cheng, others that we will go back to Liao-yang."

Until Alyosha arrived Miles and Troumestre had followed the transport along the road, but when they started again in the afternoon, he took them by a road over the hills.

They arrived at Hai-cheng at seven o'clock. Alyosha said he would take the ponies to the French missionaries; Miles and Troumestre could do as they liked – go on to Liao-yang by the next train, or stay the night at Hai-cheng.

"I must get back to Liao-yang at once, to send my story," said Troumestre.

"But will there be a train?" asked Miles.

"Perhaps not for eighteen hours," said Alyosha, "or possibly presently."

Miles said he would go by train with Troumestre; Alyosha said he would go to the town and come on with the ponies the next day.

Miles and Troumestre went to the station and asked when the next train to Liao-yang would start. Nobody knew. A train might start in three hours' time perhaps.

Troumestre said they had better go and get some food at the buffet. They went to the buffet, which was full of officers, doctors, hospital nurses, and officials. It was black with flies. Every bit of meat had to be kept under a wire cage.

They ordered some food, and they had no sooner sat down when a railway official came up to Troumestre and told him that a train had been formed, and would be starting presently.

"How soon?" asked Troumestre.

"In about an hour," was the answer.

They waited for some time. Presently the Cossack Colonel whom they had met at Kharbin came into the room. He recognised them and greeted them warmly. He sat down next to them and ordered some food.

Some Red Cross people sat down at the table opposite them; among them a young man who seemed to be of importance; he talked in a loud voice in English. Catching sight of Miles and Troumestre, he pushed away the mustard and said to his companions: "I won't eat that; it's English mustard."

He said "How do you do?" to the Cossack Colonel, who seemed uncomfortable.

"Who is he?" said Miles to Troumestre.

"A kind of minor royalty, I think," said Troumestre, "something to do with one of the Grand Dukes. I don't know his name, something German. He's in the Red Cross."

The newcomer began talking French. The others said something about the war, upon which the personage said in a loud voice: "Hush – Correspondents!" looking at Miles and Troumestre. In the meantime the second bell had rung, and the train was ready to start; but neither Miles nor Troumestre noticed it. Their friend the official came back and told them the train was just starting. They rushed to the platform; the train was moving. Troumestre made a dash for the door of a carriage, and was hauled in by an obliging soldier, but Miles was just too late; he missed the train.

He came back to the buffet, feeling disconsolate. The Cossack Colonel was kind to him, but could only say "Mister." The princeling looked at him unfavourably, and every now and then made disparaging remarks about the English in guttural, provocative English. Miles had no idea where he would spend the night. He thought he would walk to the town. He did; but when he got there, it was past the curfew hour. The gates were closed, and it was impossible to get in. He was obliged to walk back to the station. When he got there it began to rain; the buffet was deserted. He sat down at the table and ordered some tea. He felt half dead from fatigue.

All at once he heard a familiar voice saying to him: "Mihal Ivanytch, how are you?"

It was Elena Ilyin. She asked him what he was doing, and he told her his adventures.

"You can come to our train – there is a spare bed tonight; tomorrow you can go back by train to Liao-yang."

She took him to the train, and there he found Alyosha's friends whom he had met at luncheon at Liao-yang. Elena Ilyin took little notice of them, and made Miles sit down and gave him some tea. She made him tell her everything that had happened so far. She asked after Alyosha, but without great interest.

After Miles had drunk a glass of tea with some brandy in it he began to feel better. His fatigue left him. He had no wish to sleep.

"I am very hungry," said Elena Ilyin, "and as it is too late for hot food here, do you mind if we go back to the buffet, now that all is arranged? You are to sleep in Dr Schulgin's compartment – he is away – it is next door. Or are you tired?"

Miles said he would be delighted, and they went back to the buffet, where Elena Ilyin ordered some tea and some hot *bitki* (rissoles), and she lit a cigarette.

"I am very hungry," she said; "I missed the supper, and it was to get food I came here first; but I had to arrange for you first, before the others went to bed."

Miles thanked her.

"Is war like what you thought?" she asked.

"I don't know. To tell the truth, I have never thought much about war."

"How strange! And yet every man must go to war, mustn't he, just as every woman must have a baby?"

Miles laughed. "But all women don't have babies; and after all, there isn't always a war."

"Women should always have babies," she said. "I had one, but it died; and always there have been *wars* – ever since I can remember. I remember my parents talking about the Crimean War, and still more about the French war, which was just over. Then, when I was a child, there was the war with Turkey; and you too had a Zulu war, and the Prince Imperial was killed. Then you had a war in Egypt, and General Gordon was killed. Then there were two wars in South Africa – one long and wicked one – the Boers; and besides that the Italians had a war in Abyssinia and the Turks had a war with the Greeks; and I have probably left out others. You see, they never stop. Some people say there must be wars, otherwise there are too many people."

"They mean it's like people being bled?"

"Yes; but I think it's senseless all the same...it seems silly to invent engines for destroying everything and everybody – shrapnel, heavy guns, Shimosé shells – and at the same time to have all these trains, and field hospitals, and surgeons for the wounded. I think it would be better if war were as savage as possible."

"But you could not *not* look after the wounded, could you?"

"I couldn't. I should have to help. Not that I am kind. But I must be busy. I must be doing something; if there is a war I must be in it, right in it, taking part in it, seeing the worst."

"You have already seen horrible things, I suppose?"

"Yes, very bad wounds. I don't mind 'orror," she said, dropping the "*h*" and blowing rings of tobacco smoke.

"But I suppose," said Miles, "that war is good for people, good for nations."

"I wonder. I think it is only people who have not seen it who think that. They make a romance about it, especially the English, because you look on your wars as games that only a few people go to. If you have a conscript army, all is different. Then you see it affects the heart of the country. The peasant is taken away from his fields, and he has to come and fight here; he does not know why, he does not know what for, and we can't tell him because we don't know. I don't know what this war is about. We are too near to tell. What do we want? What do they want? Is it the yellow peril? Is it the invasion of the Barbarians again, or is it for our sake, this war? – for Russia – something like an operation which will pierce an abscess in our institutions and bring about something better, or something worse?"

"A revolution?" asked Miles.

"Yes, a revolution."

"If there was a revolution, would you be on the side of it?"

"I do not think so, because, although I agree with the ideas of the revolutionaries, I do not like them. I have an elemental hatred in me for the *intelligentsia*, for our Russian *intelligentsia*, that nothing can cure. I know it is unreasonable."

"But aren't you living with them now, at this moment?"

"Yes, I am. I like the people I live with. One can always do that, although I think they are foolish…not their theories. I admire their theories – if they could only put them into practice – and I *admire* them. I admire our doctors, our country doctors for instance, more than anyone in the world. I admire our men of science, I admire our teachers, our schoolmasters, our professors. I think they are right. I admire their ideas. But I don't *like* them personally. I don't want to live with them. I do it because it is the only way here."

"But then who are the people here you do like?"

"Oh, the Conservatives...people like Alyosha's uncle and aunts, whom you have met, and people like you. I like you. You don't know how different you are from the *intelligentsia*."

Miles blushed and laughed.

"You look very tired and sleepy," she said. "I will take you to your compartment. You get up early tomorrow. Before you go to bed, tell me one thing."

"What is it?

"Do you like Alyosha?"

"Yes, very much."

"I am glad; so do I. Let us go." She paid her bill, and led Miles back to the train.

When they got there they found the others had all of them gone to bed. She showed Miles his berth, and said: "Good night, Mihalivanytch," she said, pronouncing it all in one word.

CHAPTER XIX

The next morning Miles said goodbye to Elena Ilyin, and went back to Liao-yang.

"We are sure to meet again," she said.

When Miles arrived at Liao-yang he found that Haslam had left the hotel, and was living in a comfortable Chinese house. Troumestre was staying with him.

"Get any pictures?" Haslam said to Miles as soon as he saw him.

Miles showed what he had done.

"Good," said Haslam. "Now I will write up that battle, and then will begin the battle with the Censor to get it through."

The next day Alyosha arrived with the ponies, the mules, and the Staff. He stayed with Haslam and Miles; it was he who had found the Chinese house. There were rumours of fighting in the south; but nobody knew what was happening. Haslam wrote his article. Some of the letterpress was passed by the Censor, and a few of the pictures were allowed to go with it.

Troumestre said he was going back to Hai-cheng. Miles said he would like to go with him.

"Go if you like, Kid," said Haslam, " but don't expect me to go with you. I am sure going to wait for General Kouropatkin here. He has got a date with me, and he is hustling all he knows to make it."

"It is foolish to go south now," said Alyosha. "There will be no battle at Hai-cheng."

"I am going, all the same," said Troumestre.

"I should like to go too," said Miles.

"War fever," said Alyosha. "If it is like that, I'll come with you. But this time we will travel light, with no mules and no Chinamen."

They started this time with one Montenegrin servant, and the lightest of transport. But when Haslam saw them about to start he said he would go as well.

They rode along dusty roads between seas of tall green *gowliang*, and every now and then they would come to a village.

"You look quite unlike an English public school man," said Alyosha, as he looked at Miles.

It was true. Miles wore a grey sarcenet shirt he had bought at Mukden, which was not tucked in; a shiny black belt, a pair of dark blue riding-breeches bought at St Petersburg, Russian boots, and a shapeless grey yachting cap. In spite of the incongruity of his clothes Miles looked tidy. Miles always looked tidy, even if he had slept in a haystack. Not so Troumestre. He had grown a beard. Miles shaved every day, whatever happened. Haslam, too, in spite of the war and all its squalor and circumstance, remained invincibly neat. He wore corduroys, field boots, a khaki jacket, and a clean silk shirt. On his pony, with its Mexican saddle, he looked like a young American about to play polo. He had a beautiful, easy seat, whereas Troumestre rode badly.

"There are three kinds of riders," said Alyosha, as he looked at them: "good riders, who help the horse; neutral riders, who do not matter; and bad riders, who hinder the horse. Haslam belongs to the first class, I and Miles belong to the second, and Troumestre belongs to the third."

They rode all day. It was extremely hot. They had no food with them, and only some stuff-covered water bottles, which they filled from wayside streams. The water they carried grew tepid at once. They met hardly anyone. They stopped for their midday meal at a Chinese village and asked for some eggs. "*Chi-tan*," they said. The Chinese host, a grim, bronzed, impassive gentleman, said without a moment's hesitation, "*meyo*," meaning "there is nothing."

"He thinks," said Alyosha, "that we are *Hun-hu-ses*."

A conversation started between Alyosha and the host in pidgin-Russian. Finally the Chinaman reluctantly produced some pancakes and made tea. They ate and rested, and then the cavalcade went on. Haslam and Troumestre rode in front, and Alyosha behind with Miles. Sometimes they changed places.

In the evening they arrived at a post, not at a railway station but at a railway siding, where there was a small house occupied by a sergeant and four men belonging to the frontier guards.

"Can we find accommodation for the night? "Alyosha asked civilly. The senior man answered laconically "*mozhno*," which meant "possible." The ponies were unsaddled and allowed to graze. On either side of the railway lines stretched an illimitable green plain.

The sun was setting round and red over the endless sea of green millet. After it had disappeared, a dusty afterglow lingered for a time in the west.

They lay for a while in silence. Presently the senior of the soldiers came up to them and invited them to supper. They went into the little white house. A table was spread. There was soup, brown bread, and tea. The senior soldier apologised. It was, he said, the best they had. He brought some of his last delicacies – one cucumber and three lumps of white sugar, which at such a time and place were more precious than rubies – and he put them into their cups. Alyosha asked the soldiers how long they had been there; they said four years and a half.

They left the building when they had drunk tea, and they all lay down on the grass. Miles listened heedlessly to Alyosha and Troumestre as they talked to the soldiers. Haslam went to sleep.

"How wonderfully hospitable they are!" said Miles.

"Yes," said Troumestre; "that is Eastern. They look upon guests as sacred, especially if they are strangers."

"It was Western, too, in the Middle Ages," said Alyosha. "Hospitality was important all over Europe then."

"Do you agree with Rudyard Kipling," asked Troumestre, "when he says that the mistake we make is in treating Russians as the most Eastern of European nations, instead of the most Western of Eastern nations?"

"Oh, you can demolish that easily enough, if you like," said Alyosha – "that the Slavs are not Oriental, and so on; but all the same, I do not know whether it is not true... I think place plays a great part in the life of a nation... For instance, I think Germans who are brought up in Russia often become in some ways more Russian than the Russians."

"That is certainly true," said Troumestre, "about Englishmen in Ireland."

"I think," said Alyosha, "that we are more Eastern because we are near the East. We are a mixture. We have the West and the East in us. We are like those bits of country which are half like France and half like Germany; Alsace, for instance."

"To us foreigners," said Troumestre, "the first thing that strikes us when we come to Russia is the Aryan type – the tall square porters, with their fair hair and grey eyes. There is nothing Tartar-looking about them."

"I suppose," said Alyosha, "that when you land in Ireland there is nothing particularly Celtic-looking about the porters there; but the moment you have dealings with them you find there is something different."

"I think they look different too," said Troumestre. "I think you can tell an Irishman by his looks at once."

"So you can tell a Russian by his looks," said Alyosha. "But the most typical often turn out to be something else; German born, or Italians, or sometimes even English. Lermontov, our poet, was a Scotchman, and Pushkin was half African. We are like the Chinese; we are a country that assimilates other people and digests them, just as the Chinese do. We could assimilate Jews if the Jews were allowed to mix with us properly. The Chinese did. You cannot tell a Chinese Jew."

"Russians are very anti-Semite, aren't they?" asked Miles.

"It is a question of money...not of prejudice," said Alyosha. "We have no race, no colour, no class prejudice. But then there is this question... The Jews are cleverer than our *muzhiki*... Mind you, some of our peasants, like the Normands in France – what they call the *Kulaki*, 'close-fists' – are worse than any Jew; but that only proves my point: in any population in the world when you have a stupid lump which is exploited and borrows, and a clever minority which lends and exploits, the clever minority will go on squeezing and squeezing till the others will be driven to their only answer, to beat the squeezers to death and destroy their property. It is the same thing with the Armenians and the Turks in Turkey; the same thing everywhere... We do not really dislike the Jews any more than the English people do. They do not, of course, because they are nearly all of them Jews."

"What rot!" said Troumestre.

"Well, you just look at them," said Alyosha, "where do they get those sharp, aquiline features, that dark hair, and those dark eyes from?"

"Do you think Miles looks like a Jew?" Troumestre asked.

"Probably his children will look Jewish. It comes out at odd moments. But this is not my invention. There are many English people – I have often read about them – who are proud because they say they are the Lost Tribes."

"But surely," said Miles, "the Jews are much worse treated in Russia than they are anywhere else?"

"The treatment is according to the squeeze. It is the same all the world over... You would have a pogrom in Wales and

Scotland if the Jews could squeeze the Welsh and the Scotch –
only you see, there, it is probably the other way about.
Otherwise, as far as ordinary life goes, we are more in tune
with the Jews than any people in the world."

"But the peasants?" Miles said.

"The peasants have two things against the Jews. First, the
squeeze; and second, they cannot forget that the Jews crucified
their God. Other people forget this; they, never."

"They are more religious than we are, I suppose?" said Miles.

"I don't know," said Alyosha. "That would need a lot of
explaining... But, you see, they put things into practice. I do
not know if their religion is more or less than ours; but they
wear it – I mean they do not put it in a cupboard. There is no
mauvaise honte about it. If they want to say prayers, they say
them anywhere, before anybody, as a matter of course. Now,
you," he said to Troumestre, "although you are a Catholic,
might be ashamed to say your rosary aloud in a train in
England."

"I have seen that done," said Troumestre.

"I am sure the people thought it odd," said Alyosha. "Russian
peasants would have no such feeling, any more than a
Mussulman would have about kneeling on his praying-carpet at
the right time. It is to them, and to those who see them do it, a
matter of course – like wearing trousers. I do not say it is better
or worse."

It was now dark. Warmth was rising from the earth. The
soldiers brought more tea. Alyosha talked to the senior soldier,
and told him that Miles and Troumestre were English, and that
Haslam – who was now asleep – was an American. The soldier
was interested. "Englishmen are everywhere," he said. "They
took Colombo when I was there, near the Red Sea, and now
they have taken Thibet."

"Do you hate the English?" asked Alyosha. He explained his
question to the others.

The soldier smiled and said: "Oh, I know they are a clean people, and extremely clever."

He then made beds for all of them, of hay. "You will be more comfortable here," he explained, "than indoors. There are too many beasts indoors."

The soldiers retired for the night.

"He is a wonderful host, that man," said Miles.

"You see," said Alyosha, "you are guests. You will find that is a very important thing to be in Russia..."

They went to sleep in the warm July night. They woke at dawn, and saddled their ponies. They resumed their march, and reached a village about eight o'clock. There they found a Red Cross detachment, the same that Miles had met at Hai-cheng, and before at Liao-yang. They were at once invited to tea. Miles found the doctors sitting in a small *fang-tze*, the same doctors he had met before, and with them Elena Ilyin. She greeted them all with calm, and told them to sit down, and said she would make them an omelet. She talked to Alyosha, but not more than to the others, and she seemed neither glad nor sorry nor surprised to see him. They talked of the prospects.

"We are retreating," said Elena. "We are going by road; the train is full. We are going to retreat at five o'clock this afternoon."

This at once started an argument whether or not there would be a battle at Hai-cheng, and whether it was wise or not to retreat. After a while Alyosha said that they had better be starting, and the cavalcade went on once more. They arrived at Hai-cheng about an hour later. The place was full of bustle...rumours of fighting... Fighting, it was said, was still going on. Kouropatkin was at Hai-cheng. The station, they were told, was not to be evacuated, but a battle was to be fought the next day... In the meantime everybody was leaving Hai-cheng. The wounded were being moved into the train in which Miles had slept... Some were carried in on stretchers, others walked supported by soldiers…their faces were yellow like wax, their eyes wide open and staring…

"People," said Haslam to the others, after he had watched the wounded go by, "expect you to believe in a God!"

"There is no reason to disbelieve in a God because things are disagreeable," said Alyosha. "Many disagreeable things are true, all the same. You believe that if a thing is not as you like it, it is therefore not true. The world was not made for our convenience."

"But the parsons," said Haslam, "gas about an all-merciful and all-loving God."

"The difficulty," said Troumestre, "has occurred to first-class minds as well as to every street arab. I think St Thomas gives it as his second argument against the existence of God."

At that moment there was a noise of firing.

"Let us go and search for a battle," said Alyosha, and they left the railway station, got on their ponies, and rode away. A battery was firing somewhere, not far off, to the south. They rode towards it, but by the time they got there the firing had ceased. Another battery a little nearer opened fire for a time, and then ceased fire. They rode back to Hai-cheng. There was more bustle, and more wounded soldiers were brought in.

"There will be a battle tomorrow," everyone said.

They met Ivanov, the Press Censor, and he said the same thing.

"We had better spend the night," said Alyosha, "somewhere where we shall be in time for tomorrow's business, if there is a business."

They rode to a little village about half a mile north of the station. They bivouacked in the yard, and decided to get up early the next day. It was a fine moonlight night, as hot as it had been on the previous days; the rainy season, which was now due, still showed no signs of coming. About nine o'clock in the evening they settled down for the night. Hardly had they gone to bed when they were roused by alarms and excursions *without.* There was a rumour that the Japanese were in the village – and panic.

"We must go at once," the Cossacks said, "or we shall be cut off."

There was a scurrying to and fro; men shouted; somebody, a foreigner – a Montenegrin, it turned out later – was arrested because he was wearing an English straw hat, and was therefore thought to be a Japanese. He was soon afterwards released.

Alyosha, Miles, and Haslam got on their ponies and rode out from the village, and waited in the still moonlight. Nothing happened for a time. They then came across transport carts, some stray Cossacks and soldiers. These all told conflicting stories – somewhere a false alarm of an attack had been raised and caused confusion. Whether there had been an attack or not nobody knew. Not a shot was heard. The rumour had reached the transport and caused the panic. They all went back to the village, where there were no troops. Soon afterwards everything was still. The moon shone on the sleeping houses. The night was breathless. They turned in and slept, and got up early the next morning and rode to the station. There they learned that the infantry were retreating and that the station was to be evacuated.

Towards noon they started back for Liao-yang. They were joined presently by Ivanov the Censor, Jameson, Hughes, and one of the Montenegrins – his servant. There were several stray Montenegrins, freelances out for adventure, who attached themselves to any master they could find. They were bad riders, but good cooks. It was swelteringly hot. In his first march from Ta-shi-chiao, Miles had followed the transport and had met no infantry. This time they met no transport, but columns of infantry retreating. The soldiers halted every time they found a muddy stream, and drank their fill. The wells became thick with mud from being stirred up by the soldiers. The soldiers ate any green stuff they could find. It was so hot that Miles and his companions talked little. They stopped at a village to get some food, but the attitude of the Chinese was different towards an army in retreat from what it had been to an advancing one, and whenever they asked even for an egg, the Chinese slammed the door in their faces and answered one word – "*meyo.*" So they had to go without. Ivanov and Alyosha sent their Cossacks to loot anything they could find, but they came back empty-handed: there was nothing, they said. So they halted to rest in the middle of the afternoon near a clump of trees, foodless and hungry. Hughes' Montenegrin servant was riding on a small pony, as badly as the White Knight in *Alice in Wonderland.* He kept on lagging behind, and when told to hurry up and to keep in touch with the others, he sulked, complained, and said it was the pony's fault. At last Ivanov said, "I'll make him keep up with us in no time." He called him and abused him roundly, and hit him hard across the face with the scabbard of his sword. The Montenegrin burst into a storm of tears and passion, and swore that he would complain to the Commander-in-Chief. Nevertheless after that he never lagged behind.

When they arrived late in the afternoon at the station called An-shan-chan, they stayed there for the night. There was no accommodation, and they had to sleep on the platform in their mackintoshes. The next day they started early, after drinking tea, but they found it still more difficult now to find any food. They stopped at the Chinese house where they had received the pancakes on the way to Hai-cheng, but this time the host took no notice of them, said he had nothing, and slammed the door in their faces. Nor were the Cossacks more successful in finding any loot. They reached Liao-yang in the evening, exhausted.

CHAPTER XX

The Liao-yang routine began once more. Troumestre grew impatient, and said he would go back to the Brigade. Miles said he would go with him. About a week later they started once more in search of the Brigade. Haslam refused to budge. He said that if there was to be a battle, it would be fought at Liao-yang, which was obviously a battlefield – a position; if no battle, what was the use of moving?

Alyosha said he must stay at Liao-yang. The Montenegrins had all of them disappeared, with the exception of Troumestre's servant. He had been with Troumestre for years, and was a different kind of Montenegrin. Troumestre and Miles started once more for An-shan-chan, and there they were told by a volunteer whom they met on the road that General K's Brigade was in a village about ten miles to the south-west.

They found the way with difficulty, going from one village to another, and stopping at each to ask the way.

"*Do-chao-li*?" Troumestre would ask of a Chinese labourer, naming the village, and the labourer would pause, reflect, and then ask whether he meant Russian "*li*" (kilometres) or Chinese "*li*," and then answer with nice accuracy down to a quarter.

After a time they got beyond villages, and plunged into the *gowliang*. There was no more road, but there was a field telegraph, and they followed it.

At last they found the village and the Brigade. The Headquarters: two dilapidated, squalid Chinese hovels made of baked mud, at the top of a sloping garden.

The General – a new General this time – was sitting in a bare room infested with flies. Next door were the clerks, tapping a field telegraph instrument, and a corporal tapping on a typewriter placed on a packing-case, between two tallow candles.

The General received them in a friendly manner. He looked hot and tired.

"I hope you have brought some food," he said, "because there is nothing to eat here."

They found the members of the Staff whom they had already met at Ta-shi-chiao. There were additions to it: among them a young ADC who came from Tashkent.

Miles and Troumestre were billeted in the garden on the slope of the hill. It was picturesque, and surrounded by trellis-work, over which pumpkins were trailing.

Troumestre and Miles had each of them a green Wolsey valise with them. Miles had been lent his. The weather was still swelteringly hot; it was pleasanter out of doors than in.

They had a frugal meal at midday, of rusks and tea. In the afternoon they slept. In the evening they drank tea, and renewed acquaintance with their old friends. None of these could talk English, so that Miles had to carry on his conversation through Troumestre. Soon after sunset they retired for the night.

No sooner had they undressed, and got into their valises than it began to rain – not a gentle shower, but a tropical downpour. They fastened themselves up in their valises, and Miles was astonished to find that he did not mind the rain. He did not even notice it.

It stopped before dawn, as suddenly as it had begun. At sunrise everybody was up.

The doctor strolled out into the garden from a neighbouring *fang-tze*. Miles advanced to him and stretched out his hand to say "Good morning," but the doctor withdrew his hand and said something in Russian.

"What is he saying?" asked Miles.

"He says," said Troumestre, "that he begs your pardon, but he has not yet washed."

A dragoon appeared armed for the morning ritual with a kettle and a small bowl, and the doctor told him to attend to the guests; he then went away and reappeared with a small piece of soap, which he lent to Miles and Troumestre. When it was all over, the doctor shook hands with them, and they had tea.

The weather was hotter after the rain – like the steam room of a Turkish bath. They lay on their open valises and talked, and every now and then one of the Staff would visit them, and discuss the war – a long stream of desultory gossip, mingled with anecdote and speculation. They saw their friend Semenov of the rotten sausages, more enthusiastic than ever, not only about the war, but about a conquest of Thibet and India. He was ready to eat more rotten sausages. Everyone was hungry. There was nothing except hard rusks, which you melted in tea, and sometimes, as a luxury, a little brown bread. There was no sugar, no milk, no spirits, no wine. Miles and Troumestre began to long for an acid drop – for anything sweet. Strawberry jam seemed like the Beatific Vision. After Miles and Troumestre had been two days at the Brigade Headquarters, they felt as if they had been there all their lives.

It grew hotter and hotter; and whenever it rained the rain seemed to leave the weather hotter than it had been before. They lay almost all day in the garden. It was too hot to move. There was little to eat and nothing to read. They were isolated from the world. They heard no official news, but a great deal of gossip; in spite of the absence of post, telegrams, and

208

newspapers, it seemed to pass with lightning rapidity from place to place.

"It always does in countries like these," Troumestre said to Miles one morning; "it was just the same in South Africa. How news gets so quickly from one place to another in so-called uncivilised countries is a mystery. Sometimes it seems like thought transference. I always thought it made all censorship so foolish. News that was carefully kept from one by one's immediate superior is told you suddenly by a lance-corporal who hasn't shaved for a week! It is the same here."

One of the Staff came up to them – the bearded Major – and said, "Someone has brought a large tin of vodka from Liao-yang. The General invites you to come and help to drink it."

The vodka was served at the midday meal. It took place late that day, about two o'clock. The General and the Staff sat under a haystack.

There was some tough meat cooked in a pail, called *Boeuf Strogonoff*, and some brown bread. And vodka. It was privately manufactured vodka, not "state" vodka.

Miles and Troumestre thought it was almost worse than spirits of wine, because it was not quite tasteless…it had a taste, but a bad taste, a taste of rancid machinery. After the first dose – they drank it in little tin cups – Miles thought he could not possibly drink another; but after the third he minded it less. The food helped a little. The heat was overpowering. The conversation, which was loud and incessant, seemed to Miles as unreal as that in a nightmare. And yet he was happy. The General was an exuberant host. He enjoyed the sight of Miles drinking vodka, and laughed till he cried.

Troumestre talked a great deal. There was a fierce argument about nationalities. "The General says," Troumestre interpreted, "that the English are the most 'correct' people in the world, the most *kulturni*. He met a lot of English officers at Peking during the Boxer row."

"What does that mean – *cultivated*?" asked Miles, puzzled.

"Not *cultivated*," said Troumestre, "but *civilised*. He says the Russians are cultivated but not civilised; and he says our Government is detestable."

"I suppose he is thinking of the Tories," said Miles.

The General was more and more delighted at Miles' seriousness, and drank one toast with him after another. The General insisted on his drinking glass for glass, or rather, cup for cup. He followed the ritual: Three for the Trinity, four for the four corners of the house, etc. He seemed to grow bigger and more voluble, like a caricature in a comic German newspaper. His hair was untidy and the colour of tow; his white tunic was unbuttoned and had egg-stains on it. His grey eyes were bloodshot. Miles began to see everything through a haze. Troumestre didn't seem to mind. The vodka had no effect on him. Semenov, the Russian who had eaten the rotten sausages, was delighted, and drank cup for cup with him.

"*Molodetz*," he said; "*molodetz*." This was a compliment, the equivalent of saying, "You're a fine fellow." The General kept on repeating this compliment to Miles. Miles then lost consciousness. He thought that two dragoons carried the General away to one side of the haystack and himself to the other. When he woke up it was evening. He felt rested, but dazed.

Troumestre was standing up beside him, laughing.

"You have had a good sleep," he said. " It is now bedtime."

On the other side of the road beyond the garden soldiers were singing.

"It is bedtime," said Troumestre. "You are not yet awake, so it will be easy for you to go to sleep again."

Miles, still dazed, crawled into his valise.

The next day the rain fell in torrents. The little garden became a swamp. The bearded Major had had himself transferred to another unit, or to a part of a unit, which was quartered in a neighbouring village; he asked Miles and Troumestre to go with him.

"You will be more comfortable under a roof," he said.

"Very well," said Troumestre. "But before we go we must pay our mess bill."

"The General," answered the Major, "says you are not to have a mess bill. You are the guests of the Mess."

After a final meal – a sober and frugal meal this time, at which nothing but tea was drunk – they rode to the neighbouring village. Here Miles and Troumestre were introduced to a new Commanding Officer, Colonel X, who asked them to dinner. Everything here was different. Colonel X was smart, a polished man with a trim beard, and shining buttons on his spotless white tunic. The food was served on the metal plates of an elaborate English luncheon basket. It was far more civilised. There was a *pilaff*, kidneys, and some red Caucasian wine. The Colonel spoke French. The talk was of racing, Monte Carlo, and French plays – international talk.

Miles felt shyer of this polished Colonel than he had been of the untidy General whom he had just left. After dinner the Colonel retired, and told the Major to find quarters for Miles and Troumestre. They strolled through the village. Some Cossacks were standing outside a small Chinese *fang-tze*. Presently an officer walked out, shook hands with the Major, was introduced to Miles and Troumestre, and asked them all in. Inside the *fang-tze* there was the usual *kang*. Upon it were blankets; they were the beds of the officers.

These were gathered round a table drinking tea, except a few who were lying on the blankets and looking at the ceiling. It was dark; there were only two candles in the room. Miles and Troumestre were introduced to a fat, bearded man who, they were told, was temporarily commanding the battery. It turned out to be a Horse Battery. There were several young men, a veterinary doctor, and a Frenchman called Gérard. He was by birth half Russian; his father was in business in St Petersburg; he was a Russian subject, and had volunteered as a private. The Major said something about quarters for Miles and Troumestre, and the Commanding Officer said of course they must at once be given accommodation. Troumestre protested, upon which the doctor shouted to a Cossack, and told him to fetch Miles' and Troumestre's valises from Headquarters, and to spread them on the *kang*; and so the matter was settled.

None of these officers could speak English; but Miles felt at his ease with them. After they had drunk tea the Major left them, and they all went to bed.

The next day began like the one before, with the ritual of washing; but with the tea the Cossacks served up some thick pancakes.

Miles talked to Gérard in French. Gérard understood English, but spoke it imperfectly. Nothing happened all the morning. Someone had a fragment of a Moscow newspaper, six weeks old, and it was in demand. In the course of the morning the Chinaman to whom the house belonged arrived with a grievance. It appeared that a senior officer, whose acquaintance Miles and Troumestre had not yet made because he messed by himself, had committed sacrilege. He had used the metal cauldron which is to be found in every Chinese cottage, and is used for cooking, as a bath. The Chinaman felt as a German housewife would feel were she to learn that a soldier had used the house bath to wash his dog. He could not get over it. He cried and moaned, and gnashed his teeth. The doctor said it was wrong of the officer, and what could he want with a bath? The man was given some roubles, but that comforted him not; it was the spiritual indignity that he minded, and that could not be atoned for. Miles was curious to see the officer who had been guilty of this misdemeanour; but he did not appear, nor did he come to the midday meal, which consisted of soup, chunks of meat, and hard rusks. There was no vodka – nothing but tea. After the midday meal and the midday siesta, Gérard said he wished to visit the Chinese Catholic church, which he had heard was in a neighbouring village. The doctor, Troumestre, and Miles agreed to go with him. They rode to a village some miles off, and found a clean presbytery and a small church with an altar, some candles and paper flowers, a Crucifix, Images of Our Lady and of the Sacred Heart. Troumestre and Gérard genuflected, and Troumestre said a prayer. They then called on the priest, a bronzed Chinaman, who was reading his Breviary. He offered them some brandy, which they were delighted to drink. It tasted like heaven after what they had been accustomed to. They sat down in the bare room, in which there were only two chairs, a table, and a Crucifix, and the priest told them of his experiences during the Boxer troubles. He had never been to France, yet he spoke French with a French intonation, just as the English jockeys do at Chantilly. He had been condemned to death during the Boxer troubles, and led out to execution, but reprieved at the last moment. Troumestre then said he wanted the priest to hear his confession. They disappeared into the church.

"I feel sick," the doctor said, when the priest was out of the room. "Brandy always makes me feel sick. I had to drink it."

When the priest and Troumestre came back, the priest gave them all his blessing and they went away. On the way home Miles and Gérard rode together. Gérard asked whether Troumestre had always been a Catholic, or whether he was a convert. Miles explained. "And you," he said, "are you a Catholic?"

"Yes," said Miles, "but I am not a Roman Catholic; I am an Anglican Catholic."

"A Protestant?" said Gérard.

"No, not a Protestant," said Miles. "At least I was not brought up as one; my aunt was High Church, and I was brought up High Church."

"What is High Church?"

"High Church is the opposite of Low Church."

"But what is Low Church?"

213

"Low Church are people like Nonconformists, Methodists, and the Salvation Army."

"Ah, *l'armée du Salut*. But, then, why are not you a Catholic, a Roman Catholic?"

"Because," said Miles, "Roman Catholics, so my aunt says, are heretical, and schismatic in England and Wales; they introduced all sorts of new things into the Church during the Middle Ages which the Early Church knew nothing about – a lot of abuses – indulgences – images and rosaries – and new dogmas like Purgatory and praying for the dead – and dangerous things like confession, letting the priests run everything," he said rather shyly.

"But," said Gérard, "those things are not all new. Russians and Greeks have confession and prayers for the dead, and have had them ever since the earliest times."

"Oh," said Miles, "our High Church people have nothing against the Greek Church, I think. They say that one day there might be a reunion between the Anglican and the Greek Churches."

"But the Greek Church has the same Sacraments as the Romans – seven Sacraments; would they accept that?"

"I don't think my aunt would like *seven* Sacraments," said Miles. "Only two – and she is against confession, on principle. She thinks it destroys the sense of responsibility; that you can go on doing whatever you like, so long as you confess it. She thinks that is bad for one – and I must say I agree."

"The moment," said Gérard, "you abolish one of the Sacraments, you get something worse in its place. If you abolish confession to the priest, people will confess to lawyers and doctors, which I think is far more dangerous. You have no guarantee of secrecy. *Les avocats el les médecins sont souvent des crapules*, and if you give them entire liberty – " He shrugged his shoulders and spluttered. "At least the Church is a hold – a brake."

"How do you mean?"

"I mean that a Chinese priest would rather be cut into bits than betray the secrets of the confessional."

"But lawyers and doctors are just as discreet."

"Priests have to be discreet in spite of *everything*. It is a small difference, if you will, but *all* the difference. At least to me... To the person who confesses."

"But do you confess?"

"I am not *pratiquant*... I have really no faith... But I have no other faith. I am – I would be – either a Catholic or nothing."

"But it was you who made us go and see the priest, and when you went into the church you knelt down."

"*'Nous nous saluons,'* as Voltaire said when he was found making a Sign of the Cross as he passed a church. I don't altogether disbelieve, but, well – *je n'ai pas la foi.* I said that to the priest, and he told me to pray to Our Lady and to ask for it. And the doctor said, 'Of course.'"

At this moment the doctor met a friend and rode on ahead with him. Troumestre joined Miles and Gérard, and asked what they had been talking about. Gérard told him.

"Gérard is right," said Troumestre. "Every lost Sacrament means sooner or later a sham substitute. If you give up praying for the dead, you get table-turning or necromancy."

"Well," said Miles, "all that Anglicans believe – people like my aunt – seems to me most improbable and difficult to believe. And you have to believe *all that*, and things that are still more difficult and improbable...if you *do* believe them. All sorts of things that are not even in the Bible. I should have thought the Bible was difficult enough."

"The Bible," said Gérard impatiently. "That has nothing to do with it."

"Aunt Fanny says that Roman Catholics are not allowed to read the Bible."

"We can read the Bible if we want to, and it is read to us in church, whether we like it or not," said Troumestre. "Yes," he went on, speaking to Gérard, "that is the root of the matter.

215

Protestants base their religion on the Bible, and the Bible only. They think we do the same, and so naturally they think we are traitors and dishonest."

"And of course," said Gérard, "everyone makes his own version of the Bible."

"Yes," said Troumestre. "They think we have fallen away, that we are a lapsed *sect*. They don't know that as Christians we are in the majority. Macaulay noted the fact sadly; and there are far more Catholics now than in his time."

"It's all very well," said Miles. "But I see nothing in the Bible which says anything about Purgatory or Indulgences."

"No," said Troumestre. "Nor about the rosary, nor Benediction, nor Our Lady of Lourdes. But, you see, the difference between us is this: our authority is not the Bible only, although we believe it to be inspired; but a perpetually infallible Church. The Gospel for us is like a *Bradshaw*. But we believe in an infallible stationmaster's office, in which there is a succession of divinely appointed stationmasters perpetually *guaranteed*, who tell us how to use the *Bradshaw*, and what trains are running and what not."

"But," said Miles, "your title deeds are, after all, the *Bradshaw*?"

"Yes," said Troumestre; "but in that *Bradshaw* there is a notice by the first people who drew it up, saying that God had created the stationmaster's office, that it was to go on for ever, and would explain the *Bradshaw* to us rightly for ever."

"Evidently," said Gérard, "you cannot take a railway guide and interpret it as each of you likes – otherwise there will be accidents. You can deny the authority, but in that case it is better not to travel by train. But to accept a railway guide, and to dispute the stationmaster's supplementary information, seems to me absurd."

"But," said Miles, "I don't see why you should have so many monks and nuns. What do they do?"

"They do good," said Troumestre.

"But I mean those in monasteries and convents, who never come out – Trappists; what is the use of them? Wouldn't they be more useful in the world? There are enough poor people for them to help – enough for them to do outside."

"The contemplative orders pray for us," said Troumestre. "You, and a great part of the non-Catholic world, have no idea of the work they do. It is as if a savage were told there were such things as banks, and vaguely got to know that banks were places where money was hoarded by useless people. To say monks and nuns ought to leave their monasteries and convents is like saying bankers ought to leave their banks, and come out into the street and scatter the money; or that men of science ought to leave their laboratories and lecture in Hyde Park. The contemplative religious are *banking* the grace of God; it is having an enormous effect. Their spiritual life is sometimes so strong that if you were to let loose a Trappist of a kind I have heard of into the world, the world would hardly be strong enough to contain him – like letting loose radium."

"I daresay there are some monks like that," said Gérard, "but an Abbé once told me that in the lives of the contemplative religious there was often a lot of what he called *aridité*, and what I call *paresse*."

"I daresay," said Troumestre; "no society is perfect – *we live in a damaged universe*, but the *total* capital of spiritual force is immense. You see, the Catholic – or, if you like, the Christian – world (it's the same thing) is the opposite of this world. Everything in it is paradox. The poorest are of course the richest in it; the weakest, the strongest, the contemplative orders more powerful than politicians. Even in politics, as Dizzy said, it is private life that governs the world, and the people most talked about are the most powerless. Much more so in the religious life. From the worldly point of view, monks and nuns are the poorest and most insignificant, the most useless; from the point of view of the Church, they are the richest, the most influential. They are the Rothschilds of the world of poverty and the Caesars of the kingdom of weakness, and therefore the mightiest in the other kingdom, the Kingdom of Heaven."

"Yes," said Miles, "that's all right if one believes what you have *got* to believe, but surely, as a matter of common sense – "

"But common sense," said Troumestre, "takes you to a point when it is still common sense to obey, and believe your stationmaster when he tells you things that seem impossible – such as the existence of a through carriage when none is marked, even on a Russian railway – "

"*C'est vrai,*" said Gérard.

They had reached home.

CHAPTER XXI

The next day they moved into another village, into a larger house.

"War," said the battery doctor to Miles through Troumestre, "means being perpetually on the move. Directly you are more or less comfortable in one place, you have to go somewhere else."

Their new quarters were more spacious. The house was long, low, and one-storied; it was built round a courtyard, the front of which was missing, and which was full of litter and poultry. The Chinese owner of the house lived in one of the wings. In the other wing was a living room in which all the officers lived except the mysterious officer, who was apparently not second but third in command.

He was, so the others said, brilliant but peculiar; a faddist about his food.

At first Miles found difficulty in distinguishing the others – just as to a new boy at school all the boys appear to be alike; but he gradually began to sift his impressions.

He knew the doctor, who was alert, argumentative, and nearly always in opposition; then there was the veterinary doctor – suave, melancholy, and dreaming of Moscow, yearning for European civilisation, and looking up to Miles and Troumestre as representing it. There were the younger lieutenants: a Cossack, dark and slight; another, a fair-headed boy from Transbaikalia; the fat, good-natured Commander, and one or two others whom Miles hardly realised.

They were all as friendly to him as possible; but as the only English word they knew was "Mister," and as the only Russian word Miles knew was "*Seychas*," conversation did not flow easily. They talked to Troumestre a good deal. Miles seemed to himself to be living in a new world, and yet out of it; to be looking on at it from a distance, as through the wrong end of a telescope. The past was obliterated. He could hardly believe in his former life: in Madeira, Sparks, Aunt Fanny, Norfolk, the City: and the present was a dream, fantastic and unreal.

It was dawn...he was lying on the *kang* wrapped up in a *burka*, to keep away the flies – all the flies in the world seemed to have congregated in this house.

It was hot, and everybody was gradually getting up. The doctor, seeing Miles in pyjamas, said something to Troumestre.

"He says," said Troumestre to Miles, "that it is an odd thing that Englishmen dress when they go to bed. Russians take off what is not necessary."

They went out to wash. The day showed signs of being hotter than ever. Gérard was sneezing. He said he had caught cold.

"The doctor will give you something," said Troumestre. "Russian doctors know nothing," said Gérard, "especially military doctors. I will consult the Chinese doctor in the village."

Troumestre and Miles laughed.

Tea was ready. They drank it in silence. The veterinary doctor sighed... "I dreamt I was at Moscow," he said, "and that I was going to a play of Chekhov's, at the Art Theatre; and I wake up and find myself here in this horrible country."

Troumestre translated the remark to Miles, but not the discussion that ensued, which was about Chekhov. Evidently the doctor disagreed violently with what the veterinary doctor was saying.

"What is it all about?" asked Miles.

"Chekhov and Dostoyevsky...the doctor hates Dostoyevsky."

A Cossack brought in some pancakes. Outside someone was singing an air from an opera called *The Demon*.

"Who is that singing?" asked Miles.

"Oh, that is Leonid Borisovitch," said Gérard. Leonid Borisovitch was the mysterious officer who lived apart. He strolled into the room presently, and Miles was introduced to him. He wore a respirator because of the dust, but took it off. He was young and good-looking. He was full of complaints at the moment. Nobody took much notice.

When tea had been drunk Miles, Troumestre, and Gérard strolled out into the yard. The horses were munching corn. The Chinese host was sitting in tears; this appeared to be his normal condition.

Gérard asked him in pidgin-Chinese what was the matter...a long explanation followed...they did not understand each other. At last the Chinaman led them to one of the windows in his house, and pointed to the paper window-pane. It had a slight tear. He pointed to a Cossack. He meant it was his doing.

"They respect property," said Troumestre.

"*Tant pis pour eux*," said Gérard; "probably before long this house will be shelled to bits – or looted by the Japanese."

The sun was blazing by now. It was too hot to stay out of doors. They went back to the house. There it was hotter still. The officers were lying down on the *kang*. There was nothing to smoke except imitation Russian cigarettes made by the Chinese, and Miles could not smoke them.

Miles sat down on the *kang* and wrote a letter to Aunt Fanny in his pocketbook with an indelible pencil. He was disturbed by the sound of a heated discussion going on, as usual, between the doctor and Gérard.

"What are they arguing about?" he asked Troumestre, who was lying down next to him.

"Oh, whether it isn't absurd to have hospitals and doctors in war time, when the real aim is to exterminate the enemy as quickly and as thoroughly as possible."

"I have heard all that," said Miles; "who was it saying that to me the other day?"

"The doctor says," Troumestre went on, "extermination is the only logical thing, and Gérard says he would never carry out his theory into practice."

"I don't suppose he would."

"Of course he wouldn't," said Troumestre.

Troumestre was reading in a little book, and went on reading. Miles, who was describing the scene in his letter to Aunt Fanny, wrote: "*Troumestre is reading Dante. I asked him if it wasn't rather dry reading for such hot weather, and he said it was only in moments like these that he could read books of that kind. He had read all 'Paradise Lost' during the Boer War, and nothing else. There is, as a matter of fact, nothing to read here, and I would give worlds for a copy of the 'Strand Magazine.'*"

Soon (much sooner, Miles thought, than appeared to be possible) it was luncheon-time, and they all sat round a table and ate beef – hunks of beef from the pail, called as usual *Boeuf Strogonoff*. The Cossack cook who brought the pail had a cunning face.

And just before they began, the men's soup was brought to the officers for them to taste.

The younger Cossack officer asked for a portion. It was explained to Miles that he had lost a lot of money playing *Macao*, a form of *vingt et un*, and to escape a Mess Bill he was feeding at present on the men's rations. Miles was given some of the soup and thought it delicious, much better than the officers' *Boeuf Strogonoff*.

The morning's discussion still smouldered at luncheon, but without flaring up.

The officers chaffed Miles because he always refused to be served first. This trait in Miles irritated the doctor, who said that in war time all *delikatnost* (delicate scruple) was out of place, and he affected an exaggerated brusquerie.

They spent the rest of luncheon teaching Miles a few Russian words, especially the Russian for "soap," which Miles found impossible to pronounce; they all laughed at his ineffectual efforts.

As soon as the meal was over they had a siesta. Miles could not sleep. It was too hot and the flies were too troublesome. He was even forced to put the stuffy *burka* over his head for protection. He lay thinking...and wondering whether he was really alive; whether this was reality, for – as sometimes happened to him when he was a child – he seemed to lose all sense of reality. He seemed to be in that world in which one wanders when one is coming to from chloroform or laughing-gas. The world seemed to spin and disappear. He was on the edge of the planet...and then he said to himself, "Where am I? and who am I? what am I?" The question revolved and spun in his mind, and there was no answer. His personality had vanished; he was nothing; a whirling atom in a dim abysm.

"No, Gérard, you can't have that... I'm in the middle of it."

Miles was brought back to reality by the voice of Troumestre, in which there was a peevish note. Gérard had taken a Russian magazine from the *kang*. It was lying beside Troumestre. Troumestre had been reading it, but he had put it down and dozed off to sleep.

"So am I," said Gérard, "also in the middle of it." He spoke English, which he only did when he was annoyed.

"No, please give it to me. I want to finish the story." The story was a translation of Wells' *Food of the Gods*. Gérard took no notice, but sat down at the table and began to read.

Troumestre jumped from the *kang*, went up to Gérard, and tried to snatch the magazine from him. Gérard clung to it desperately. They both rolled on the floor, wrestling, kicking, and even trying to bite each other. The struggle went on silently for a few moments. The Russians watched it with amusement.

"How savage Mister is!" one of them said; "we thought he was so meek!"

The battle was drawn, but by the time it was over the magazine had been torn to bits.

Troumestre and Gérard rose from the ground panting, and Troumestre laughed...they both laughed, after a time. "Now," said Troumestre, "we shall never know the end of that story...it's a pity, because it was interesting."

They all sat down to tea once more. Gérard said his cold was worse, and that he must consult the Chinese doctor in the village.

"You don't really mean that seriously, do you?" said Troumestre.

"Of course."

"Of course he doesn't" said the doctor.

"I'm going to the village now."

"Don't be such a fool," said the doctor.

Gérard got up. "Come on," he said to Troumestre.

"How will you explain your symptoms?" asked Miles.

"I will take the interpreter."

There was a Chinaman attached to the battery who spoke Russian fluently.

The doctor shrugged his shoulders.

Gérard and Miles and Troumestre set off for the village with the interpreter, who grinned when he was told where they were going.

They found the doctor at home.

He looked, Miles thought, like a wizard; he wore large horn-rimmed spectacles.

"Tell him," Gérard said to the interpreter, "that I have got a cold and can't get rid of it."

An interminable conversation took place between the interpreter and the doctor.

The doctor nodded and left the room. He came back presently with a brew. He brought this in a wooden cup which had no handle. It was broad and filled to the brim with a thick liquid, dark as Munich beer, which had a strong aromatic smell and a slight whiff of rotten eggs. There were vague lumps floating in it.

"Doctor he say you drink this; get quite well three suns," said the interpreter.

"But surely you are not going to drink that?" said Miles; "it looks like toadstools."

Troumestre laughed and quoted:

> "Eye of newt, and toe of frog,
> Wool of bat, and tongue of dog."

"Of course I shall drink it," said Gérard. "Chinese doctors are the best in the world."

The Chinese doctor presented the bowl to Gérard, with a gesture of matchless courtesy. Gérard took the bowl. It was difficult to hold, but his hands were steady. He drank it to the dregs. He made rather a wry face and said nothing.

"Well, you are the most obstinate and pig-headed man I have ever seen," said Troumestre; "but I must say the brew was beautifully presented. It proves that everything in the world depends upon how it is presented."

He then turned to Miles and said: "Gérard has only done this to annoy our doctor; it will probably kill him."

Gérard asked the doctor through the interpreter to name his fee. Another long conversation took place in Chinese. The interpreter said there was no fee. He explained that the Chinese only took fees as long as their patients were in good health, never when they fell ill. He added: "He says you very well tomorrow."

"How do you feel?" Troumestre asked Gérard.

"No worse," he answered.

"I wouldn't have drunk that brew for a thousand pounds," said Miles. "I think you are the bravest man I have ever seen."

"No, not brave," said Troumestre, "reckless and obstinate, with an *amour propre du diable*."

"Well, I confess," said Gérard, "that I do want to prove to our doctor that he doesn't know *everything* in the world – that he is not infallible."

They said goodbye to the Chinese leech, who ushered them out with a number of bows and hesitations, and they walked towards home; but they did not go straight home. They walked down to the lake which was near the village. The sun had set. It was cooler.

There was in the lake an island of pink lotus-flowers which were as broad and stately as water lilies. On the banks there were a few delicate willow trees. The new moon had just risen in a sky that was as pink as a hydrangea.

The petals of the pink lotus-flowers rested on a tangled mass of green leaf which was grey in the twilight; the sky was dim, the water silvery.

The Cossacks were bathing naked on horseback. Miles and the others stood by the lake and watched.

"And to think," said Troumestre, "that we should be at war on an evening like this!"

Gérard sighed: "*Aprés la guerre*," he said, " I shall go to Europe. I shall never go near the East again. I shall leave Russia and settle in Paris. It is, after all, the only place to live."

"I shall never go to another war," said Troumestre, "as long as I live. That I swear."

He knew little that eight years later he would be in another war in Turkey – a week after the declaration of hostilities, a war from which he would not return.

"I don't suppose that I shall go to a war again – that any of us will," said Miles.

"One war is enough for a lifetime," said Gérard.

They were silent and pensive for a time. The Cossacks were riding their horses home.

"Let's go," said Troumestre. "It's time for supper."

When they got back the doctor greeted them with a sardonic smile.

"Well," he asked, "what did the doctor say?"

"He gave me some medicine," said Gérard defiantly.

"And I suppose you took it?" said the doctor ironically.

"He did take it," said Troumestre, "and you should have seen the stuff!"

The doctor was almost too angry to speak.

"Of course, if he wants to kill himself, it is his own affair. I don't care."

"The Chinaman's medicine," said Gérard, "is certainly no worse than some of the brews you European doctors give us to drink."

"Toadstools," said Troumestre.

The doctor laughed.

"It's all very well to laugh," said Gérard, "but why are toadstools worse than the glands of guinea pigs or the putrid juices of calf which they call vaccine and inoculate us with?"

"A hundred years ago," said Troumestre, "a pastor near Dresden carried on a brisk trade all over Europe with magpies burnt to coal and powdered, as a remedy for epilepsy."

"Well, I don't care," said the doctor. "Take what you like."

Outside the Cossacks were singing their evening prayers. The voices rose in high, strong concent. The attack of the chant was clean, sharp, and clear. Miles had never heard anything like it in his life. It began as suddenly, as sharply, as someone diving off a springboard into a stream. There was no hesitation. The voices seemed to rush into the breach. The tenors were higher and sharper than any Miles had ever heard or could imagine, and the basses were like the deepest organ pedal-stop in a cathedral. Yet sometimes the basses seemed higher than the tenors. Miles and the others listened in silence.

"What did that mean?" asked Miles, when it was over.

"It is the Prayer to the Holy Ghost," said Troumestre. "It means something like this:

" 'Heavenly King, our Comforter,
Spirit of Truth,
Who dwellest everywhere, and pervadest everything,
Treasure of Goodness, and Giver of Life,
Come and abide with us,
And deliver us from all that defileth,
And have mercy upon us,
Oh! Thou most merciful,
And save our souls.' "

"It's wonderful," said Miles.

"Let's go and have supper," said Gérard. "I feel better already."

The next morning his cold was cured.

CHAPTER XXII

Troumestre was obliged to go back to Liao-yang to send off a dispatch to his newspaper, and Miles went with him. The day after they arrived they heard rumours of fighting, and they settled to go south again. Alyosha was nowhere to be found. It seemed most probable that a big battle must happen soon. They left their servants at Liao-yang. When they were with the battery, they were looked after by the Cossacks.

They started in the morning down the long road along the railway line which by this time had become familiar to them. They passed a regiment of Cossacks encamped near the railway, and a battery ready for action on a hill.

They reached An-shan-chan in the afternoon. There was an uncanny stillness brooding over everything. The little station was deserted.

"How shall we find the way," said Miles, "without the servants and without Cossacks?"

Troumestre caught sight of a Staff Officer. He went up to him and explained his difficulty. The officer took him into the buffet and drew him a sketch map.

They started once more on the way to the village, where they had left the battery.

It was getting late; the Staff Officer had marked two villages for them on the map. They passed through these. After that they were to follow the field telegraph, and then a road.

They had followed the field telegraph for a time when Miles said to Troumestre: "Do you think this is the right road? I don't remember it."

"No more do I."

They halted. The ponies seemed to tell them they were going wrong. About five miles to their south there was a small hill, rising isolated out of the green *gowliang.*

"I remember that hill," said Miles.

"So do I. Shall we make straight for it?"

"When we were in the village that hill seemed a long way off. It may be occupied by the Japs by now."

"We must try and find the main road," said Troumestre.

"What? Go back?"

"Yes, back, and I think a long way round."

"But what does the map say?"

"We are off the map. I mean we've lost the road the map marks...but we can't be far off."

They turned back towards the setting sun. They did not meet a soul. The sunset was red and threatening. They rode on in silence.

"I wonder if we are going right?" said Miles.

"I think so," said Troumestre; "as long as I don't think or look at maps, I find the way all right. I think my pony thinks we are going right...this pony is quite tame now."

They came to a village.

The sun had set. Chinamen were standing outside their houses. They looked at Miles and Troumestre, who were wearing red brassards on their arms, and said, *"Ti-fu"* to each other, which meant doctor.

Troumestre asked the way: *"Davan-tien-tung doshao li?"* (How far is it to Davan-tien-tung?)

The Chinamen pointed down the road and grinned.

"I believe," said Miles, "they are telling us wrong."

Troumestre took out a coin and showed it to a little boy and asked him to be their guide.

He nodded, and pointed to a road, and led them until they came to a sea of *gowliang*. There he disappeared.

"Damn the boy!" said Troumestre. "I wonder if he has taken us right. Wait here, Miles. I will just trot down that track and see if it leads anywhere – if not, we will go back to the village."

Troumestre trotted off. Miles felt a sense of despair alone in the *gowliang* in the deepening twilight, so far from everything and everybody, not able to speak a word of any necessary language. Nor did he believe in Troumestre's sense of locality.

"He may find himself with *Hun-hu-ses* or Japs," he thought.

But Troumestre came back presently.

"I think it's all right," he said. "The only thing to do is to go on."

They did.

They met a Cossack. Never had Miles seen a more welcome sight.

Troumestre named the battery, and asked where it was to be found. The Cossack pointed to the first house. The battery had moved since they had left, and they had come accidentally straight to its new quarters.

They were welcomed and told the news.

The battery had been standing to arms all day, and the Colonel had come back. He was better.

"Is there going to be a battle?" asked Troumestre.

Gérard shrugged his shoulders.

"So they say," he said.

They had supper and went to bed. At two o'clock in the morning they were suddenly roused by a Cossack.

There was a buzz of talk. Everybody got up.

"The Japanese," said Troumestre to Miles, "are advancing on the village. We've got to do a bunk."

"Off we go again," said the doctor.

They took some time to get ready. There appeared, so Miles thought, to be no violent hurry.

It was dark and raining. They assembled in a field. Miles and Troumestre rode together at the head of the column behind the two trumpeters, in silence. Before sunrise they reached a village and settled in a house. They drank tea, and had their midday meal as usual. They then suddenly got orders to get ready for action. The guns were placed in a garden pointing to the village they had left early that morning, where they had spent so many lazy days.

The Colonel, not of the battery but of the unit, with whom they had dined, rode up and made a speech to the men.

The men shouted their salutation. The fat Commander seemed excited. He and another of the younger officers disappeared behind a hedge and presently reappeared. Miles wondered what would happen next… Was at last something going to happen? Would they perhaps all be blown to pieces in half an hour's time? The fastidious lieutenant seemed happy. He was humming his favourite tune from *The Demon*. The Colonel, whom Miles could now observe properly for the first time, was giving orders. He was bent, grey, and looked ill. He had a studious face and kind eyes. He had a squared map in his hand, with a mica cover over it. He got off his grey horse and went with the fastidious officer to give the range. Presently the guns began to fire.

"Ça y est," said Gérard.

"What is going to happen," thought Miles.

He and Troumestre and the doctor were standing behind the guns. Nothing happened. The firing went on and on.

After a time the tension, that everyone seemed to have been feeling, relaxed.

"Do you think we are shelling the old man's house where we lived – the old man who cried?" asked Troumestre.

"I think most likely," said the doctor.

At five o'clock the battery ceased firing.

They moved in the evening to another village, and there Miles and Troumestre occupied a small temple. They unsaddled their ponies and lay down on the clean matting.

"Thank God! thank God!" said Troumestre; "sleep at last."

He had scarcely said the words than there was a scurry, a noise, and some shouting.

Gérard rushed in.

"The Japanese are upon us, only a verst from here," he said. "They rode into the village we evacuated, just as our dragoons were going out at the other end. *En avant mes enfants!*"

The force of which they now formed part was small – only a detachment of dragoons and the battery; the rest of the brigade had started earlier in the morning.

They heard shots fired...orders were given to get away as quickly as possible.

Miles and Troumestre saddled their ponies and got on them mechanically.

"It has been going on like this," said the doctor to Troumestre, "ever since Wa-fan-go."

A long march began. Miles and Troumestre rode together in silence, and Miles almost went to sleep as he rode; at one moment he was conscious of having slept.

Towards midnight they halted in a village. There they dismounted, and fell asleep on the floor of a little house – but only till dawn. At dawn they were in the saddle once more.

They started for Liao-yang by a roundabout route. They arrived there about three o'clock in the afternoon, and settled down in a village on the railway line, less than three miles from the town.

It was the first village that Miles and Troumestre had passed through every time they had gone south. They knew the inhabitants.

They lay down on the grass outside the little house, unstrapped their valises, which had come on a mule, and slept.

They woke in the evening, and Troumestre said to Miles: "It's only in war that one gets just that kind of sleep. I wish one could sleep like that in ordinary life."

"Yes," said Miles; "it's rather like the sleep one has in a theatre when one is tired, and one suddenly feels sleepy, and tries to keep awake and can't."

After supper they were able to sleep uninterruptedly all the night long. The next morning they rode into Liao-yang, to see the Censor, Ivanov, who was sitting in a bare room at the station.

There they met Alyosha, also Berton and Maurel.

There was a buzz of talk, greetings, questions, answers, gossip. Ivanov opened a bottle of beer.

"Is there going to be a battle? "Troumestre asked.

"Kouropatkin says," Alyosha informed them, "that he will put up a large candle to Our Lady if the Japanese attack him here. It is a wonderful position."

"And do you think they will?" asked Miles.

"Of course they will," said Ivanov.

Troumestre sent off a telegram. He and Miles went to their old quarters in the town and found Haslam.

"You see the Front has come to me," he said. "I shall have as good a view of the battle as anyone. And I've got everything fixed in case we have to beat it."

In the evening Miles and Troumestre rode back to the battery, and drank tea in their garden.

Everything was peaceful and idyllic once more.

On one side of them there was a range of blue hills, on the other side a plain of *gowliang*, to the south a tall hill, to the north the town, with the pagoda.

It was a radiant evening; a captive balloon soared gently into the still sunset.

"They say there really is going to be a battle tomorrow," Troumestre said to the doctor.

"Mister," said one of the young Cossacks, pointing to Miles, "will have to be an honorary bombardier."

They all laughed. Troumestre translated the remark and Miles blushed.

"He blushes," said the doctor, "just like a girl."

They all laughed again.

"There won't be a battle," said one of the officers; "don't believe it…it is always the same story. The Japanese won't attack us, because we expect it. They will do something that we don't expect."

They had supper out of doors.

Miles was so used to hearing the flow of unintelligible conversation going on all around him that he hardly ever answered a question when it was first addressed to him; so when the doctor suddenly asked him in broken French, "Have you made your will?" – it was a joke – he took no notice. Troumestre had to call his attention to the question after the doctor had repeated it to him twice.

"Yes," said Miles seriously; "my will was made when I came of age."

When his answer was interpreted everybody laughed. Before they went to sleep that night orders were given to the battery for the next morning.

"There will be a battle," said Troumestre to Miles. "Ivanov told me it was quite certain."

They prepared to go to sleep, but just as they were lying down, fresh orders came for them to move eastwards at once, to a village about three miles distant. There they established themselves once more, and there they were allowed to remain.

Miles fell into a heavy sleep. Before dawn he was roused by a sound he had never heard before – the sound of rifle fire. Miles and Troumestre and the others silently and automatically got up. It was still dark, but the sky was glimmering. They were in a field, a squat *fang-tze* was in front of them; sitting at the window was one of the Cossack officers, bending over something. Miles thought it was one of his friends, one of the officers who chaffed him and taught him Russian. He walked up to the darkling window, and was about to give the officer a friendly pat on the back, when a grey, grim face turned slowly towards him, looked up and grunted. It was the Colonel. Miles murmured something and fled.

Faint streaks began to glow in the eastern sky. They were among the hills, and the village itself was on a small hill; but there were higher hills all round them.

There was now a noise of guns as well as of rifle fire. The battle had begun. They were just going to have tea when they were told to move from the village to a hill not a hundred yards off; here there was an open space, but the view they had was limited.

"Is this a battle?" Miles asked Troumestre.

"Yes, it's a battle all right."

Two regiments of infantry were standing at ease on the slope below them. Beyond this, and below, was the village they had just left. Suddenly a General in a white tunic, with a glittering staff, rode through the village; the men rapped out the salutation – loud, crisp, and clear.

"Is that Kouropatkin?" asked Miles.

"They think it is," said Troumestre, "but I think it is Stackelberg. It's silly of him to wear a white tunic. It makes such a good target."

On the rocks of the various knolls officers were looking at the position through their field glasses. The sky was grey and splashed with watery fire – an angry sky.

A shell burst in a compound below, where some dragoons had halted.

" It looks like the picture of a battle, doesn't it?" said Miles.

At that moment they got orders to move again.

They were sent back to the west again. They went off at a brisk trot. When they reached the road and the railway line, the guns were placed at the edge of the plain of millet, below the tall hill where they had been the night before. The Colonel climbed up the hill and sent his orders down through transmitters. The battery opened fire at once.

Miles, Troumestre, and the doctor climbed the hill. The sky was grey. They could see nothing but *gowliang*. The noise was deafening.

The fastidious officer was giving the range. The Colonel was lying next to him wrapped up in his black *burka*, his face white and pinched with pain.

"What are they firing at?" asked Miles.

"At a Japanese battery about five thousand yards off."

Troumestre looked through his Zeiss glass.

"Can you see anything?"

"Yes, I saw a flash just now. They haven't got the range. The Japs, I mean. Their shells are falling to the right of our battery. Would you like to look?"

" I can't see through those glasses... I can see troops in that clearing over there. They look like tin soldiers."

"Yes, or ants."

The doctor asked Miles if he were hungry.

"No," said Miles. The doctor laughed.

They stayed there watching the fastidious officer giving the range. The Colonel said something to the doctor.

"We had better go down again," said the doctor to Troumestre.

They went down the hill.

At the bottom of the hill was a road at right angles to the railway. On the other side of the road, *gowliang*.

When they got to the bottom of the hill they walked to where their ponies were tethered with the transport, and the doctor found a tin of potted meat in his saddlebag. There was very little meat left in it. The doctor offered Miles some.

"After you," said Miles.

The doctor was irritated.

"You are annoying him," said Troumestre. "For God's sake, help yourself."

"I'm not hungry," said Miles; "I couldn't touch it."

The doctor shrugged his shoulders and poured out a flood of Russian.

"He thinks you're absurd," said Troumestre, "and obstinate."

The doctor left them. He had work to do.

Miles and Troumestre climbed the hill again. The situation seemed unchanged. They came down again. They remained with the transport for a little while. They met Gérard and talked to him. The time passed slowly and quickly. The noise never ceased for a moment.

In the afternoon the attack shifted, from the south to the south-west.

Three of the six guns of the battery were taken and placed on a knoll at the foot of the tall hill. They pointed due west.

Miles and Troumestre walked from the *gowliang* to a road which ran parallel with the base of the tall hill; they then turned to their right, down another road which ran parallel with the railway line – the road which led south to An-shan-chan and north to the town; the road, now so familiar to them, by which they had so often travelled southwards.

"What time is it?" said Miles.

"Just five."

The noise was so loud they could hardly hear themselves speak.

They met one of the young officers, the dark young Cossack.

"You here, Mister?" he shouted.

He was hoarse and deaf.

"What does he say?" shouted Miles.

The Cossack said something else.

"He says," shouted Troumestre, "that you are a *lyubitel silnykh oshchushcheniy* – an amateur of violent sensations."

"What sensations?" shouted Miles, bewildered.

Troumestre laughed and shook his head. A bullet hit a stone on the road and spluttered.

The Cossack took a tin of potted meat out of his pocket. They shared it. This time Miles did not refuse to eat. The young officer had been shouting words of command all day, and had lost his voice.

"I must go back," he said.

A shell whizzed over their heads, and burst somewhere far away to the right, out of sight in the *gowliang*.

"It's like a firework," shouted Miles.

It began to rain; the sun as it set became visible, a red ball...the guns were firing towards it. As soon as it began to grow dark the firing ceased.

Miles and Troumestre walked back towards the transport.

"I must send a dispatch," said Troumestre. "You had better stay with the transport, and I will come back as soon as I can."

They met Gérard on the way; he was on horseback.

"*Cela marche bien*," he said. "The Japanese attack has been driven back and we've had no casualties. I am going to sleep in the town. Come with me."

Troumestre said he would catch him up later. Gérard rode off. Miles and Troumestre walked along the road and then turned to the left. They met a procession of wounded men – some walking, some on stretchers; they were bandaged, and sometimes the blood had soaked through the bandages.

They passed one man walking quietly, his face bandaged; his lips had been shot away.

At the transport they found no one except Cossacks. Troumestre got on his pony.

"I will be back very soon" he said, and rode away.

Miles wanted to find the officers. He walked to the small knoll, and there he found the Colonel wrapped in his cloak, and the fastidious officer, who said something to him he didn't understand; but he realized he was to follow him. It was now dark. The officer explained in pidgin-French that he had sent a

Cossack to find quarters for the Colonel – at least, that was what Miles thought he was saying.

"*Et Cossaque pas revenu... Mister,*" he said.

"*Les officiers?*" asked Miles.

"*En ville pour dormir.*"

"*Et le Colonel?*"

"*Colonel malade, beaucoup malade, pas bouger.*"

They arrived at a village. They entered a little house. Some soldiers were in one room warming themselves at a fire...there were two more rooms: one occupied by Japanese prisoners, the other by Russian dead.

"*Occupé,*" said the fastidious officer to Miles.

The Cossack who had been sent there to find a billet explained this, and pointed to a shed, full of refuse and dirt.

The officer shuddered.

"*Moi ville,*" he said, "*vous ville, ici pas possible.*"

"*Moi rester,*" said Miles. He felt he must stay in case Troumestre came back.

The fastidious officer left in disgust.

Miles stood warming himself by the fire.

Presently some officers of an infantry regiment walked in, drenched and exhausted. The Cossack met them and said something. Miles didn't understand what they said, but he caught the word "officers" and "battery," and he guessed the Cossack had told them the billet was reserved for the officers of the battery, for the infantry officers left immediately in anger and despondency.

"What shall I do without my pony?" thought Miles.

He walked back to the knoll. It took some time.

The Colonel was still there, and the doctor, and the young Cossack officer, and Gérard, who had stopped at the knoll before going on.

The Colonel refused to move. The doctor, Miles, and the young Cossack and Gérard left him wrapped in his Caucasian cloak, his eyes shut.

The words, "They all forsook Him and fled," came into Miles' mind. He pointed to the Colonel, and asked Gérard whether he wasn't coming. The doctor shook his head and Gérard said: "He is too ill. He can't move."

They walked to the transport and found their ponies.

"*A demain*," said Gérard. "I am going to the town." He rode off.

Miles and the doctor rode to the village, where they found the Cossack regaling the soldiers with an excellent supper of tea, sausages, and a bottle of vodka, in the room with a fire.

As Miles warmed his hands by the fire, he thought of the Colonel lying alone on that knoll. He thought of St Peter, as he warmed his hands.

"*Colonel manger?*" he asked the doctor.

The doctor shook his head.

After they had had some food, they lay down to sleep. About one o'clock in the morning there was a rattle of bullets; they got up and saddled their ponies in a hurry, and rode out into the dark. Miles lost the others at once, and then lost his way trying to find the battery.

After wandering about for a time, he struck one of the main roads, and reached a Red Cross detachment, which was stationed in a temple – the very place where he had once had luncheon – and there too was Elena Ilyin. She gave him some tea, and he slept in the yard of the temple on some stones, near a blazing fire. The noise of the firing had ceased.

Miles woke up early the next morning at sunrise. Everybody in the temple was astir. Elena Ilyin told Miles that she had been working with a flying ambulance column the day before, and had given first aid to the wounded.

She was going to do the same today. She was dressed in a grey riding habit.

"We must drink tea quickly and go," she said. She boiled an egg for Miles.

"How do you think things are going?" asked Miles.

"Things went well yesterday," she said. "They say the Japanese only took one trench, and they were turned out of that... By the way, where is Alyosha?"

" I haven't seen him since the battle began," said Miles. The doctors came up bustling; tea was over. Miles, after he had fed his pony, said goodbye; everybody began to move. Elena Ilyin got on her pony. She looked, so Miles thought, graceful on horseback.

"Where are you going?" she asked Miles as he said goodbye.

"Back to my battery."

"Well, *au revoir*," she said. "I think we shall meet again," and waved to him. They separated at once. The Red Cross people went west, Miles south. He soon found the old familiar road leading south – the way seemed so easy to find now in the daylight; the night before it had seemed so impossibly difficult.

After he had left Elena Ilyin and her friends, and had ridden on some way, he became conscious of a certain stillness. It was not that the guns had ceased firing; they had been firing ever since sunrise; but while he had been at the temple, and for some way down the road, he had been aware of the stir of life; he had met people, heard voices. Now he seemed to have passed a line into another world – a world that was silent save for the noise of the guns – that was incessant, it is true; but it was the more striking by the absence of all the other ordinary noises of life; there seemed to be all of a sudden no signs of life anywhere.

He found the battery where it had been the day before. There was the transport; there was his mule, his portmanteau; and then further on, in the *gowliang*, there were the guns. None of the officers were there; they had not arrived. The battery was in action; the sergeant was shouting the words of command which were transmitted to him, and they came from whom? Miles wondered, as he stood watching the men serving the guns. He left the *gowliang* and crossed the road; it only took him a few moments. He walked up the knoll on the other side of the road, and there was the Colonel in his cloak, giving the range; the doctor was with him. No one else.

Miles said good morning – he could say nothing else – and walked back again to the transport. He wondered what had happened to Troumestre and to everyone else.

There was no one to whom he could speak. Presently some of the officers arrived; the fastidious officer, who at once went and took over the command from the Colonel; another officer, and Gérard; but no Troumestre. Miles asked after the young Cossack he had talked to the evening before. He had been wounded in the night. He stood with Gérard near the guns; there was no news.

"The Japanese are getting the range," said Gérard. "They have won back the ground they lost last night. They have spotted our battery. Shells are bursting on the road."

Gérard left him after a time; he said he must take some rusks to the Colonel, and Miles was left to himself. Miles thought he would go on and see what was happening on the knoll. When he got as far as the end of the road, a shell burst, and soon after another, beyond it, in the *gowliang*, and Miles couldn't cross the road. He felt he could neither go backwards nor forwards. The journey seemed suddenly an immense, portentous adventure. Then Gérard reappeared; he had taken the bag of rusks to the Colonel.

"We had better go back to the transport," he said.

No sooner had they gone back than Gérard was sent for by a Cossack, and Miles was left alone. Miles soon wearied of this, and made up his mind to cross the road and get back to the others, come what might. A Cossack was crossing the road carrying a pail of soup for the men on the hill, the "transmitters," who lay on the ground forming a ladder higher up, and about a hundred yards to Miles' right. The Cossack was in his shirtsleeves. He said something to Miles as he passed him, and laughed. Miles couldn't understand what he said. The Cossack walked on. A shell burst on the edge of the road, and a long space of time seemed to have passed before Miles looked again at the Cossack, who by this time had got to the knoll, and seemed to be quite out of reach. Was it his imagination, or were his arms red? Red? They hadn't been red before – had they? His shirtsleeves were rolled up – had they been rolled up before? Why were his arms red? "I must join the others," thought Miles to himself. And then once more he felt paralysed; the road seemed to be a hundred miles broad; and yet, save for the noise of the guns firing, and the whizz of the shells through the air, which made a noise like rockets, what a deadly stillness between the shots! What a complete absence of the hum of life! Miles crossed the road slowly. It seemed to him to take an eternity. At last he reached the knoll, and began slowly to climb it. It was not high. On the top, sitting on a rock, Miles found the Colonel, the fastidious officer, and Gérard. Shells whizzed high over their heads, but Miles no longer minded, now that he was with the others. He felt all at once secure. The fastidious officer was obviously happy; he positively enjoyed being under fire. The Colonel lay in his cloak, silent and worn with pain. The doctor smoked and talked. He talked more than usual, a little feverishly. Gérard said nothing. The noise was terrific; it became louder and louder. The Japanese were firing, so Gérard told Miles, from a battery about three kilometres distant: shrapnel and *shimoze* shells. Sometimes when the Cossack battery fired a salvo, and the Japanese shells were bursting at the same time, Miles felt as if his head would split. Gérard told Miles that the Cossack who had brought the soup for the transmitters had been wounded by shrapnel, in the *gowliang*, just as he was starting. He had not noticed it at once. The doctor had bandaged him. It was a slight wound – nothing.

Gérard told Miles that the Japanese shrapnel was bursting too high. Just as he said this a bit of metal from a common shell hit a rock near them, and a tiny fragment of it grazed the skin of Miles' thumb.

The doctor laughed. "Now you've been wounded," he said.

Miles felt curiously excited, as if he had taken a tonic, or a dose of the "accelerator" imagined by H G Wells. Everything seemed to go faster; he no longer felt a vestige of panic.

The doctor gave him a little potted meat. There was a look of satisfied triumph about the fastidious officer; the expression of an artist at last able to do his job, and happy at it.

Towards one o'clock Miles thought he would make a last effort to find Troumestre. He crossed the road again. He did not mind crossing it this time. He found his pony and rode north towards the town. He passed the temple where he had slept the night before; it was now occupied by another detachment of the Red Cross. These were strangers to Miles, but they welcomed him and gave him some food. Presently Troumestre rode up; he told Miles his adventures. He had been in another part of the field with General Stackelberg. He had not been able to get back the night before. They stayed there a little time with the Red Cross, and then they rode west and watched an infantry regiment going into action through the *gowliang*.

"Let's go back to the battery," said Troumestre after a time.

"Very well," said Miles.

They started to go to it, but presently they met an officer, and they asked him where the battery was.

"It's moved," he told Troumestre, "moved right over to the east. It's no good going back to where they were this morning."

This, as it turned out, was untrue. The officer thought it unsafe for them to go to the battery, and so deceived them on purpose, and he probably thought they would be in the way.

So Miles and Troumestre turned back. Wounded men kept walking on down the roads to the Red Cross station, and from the station an unbroken column of ambulances, stretchers, and bandaged men on foot streaming towards the town. The roads were strewn with bandages soaked in blood.

Miles and Troumestre rode to the east, and there, too, they watched the infantry disappear into the *gowliang*.

When the sun set they decided to go back to the town.

"We shall never find the battery," said Troumestre.

"Let's look up Ivanov; I must send a dispatch."

They rode to the station. There they found Ivanov. He told them that Haslam had started for Mukden with all their heavier belongings, and such stuff as was left to them.

"Why?" asked Miles.

"He thinks there will be a retreat."

"Will there be a retreat?"

"No; I don't know," said Ivanov.

There was no news of Alyosha; Ivanov had no idea where he was.

"You had better both of you sleep here," said Ivanov. Troumestre sent off his dispatch. They had some food.

An officer arrived presently with news. He was in high spirits. The Japanese had been driven further back to the west. Ivanov and his guests went to bed. When they awoke the next morning, there was an unaccustomed stillness. Not a gun could be heard. Ivanov went to get news.

He came back with news – was it news to him? A turning movement as usual, by Kuroki, in the east. Orders had been given for a general retirement. Two corps had already crossed or were crossing the river. At Liao-yang the forts were left to defend themselves, while the rest of the army crossed the river.

"We must start at once," said Ivanov.

All such belongings as Ivanov and Troumestre had with them – Troumestre had moved his things from the town to Ivanov's office – were put into a Chinese cart. They started with Ivanov's Cossack servant, who was horseless and sat on the edge of the cart, and Troumestre's Montenegrin.

They went to the station and to the telegraph office. It was being moved into a train. Troumestre sent off a telegram. Trains were being sent off one after another. On the platform they met the Russian man of business whom they had met on their way to Kharbin, and who had given them so much trouble.

"It's all up," he said to Troumestre, waving his hands. "The war is over."

Troumestre was in doubt about his wire. He wanted more news.

"I shall go to the town and find out; I must send it," he said to Miles. "You go on with Ivanov, and I will meet you at the river at the first bridge; but for Heaven's sake get the stuff away."

Ivanov and Miles went on. They reached a bridge and halted at a Red Cross hospital just beyond it. There was no sign of Troumestre. They waited there two hours and a half.

Rumour said that the army would leave Mukden to its fate and go right back to Tieh-ling. Hundreds of carts, ambulances, and wagons and every kind of transport were crossing the river by the bridge.

The Japanese were firing, and the station and what was called the new town, the little brick-built offices that had grown up round the town, were being shelled. Miles and Ivanov were bound for Yen-tai. Presently they met Jameson and Maurel. They had no fresh news. They had lost all their belongings, as they had left the new town too late, when it was being bombarded. Troumestre, they said, was all right. He had started a moment or two before them, but it was impossible to find anybody in the confused mass of transport. They all rode on till they got to a siding. There was a train which was full of provisions from all the European shops of Liao-yang.

The train had stopped. The soldiers, discovering what was in it, began to loot it. They stormed the train, and hurled bottles of beer and packets of cigarettes to their comrades below. Miles drank a bottle of beer. He was parched with thirst.

They rode on till the evening, and halted with some Cossacks who were bivouacking by the railway line. Miles' head was splitting from the sun. He had lost his cap, and a Chinese substitute he had been given by a soldier had proved inadequate. He was faint from hunger and fatigue. He sank into an exhausted stupor, but instead of sleeping he began to rave.

He had caught a sunstroke. He spent the night in delirium. The next morning a hospital train stopped at a siding close by, and Miles was carried to it unconscious by Ivanov, Jameson, and his Cossack. He was put in charge of a nurse, who happened to be Elena Ilyin, and sent to Mukden. Ivanov's Cossack took charge of his pony.

CHAPTER XXIII

It was more than a sunstroke that Miles had caught during the strenuous days of the battle of Liao-yang.

It was dysentery. He was taken to Mukden, to a hospital outside the town, and there he was nursed till the end of September. He was not seriously ill, but not well enough to go on taking part in the campaign. Haslam, in the meantime, had been recalled by his editor. He was going back to America, *via* Japan, a route which had been forbidden to all other correspondents. He had arranged this with Diettrich. Miles wanted to stay; Haslam said he could stay as long as he liked, calling himself the correspondent of *Skreibners'* , provided he paid his own expenses; he could send any photographs which he took; the magazine would gladly put them in if they were interesting enough.

The hospital where Miles was living was in a temple, near a grove of trees. In one small part of it the priest still lived, and minded the painted gods in their wooden pagoda. It was a large compound: three quadrangles surrounded by high stone walls, and Miles enjoyed for a month the calm, mellow approach of the autumn. The *gowliang* was reaped. There was a subtle thrill in the air. Sometimes skeins of wild geese flew overhead.

In the grove the pheasants were loud. The leaves were brown, but the foliage was still intact. The hours to Miles, as he lay in his bed and watched the low sunshine, seemed to go by gently, to the silvery noise of the Chinese gongs which chimed the hours. On the right of him in the ward was an officer who talked a little English; to the left, one who talked French.

Elena Ilyin, and the staff of doctors whom he had originally met at Liao-yang, were all of them still at Mukden, in a train. Elena's husband had been killed during the battle of Liao-yang. Her unit was not attached to Miles' hospital, but she visited Miles almost daily.

One fine afternoon in the middle of October, soon after the midday meal, as Miles was lying out in the sunshine on his camp bed in the quadrangle, Gérard walked into the yard.

He had come to see a friend, and he was overjoyed to see Miles.

"The battery has come back," he said. "We are here, quite close. We were sent right up to the north, to rest after the battle, but resting meant going all the way to Kuan-chen-tse and all the way back."

"And what are you going to do now?" Miles asked.

"They say there is going to be another battle, that we are going to attack; but we – the battery – thank Heaven! are in the deepest reserve."

Gérard asked after Troumestre.

"I haven't seen him since Liao-yang," said Miles, "but one of the correspondents told me that he had gone right out to the west, to be with Mishchenko. I expect he will be back soon."

Miles asked after everyone in the battery. The Colonel was with them, but still not well.

When Gérard said goodbye, he promised to come again soon.

"We shall probably be here for days, and we are quite close; I will bring some of the others to see you."

A little later Elena came to see Miles. He was anxious to hear what she thought of the news.

"They say there is going to be another battle," he said.

"Yes, it is quite true; and this hospital will probably have to move. Our detachment is going south again to the front, and you will be sent in the train to Kharbin – or to Moscow, if you like – "

"But I'm quite well now," said Miles. "I can come to the Front. My battery is here next door."

"No," said Elena, "you are not at all quite well. You had better go straight to Moscow and then home to England."

"I can't do that."

"Your aunt must be anxious."

"All she knows is that I had a sunstroke and she thinks I am quite well. If I told her more, she would come out here; and it wouldn't do – it would be difficult; Aunt Fanny wouldn't understand. When do you think the battle is going to begin?"

"Quite soon. We shall perhaps start tomorrow, or the day after. You must go to Kharbin. If you had been better, you could have stayed at Mukden, with the Correspondents, at the hotel there, or with the Missionaries, but you are not well enough; it would be too uncomfortable, and you still want looking after – and then you must go home. You have been away long enough."

"I shan't go home," said Miles. "I will stop at Moscow and learn Russian. I have settled that. I have got the address of a lady in Moscow who takes in English pupils. Jameson gave it to me, and then, when I know Russian, I will come back here, if the war is still going on. If it isn't, I will travel in Russia."

"And your business?"

"Saxby will go on looking after that."

"I hope he is looking after it properly."

"Better than I should – or could."

"Is he honest?"

"Of course he is – "

"Why of course?"

Elena was called away to see someone in the hospital, and as she left Miles, he felt as if the sunshine had gone with her.

He realised now what he had vaguely thought before, but never put into words – that he could not imagine life without her.

And then the old question came back to him, in a flash – the old question that Alyosha's aunt and cousins had put to him in that restaurant in Paris, a question which had already once changed the course of his life: "Why not?"

"Why not?" Why should he not marry Elena Ilyn? Her husband was dead – she was free – he was free – he was well off. She had few relations – a brother who was doing something somewhere. He didn't know Russian, but what did that matter? He would learn it. He already knew quite a lot of words, and he was getting used to the sound of it. He would propose on the first possible opportunity – this very day – *now*, if she would only come back. Was it too soon? Presently be would be taken back to the ward, and then it would be too late.

He loved her – there was no one like her; he had met nothing in his life to compare with her frank directness, those clear eyes, and that simple serenity; she understood everything, one had to explain nothing…she was so much more natural than anyone he had ever seen in his life. What would Alyosha think? Alyosha was married, in the first place, and then his life was fixed – that was all over. Alyosha would be pleased. Where was he now, Alyosha? He had not seen him for months, not since the retreat – what a long time ago that was! – would he ever see him again? He must ask Elena…the figure of Alyosha had become dim to him, as if he were someone he had read about in a book, instead of someone he had known.

As he was thinking these thoughts, and they were becoming more and more dream-like, Alyosha and Troumestre appeared at the gateway.

"I have brought you a friend," said Alyosha.

"I have come to say goodbye," said Troumestre; "I have found the battery, and we are starting tomorrow."

"I will leave you two to talk," said Alyosha, "I want to speak to someone inside."

Alyosha went inside the hospital, and presently he came out again with Elena.

"We are going for a walk," she said to Miles as they passed him, "but we won't be long, and we will come back and have tea with you."

She seemed happy and gay, and Miles felt a pang of jealousy, but scolded himself for being absurd.

Troumestre sat down next to him, and told him all his adventures during the last month.

He was glad to be back...glad to have found the battery...his old friends...they thought they might start the next day – he didn't know...they were in the reserve; possibly they would not take part in the fighting at all this time.

Miles asked after all the others, and Troumestre told him all the news that he could.

Troumestre stayed over an hour, till it was time for Miles to be taken indoors. One of the nurses came for him. Troumestre said goodbye. Elena and Alyosha had not yet come back.

"Come and see me tomorrow, if you are still here," said Miles.

"Of course I will; we are quite close to you."

Half an hour later, Elena and Alyosha appeared; but Elena said goodbye at once. She must, she said, go back to the station...

Alyosha sat in the ward next to Miles' bed.

"I will come and see you tomorrow," said Alyosha; "I have something important to tell you. I cannot tell you now." He glanced at the other patients who were within earshot. "We shall all still be here tomorrow, and perhaps the day after," said Alyosha.

The next day everything seemed as calm as usual.

Everything, too, in the hospital seemed to be going on in just the same way. There was no sign of packing or of a move. The routine of Miles' day was the same as usual: after his noontide siesta, he was taken out into the quadrangle, and lay in the sun.

Elena came to see him.

"At last," thought Miles; "now the moment has come."

"There is not going to be a battle just yet," said Elena; "that is to say, not tomorrow; we shall have a few days' peace – and perhaps, after all, it is only a rumour. The train is not to go. I have seen everyone. You will probably not go till tomorrow, or the day after. But it is all arranged. You are to go to Moscow, and there is Petrov – a doctor who talks English, and he will look after you. I have told him all about you – "

"And you?" said Miles. "Will you go with the train to Kharbin?"

"No; I shall go to the Front with my *otriad* as before."

And shall you stop out here till the war is over?"

"No, I may have to go back first – perhaps soon – but I don't know; that depends on so many things. Who knows? I can't go until the next battle is over – if there is a battle; and if there is a battle, anything might happen."

"But then you will go home?"

"I have no more real home. I have no place in the country. We live at St Petersburg, and sometimes I had a *datcha* at Terrioki. I have few relations, a brother – he is out here – and then there are my husband's relations – they live everywhere; but I have affairs to settle."

"But the Kouragines?" said Miles.

"They are not relations, only friends…"

"But you used to go there and stay with them?"

"When I was little – when I was a girl."

"Now," thought Miles, "now is the moment – now or never – " but at that moment Alyosha strolled into the quadrangle smoking a cigarette, and said, "How do you do" to Elena Nikolayevna.

Miles noticed that her face lit up as she looked at Alyosha, but he attached no importance to this – not with his mind – not with his reason; but at the same time some instinct stirred in his heart; it was as if it had heard a knock at the door – whatever it was, his mind, not he, turned from it, ignored it, refused to admit, to see, or to hear.

They talked for a moment together about the prospects of a battle and the latest news. Then Elena said goodbye. As she went, she said to Alyosha: "I shall be free at four o'clock. I will come for a ride with you, if you will come and fetch me."

As soon as she went away, Alyosha sat down on the grass on a blanket, next to Miles' chair, and said: "I have a great deal to tell you. I will not tell you all, but you must guess what I do not tell. It is shortly this: that I do not think I will ever go back to my wife again; and if we come through this war – if we come through this next battle – "

"Oh," said Miles. He did not know exactly what to say. "Has anything happened?" he asked after a slight pause.

"Yes, and no," said Alyosha; "nothing has happened, and yet in a way everything has happened; I feel I can no longer live with my wife; or rather that I shall no longer be able to live with her; if ever this war comes to an end – I shall be a different person. The long and short of it is, I am in love with someone else – someone I saw at Kharbin."

The supper at Kharbin rose quickly in Miles' mind – "Not that lady who – "

"No, not Marya Ivanovna – it's somebody else – nobody you know."

Doors had been flung open violently in the soul of Miles; at that moment they were softly closed.

"Are you engaged to be married?" he asked after a moment.

"Yes and no," said Alyosha; "it all depends. She has told me she may be willing to marry me, but there is my wife; she would only be willing to marry me if my wife consented... I am to tell her the whole story, but not now, only when the war is over. Of course, anything may happen before this."

"But will your wife consent?"

"I think she will when she knows all that has happened."

"But will you desert her? How will she live?"

"As she lives now; she will have the tobacco store. She manages it all now as it is."

"But how will you live?"

"Oh! I will always find some job or other."

"And if she refuses?"

"She will not refuse. She knows I have never – well, she knows me, and all about me – she is very sensible."

"Won't she be jealous?"

"I think no."

"She must be a wonderful woman."

"She is. You see, after all, I went to prison for fifteen years and lost everything, not for her...my wife knows all that; she will understand perfectly... It was always understood between us that if ever there was a moment in the future – and I never thought there could be a moment – but she knows that if ever there should, by a miracle, be a chance of my being in love – really in love – again, I would of course take it. It only shows that nothing is too extraordinary to happen. I never thought the chance would come – and now it has come."

"I suppose not," said Miles, but he hardly listened now to what Alyosha said, for it was a matter of profound indifference to him whether Alyosha married or deserted his wife or not; the only thing that mattered was that it was not Elena whom Alyosha had meant, and that meant that his hope was not ended. "I won't, certainly won't go home," he thought. "I will go to Moscow."

The next day Elena Nikolayevna, the battery, and everyone else went south to the Front. Elena came for a moment to say goodbye to Miles.

"Are you really going to stop at Moscow?" she asked.

"Yes," said Miles. "The doctors say I had much better, and not go straight to London. Not that I really care where I go now."

"Why not?"

"Well, all the interest of the war is over for me now that I can't be at the Front…and as I can't be at the Front, I don't care where I go – Moscow, Madeira, London, it's all the same."

Elena looked at him attentively. "I didn't know you were so interested in war," she said.

"I didn't know it either, till it came to going away."

"Everything is arranged for you," she said; "your train goes tomorrow. Dr Petrov will be kind to you. He talks English; he was at Cambridge for a long time, or Oxford, I forget which."

"And shall you come back to Moscow?"

"Oh, I have made no plans. It all depends on this battle, and on everything else; a multitude of other things."

"If you do pass through Moscow, please let me know."

"Then you think you will stay there?"

"I shall certainly stay. I mean to learn Russian now I am here. I shall stay with a Russian lady; Jameson has given me her address. Here it is on this card. You can keep that; I have copied it out in my notebook. If you lose it, you can always ask the British Consul; I shall give him my address."

"But after all, what is the use of your learning Russian?"

Miles blushed. Here was the Heaven-sent opportunity – why was it that he could say nothing? Yesterday it had seemed so easy, so possible. Was it the recent conversation with Alyosha? But Alyosha had told him it was no one he knew – that it might be Elena was absurd. Be it as it may, he felt it was impossible to speak out now. If only she would guess, if only she would help him – and then he was so afraid of spoiling everything.

"They say Russian is so useful in business now," he said, "and our firm does business with Russia – the Russians drink Madeira. And then I should like to read all that poetry you have told me about – in Russian – Pushkin."

Elena laughed; she got up.

"Well, goodbye," she said; "don't forget me."

"I won't; and – please take care of yourself."

Now at the last moment Miles thought he might say something, but Elena shook hands with him in a friendly way, and said, "Goodbye, Mihalivanytch; I am very glad we are friends. I shall certainly try and find you if I come to Moscow, and if you are still there, which I doubt. Alyosha asked me to say goodbye to you for him."

"Has he gone to the Front?"

"He has gone on a mission – I don't quite know where to. He sent you lots of messages. He had to start in a hurry, and hadn't time to come and say goodbye."

"Please give him my address," said Miles.

"I will."

"Will he come back soon?"

"Who knows? Perhaps soon, perhaps never; we know nothing, do we? Everything is uncertain always, but in wartime... Goodbye. If ever I do see him again, I will give him your address. *Dosvidania.* I wish you the best."

She left him. The next morning Miles started in the hospital train for Moscow.

CHAPTER XXIV

The journey to Moscow took nearly a month. When Miles arrived there he was convalescent.

The first thing he did was to visit the British Consul, and make inquiries about the lady whose address Jameson had given him. He found at the Consulate several letters waiting for him from Aunt Fanny; Miles had given "The British Consulate, Moscow," as his most reliable address.

Aunt Fanny was resigned to his absence. Now that the deed was done, she thought it, on the whole, not a bad thing that he should see the world, although she would never have suggested it herself. If consulted, she would certainly have thrown cold water on the idea, on the grounds of common sense. If anybody had suggested Miles going out to a war, as a photographer, she would have thought the suggestion insane. But now that it had happened, and had proved successful – some of Miles' pictures had appeared in *Skreibners'*, and been talked about – Aunt Fanny took credit for the idea, and talked as if it had been her own suggestion.

Miles had told her little about his illness. He had merely mentioned a slight sunstroke. She was not expecting him home; and when he telegraphed to her, answer paid, that he was at Moscow, and intended to stay on, he was surprised to get an answer saying, "Quite understand." Aunt Fanny had consulted Saxby, who, instead of being in favour of Miles' immediate return, as Aunt Fanny had expected him to be, said that it was a good thing for the young to see the world, that one was only young once, and other remarks all tending one way: the protraction of Miles' absence.

Miles was staying at the *Dresden*, where he had stayed during his first visit with Alyosha. He visited the lady whose address Jameson had given him with a letter of introduction from the Consul.

This lady, whose name was Bloum, lived in part of the ground floor of a two-storied wooden house in a small street (called a *pereulok*), some distance from the centre of the town.

Miles called on her at tea time, and found her at home. He was shown into a dining room, which was also a sitting room, not unlike the room where he had had supper at Kharbin with Alyosha's friend, Marya Ivanovna. There was a long table covered with American cloth; a lamp hanging from the ceiling; a samovar on the table; pictures of Herzen, Tourgenev, Pushkin and Beethoven on the wall. A large white stove was flush with the wall. There was a palm tree in a pot near the window.

The inmates had finished dinner and were drinking tea. There was the husband, Ivan Borisovitch Bloum, a schoolmaster; he was introduced to Miles by the lady of the house, and got up from the table, where he was doing a Patience, and extended a limp, welcoming hand. It was evident that his wife, Elizaveta Ivanovna, managed the household; and indeed it was she who took in and looked after and taught the foreigners who boarded there. Miles saw no Englishmen at the table, but several Russians; one in the uniform of a civil servant.

Miles was welcomed warmly by Elizaveta Ivanovna, who was an oldish lady dressed in black, with intelligent eyes and an air of bustle that reminded Miles slightly of Aunt Fanny. She asked a great deal after Jameson – Harold Franzovitch she called him.

"Oh, such a talented man – very capable (*ochen sposobni*), and learnt Russian so quickly, but alas! too little application." She sighed: "Here today, gone tomorrow…he might just as well have been a Russian."

Elizaveta Ivanovna looked at her husband as she said this. He looked exceedingly meek, large, comfortable, and shabby, as he sat rolling a cigarette in an interval of his Patience.

Yes…she had a room vacant…so Mr…so Konstantin Ivanytch…no, Mihal Ivanytch, ah yes – wanted to learn Russian?… Was it for the Staff College? No? For business?… Ah yes; and he had been to the war…just fancy! How long would it last? When would it be over? How was Kouropatkin getting on? There followed an interruption; a flood of questions from the husband, and a digression about the internal political situation, which went on till his wife put a stop to it, after bearing it patiently for some moments.

"I have already two Englishmen here," she said, "Captain Wilson and Mr Roberts… One is in the army and working for the Staff College, and the other to be an interpreter; they are both of them out today… But I have a room vacant. Mr Welby has gone home for his examination… When would you be ready to come?"

Elizaveta Ivanovna, seeing that Miles was the kind of man who can never bring himself to mention terms or bring the word "money" across his lips, and being used to the shyness of Englishmen, helped him out of the situation, stated the terms – which included lodging, board, and two hours' daily tuition – showed him his bedroom, which was warm; it was arranged that he should move in on the following day.

Thus another chapter of life began for Miles. It reminded him of life at the Mourieux', but there was this great difference: he was older…and his companions were older. He was different too; he made friends easily now with the two Englishmen. He felt much older than the younger of the two, who was working for an interpretership, and no younger than the Captain, who was his senior by some years. They showed him the sights of Moscow. His life was as regular as when he had been working at the Mourieux': coffee at nine o'clock in the morning, or later; then work. Two hours' tuition with Elizaveta Ivanovna were got through in the day; sometimes in an unbroken stretch from ten to twelve, or from twelve to two, or sometimes broken up into two separate hours, or into an hour and a half and half-an-hour; the second dose being given in the afternoon or the evening. It depended on the others. Only Russian was talked at meals. The important meal was supposed to be at two o'clock in the afternoon – often it was later, at three or four. After it, Miles would go out, and sometimes the Englishmen would take him to a restaurant in the evening, or to the theatre. Miles had to be careful. He was still in a delicate state of health.

Often, in the evening, Russian friends would drop in. There would be supper at nine or later, after which tea would be drunk, and everyone would stay up, sometimes till two in the morning. The Englishmen would usually go to their rooms after supper, to work, and come back later.

The snow was beginning to fall when Miles arrived. Then it thawed; it snowed again a fortnight later; it thawed again, and then snowed once more at the beginning of December, for good. Miles bought a fur-lined coat, a fur cap; the cabs had been replaced by sledges.

Miles received a postcard from Elena, saying she was coming home in the spring. From Alyosha he heard nothing. But he had a card from Troumestre, a few weeks after he had arrived, saying that he had taken part in the battle of Sha-ho, and that he was going home for Christmas. It was impossible to get any dispatches through. Troumestre passed through Moscow just before Christmas. Miles went to see him at the station. He was going straight on by the express to London. He had about an hour's wait. They went into the buffet and ordered some vodka, and sat down at a table. Troumestre told him the news.

Most of the correspondents had gone. Some were staying. It was useless, really; one couldn't send any news. The newspapers wouldn't stand it.

Troumestre had seen Elena Nikolayevna at Mukden after the battle... They expected the war would last a long time yet.

"There won't be a decisive battle?" said Miles.

"There can't be," said Troumestre. "And then things will warm up here. I hear they are warming up already."

"I should think they were," said Miles. "Do you know what they dared do?"

"Who are 'they'?" asked Troumestre.

"Why, the Government, of course. They have banished Prince Viazemski to the country! For a year! Because he protested about the action, the disgraceful behaviour, of the police when the students had a meeting at the Kazan Cathedral the other day! Prince Viazemski, a member of the Council of Empire!"

"Oh really," said Troumestre, not interested.

"Yes, and that's not all. They've closed the University here for no reason at all. Just because the students showed themselves in the streets! It is a *shame*, and silly too – they are asking for revolution. It's the French Revolution over again."

Troumestre laughed. "You have become a regular Russian," he said. "I suppose you talk Russian like a native now?"

"Oh no, but I can follow everything that is being said. I can read a newspaper, and make myself more or less understood in simple matters."

"Aren't you coming back to England?"

"Come back *now*? Just as it's getting interesting? Oh no!"

"I don't think anything will come of it. They've got no one, no big man; the only capable man they've got is Witte."

"Witte!" Miles said with scorn; "nobody trusts him. They won't have anything to do with him!"

"But who else is there?"

"Well, there's Shipov, and many others, leaders of the Zemstvo."

"Girondins," said Troumestre.

"Well, after all, Girondins made the French Revolution."

"They ruined the monarchy, and got their heads cut off. But you are enjoying yourself? Are you comfortable? What are the people like you are staying with?"

"Oh, as nice as possible. There are two Englishmen there, both very nice; they are learning Russian; they are very good to me, and I like them awfully... Of course they are both very reactionary."

Troumestre laughed.

"There, the second bell," he said; "I must go. Don't become too much of a revolutionary. Don't get locked up or massacred. Remember it's not our affair, not our funeral."

"It's everyone's affair," Miles said hotly, "everyone who cares for liberty."

"Well, I confess I don't care a rap for liberty," said Troumestre. "I see precious little trace of liberty in Russia – least of all among your Liberals. They are the most tyrannical and arbitrary people I have ever seen. The only liberty worth having is that which proceeds from authority: the rest is not liberty but licence."

" But," said Miles, "you must admit – "

"I shall miss my train; I really can't stop to argue now. Goodbye, and take care of yourself; you don't look well."

Troumestre said a hurried goodbye and jumped into the train.

"You won't come back?" said Miles.

"No, I don't think so. I am wanted at home, and it's no use staying here, from my point of view."

The third bell sounded, and the train started.

When Miles got home he found a letter from Aunt Fanny, asking whether he wouldn't come home for Christmas, to

Norfolk; his cousins would be there. Miles wrote to her at once, explaining that he was just beginning to understand Russian, and that if he were to come home now he felt he would snap the thread. He was sure he would never go back to Russia. He thought it wiser to stay. He was determined to stay on for three reasons.

In the first place, Elena; he would not leave till he saw her again. In the second place, he was more comfortable and at ease in the somewhat comfortless surroundings at the Bloum's than he had ever been before. In the third place, he had caught the infectious disease of Russian politics. He was more than interested in what was happening. He was violently keen; his Whig blood and upbringing were aflame. Everyone was talking politics. The war was forgotten; and when the bad news reached Moscow from the frontier – the discomfiture of Kouropatkin, the fall of Port Arthur – it was received by the Bloum household without regret. They thought it would hasten the end of the war. A series of sporadic strikes and disorders began all over the country; and in February, as Miles was walking under the gate of the Iverskaya, he heard an explosion: the bomb which blew up the Grand Duke Serge.

News came of agrarian disturbances in various parts of the country. Miles wondered whether this would affect Elena's movements. In the meanwhile life went on as usual, and the riots in St Petersburg (Father Gapon), the bad news from the Front, the news of the Prime Minister's resignation, the appointment of Trepov, made little difference to the tenour of life in the *pereulok* where Miles now lived. It merely provided food for discussion. By Easter Miles could understand Russian, and read it without difficulty, and make himself understood.

When news of the battle of Mukden reached Moscow, the Bloums said it must mean the end of the war. They had said so after every untoward event, but the war went on in spite of all. Both the armies, whatever happened, seemed to be in a perpetual state of "as you were." It looked as if a huge game was being played which could but end in stalemate.

Ivan Borisovitch rubbed his hands when the bad news reached him, and said, "*chyiem huzhe tiem luchshe*" (the worse it is, the better).

His wife made no comment, but compressed her lips and looked grim; the two Englishmen took Bloum seriously to task for his want of patriotism. Ivan Borisovitch told them they didn't understand, and couldn't understand. Miles backed up Ivan Borisovitch, and waxed hot in discussion; but all the time he was wondering how far this event would affect Elena's plans; would it make it more difficult or easier for her to come home?

One day he received a postcard from Alyosha, from Verkhneudinsk. So he had gone back to his wife after all, or had he gone to arrange matters? All that Alyosha said on it was, "*Christos voskresse*" (Christ is risen). It was sent for Miles to receive at Easter, and it was only a week late.

Easter was celebrated as usual that year at Moscow, and the Bloum family took part in the national festivity and observed all the ritual.

The Blooms were not specially orthodox. Nevertheless, during Holy Week, nothing but Lenten food was eaten by them. Traphim, the boy who did the rough work of the household, fasted a whole day preparatory to receiving Holy Communion. When he came back from church after receiving it, everyone congratulated him. On Maundy Thursday Miles heard the Gospel read out in a number of tongues. On Easter Sunday they took him to the midnight service – Matins and then Mass; to the *Hram Spasitelia* (St Saviour's), which was packed with poor people, so that to get in, and still more to get out, was like taking part in a football match in which all the spectators were playing as well as the two teams. When Matins were over, Miles heard all the bells of the city ringing. There was no more snow; the dawn shone on the white river as they drove back to the *pereulok*, and partook of the *Paskha*, the Easter cake: the Blooms, the two Englishmen, and an old-maid friend of the family.

Just as they were sitting down the bell rang, and a good-looking, fair-haired girl, about twenty-five, dressed in a way that suggested artistic Paris, with an ornament made by Lalique hanging around her neck, came into the room accompanied by an older girl, with black hair parted in the middle, and dressed in a striped black and white Munich *reformkleid.*

"Vera Petrovna, and Liza!" Elizaveta Ivanovna exclaimed: "Just fancy!"

There was a chorus of greetings.

Miles was introduced; explanations were poured out to him. Liza (Elizaveta Borisovna) was a niece of Bloum. Vera Petrovna was her intimate friend, the daughter of a General.

"Last year," explained Elizaveta Ivanovna to Miles, "Vera Petrovna came in here one day, just when the war was starting, and said she was going to the Far East. She was going as a nurse. She got everything ready, made all arrangements, had taken her ticket, and then – just fancy! – the day she was to start she came here again, and said: 'I'm not going to the Far East. I am going to the Far West! I am going to Paris!' and she has been away ever since. Now tell us what you have been doing all this time."

Vera Petrovna sat down opposite Miles. She had disconcerting eyes, and dazzling hair, with red lights in it, and the neatest of figures. Smoking cigarette after cigarette she talked with great animation of Paris: the theatres, music, the books, the pictures, the artists, the journalists, the cafés, the night restaurants, the cabarets, Montmartre, the studios – all sorts of names came up that Miles had never heard of. The others listened. The dark girl sat looking in front of her, silent and expressionless and ominous, like a tragedy queen. She did not seem to be listening.

"And now that you are back, Vera Petrovna," Ivan Borisovitch said after a pause, " I hope you are going to stay with us. Here everything is becoming interesting. Things are beginning to move."

"Oh, politics! I can't bear politics. I am sick of it all! I have just come back from Simbirsk, from my estate; and it is my brother who is looking after it. It is mine really, but he is looking after it – and he is doing dreadful things! I am in favour of total expropriation. It is the only means of saving anything; but Alexander is so obstinate, he will not hear of it. He will not sell anything, and there have been disorders quite close to us – a house burnt, and the Governor shot at – and Alexander will not listen to reason. I hate him, and he has taken to drink, and he says force is the only way. What force have we got, if you please? I would like to know. It is a wonder we have not been murdered; happily the peasants know that I am on their side, and the estate is mine. Our steward is on my side too; he is good-natured, but weak – a fool! What can one do? So you see I am sick of politics. I have come here to forget all that...for the moment."

"You won't forget it here," said Ivan Borisovitch. "Here we are resolved to see the business through," he said energetically, thumping the table with his fist. "We will teach them a lesson."

He looked so mild, so fat, so good-natured, so fundamentally weak, as he said these inspiring words that Miles wondered for a moment whether Troumestre might not, to a certain extent, be right. Liza uttered a profound sigh.

"Everything is awful," she said, "awful! I cannot sleep at night for thinking of all the awful things that are happening; and this terrible war, when will it end?"

"The worse the better, the worse the better," Ivan Borisovitch said cheerfully.

"It is shameful, shameful, Ivan Borisovitch, to talk like that! How can you?" interrupted the old maid. She was fat, short, and plain; her hair was parted in the middle and brushed back;

she wore a cameo brooch. She was the wife of an official, and considered by the Bloums to be reactionary. She looked in almost every evening. "It is the dreadful things that the revolutionary youth are doing that are bringing this trouble on us. Ah! we shall pay dearly for it! They believe in nothing!"

"It is entirely the fault of the Government," said Ivan Borisovitch.

"I will have no political arguments on Easter night," said Elizaveta Ivanovna decidedly, as she poured out some *nalivka* for the guests – "I am sick of it. Not tonight, please."

"So am I!" said Vera Petrovna. "Let's enjoy ourselves. And so you have learnt Russian, Mihal Ivanytch?" she said, turning to Miles and speaking English to him. "I hope you go often to the theatre; that is the best way. I am going next week to hear a new play read out at a friend's house. Stanislavsky is going to do it next season. They have nothing like our theatre in Paris. I am mad about the theatre. I saw the Duse in Rome; she is a wonder – but badly supported; here at least you have an *ensemble*; but next week I mean to see what there is to see."

"I can't think how people can go to the theatre in these times!" said Liza.

"On the contrary, I find one must go *now*," said Vera Petrovna feverishly. "I want to forget; I want to live – and I am going to live; to enjoy myself, to be gay, in spite of everything. I find one has the right to live – one has only one life. Youth is youth, the spring the spring; they are both short – and now that the spring is coming I mean to enjoy it."

"Have a little tea," said Elizaveta Ivanovna, handing a glass to Vera, "and please speak Russian to Mihal Ivanytch."

The old woman looked at Vera Petrovna anxiously; evidently the younger woman made her uneasy.

"Have you just come back from Paris?" Miles said to Vera Petrovna.

"I have been back a fortnight. I went to the country for a few days, but I have been in France or in Italy all the year," she said in Russian.

"I wonder," said Miles, "if you met some people called Dashkov in Paris?"

"Dashkov... Pyotr Ilyitch and Elizaveta Sergeevna, and their daughter Sandra. Of course I met them." She broke into English: "And Mary Kouragine, their niece. I met them at Madame le Clerc's – you know, the artist; she paints haystacks in the sunlight, and sycamores...she had a musical evening one night I went, and it was oh! so interesting. Guitry recited some verses, and Raphael Luc sang... Fauré's songs; and an Englishman, a Mr Lawrence, played the piano. He is very strong in music, and will soon be being a professional; and there I met the Dashkovs. I knew them before, of course, and Mary Kouragine, very well, and her Aunt Kitty. They are all musical, the Dashkovs; especially Elizaveta Sergeevna."

"I suppose they are back in Russia now?" said Miles.

"No; they are not coming back. Pyotr Ilyitch has sold his property; all except the *usadba* – *et il a raison*. I want to do the same. The *usadba* for the moment has been turned into a hospital for convalescent officers. They are not coming back this year, at any rate; they will stay the winter at Nice. It is better for the old man."

The old maid sighed.

"If all the decent people leave Russia, what can you expect?" she said.

"I beg your pardon, Sofia Drimitrievna," said Bloum to her; "it does not matter what the nobility do; they are finished, the sooner they go the better... They are rotten to the core."

"And do you mean to say the *intelligentsia* will do better?" asked Vera Petrovna in Russian, with flashing eyes.

Bloum stood up and began solemnly and slowly: "Every man who is not a born idiot knows – "

But Elizaveta Ivanovna cut him short abruptly: "Enough, enough, my children... I cannot have disputes on Easter night...let us drink to the dawn of better things."

"The dawn," said Liza, and sighed deeply; "the dawn! I wish one could go to sleep, and that there were no such thing as the dawn."

Sofia Drimitrievna, the old maid, snorted, and said half aloud: "All that decadent stuff!"

"Well, let's drink to the dawn...the dawn of better things," said Bloum cheerfully, and he poured out a glass of *nalivka*.

CHAPTER XXV

A few days after Easter, Vera Petrovna appeared again at the Bloums', and told Miles that she wanted to take him to the theatre with some friends. She was dining with Losov, one of the rich Moscow merchants, the following evening, and Losov had asked her to bring Miles: he liked Englishmen, and knew all about Miles' firm. He was a kind man, and an amateur of the fine arts.

Miles accepted, and the next afternoon Vera Petrovna came to fetch him, and took him to Losov's house. This was in sharp contrast to the Bloums' apartment in the *pereulok*, and unlike any other Russian houses that Miles had seen up till then. The rooms were large and high, with arched ceilings, in the old Russian style, like the rooms in the Kremlin, or in historical pictures of the palaces of the old Tzars of Moscow. There were shiny parquet floors and stoves in dark green faience.

The rooms were sparsely furnished, but the walls were covered with pictures, all of them modern: French Impressionist landscapes, English portraits of the Glasgow school; some Danish oil paintings, some Spanish pastels, and some fantastic imaginative pictures by a young Russian.

The master of the house was bearded, fat, and friendly. There was an artistic wife dressed in the *art-nouveau* fashion, with wide fair hair, a girl with plaits, a schoolboy; Nadezhda

Mandel, the actress – handsome and haggard, famous in Ibsen parts; Stepanenko, the subtle comedian, with his resonant voice and quaint woe-begone face; Bielov the eclectic composer; pale, with his dark hair *en brosse*, and dressed with the utmost correctness in a frock-coat, looking like what in private life he was – a model government official; Vladimir Oleg, the poet, who looked like Swinburne, and wrote *vers libres*.

Dinner was at six; the *hors d'oeuvres* were a meal in themselves. They were divided into two series: hot and cold, and Miles, after he had feasted on smoked salmon and caviare and *sig*, thought he had eaten enough for the evening; but the cold dishes were quickly succeeded by hot mushrooms and other tempting little dishes; these were interspersed with glasses of vodka, which Miles thought stronger than the ordinary vodka. It was called *starka*.

Then they went into another room for dinner. There was *borshch* and a marvellous fish, a roast sucking-pig with buckwheat, hasel-hens cooked in cream, and cranberry jelly called *Kisel*.

After dinner they had tea in another room and smoked. Bielov played parts of an unpublished symphony. It was quite unintelligible to Miles. More people dropped in: artists, singers, and writers, and one of the leading Zemstvo leaders.

Nobody talked politics. Oleg recited some verse translations of Mallarmé, and of Shelley in honour of Miles, who, never having read the original, could not follow the translation. A famous stage producer arrived. There was immediately a hot discussion about the production of Shakespeare, and indeed all plays, between him and the actors present.

He belonged to a new school. He was violently opposed to the realism of the Art Theatre, scornful about Shaw and Ibsen and the *Théâtre Antoine*, but an admirer of Gordon Craig. He wanted to stage Byron's *Cain* – so did the Art Theatre, but they disagreed about the manner of the production. Later on Vera

Petrovna, Bielov, Oleg, and Stepanenko took Miles to a small cabaret where short plays, parodies of current productions, of Chekhov and others, were performed. They stayed there till past midnight, then Stepanenko suggested going on to his flat, which they did. He lived in a large studio, in another quarter of the town. There they had supper: vodka, sardines, tomatoes with onions, hot mushrooms, and small sausages, and more and more vodka.

Other friends arrived; Bielov played songs, and Zurova, a well known *diseuse*, sang. Much later, a tall man entered, and everyone greeted his arrival with cheers. He was introduced to Miles as Tsezarin, the great singer. He was the idol of St Petersburg and Moscow – a great artist. He ate his supper quietly, and drank some vodka; they asked him to sing, but he said he was out of voice. They did not press him, but Bielov sat down to the pianoforte again, and began playing a listless accompaniment badly on purpose. Tsezarin pushed him from the piano and said: "No, it should not be so…but so, like this," and with one finger he picked out the tune and indicated the rhythm. Bielov nodded. "Is this better?" he said, and played it perfectly. Tsezarin answered by bursting into song. He went on singing. His voice filled the room. Miles had never heard him on the stage; he had never been able to get tickets when he was singing at the Opera. He had never heard anything like it. It was so easy, and at the same time so tremendous. When he had finished the passage from the opera (*Prince Igor*), which was highly dramatic, he passed on to some Russian songs; everything he did seemed to be infallibly right. He sang a song of Schubert's; it was heartbreaking – the natural language of despair; and then a trifle about a drunken *chinovnik*. It was perfect; there was no trace of exaggeration; just a picture of imbecile, maudlin futility, indicated in a line, as it were, by magic. He acted every song, and seemed to snatch the idea from its secret hiding place in the soul of the composer, and to present it without ornament or explanation.

They went back to the supper table. More vodka was drunk. It was nearly three o'clock in the morning, but no one thought of going away. Some of the guests were playing *vindt* in the corner of the studio. Zurova sang again, and as she sang Tsezarin listened in ecstasy, appreciating every detail of her slight but exquisite art, without a twinge of jealousy or impatience. Tsezarin sang again – a sad folk song in a minor key – about the autumn and the night, and then said he must go home; but he made no move.

"You mustn't all go home," said Stepanenko; "you mustn't go home, Mister," he said to Miles.

"Let's go to Yar," said Vera Petrovna. Yar was a restaurant outside the town.

"It's too late," said Stepanenko. "Let's stay here."

"Mihal Ivanytch must see Yar," she said.

"He has heard *tzygane*, he tells me, in St Petersburg," said Stepanenko.

"They are better here," said Vera Petrovna.

Some were for going, some were for staying, and all the while the talk went on: talk and argument. Some argued about whether they should go to Yar or not; others went on with the literary and abstract discussions in which they were already engaged: arguments about stage, books, poetry, authors, actors, artistic ideals and schools – philosophy – religion. Verse was quoted by the ream, interspersed with snatches of song. Everyone was talking; no one was listening. Stepanenko did some imitations, and then fetched a *balalaika* and began to play. A special favourite was asked for; Zurova forgot the words in the middle; Tsezarin could not remember them either.

"Let's go to Yar," said Vera Petrovna, "we *must* have that song."

"Very well," said Stepanenko; "let's go to Yar."

"Yes," said the others; " let's go to Yar."

The card players paid no attention to the discussion. They went on with their game. But no sooner had the majority decided to go to Yar, than the party seemed to be immobilised.

"One moment," said Bielov to Vera Petrovna, "do you know this?" He sat down at the pianoforte and played an air.

"Skriabin?" she asked.

"Yes." He went on playing. Everyone sat down.

She sat down on a chair near the pianoforte, but she did not look at the player, nor did he look at her; he seemed to be playing for her, and she seemed far away from him; in a different plane or planet.

The music went on.

The discussions and arguments grew lower in pitch, but did not cease; the card players went on with their game, loudly as before. A winning card was triumphantly thumped on to the table; a piece of bad or good luck was vociferously underlined. Tsezarin had not gone; he was listening to the music, too absorbed to comment... Bielov was playing Chopin now... He played the pianoforte as composers do, with immense richness and understanding, although he missed a note here and there...he had forgotten his surroundings.

His mother was a Pole; he understood Chopin...he played and played. Miles was spellbound...through the music he saw the face of Elena; it seemed to him to be about her, and nothing else...he had never experienced anything like this since that Lamoureux concert the Dashkovs had taken him to; and this impression was still more wonderful... He was not being stunned this time; he was sailing through the blue...he hoped it would never stop; he looked at Tsezarin...his face was a study, a mixture of ecstasy and pain... Oleg looked sad too...he was not musical, but art in any form appealed to him. Zurova was crying. The dawn glimmered through the double window-panes. The sun rose. Still Bielov played on. Even the *vindt* players had left off playing and had come to listen. Nobody knew what he was playing: he did not know himself…a god was there, whispering tunes to him.

He was playing something triumphant now, a hymn to the rising sun.

Suddenly the door was flung open, and a shabby man, quite drunk, with towzled hair like tow, green eyes and a blotched face, burst into the room.

"I declare to all gentlemen – " he said, then, looking round the room at the company, he stopped and bowed; and then, catching sight of Tsezarin, he bowed again and said: "Leonid Andreyevitch! My respects."

"All friends – " he began again.

Stepanenko led him gently to the table, and he sat down, and buried his face in his hands.

Miles was told that his name was Golovachev, and that he was an artist who shared the studio.

Bielov had stopped playing. The spell was broken.

They sat down again at the table and had a final supper. Some more hot food was brought in. More vodka was drunk. Zurova sang again, and everyone toasted her. Tsezarin made a speech, and drank *Brüderschaft* with Miles. So did Stepanenko. Miles had drunk little, but he was morally intoxicated. Golovachev became talkative, and made a harangue distinguished by the curious dream-like logic of the intoxicated. Stepanenko, who had been drinking vodka all night, seemed perfectly sober. At least he talked with the utmost seriousness; but Oleg began to make professions of faith and friendship to everyone, and quoted unpublished verse which seemed to be, if possible, more obscure than usual. He drank the health of the English poets, and made an impassioned address to Miles on the subject of Swinburne. Tsezarin caught fire at the word English, and went to the piano and played "Drink to me only with thine eyes" with one finger. He had been taught the tune, he said, by an Englishman at Monte Carlo. "It is so noble," he said, and hummed it exquisitely. Then he sighed and said solemnly: "Children, I must be off; I am singing tomorrow night."

It was eight o'clock in the morning when the party broke up. Stepanenko insisted on driving back with Miles. He, Bielov, and Vera Petrovna all went in one cab; they took a roundabout way by the Kremlin, because Stepanenko wanted to see the river.

It was a dazzling, pure spring morning.

"It is a good thing to be alive," said Stepanenko. "After all, things might be worse – we might be dead."

"We are dead," said Bielov, "dead, all of us – that is the trouble – *und wussten es selber kaum*," he murmured to himself. These were the only words he spoke during the whole drive. Vera Petrovna said nothing either. It was nearly nine o'clock before they reached Miles' house.

Nobody was up yet, but Traphim was bringing the coffee. He smiled as he saw Miles, and merely said: "*Pozdno*" (late).

Miles went to bed, and slept till four o'clock in the afternoon.

When Miles woke up he felt ill. It was not merely a headache after the last night; he felt a return of his illness. Elizaveta Ivanovna sent for the doctor, Philipov. The doctor was a man whom Miles knew well. He used to drop in at the Bloums' house in the evening and play cards. He knew Miles' "history." He examined him, and said: "No more vodka, Mihal Ivanytch; no more champagne. Moscow is bad for you…you cannot stand those hours – the sitting up – not in your present condition. You ought to go to the country…to some quiet place in the south – Yalta, for instance." He looked at Miles with his quiet grey eyes and lit a cigarette.

"I can't go to Yalta," said Miles; "I know nobody there."

The doctor shrugged his shoulders. "Well," he said, "if you stay here you must be careful, or else I will not be responsible for you."

Before leaving the house Philipov had a long talk with Elizaveta Ivanovna about Miles.

"He had injured his constitution," he said, "out there in Manchuria, and he was just getting well; and now he undoes all the good his treatment has done him. He must be careful…if he is careful, he will be all right. I am going to give him injections, but while my treatment lasts he is not to touch a drop of vodka or wine or beer."

Elizaveta Ivanovna agreed. "It's Vera Petrovna's fault, Aleksei Ivanovitch," she said; "she threw him into that Bohemian world. I don't know what has happened to the girl! She has quite changed. She used to be serious, capable; but now, ever since she has come back from Paris, she is another being. I don't understand it, because it is not her nature. She is serious by nature. She has read a great deal; she has studied. She has a head for business… I have seen her at Committee meetings. I looked upon her as one of the rare exceptions of her class – but now, just fancy! To sit up all night at Stepanenko's studio, and then to want to go to Yar!"

"Perhaps she is in love."

"She had a love affair, I believe; someone who went to the war, and nothing came of it…perhaps that was why she did not go; and Liza says that Bielov loves her madly, but that she will have nothing to say to him. Whatever it is, it is a pity, a great pity. She will be a lost being if she is not careful, but I will not have her ruin Mihal Ivanytch. I will speak to Liza about it."

"How is she?"

"As depressed as ever. I can get her to do nothing. All the world has become hysterical."

"It's the war. It happens in war time."

"I wish it would end…and then what will happen next?" she sighed.

The doctor went away, and Elizaveta Ivanovna rang up Vera Petrovna on the telephone, and said she wanted to speak to her seriously.

Miles stayed in bed all that day; he felt ill, and not much better the next day. The doctor came to see him again.

Elizaveta Ivanovna had a serious talk with Vera Petrovna, who was most penitent. She had no idea that Miles was delicate, and she promised not to do it again.

The next day Miles got up.

In the morning he was startled and delighted at receiving a note brought by a commissionaire from Elena Ilyin, saying she had arrived at Moscow, and asking him to come round and see her at the *Dresden*, where she was staying.

Miles found her there in the afternoon. The first thing she said to him was: "You look ill...worse; what have you been doing?"

Miles told her what he had been doing during the last month and the last days.

"You must leave Moscow at once, that is clear," she said. "Now I will tell you something. The Dashkovs' house in the country has been turned into a hospital. They have sold everything, except the *usadba*; that means just the house, the garden, the stables, and a few fields...not a real hospital, but a convalescent home for officers for the summer. There will not be many people there, but there is a doctor and nurses, and my brother has gone there. I had to come home to put my affairs in order. My brother was ill after Sha-ho, and was sent home. He needs a long rest and looking after. It is a nice house, in the middle of Russia, and in a quiet place; and there will be no disturbances there, as the peasants have got all the land they want: as much as they can swallow, and more than they can digest. I am going to look after my brother. I will arrange for you to come there too, if there is room. I am going to start to-morrow, I believe, and I will send you a telegram. Why not come there and rest for a month till you are well again? Then you can come back here, if you like."

Miles thought a moment and then said: "I should like to do that immensely."

"Have you learnt Russian?"

"I can read Pushkin." Miles blushed. "I like his poetry; I think he is wonderful."

"Let me hear you talk."

The talk went on for a while in Russian.

"Very good, very good indeed, and it will be still better; you will be able to talk at Susieki. That is the name of the place. You will love it; it is the place I like best in the world, and I have not been there for a long time. I am longing to see it again."

"How are all the people in Manchuria? How is Alyosha?"

"I have not seen Alyosha for weeks, not since Sha-ho. He went to Verkhneudinsk, and I believe he is still there."

"Will he come back?"

"I don't think he will."

There was a pause.

"And you?"

"When I have put my affairs in order, and if my brother gets well, I shall go back again, but not till then...the war is not nearly over."

"Here everybody is much more interested in politics than in the war."

"I suppose they are. That is one of the reasons I should like to go back to Manchuria."

"But don't you think things here are getting very interesting just now?"

"I find it, on the contrary, all very disgusting."

"But if all decent people refuse to have anything to do with politics, everything falls into the hands of people who are not decent. I believe the people here have begun to realise that; and that is why the Zemstvo people are doing such a lot of good."

"Possibly; I don't know... I know the Liberals are always right, but I do not like them."

"Perhaps you don't know them?"

"Know them?"

Elena laughed.

"I know them better than you do, my dear Mihal Ivanytch. I have known them all my life."

They talked on for about an hour, and it was settled that Elena should let Miles know by telegram directly she got to Susieki whether there would be room for him there or not.

"Tell me about your brother," said Miles; "what is he like? Shall I be able to get on with him?"

Elena thought for a moment.

"Yes," she said; " I think you will be able to get on with Valia. He is younger than I am. He likes balloons and poetry. He is very comfortable. And now I must leave you. I have a visit to make."

Miles took leave.

CHAPTER XXVI

Two days later Miles received a telegram from Elena, telling him that a room would be ready for him in a fortnight's time.

He started for Susieki at the beginning of May. The doctor thought the idea an excellent one. Elizaveta Ivanovna approved also, although she was sorry to lose Miles.

Susieki was in the Government of K——, a night's journey from Moscow. Miles started in the evening, and arrived at a junction at three o'clock in the morning, where he had to change, and wait several hours for a local train. It was still dark when he got out of the train, and he watched the dawn from the platform of the station. He remembered Alyosha's telling him that he would see this some day. The sky was covered with a grey cloud, as with a curtain, and all at once it lifted, and underneath it there was a great gulf of lemon-coloured light, the essence of dawn. The grey curtain broke up at the base into strips, which gradually grew soft and pearly, and the thinner fleeces turned pink. The barns, the ricks – huge brown shapes – gradually grew distinct, and loomed large, just as Alyosha had described them; presently the cloud lifted still higher, over a space of dazzling azure, and the sun rose.

The station was full of peasants, soldiers, and public servants. Miles sat in the waiting-room and drank tea. He still had four hours to wait. He inspected the bookstall. The fare

283

was uninviting: translations of Herbert Spencer and John Morley; some Russian magazines... Finally he bought *Three Men in a Boat*, by Jerome K Jerome, in Russian. About eight o'clock the local train arrived, and Miles got into it. It crawled along, stopping a long time at two stations. He arrived at half-past eleven.

Elena met him at the station in a small one-horse carriage, driven by a coachman in a loose red shirt.

They drove through the village – a small, straggly conglomeration of straw-thatched, log-built houses, with gaps here and there caused by recent fires. It was a soft spring day, but the trees were not yet green. Presently they reached some palings and a gate, beyond which were trees. They drove through the gate along a carriage-drive, up a hill, and passed a garden full of flowerbeds, which were gay with wallflowers and primulas. They drove past the garden front of a house, and a verandah which faced the flowerbeds. The house was made of wood. It had been built at the beginning of the nineteenth century. It was a dull light red – burnt sienna – in colour, with a roof of sheet iron painted grey. There was a central classical block, surmounted by a pediment, two wings with two windows in each wing. The centre of the house curved outwards and formed a verandah from which a flight of stone steps, fringed with flowers and creepers, led to the garden. Three large windows opened on to the verandah. Its wooden pilasters supported a balcony behind whose low wooden balustrade a window inserted in a segment of wood, painted sea-blue, led to a bedroom. Over this window a strip of sea-blue wood formed an arch.

The house was given up to the patients – four officers, besides Elena's brother, and Miles, a doctor and a nurse. Downstairs, on the ground floor, there was a library, a small billiard room, with a bagatelle board in it, a large sitting-room looking on the garden, and a dining-room. All the officers were well enough to get up during some part of the day, except

Elena's brother, who kept to his room. Miles was not introduced to him till later.

They had luncheon soon after Miles arrived. He was introduced to the officers, who were mostly from line regiments. One was a Cossack, one a gunner; two were riflemen, from the Eastern Siberian Corps. The doctor was out. They were all of them friendly to Miles, who got on with them easily. They were just like the people he had met in Manchuria.

After luncheon, Elena showed Miles the house and the garden. They were on high ground, at the edge of a wood. The garden was full of lilac bushes, and surrounded by trees. The officers used to sit out in long straw chairs on the verandah, where there were rose trees in tubs and agapanthus in pots.

"Would you like to go for a little walk through the woods," Elena asked Miles, "or are you too tired?"

"I should like a walk," said Miles; "I am not at all tired."

They started presently. Elena gave Miles a short biography of each of the officers.

"There is nobody very interesting," she said, "but they are all of them nice, and *comme il faut*. The doctor, Arsenev, is interesting; he came here first, because he is too ill to be at the Front any more. He was wounded, but he is well enough now to look after the others. You will see him later – he had to go to the town."

"I think it's a lovely place," said Miles.

"It isn't exactly lovely, but it has charm; and it will be lovely in a very short time, *for* a short time, when the trees come out; they will be out in a fortnight."

"You used to come here very often?"

"Every summer, at one time. Sandra Dashkov and I were almost the same age, and inseparable. I used to call Pyotr Ilyitch Uncle Pierre. But I haven't been here for a long time."

"Do you think the Dashkovs will never come back?"

"Who knows? He is getting old, and he likes the south; in the summer they go to Switzerland or to Berchtesgaden. It is better for him, and the journey to Russia fatigues him; and now that he has sold most of the land, there is no point in his being here."

"But aren't they fond of the place?"

"Oh yes, very; but there it is...the lilies of the valley are not yet out," she said. "This wood will be full of them...but look at the ferns, the little ferns uncrumpling; they are called *paporotniki*." They walked along a thick glade, and presently through the birch trees they caught sight of a small river.

"In the flood time," said Elena, " that river floods all those fields beyond...it all looks like a big silver sea. Would you like to go down to the river? there is a path here."

They followed the path through the bushes down to the river's edge, and followed its winding course. Presently they came to a mill. Its wheel was working and grumbling. The river divided here; on one side of it there was a weir.

"Does Alyosha's sister always live with the Dashkovs?" Miles asked presently.

"Nearly all the year round; sometimes she stays in the country at her Aunt Kitty's in the south, near Kiev; the Dashkovs are very fond of Mary."

"She is younger than Alyosha?"

"Oh, much."

"And pretty, don't you think?"

"Yes. Many people have wanted to marry her, but she will never make up her mind. She was engaged once to a Count Oesterwald. It was broken off...and now I think she is fancy-free, and she – " She stopped, then she went on: "My brother is fond of her. He wanted to marry her before the war, but it was thought unwise; he was delicate and had bad lungs, and he is younger than she is – only twenty-two – and just beginning everything...and then there were other reasons."

"What does he do?"

"Well, before the war broke out, he had just finished being a student, and had done his military service, and was going to

America to learn to be a civil engineer – he is clever about such things...then he volunteered...he was wounded and got ill...and his lungs are bad now; the doctor says he ought to go to Yalta, or to Switzerland. He will not go; he is obstinate – you will see."

"But is he getting better?"

"He is better than he was...but one can't tell... It was madness to go to the war, but he insisted; he is capable, and knows all about balloons; his dream is to invent a flying machine. He is always drawing plans."

"I'm afraid I shall be out of my depth with him. I know nothing about mathematics, and all that sort of thing."

"He does not only like that; indeed you might know him for years and not know that he cared for mathematical things. I know nothing about them either... He is fond of books; he has published a small volume of poems anonymously. He is fond of poetry, especially English poetry."

"He speaks English, then?"

"Oh yes, better than I do; and French and German. You shall see him when we get back. He was not so well today; generally he comes down to luncheon. He is so pleased that you have come; but you must not talk English to him, or you will forget your Russian; we must not talk English any more either. I think it is time to turn back. I must not be out too long. I have things to do."

They turned back and walked along the river bank, past the mill. They walked up the path through the undergrowth of the wood, and so back into the garden.

"Before we go in, I want to show you this," said Elena. She led Miles along a path down to a wide pond surrounded by tall lime trees, with a seat under the largest tree.

"Isn't this a pretty place?" she said. "In the summer we used to sit out here in the evening; you can hear the people singing in the village. There is a road on the other side of the pond beyond the trees... I think it is so well framed, and such a dreamy place. I used to think *nixen* – pixies – lived here, when I was a child."

"It's enchanting," said Miles.

"Now we must go in. Sit wherever you like; take any books you like from the library. If you are bored with the people, go to your room. If Valia is well enough, he will come down to tea; if not, I will take you up to him."

They went back to the house, and Elena left him.

Two of the officers were sitting on the verandah reading magazines; the two others were playing bagatelle.

Miles strolled into the library and looked at the books. They were most of them old books in calf bindings or faded marbled paper. There was a first edition of Pope's *Iliad*, in large folios, bound in calf; early editions of Byron, and the first collected edition of Goethe's works; several small volumes, printed between 1789 and 1793, with delicate coloured engravings; there were early editions of Pushkin and Gogol, and the complete works of Voltaire, besides other French classics.

There was some pretty mahogany furniture in the room, and one or two family portraits: a portrait of Uncle Pierre's mother by Winterhalter, and a picture of his father in uniform, of the time of the Emperor Alexander I.

At tea-time Elena came down again and said: "We will have tea indoors; Valia is not coming down, but I will take you up to him when we have finished tea."

They had tea in the dining room; Arsenev, the doctor, came back for tea. Miles was introduced to him. He had a black beard and bushy eyebrows, and a sympathetic expression. They all talked of the war; and when they had finished tea, Elena asked the doctor whether Miles might see Valia.

"Yes, but he mustn't stay too long; and when you have finished I should like to have a talk with Mihal Ivanytch myself."

Elena took Miles upstairs to Valia's bedroom on the first floor. He was lying in bed, in a blue dressing gown. Next to his bed was a chair with a pile of books on it – French and German technical works. He had a small square head, short black hair, and large black eyes, which seemed larger now owing to the pallor of his face.

He leant forward and smiled, and held out a thin hand to Miles.

"I am glad you are come here, Mihal Ivanytch," he said in English. "I believe I ought only to talk Russian to you."

"Oh, let us talk English today," said Miles.

"Tomorrow I shall be downstairs. Today they would not let me get up; it was a shame and nonsensical, as I really feel very well, and I wanted to get up to greet you." The effort of talking made him cough.

Elena made a sign to Miles.

"Mihal Ivanytch will come back later," she said, and went.

"Yes, later," said Miles. "Goodbye for the present," and he left him. Downstairs he met the doctor.

"Vladimir Nikolayevitch is coughing, I suppose," the doctor said. "Now I should like to talk to you, Mihal Ivanytch," and he took Miles to his room and examined him and asked him questions. Miles was ordered to take things easy for the moment. He was given some medicine.

"You must be careful not to excite Vladimir Nikolayevitch," he said. "He is much worse than he thinks."

A period of leisure began for Miles. He gave the Russian officers English lessons, which was good for his Russian; he read; he sat in the garden; he talked to Elena, but he did not see much of her, as her time was fully occupied.

Two or three days later, Valia came down and sat in the library. He had a long talk with Miles, and asked him to tell him the story of his life. Miles found Valia knew about English things, although he had never been to England; he seemed to understand the wine business. He had read English books too, more books than Miles would ever hope to read.

He talked much of the future, of what he meant to do when the war was over, of his journey to America. His parents were dead. He had inherited a small property which he had sold. He had been left well enough off to be able to follow his own bent. He took a passionate interest in all sorts of things; and what interested him most was the problem of flight. He was convinced that the solution of the problem was at hand, but his ambitions soared higher and further than to a flying machine. He was already dreaming of a man who could fly: the Lilienthal idea…he astounded Miles by the many-sidedness of his interests and his ambitions.

"I don't know if it's any use being ambitious here *now*," he said; "we are living in a crumbling old world that is going to pieces… I mean the rubbish on the top. We are casting the skin like a snake; but it will take years before the skin is cast, and the new skin underneath is not ready… Then Russia may be an interesting country to live in…who knows? I shall not live to see it."

"You will live to see more than I shall," said Miles.

Valia smiled.

"Who knows?" He said nothing for a moment or two, and then suddenly: "You saw Alyosha Kouragine at the war, and you met his sister with the Dashkovs at Paris?"

"Oh yes," said Miles. "They were so kind to me."

"They are nice people," said Valia. "Alyosha has gone back to Verkhneudinsk. Elena tells me you were kind to him."

"He was kind to me. I don't know how I should have got on without him."

"You did not know Russian when you started?"

"Not a word,"

"You were right to go… One must do that kind of foolish thing when one is young. They all told me it was foolish of me to go to the war; but I would not have missed it for anything;…it shows one life in a way nothing else can… It makes all other work more interesting afterwards. I would never have got over it, if I had not gone. And now you will go back to England?"

Miles blushed.

"Not just yet."

"Well, there is no hurry. You must stay here till you get well."

This was the first of many conversations. Miles thought that Valia was like his sister in some ways; but whereas she seemed to be looking on at life, or looking back at it, he seemed to be looking forward: to live in the future; to be thirsting for all kinds of knowledge. In talking to him Miles felt as if he were talking to someone older, and not far younger, than himself.

Miles was happier than he had ever been in his life; and happiest in the presence of Elena. He did not often see her alone, after their first walk. She was busy, and impartial in her attentions to the patients... She helped to manage the house... She saw many people... But to live in the same house, and to see her at meals, was enough for Miles.

He thought her more delightful every day. He watched her with the doctor, with her brother, with the officers, the neighbours: the schoolmaster and his wife; the Dashkovs' steward – a fat Pole – and his wife; with the servants and the peasants... She was always right.

"I will propose to her one day before I leave," he said to himself. Then another voice within him would answer, "She will never marry you." And the first voice said, "Why not?" "You are too stupid and ordinary for her." "That is true, but women often do marry people more stupid than themselves." "Yes," said the other voice, "because they happen to love that particular stupid person, but have you any grounds for thinking she loves you?" "No; but why should I not try?" "You can try, but do nothing foolish or rash," said the other voice. "Do not rush things, or you may spoil everything."

The days went by: it grew warmer and warmer. Suddenly one morning Miles noticed that the birch trees were green, a bright green, such as he had never seen before nor dreamt of – so bright that the colour hit the eye and almost hurt you...

"The spring has come in a night," he said to himself.

He met Elena that morning on the verandah. She was sitting with Valia.

"The spring has come," said Miles.

"Yes, and it will not last long," said Elena sadly; "only a fortnight. It makes me feel so lazy; I ought not to be here doing nothing."

The lilies of the valley were out in the garden; nightingales were singing loudly in the bushes. Miles had never heard a nightingale; he asked what they were; Elena and Valia laughed.

"Nightingales," she said. "Fancy you never having heard one before! A long time ago we used to call a nightingale that sang in that bush 'Battistini.' "

"Who is Battistini?" asked Miles.

"A famous baritone," said Elena. "But with all the trills of a tenor. You've never heard him, have you, Valia? You must go for a walk in the woods this afternoon," she said to Miles. "You will see how lovely they are."

Miles remembered what Alyosha had told him about his courtship of Elena; he wondered whether she was thinking of it.

"I should like to see the spring in England," said Valia.

"It comes much slower," said Miles, "and it is often bitterly cold in March and April – at least, where I live. By this time it is nearly summer now at home."

"People say the autumn is the sad time of the year," said Elena, "but I do not think so. I think the spring is the saddest season... In the autumn I feel energetic; I like the nip in the air, and the first frosts; but these days make me feel foolish and melancholy and lazy; disinclined for duty."

"It is your duty to amuse us," said Valia. "We want to be amused; and as we are your patients, we have a right to be amused."

They were joined by some of the other patients. They all sat basking in the warmth, smoking cigarettes.

Every now and then someone would come and ask a question: Andrey, the coachman, to know whether the horses would be needed; Ivan, the cook, would propound some food problem.

Marusia, an old woman who had nursed the Dashkov children, and who wore a yellow kerchief round her head, came and announced that Mihal Ivanytch had not got one pair of socks that was fit to wear. They were all in holes, and too far gone to darn. He must have some new ones. He couldn't, of course, be expected to choose them himself; Elena Nikolayevna must buy him some next time she went to the town.

The doctor joined them. He, too, sat down and smoked; they sat on till the bell rang for luncheon. After luncheon they went back to the terrace, which was now in the shade. It was hot enough now to enjoy it. Presently the postman arrived; there were letters for Elena, Valia, and a letter to Miles, forwarded from Moscow. It was from Aunt Fanny. She told him the news. She was a good letter writer. She confined herself to facts.

"We are all very glad," she wrote, *"that you are getting on so well with your Russian. Saxby says it will be useful to you in business, and a good thing for the firm. We all think it is so clever of you to have learned such a difficult language so quickly. Last Sunday M. Mourieux called, and he said he always thought you had the gift of languages. We are going to Wheatham for Whitsuntide. I do hope you are taking care of yourself. All the news from Russia seems very bad, and they seem to be doing* dreadful *things everywhere, especially in the Black Sea. But I suppose you will be safe at Moscow.*

"Do wrap up warm when you go out, and remember that May is the most treacherous month in the year, and the east

winds and cold nights so sudden – 'don't cast a clout' till we are well into June; perhaps you are well into June already! I know the dates out there are so different."

"I have had a letter from Alyosha," said Valia, and he handed it to his sister.

CHAPTER XXVII

As Elena had foretold, the spring was only too swift. A fortnight later, all the trees were green, and the wood was carpeted with lilies of the valley. It grew hotter and hotter. Every now and then there would be a thunderstorm.

The nightingales in the garden sang loudly day and night. Miles felt well, but he was overcome by lassitude. He felt as if he had been stranded on an island of lotus eaters; he was losing the sense of reality; life seemed too good to be true.

It was the presence of Elena that made him feel thus; he was living in a world of romance, and she was the centre of it; he was afraid of shattering the dream. He knew, although he would not have admitted it, that it was fragile. Alyosha had not been mentioned since the day Valia had said he had heard from him.

Valia was better. The warm weather suited him; almost every day he would come down and lie on the verandah.

One hot afternoon, when he was there alone with Miles, and the others were sleeping indoors, he said to Miles: "It must have been annoying for André Chénier to be guillotined, when he felt he had something there." He pointed to his forehead.

"Who was André Chénier?" asked Miles.

"A French poet who was guillotined in the Revolution. One of the best of the French poets. You will think I am mad, but I feel the same thing. I am afraid I shall be guillotined before I have time to tell the world what I have got here." He again pointed to his forehead.

"Do you think there will be a Revolution and a Reign of Terror?"

"Most certainly, some day; but I was not thinking of that. I meant guillotined by my illness. I meant that I shall die before I have time to do what I want to do."

"Alyosha has a theory that everybody does what he can do, however soon he dies," said Miles, "and that all the people who died young, like Byron, had finished their job."

"That is Goethe's idea," said Valia. "It is perhaps true. Perhaps all that I can do is to help others. One's work may act as a stepping stone, however incomplete."

He sighed. "Perhaps not even that – perhaps it is only a hindrance – an obstacle; but I had hoped – I still hope – it may be more. I fear I have come too soon – like Lilienthal."

"Who is Lilienthal?"

"The greatest aeronaut since Daedalus. I am sure the ancients knew how to fly. I am sure, if I live, I shall be able to fly. That's what I've got here." He pointed to his forehead. "Of course you will think me mad – inventors are always thought mad – and yet they do invent things."

"Have you ever been up in a balloon?"

"Of course; often."

"Is it dirigible balloons you are interested in?"

"No. Not machines lighter than air, nor really machines heavier than air – although I have been working at that problem. I am interested in flight – the principle. I want to invent a machine that will enable a man to fly, and alight on the ground, like a bird. I want to carry on Leonardo da Vinci's work."

"And do you think you will succeed?"

"I am sure I shall succeed, if I live. Probably someone is doing the same thing – perhaps at the other end of the world –

at this very moment. It often happens that people invent the same thing at the same time. Ideas are in the air, like microbes; they are infectious. I do not think that flying will be a benefit to mankind; but *tant pis*, flying will no more be a benefit to mankind than printing or the automobile."

"But surely," said Miles, "the printing press has been a benefit? Think of the thousands of people who are able to read now."

"I find that a pity. Before they could read, they spoke a beautiful pure language, as our peasants do; they knew by heart epics like the *Iliad*, and sagas; now they talk jargon, and read bad novelettes. Do you think it is an improvement? I am not talking paradox. I am speaking the truth when I say that the printing press, and especially the newspapers, have brought nothing but enormous misery to the world. Look at the newspapers, at all the harm they do. Every modern thinker in the world has recognised this. Read Balzac, and see what he says about it. Take the opinion of any journalist – you must have met journalists in Manchuria; surely they said the same?"

"Yes," said Miles; "I met two French journalists, Berton and Maurel; they certainly said the same thing. They thought the press was entirely harmful; at the same time, Maurel said he was its willing slave; that he wouldn't be free even if he could."

"Maurel – Maurel. I know about him; he has been an aeronaut too, and has written in the *Geographical Review*."

"Yes, he is fond of travel and big game shooting."

"Well," went on Valia, "I think that flying will probably be the most annoying of all inventions.

"Do you know that there was a Russian, long before Lilienthal's day – in the fifteenth century – who flew from the top of a church; he did modern gliding experiments. The Tsar *Ivan Grozni* – the man you call Ivan the Terrible – had his head cut off. Ivan the Terrible was right. Flying will be a curse. But one can't help that; man must invent, just as plants must grow. There is this consolation: man's inventions last a short time.

There comes an earthquake, a tidal wave, an invasion of the barbarians, and everything is swept away; he has to start all over again from the beginning. I am sure we should seem uncivilised to the Egyptians; just compare our buildings with the remains of theirs. As architects and engineers, they would look upon the Eiffel Tower and the skyscrapers as childish; and the inhabitants of Atlantis would probably think the Egyptians and all their works just as childish. And so the world goes on; but it does go on – that's the point, or the trouble. It doesn't stop; and we who are in it have to go on with it. We know it is all vanity, *vis-à-vis de l'éternité*; but this doesn't prevent us minding so terribly, and taking our toys seriously."

"Do you believe in another life?" asked Miles.

"Of course I do," said Valia, "but that doesn't prevent this life seeming too short, because, with our present apparatus of senses, we only see *this life*."

"I can't imagine," said Miles, "wanting another life where everything would be perfect. Does anybody want such a thing? For instance, take a man like Alyosha. I like him as he is, with all his faults, and because he is so human; but I can't imagine an Alyosha with wings or without faults – can you? At any rate, I shouldn't care for him. I want Alyosha as he is, here."

"One can't judge the things of another world in terms of this world," said Valia. "It is just as if someone were to say, 'I don't want to taste a peach. I am quite happy with an apple; I don't want a celestial apple'; or as if one said, 'I have no wish to hear the music of Bach or Chopin; I am quite satisfied with the tom-tom; I don't want a transcendental tom-tom; I like it because it is a tom-tom.' Of course you do; that is the point; but there may be something else you would like better that you have not yet heard or tasted."

"But then that something else would no longer be a tom-tom or Alyosha."

"Yes, it would. You may not know Alyosha really, now, at all; not the real Alyosha. What you like in him may be the hint of something you would like still better, if you knew it."

"But," said Miles, "that is just what I can't imagine."

"Of course you can't imagine it."

"But I can only like what I can imagine."

"I believe that you are being deceived; that this is an illusion. What you like in Alyosha, or in anyone else – what you call his faults – is really a *flavour*, which is different from that of anything else. You say, 'I like it because it is imperfect,' or 'because it is weak, human, foolish, or drunken, or false' – anything you like; but that is an illusion. It is not the fault you like; it is the essence or flavour behind the fault. You may like a mango with a slight taste of turpentine, but it is not the taste of turpentine you like, but the mango; the flavour of the *whole* mango, the mango *an sich*; now, in another world you might get the Alyosha flavour, or the mango flavour, to the n-th, so perfectly, that you will be satisfied, and yet know it *is* Alyosha, or the mango. And if you are fully satisfied, one can't go further."

"I don't understand that," said Miles, "and I'm not sure that I want to. I don't think I want another world; this one is difficult enough, as it is. I can imagine nothing better than going to sleep for ever when it is over."

"Very comfortable, no doubt; but there is nothing in the plan of the world, as far as we can guess at it, to make us think your wish is more probable than the opposite. The ancients thought otherwise, and they were wiser than we; and the Church says the truth is otherwise, and the Church is wiser than we are."

"But the Churches are obliged to think that, aren't they? and weren't the ancients very limited? They thought the sun went round the earth."

"Yes, they did, and I, for one, believe that, so far from their being backward in their geometry and cosmography, we are far behind them; and that in thirty years' time many mathematicians will say the same."

Miles looked at Valia with astonishment.

Valia laughed.

"You think I am mad, and the matter is too technical for me to go into; but please remember that I said this to you. After I am dead, in thirty years' time, there will be serious mathematicians, honoured by our universities, who will look upon all our system of mechanics, and on the Euclidean principle of geometry underlying it, as silly and out-of-date, and who will say that perhaps the Greeks were not only right but ahead of us in their cosmography."

"That the sun goes round the earth?"

"Certainly. I don't say they will all say it; but they will admit that those who do say it *may* be right, and that Dante's journey through Hell and Paradise is no more improbable than Captain Cook's, and as accurate as a railway guide."

"And do you really think that?"

"Yes; and please remember that I said so. Write it in your tablets; for I shall not be alive in thirty years' time."

"You have as much chance of being alive as I have; but, if we are both of us alive, I will remind you."

At that moment one of the officers, called Bakmanov, a good-natured man with a smiling face, came up to Miles and asked him if he would like to go on the river. He wanted to fish. Valia said that he was too tired. Miles consented, and they strolled through the woods down to the river, and found a boat.

"We may catch a perch," said Bakmanov.

"It's so hot, I should like to bathe," said Miles.

"I would advise you not to; I think it would do you harm."

"I can't help it; I must," said Miles.

On the banks of the river there were oak trees, ashes, and willows, and bushes of sweetbriar, which were now in flower. It was a stifling afternoon; there was a threat of thunder in the air. The sky was grey; the water as smooth as oil; it seemed as hard as glass, and there was no ripple except every now and then the splash of a rising fish.

Miles undressed and plunged into the river. The water, which was very deep, was as cold as ice. Bakmanov sat on the bank, smoking; he made no protest. He saw it was useless.

"It's delicious," said Miles, gasping; "you had much better bathe."

"No," said Bakmanov; "I swim badly, and I am frightened of being drowned."

Miles got out presently and dressed. He was shivering. Even when he was dressed, he still felt cold, in spite of the heat. They got into a boat, and drifted down towards the mill, past islands of rushes, and a tangle of water lilies. Near the mill, the river broadened. Thunder began to mutter; a rainbow glimmered in the grey; everything was still, except for the laughter of some children who were bathing in the distance. Bakmanov went on fishing in silence; he caught nothing.

"It would be nice to go on living like this," he said presently, "but everything which is good has an end."

"You are not staying on?" asked Miles.

"No, I am well again. At the end of the month I go back to my regiment, back to all that discomfort and those unpleasantnesses, and to that disgusting country; in all probability I shall be killed, or worse, wounded. It is a silly war, all about nothing; but after all, it is not worse than peace. In peace time our regiment was at Chita; it was so boring, so monotonous. I hate military life; but what else can one do? Nothing! It is perhaps best to be killed, yet I do not exactly want to die."

"How do you think Valia is?" Miles asked.

"Very ill, I think; he has been better lately, of course; but that is only relative, and makes no difference. I do not think he will ever get well, and I do not think he will live more than three months, if as much as that."

"Really?"

"Yes; he will certainly not live through another winter. He ought to go away, but he does not want to; and perhaps he may be right, for it is probably too late now. He ought to have gone long ago to the south, and never to the Far East. It is a pity, for he is a nice man."

"Yes," said Miles, "and wonderfully clever, isn't he?"

"Oh! his ideas? They are all rather mad, but he has written some good poems."

"Do you think all his ideas about flying and mathematics are mad?"

"Quite. That is only part of his illness. He is a poet, you see; most good poets are a little mad."

"But he seems to me practical and sensible."

"Yes, he is – apart from his *idée fixe*."

They rowed back to the place from where they had started. It had become hotter and more sultry. A kingfisher skimmed low, from the foot of a willow tree across to the other side of the river, and disappeared into the bushes.

Miles felt as if he had seen all this before. He then remembered that Alyosha had described to him just such an evening on the river, in the train, on their way to Kharbin.

"I think there is going to be a thunderstorm," said Bakmanov; "we must go home."

"I feel rather cold," said Miles.

"That means you have caught a chill, because it is very hot."

They walked fast and in silence back to the house; just as they got indoors the rain came down in torrents; sheets of clear, clean, cool, straight tropical rain. It was a great relief.

Miles watched it from the library.

The storm lasted about an hour, and then, as if by magic, the clouds rolled away in a moment. The leaves of the lilac bushes rioted in the moisture. The world was washed clean; the sky was soft and pink as the petal of a rose; nightingales began to sing with all their might.

Everybody was relieved, but Miles still felt hot and cold alternately.

It was a beautiful evening – a June evening; the roses were all out on the stone terrace; the syringa and the guelder roses were in flower.

After dinner, Miles and Elena sat on the verandah. Valia and the others were in the sitting room, playing *vindt*; Miles could see them through the window. The lamps were lit indoors; moths fluttered round them.

Miles had not seen Elena alone for some days; that morning he had made up his mind to speak. He now thought the setting was appropriate. The air was still and warm; the moon had not yet risen, but there was a faint halo rising from beneath the trees, the presage of moonrise. The frogs were croaking in the pond; every now and then a dog barked. The nightwatchman was shaking his rattle. Someone beyond the palings was singing, an interminable drunken song, which had only four bars, repeated over and over again:

Someone, somewhere, was playing an accordion, and there was a stamping of feet.

"Did you see that?" asked Miles.

"What?" said Elena.

"The falling star."

"Was it a falling star?"

"Yes," said Miles.

"They say it is lucky," she said.

There was a pause.

303

"Bakmanov," Miles said presently, "says he is going away at the end of the month. That's soon, in about a week. I suppose I shall have to go soon too."

"You will go as soon as the doctor allows you to, not before."

"But I am quite well; at least, I feel quite well. This morning the thundery weather made me feel uncomfortable. Thunder always gives me a headache; but as soon as the storm was over, I felt better."

"It was not the thunderstorm," said Elena, "it is because you bathed that you feel ill. It was foolish of you, Mihal Ivanytch."

"I couldn't help it; I suppose it was foolish. I felt I might not have another chance."

His own words echoed in his heart. "I felt I might not have another chance." That was surely the truth.

This was the moment. He must speak; now or never. He was slightly feverish; he had caught, although he did not yet know it, a touch of malaria. The fever gave him the wish to be bold. He felt he could speak now, if ever.

"I am going to speak," he said to himself, "now; the moment has come."

At that moment a nightingale began to sing.

"That is Battistini," said Elena softly.

And these words, and the way they were spoken, brought back to Miles Alyosha's story; how he had proposed to Elena years ago, in this very place, in just such a setting.

There she was, dressed in white, now as then; could she have been more beautiful then? Could she have been as beautiful? Miles, too, could see her eyes shining in the darkness, The moon was not up, there were no stars; or, if there were any, they were so faint you could not see them, except when they fell; the nightingale was singing now as then... How could he speak? And yet, was it not foolish not to speak? All that had happened long ago; it was forgotten. But was it forgotten?

There was a long silence. The bleating tune of four bars went on, and in answer to it the nightingale sang.

"That's Ivan's father singing," said Elena. "He is drunk." Ivan was a boy who worked in the stables.

Miles felt the opportunity was lost. "But never mind," he thought, "I will choose a better moment; this is too romantic. Perhaps I had better write it – I must be matter-of-fact, practical, sensible. There must be no nightingale."

"I heard from Alyosha today," said Elena.

"Really? How is he?"

"He is well. He has left Verkhneudinsk, and he is back at the Front, at Headquarters."

The mention of Alyosha's name made it impossible for Miles to speak; he acknowledged the impossibility. "I shall never do it," he thought; "the only way will be to write when I have gone; and the sooner I go the better; it is useless to stay here. I am quite well." As he said this to himself, he shivered.

"Are you feeling cold?" asked Elena.

"Yes, I do feel a little cold."

"Then we must go in at once; you ought not to have come out at all. Come."

She got up, and walked into the sitting room.

"How sultry it is again!" the others said, as Miles and Elena walked into the room.

"Mihal Ivanytch isn't feeling well," said Elena to the doctor. "He bathed this afternoon, and I think he must have caught a cold."

The doctor got up from the card table.

"I will be back in a minute. Come with me, Mihal Ivanytch," he said to Miles, and he led him upstairs. They went up to Miles' room; the doctor took his temperature.

"You must go to bed at once; I will send you up a small dose presently; you are not to get up tomorrow before I have seen you."

After the doctor had sent his *feldsher* for the medicine, he went back to the others.

"Well?" asked Elena.

"He has got a touch of malaria," said the doctor. "Foolish boy, to bathe in the river! It may be a long time before he gets rid of it. I am giving him some tincture of sunflower. He may throw it off."

Miles did not throw it off. The fever recurred during the next days at regular intervals, when, after a period of shivering, his temperature would rise. He said Miles had better not go to Moscow, because he needed looking after, and he could not get such good attention at the Bloums' as at Susieki. Miles consented to stay. He felt it was more difficult than ever to say anything to Elena. At the end of the month, Bakmanov went back to the Front to rejoin his regiment. Everything else went on as usual. Valia seemed fairly well. He liked talking to Miles, and found his society restful; but his cough was still bad. A few days later Miles and Valia were sitting downstairs in the library after luncheon. They were alone.

Valia mentioned Alyosha.

"Elena Nikolayevna," said Miles, "told me she had heard from him last week."

"Yes," said Valia; "so did I. He says he is going to be separated from his wife."

Miles felt that this piece of news was ominous.

"Will they be divorced?" he asked.

"Oh no; but I am afraid he may leave her when the war is over."

"Do you know her?"

"No, I have never seen her; but I am told she is very nice – an excellent, practical woman, and very fond of him."

"Do you think – "

"It was she?" said Valia, finishing the question for Miles. "No, I know it was not. It is Alyosha. He wants to marry someone else."

"Yes; he said something to me about that before I left Mukden," said Miles.

"Did he tell you who it was?"

"No; he said it was someone I didn't know. I was afraid it might be that woman who lived at Kharbin."

"Marya Ivanovna?"

"Yes; you know her?"

"I only met her once, but I know all about her. No, it is not she; it might very well be; it would be, if she wished."

"I didn't understand her fascination," said Miles. "Perhaps it is because I didn't understand Russian when I saw her; but I couldn't see that she had any charm."

"No; but she has something else – *du chien*, as the French say. Poor Alyosha!"

"Poor Alyosha!" said Miles.

At that moment Varvara Dimitrievna came into the room and announced the arrival of visitors. She said that Valia must at once go upstairs so as not to be caught by them. Elena Nikolayevna was with them, and she had sent the nurse to get Valia away; the doctor said it was bad for him to see many people at a time. Valia was led away upstairs. Presently who should walk into the room, led by Elena, but Vera Petrovna, and with her the Bloums' niece; Losov, the merchant, whom Miles had dined with at Moscow, Bielov the composer, and Nadezda Mandel the actress. They had come from the town of O—, where Bielov and the others were to stay the night. Bielov was giving a concert there. Vera Petrovna greeted Miles warmly.

"We arrived at O— this morning," she said, "by the night train from Moscow, and we had nothing to do all day. And then I remembered Susieki. You must be very happy here in this beautiful, this enchanting house. Isn't it picturesque? Isn't it original? We have been telling Alexander Feodorovitch " – that was the merchant – " that he must have a look at it."

307

They all went round every room slowly, and saw everything in detail, going into ecstasies over every picture, each bookcase, each table, each chair; the books, the pianoforte, the harp, the bagatelle board, the astronomical globes, the albums, and the ivory cup and ball on the table. They then went into the garden and made a thorough inspection of it, and walked to the pond. Miles followed them. They were enthusiastic about the garden, and especially about the terrace and the pond.

They had tea on the verandah.

"It's so perfect in style," said Vera Petrovna. "And just the right kind of flowers – those sweet forget-me-nots, those lovely lilies of the valley!"

"I should like to act here," said Nadezda. "If Alexander Feodorovitch buys it, we will get up a performance of *The Cherry Orchard* here. It is really old-fashioned, really old-world."

The Bloums' niece uttered a deep sigh, looked tragic, and said nothing.

"And is it really true it's for sale?" asked Vera Petrovna. "And do they really only want sixty thousand roubles for it? Why, it is nothing! A mere song! Alexander Feodorovitch will be mad if he doesn't buy it at once – mad, won't he?"

"But I have already got one *datcha* (a wooden villa in the suburbs) at Tsaritsino," the merchant said, "and in these troubled times – "

"Oh, all that will pass," said Vera Petrovna; "one must never let such an opportunity slip. It won't come again. It would be a crime to miss it. Good gracious!" she said, looking at her watch, "it's five o'clock! We shall be late! We have got to drive fifteen versts! We must go at once!"

They said goodbye and rushed off, still ejaculating enthusiastic and extravagant adjectives until they reached the front door, where their two carriages were awaiting them.

CHAPTER XXVIII

The next weeks passed swiftly for Miles; one day he realised that what he would have called in England "the summer" was nearly done. The corn was ripening. On one side of the house, to the east, there were plains of corn, stretching out into the distance; sometimes he would drive through this undulating sea with Kabylski, an officer who was still at Susieki. He was a fair-haired boy from Transbaikalia. He had been wounded at Liao-yang, and complications had followed; his leg had had to be cut off. For a time he had been seriously ill, now he was convalescent. There was no question of his going back to the Front. He was a simple, matter-of-fact man, fond of music, and a competent player on the *balalaika*.

Miles had not spoken to Elena; he had now settled not to until he left Susieki for good. "Then," he said to himself, "I will write; I shall be able to explain everything better in a letter."

Life went on in the same way. Miles, under the doctor's treatment – injections of arsenic every day for twelve days, to be repeated after a certain interval – felt much better. The doctor took his temperature twice a day; he was not allowed to go out in the evenings. Every day he spent a few moments with Valia, who seemed better, but had become more silent, and was more easily tired. He had fits of coughing at intervals, and restless nights.

Miles took lessons in the morning in Russian from the local schoolmaster; he read Russian books, and gave English lessons to Kabylski.

One afternoon, at the beginning of July, Miles was sitting by himself in the cool library after luncheon. Kabylski was asleep in his room. Elena and the doctor had gone to spend the day in the town of O—.

Miles was reading a book by Gogol, in Russian; every now and then he dozed; through the yellow blind in the open window came the sounds of summer. The nightingales had been silent for some time; the bees made music instead of them.

Lieskov, the doctor's *feldsher* (orderly), a man who looked like a good-natured stiff sergeant, came into the room and announced that Vladimir Nikolayevitch wished to speak to his honour. Miles followed him upstairs.

He found Valia lying propped up against pillows. The nurse was in the room. She met Miles at the door and said: "Vladimir Nikolayevitch wants to see you; go away," she added in a whisper, "if you see he is tired."

Miles nodded.

"Sit down," said Valia. He looked round the room. "Yes, that is right," he said, when he saw she had gone; "I want to speak to you alone. Do you want a cigarette? Listen to me, Mihal Ivanytch; this is perhaps the last opportunity I shall have of a real talk with you, so I want you to stay till I tell you to go. I know quite well that Varvara Dimitrievna told you you were not to stay long; but this time you must obey me and not her. I will tell you when I am tired – when I have finished. It would tire me more not to speak to you than to speak to you now. I have chosen this day because the others are away. Arsenev gets on my nerves. He thinks I don't understand. All doctors are like that; they think one is taken in. He tells me I am better and I tell him I am better, and he thinks I believe it. He thinks – I have heard him say so when he thought I was asleep, but I knew it without that – that people with my disease never know when they are dying. It may be true in some cases. Not in mine. I know I am dying – don't interrupt, please – I know I am dying quite soon. I minded at first – now I am minding less. Now I have some things to say; it will not take long.

"In the first place, tell me what are *you* going to do?"

"The doctor says," said Miles, "that I must finish my course of arsenic injections – then I can do what I like. I have had one whole course and nearly all the second. After a week I shall have the third. That will take me to the end of the month. Then I shall go back to Moscow or perhaps home, I'm not quite sure."

"You won't go back to Manchuria?"

"Well, that is just what I *do* want to do; just what I was thinking of doing. I shall have to go on my own – I mean pay my own expenses – but I don't mind that; I shall still nominally be correspondent for *Skreibners'*, and send them pictures if I want to. I have got all the necessary papers. I got them before I left."

"I thought you would go back; I shall be glad if you do, because I have got a commission I want you to do for me."

"Of course I would do anything. What is it?"

"I will tell you presently. But before I tell you, I have got something else to say. I want you to do two things for me. I want you to send off this telegram for me. Don't give it to Andrey, or to Elena, or to anybody here. I want you to go to the village and send it off yourself. It is to Petersburg. Here is the money."

He handed Miles a sheet of paper on which some words were written in pencil, and a paper note.

"You can give that piece of paper as it is; they will stick it on a form at the office. Send it off today, if possible. That is the first thing. The second thing is this: I want you to burn all this."

He took from a small hand portmanteau he had on the table next to him a copybook full of MSS notes, and a roll of diagrams on tracing paper.

"That," he said, "is my life's work. I want you to burn it."

"Burn it?" said Miles, dismayed.

"Yes, burn it. For this reason; it is either nonsense or it isn't. If it is nonsense, it doesn't matter. If it is not nonsense – and I don't think it is – it will be of no use to anyone. I haven't got far enough, and the others who are doing the same thing will have found, or will find, all I have found without difficulty. I have just stopped short of the crucial difficulty. I am not strong enough to deal with that, and I never shall be; but I don't want people, when I am dead, to say either that I was mad or that I was one of those unfortunate, misunderstood geniuses that came too soon. It would make Elena and others unhappy. That is why I want you to burn it. You can wait till I am dead if you like, if you are still here when I am dead. I think you will be; if not, you must burn it before you go. No, on second thoughts I would rather you burnt it this afternoon, so that you can tell me it has been done. Will you promise?"

"If you really want me to, yes, I will; but don't you think it is rather a pity?"

"My dear Mihal Ivanytch, Virgil wanted his friends to burn the *Aeneid* when he was dying, and he was right; but they didn't...they played him false."

"I don't agree at all."

"But if I think like that – and if I ask you to do this as a favour, will you refuse me? If so, I must get someone else."

"I will do it if you wish."

"Today – word of honour?"

"Yes; word of honour."

"Well, here it is. I will tell you what it is. It is, for the most part, designs for a flying machine heavier than air; but not on the system, not on the lines along which people are experimenting now, gliding...it is further than that. I have tried to find out the part the feathers play in the flight of the bird. What I am aiming at is a direct lift, but I won't go into that; it is too technical. I think I am probably thirty years ahead of my time, and everyone will waste time on side issues before they begin to attack the real problem – but it will come."

"But why not leave your work? – it may be useful to others."

"No, please not; it is my *Aeneid*; it is a question of *amour propre*. It may be silly, but I am like that. I ask you to do this for me as a friend. If Virgil had had a friend, the friend would have understood; a real friend would have burnt the *Aeneid*: but Virgil had no real friend. There are some verses, too, in that copybook; and they, too, are ahead of the time – in ideas – and they, too, are not good enough for – not finished."

"I will do whatever you like; but I do think it is a pity."

"Think me mad, if you like, mad with *amour propre*...you see, I am in love with my ideas... If you have ever been in love, perhaps you have been – "

Miles blushed scarlet.

"Of course you are – I had forgotten; you *are* in love. Well, you ought to understand. When one is in love, one cannot endure the second best; it must be the first best, or nothing. Do you understand?"

"I do understand what you mean."

"I thought you would. Now I want to tell you a few things about yourself." Valia was silent, and then, after a pause, he said: "You know Alyosha's story?"

"Yes, I know Alyosha's story," said Miles. "He told me."

"Well, the curious thing is this. I believe – I may be wrong – that Elena, who thought she could never marry – now almost thinks she could – almost thinks she will... There was, of course, every reason to prevent her. I don't mean the old story only. I mean *all* that has happened... And Elena is a sensible person, full of heart, and would not like to hurt a fly. Alyosha says that matters have come to a crisis: but is that true? And if it is true, does it make any difference? I think not; and I know Elena thinks not, but it may be *plus fort qu'elle*. I want you to go back, and if you see Alyosha, beg him if possible not to... It may be too late... It may be impossible. If they both say they

313

cannot help it, then let it be – one cannot prevent these things. They are fated... That's all about that... But I hope it will not happen, as they would both be unhappy. The only happiness for Alyosha is to remain in Siberia. He knows that. He could never really live anywhere else."

As Miles listened to these words, he knew that he was hearing what he had been expecting to hear some day, at some hour, for months – ever since Alyosha had spoken to him at Mukden, before that; ever since he had seen Elena's face when she met Alyosha at the hospital at Mukden...perhaps even before *that*... Ever since that moment Miles had been like a prisoner who is condemned to death, and knows that the jailer may come into his cell at any moment and say, "It is now."

But he had never for a moment admitted this to himself; he had put away the thought; ignored it; pretended it did not exist; said to himself he was mistaken; that he had imagined what was not; and now that it had happened – now that he knew it to be a fact – he was astonished at himself; astonished to find how calmly he took the final end of his romance, the destruction of his lovely castle in the air. Perhaps this destruction had been effected unconsciously, gradually, without his knowing it. Yet Valia's words changed the colour of the world for him in a moment.

He felt that everything had turned grey; the sunshine had gone from the world; yet he managed to look unconcerned, and to say in the most matter-of-fact voice, with hardly the hint of a strain in it, "Where would they live?"

"Heaven knows!...you see Elena hates towns...the only place she has ever loved in her life is this place. She loves it. It is the home of her soul, for it is the only place in her life where she has been happy."

"And I suppose she could never live here now?"

"They might buy the *usadba*, but I don't think Alyosha and Elena could do that; besides, what is the use of an *usadba* in Russia now?"

"Then you think there *is* going to be a revolution? that the revolution has begun? That is what I feel," said Miles.

"No, I do not think so; not now. It may be the beginning, but the *real* revolution won't happen now. You are thinking of other revolutions; you forget that Russia is a very big country, and that things take much longer to happen here than they do anywhere else."

"But," said Miles, "surely the old régime is at its last gasp; surely everyone is tired of the autocracy and the war; surely the whole system is rotten to the core. You said yourself to me that the top was crumbling."

"Revolutions," said Valia, "don't happen because things are rotting and crumbling. In a way the top has always been rotting and crumbling, and always will be, however many revolutions happen. But revolutions happen when the nation is full of sap, like young plants growing up and pushing the dead branches out of the way. That is what happened in France; but I don't think the sap is strong enough here, at this moment. The war may help to make it stronger; but this war is only an adventure after all; it would need a bigger war – a *real* war – to make a real revolution; an unsuccessful war, of course – to give it the kick-off; but besides that, there is something else necessary...the shock is not enough...you must have a state of things in the background to work on. A revolution will only come when the Government of the moment is too little appropriate to the actual needs of the nation...when it fits too badly...and not because there is or is not a tyrant, or a tyrannical Government...the tyrant, the despot, is always the *result* of a revolution...never the cause – I mean of a real revolution, not a Court revolution."

"That's just what my old tutor, M. Mourieux, used to say," said Miles; "but surely nothing could be more inappropriate to the nation than the present Government?"

"Do you think so? I am not sure. At present there is a time of trouble going on – a ferment; the pot a-boiling; one side will

come out on the top, either the Government or the Zemstvos –
the revolution if you will. I see no one on either side capable of
organising victory – no Danton, no Carnot – capable, that is to
say, of being a despot."

"But do you mean to say the only result of a revolution here
would be to have another despotism?"

"Of course. Russia will either be governed by despotism or
not at all: Despotism or Time of Trouble. That is the formula of
Russian history."

"You mean to say there never will be a time when there will
be a constitutional Government."

"I hope not, and I don't think so."

"In Manchuria, our doctor used to declare that if there was
no constitutional Government soon, he would rather be
a Turk."

"He is probably half a Turk already. You judge everything
from the English point of view. Talk to Arsenev, disagree with
him, ask him to accept the vote of a majority, and he won't.
He'll say it's not fair."

"But, Valia, a great many Russians disagree with you."

"Probably everyone, but I don't believe in the *intelligentsia*.
I think they are doomed. I don't know what will happen, but the
fight will ultimately be between the peasants and the towns,
and I back the peasants."

The nurse came into the room.

"Vladimir Nikolayevitch has talked enough," she said. "It is
time for him to rest."

Miles got up.

"Very well; one moment, Varvara Dimitrievna," said Valia.
"Come back in two minutes…

"…There is one thing more I want to say. I see you have
caught the infectious disease called Russia. You will probably
come back, so remember this. When there *is* a revolution, it
will mean the real thing – wholesale killing…"

316

"Then do you think Alyosha and Elena Nikolayevna could never live here?"

"Why not?"

"If there is a revolution?"

"But I have already told you I don't believe in it *now*. I was talking of the future."

"But you said just now, what is the use of an *usadba now*?"

"I meant life can never be the same as it used to be, but I was silly in a way. There is in a way just as much use in an *usadba* now as there ever was. There never was any real use in an *usadba*. It's pleasant while it's there, and that's enough."

"Then you don't think it would be mad to buy an *usadba* now?"

"Certainly not, if one wanted one."

"But agrarian disturbances?"

"That depends on the place; there won't be any here. The peasants have got everything they want. What I mean to say to you is this: if you are still in Russia in the days when a revolution comes – it may be years hence – don't think it will be all right for *you* just because you are a Liberal, and live with enlightened *intelligentsia*; they will be the first to be killed. Now you had better take these papers and go, and don't forget the telegram."

He shook hands with Miles and smiled.

"Come and see me tomorrow. Remember the papers. Today – you promised."

Miles left him and walked through the village to the railway station, where he sent off the telegram. He then went back to the house and strolled into the woods. He walked down to the river, and there he picked some briar roses. Then he walked back through the undergrowth to the top of the hill. He noticed a dragonfly gleaming in the sun. He followed it. It was hovering over a patch of marshy ground, a pool at the edge of which grew a few purple irises; he picked one of these. He then chose a patch of dry ground where there were some dry grass, and he made a small bonfire with Valia's papers. He threw the iris and the briar roses on to the flames.

"There goes Valia's *Aeneid*," he said, as he watched the papers slowly burning, but he felt it was more than Valia's *Aeneid* that he was destroying. He was burning his own, his first and only romance. He waited till the papers had been reduced to a heap of ashes. He was careful to leave nothing behind.

When he got back, he found Elena and the others at tea.

"Valia wants to see you for a moment, after tea," she said to him.

Miles had tea and went up again to see Valia.

"Have you done it?" asked Valia.

"Yes, I sent the telegram."

"And the papers?"

"I burnt them."

"All of them?"

"Yes, all of them – to the last scrap."

"Where? In the wood?"

"Yes, in the wood. I threw some flowers – some sweetbriar and a purple iris – on the funeral pile," said Miles, blushing.

"That is right, and quite Virgilian, as is proper, *manibus date lilia plenis*...quite right for a kind of Marcellus. Goodnight. I am too tired to talk any longer. Goodnight, goodbye, and thank you."

When Miles got downstairs, Elena said to him, "Valia is not looking well, is he?"

"I think he is rather tired," said Miles. "I hope I didn't stay too long."

They could hear him coughing through the open window. The next day he was worse; he saw nobody but the doctor and Elena. Miles asked Arsenev whether he was very ill.

"He is dying," said the doctor, "but he has no idea of it. He was talking this morning of spending Christmas at Yalta with

his sister. When people are dying of consumption, they never
know."

"It is consumption?"

"Oh yes, and there are complications. I don't think he would
have lived long anyhow. He had too weak a body for his
intellect."

"He is very clever, isn't he?"

"Capable, yes, full of capacity, but fantastic; too reactionary
for our times. He would never have done anything in the world.
He ought to have lived two centuries ago."

"Or perhaps," said Miles, thinking of what Valia had told him,
"two centuries after us."

Arsenev smiled, thinking that Miles, contrary to his custom,
had ventured on a paradox.

"He is good-hearted, a very good-hearted man – but as for
his brain – " The doctor touched his forehead.

The next day Valia rallied a little.

Elena received a telegram in the evening, and when she had
read it she said to Miles: "Alyosha's sister is coming here on her
way to Kiev, where she is going to stay with her Aunt Kitty. I am
glad. It will do Valia good."

"When is she arriving?" asked Miles.

"Tomorrow morning, for luncheon."

Mary Kouragine arrived the next day by the same train Miles
had come by from Moscow.

Valia, they said, was a shade better, but still very ill. He saw
her in the afternoon, but she was not allowed to stay more than
a moment with him. She was delighted to see Miles again. She
talked to him a great deal about Alyosha and Manchuria, and
said she was so glad the whole thing had been a success. She
had had no idea he was here. She would write and tell her Aunt
Lizzy at once. She left Susieki that evening for Moscow.

The next day Valia said he wished to receive the Sacraments.
He explained to Miles that it was not a case of the "Last"
Sacraments; that the orthodox often sent for the Holy Oils

when they were ill, so as to get well, just as the early Christians used to.

When the priests had gone, Elena said to Miles: "He knows he is dying all the same; he is much worse today."

"Arsenev," said Miles, "told me the other day that he had no idea how ill he is."

Elena smiled.

"I am glad he saw Mary," she said; "that made him happy."

Valia died between three and four o'clock the next morning. He was buried in the village two days later. Miles attended the funeral.

He had not seen Valia again after the evening he had burnt the papers.

CHAPTER XXIX

On the day of Valia's funeral Elena told Miles that she was going away; she had to spend a few days in St Petersburg, to see her husband's family and attend to some business matters. She was then going back to the Far East.

The peace negotiations were going on at Portsmouth.

"Do you think it is any use going back now?" asked Miles.

"I am going back, peace or no peace," said Elena. "I shall certainly stay in the Far East till the war is over."

Miles understood.

"But you must stay here," she went on, "till your treatment is over. Arsenev and Varvara Dimitrievna will be here, and the hospital will be open until the beginning of October."

"I have only got to have three more injections," said Miles. "When they are finished, I shall go to Moscow. I am quite well."

"And then?"

"Then I, too, shall go back to the Far East."

"Will that be worthwhile?"

"I want to say goodbye to my friends in the battery...and then, who knows? Perhaps there will be no peace...there may be another battle; the tide may turn; the situation may change... I should like to see the end."

"If you do come out, perhaps we shall meet."

"And I want to say goodbye to Alyosha."

"Yes," said Elena. "He will be glad to see you. He is at Headquarters. He did his last mission very well. He has now got something better."

"What was his last mission?"

"I don't know... Something to do with the Chinese. They are pleased with him, and he is pleased. I heard from him yesterday."

Until this moment Miles had not really made up his mind to go back to the Far East. He felt that he ought to do Valia's commission, and to deliver his message to Alyosha...otherwise he had no wish to go back. He would rather go to London, to Madeira, anywhere... And yet he knew that this was not quite true. He would find it difficult to go away. He wondered whether Elena knew that he knew. Had Valia said anything to her? She said nothing more, but left him with a smile.

As she was going out of the room, she stopped at the door and said: "I suppose it would be wiser for you to go home, Mihal Ivanytch? But if you do come out, I shall be very glad to see you again, and I am sure Alyosha will be glad too."

She said this so naturally that Miles was baffled. "However much she knows that I know, she does not care," he thought to himself.

"I shall be sorry to go," she said. " I have always loved this place more than any place in the world. It is the only place I have loved – I love it still better now – more than ever – because Valia spent his last days here and is buried here. It is dreadful to think I shall never see it again."

"But won't you see it again?"

"I don't think so. You see it is to be sold... The hospital must be shut on the 1st of October. The house would be too damp. Nobody could live there later. Then I think it will be shut up altogether. It will probably be bought by some rich Moscow merchant...and, like *The Cherry Orchard* – you know the play?"

"Yes; but why do the Dashkovs sell it?"

322

"Because they would never come back here in any case. Uncle Pierre must live in a warm place in winter, and they are used to being abroad now… However, everything must have an end, and this is the end of Susieki for me. I am glad you have liked it, too. I am sure you have liked it."

"Oh, I have loved it."

"One always has to begin again in life… It is no use thinking one can go on with the same thing, or have something over again; but we are all of us so childish – we can't help clinging to things."

"No, we can't," said Miles.

"Goodbye for the present," said Elena, and she went away laughing. But there was something poignantly sad about her gaiety.

The next day Miles received a letter from Alyosha, written from Headquarters. It was quite short. He said that he was well, that Miles' friends asked after him, and added at the end of the letter: "The affair I told you about is settled. My wife has consented, and we are to be separated." As he mentioned no names, Miles didn't feel he could talk about it to Elena, unless she spoke of it to him first. She said nothing. She left for Moscow that afternoon. Miles thought that she was looking happy, considering things.

The next day Miles felt desperately lonely. He felt the death of Valia more sharply than before; he had only one more day at Susieki. He might have left on the same day as Elena. It was not only to have his last inoculation that he stayed; it was to execute a plan that had been taking shape in his head ever since his last conversation with Valia.

The plan was this: to buy Susieki, and to give the *usadba* – that is to say, the house and what was left of the land – as a wedding present to Alyosha and Elena if they got married. If they would have none of it, he would keep it himself.

The day after Elena left, he called on the Dashkovs' steward and told him his wish. Karl Zygmundovitch, the steward, was not surprised. He thought that all Englishmen were more or less mad; that Miles was perhaps madder than most. He told him the price, 60,000 roubles (£6000), and the steps they both would have to take. Miles said he would telegraph to his banker for the necessary sum; he arranged to meet Karl Zygmundovitch in Moscow during the next week, and went through the preliminary formalities.

Miles felt he could well afford it; he telegraphed to his bank, asking them to sell securities, and to transfer the necessary sum to a Moscow banker whom he knew. The next day he started for Moscow and went to the hotel. The Bloums had left the city for a *datcha*, just outside the town. He spent the day with them there.

A few days later Miles received the money at the bank. He stayed on in Moscow until the necessary formalities of the sale were accomplished, and when he left for the Far East at the end of the first week in August, he was the owner of Susieki. He had bought it lock, stock, and barrel, with the exception of a few pictures and objects that Pyotr Ilyitch wanted to keep.

He felt strange as he started on this journey the second time; it was still stranger to him to be able to speak to the people – the guard, the porters, his fellow-passengers – and to be able to understand what they said to him.

The weather was hot; the topic of peace absorbed every one's thoughts, and was the sole subject of conversation. Miles crossed Lake Baikal in a steamer; he arrived at Kharbin towards the end of August. He found it had grown out of all recognition since his absence, and there was a huge new *Art Nouveau* railway station.

As soon as he arrived at Kharbin, Miles asked for leave to go to the Front, and was told it would be given to him in a few days.

Miles was glad that he had come. He asked for news of Elena at one of the hospitals, and was told that she was probably with the hospital train at Headquarters. He heard nothing at all about Alyosha. Ivanov had left, and had been replaced by another Censor, who was at Headquarters. He met none of his old friends. Linevitch, the Commander-in-Chief, did not allow officers to go to Kharbin.

The next day peace was officially announced at Kharbin. The people in the streets tore the telegrams and printed news from each other's hands.

Towards one o'clock Miles went to a new restaurant which had sprung up opposite the bank during his absence, hoping to find a friend with whom he could discuss matters. A band was playing the overture to "William Tell." The first person Miles saw as he entered the restaurant was Alyosha, who rushed up to him and greeted him with warmth: "You must have luncheon with me," he said, and he ordered some vodka and food. "Tell me all that you have been doing since you got back; I hear you talk Russian better than I do. You shall talk Russian to me, and I will talk English to you; that way we will both be learning something."

"I have been staying at Susieki," said Miles, "and I saw your sister."

"I know," said Alyosha; "Mary told me."

"Told you! Have you seen her?"

"Yes, of course; she is here in one of the hospital trains. She came out directly Valia died."

"I thought she was going to stay with her aunt."

"Perhaps she was; but none of my family ever tell the truth, if they can help it; she probably did not want the bother of explaining everything at Susieki."

"I have a message for you from Valia," said Miles; "a message he gave me for you the last time I ever saw him."

Miles felt fearfully embarrassed about delivering this message.

Alyosha, as if divining his embarrassment, said: "Perhaps he wanted to congratulate me; but I must tell you at once that what I wrote you about my new marriage being settled is no longer true. That is all over. The truth was, I found I could not leave my wife. She consented, but it was just *that* which made it impossible – and the other person was no longer willing, for the same reason. It was perhaps about that that Valia talked."

"Ye – es," said Miles, still embarrassed.

"He told you who the other person was, of course?"

"Yes, he did."

"And she, of course, said nothing?"

"Of course, nothing."

"Well, it is all over; so you need deliver no message. I am sure I know what the message was; it was 'Don't.' "

"Yes," said Miles; "but you told me it was no one I knew."

Miles did not feel quite certain there might not have been someone else.

"I thought it more comfortable for you and for me. I thought you would know without my telling. I had already told you enough before – I supposed you would be guessing."

"Not till Valia told me," said Miles, blushing.

"I see, I see, I see…" said Alyosha.

There was a pause.

"Well," Alyosha went on, "I went to Tsitsihar. I was sent there, and then to Verkhneudinsk; there I saw my wife, and I told her everything – the whole story. That the miracle had happened. She said to me: 'I understand, Alyosha. I will give you up, because I know that you do not really belong to me; why should I keep you? and if she consents to take you, I will set you free.' And when Elena knew this, she felt she could no longer marry me; and I, too, felt it would be wrong; so we said goodbye. And now I shall go back presently to Verkhneudinsk, to my cigar store; and I hope that we may live happily ever afterwards… At any rate, we have missed committing a crime. We should not have been happy. I should not have made Elena happy."

"That is what Valia said," said Miles.

"Ah, that is what Valia said?" Alyosha repeated after a pause.

"Yes; he said that of course if it had to happen, if there was no help for it, he would understand… But he told me to ask you not to do it…unless you both knew you couldn't do otherwise."

"Providence carried out his commission by means of someone else. Did you like him?"

"Yes, very much. I thought he was very clever."

"He was a very bright boy. It is a pity he has died. He was full of talent."

"Yes; all his ideas about flying."

"Oh, that… I think he might perhaps have become a good writer."

"A poet?"

"People always begin by writing poetry. I think he might have been a good writer of articles – perhaps on political economy."

"But surely he would have been more than that."

"Possibly; who knows?"

They had luncheon. Miles' impressions were confused.

The idea of giving Susieki to Elena and Alyosha as a wedding present had to be flung away. There was an end of that. What would he do with it now? He could not help asking himself whether there might not once more be a chance for him. It was more than improbable; but after all, the improbable might happen.

As soon as they had finished luncheon, Alyosha left in a hurry. He had, he said, an important official engagement. They would meet again the next day.

"I am here for the next week or two," said Alyosha, "till I go home, which will probably be soon."

Miles walked back to the hotel. There he met his business friend, Rosen, who asked him what he was doing that afternoon.

"Nothing at all," said Miles.

"Then come with us…we are going for a *partie de plaisir* on board a steamer down the Sungari," and Rosen named a banker, a General and his wife, and some others.

"Very well," said Miles.

"We must make haste," said Rosen, "because we are late."

He called a cab, and they drove down to the quay, which was some distance off.

"You will meet a charming lady," said Rosen, as they drove, "the wife of one of the officials here, a man called Zhilkov – Marya Ivanovna."

"I know her," said Miles, and the name started a new train of thought in his mind. "Has she still many admirers?"

"Oh yes, as many as usual… Vassilevski wanted to fight a duel with the head of the Customs about her last week…but it was arranged."

"Do you admire her?" asked Miles.

"Of course I do… *Nous avons tous passé par là*, but I got over it early; and once bitten – "

"But I thought," said Miles, "that her *spécialité* is to keep people."

"So it is…luckily I was inoculated…soon enough."

When they reached the steamer, which was a large one, and walked up on deck, they found a large party of people – ladies, officers, officials, and business men. The steamer was just starting. Miles was introduced to several people, some of whom he remembered meeting before.

It was not until the steamer had started that he noticed Marya Ivanovna sitting with Alyosha, apart from the others. Alyosha beckoned to him. Miles said "How do you do?" in Russian to Marya Ivanovna, and she smiled.

"How quickly you have learnt Russian, and how well you speak it!" she said, but Miles knew, in spite of her amiability, that she had no use for him.

She talked to him for a few moments, dragging him into conversation, and yet he was conscious that she was only doing this to clinch the imminence of his departure; that in a moment or two he would find himself gone. And so it happened. After the conversation had flowed on breathlessly for a few moments on various topics, Miles heard himself saying: "Goodbye for the present," and Marya Ivanovna answering, "You must look in tonight at our house for supper; Alexei Nikolayevitch will bring you."

Miles joined the others, and was introduced to a General's wife, who talked to him for the rest of the afternoon. They got back in the evening, as they were all of them invited to Marya Ivanovna's for supper. Miles dined by himself at the restaurant.

Alyosha strolled in as Miles was finishing his coffee, and sat down at his table.

"I suppose you have guessed?" said Alyosha.

"What?" asked Miles.

"Well, Marya Ivanovna."

"Has it happened?"

"Nothing has happened, except that she has made my marriage impossible. I have been lying to you; but you may as well know the truth now. I have been to Verkhneudinsk; I told my wife: she agreed... Not quite so much as I told you... She was refusing to hear of a divorce. But what I have not told you was that I was determined on the other thing, all the same...and it would have happened, but for Marya Ivanovna. I was sent here, and I saw her again. She had heard the story, partly from others, partly from myself. I have told her; and she got me back at once. As I told you, I knew she always could if she chose. She did choose; and there it was. It was seen, or guessed; of course it was all broken up, or off – how do you say?"

"I think Marya Ivanovna must be a very wicked woman."

"Wicked? Not in this case. She did it for my wife."

"I can't believe that."

"I am certain of it. The proof is, she is sending me back to Verkhneudinsk. In a fortnight's time she will no longer see me at all, and I shall never see her again."

"Really?"

"Yes, really. She has a hook in me, and she does with me what she wishes; but she has no wish to keep me. She has never loved me, not for one moment, and she never will."

"Has she ever loved anyone?"

"Yes, I think so – twice…the first time it was her first husband."

"Then Zhilkov is her second husband?"

"Yes; her first husband was high up in the railway service at Odessa. He was a great big man with huge shoulders and a red beard, and small, clever eyes. She loved him; she was afraid of him. He was clever and didn't care. He treated her like dirt, and then he died. Some people say she killed him, poisoned him – but that is silly; she is not melodramatic, and she loved him; it is false psychology – and then, later, she loved an officer, who, although quite unlike her husband, was rather the same type, big and tall and fair, with a face like a moon, rather cunning, and very stupid. She adored him because she knew he would have beaten her. He did not care either… He used to get very drunk at times, and when he was drunk he was dangerous. Then he was killed at Liao-yang…since then she has loved no one."

"And now?"

"Now there is nobody."

"Rosen told me there was nearly a duel about her the other day."

"There is nearly a duel about her once a week; but that means nothing."

"And do you care for her as much as ever?"

"Oh, more than ever… I told you before it is an incurable disease. I would give up everything and everybody for her."

"Then do you think you will really go back to Siberia?"

"Yes; but only because *she* has made up her mind that I shall, and made it impossible for me not to. She has been perfectly frank with me. She told me herself that directly she heard I might be going to be married, she made up her mind to stop it."

"But does she know your wife?"

"Not at all. But she has determined that no one else should break up my marriage – my first marriage, I mean. She is not in the least jealous of my wife."

"Then she must have some good in her."

"It is not done out of goodness. Don't you understand that she would never hate my wife, and that she would always hate anyone else?"

"I can't understand the fascination you all see in her."

"Would you like to?"

"Not at all – why?"

"I would only have to say a word to her – I should only have to tell her that – " He stopped.

"What?"

"Oh! anything; and she would make you understand…but I will not; it would be a pity. Why should she make you unhappy?"

"I am going to the Front in a few days."

"For the new war?"

"What new war?"

"They say that the peace will not be ratified; that there is a revolution in Japan, and that the General who was with us to-day has just now received orders to go to the Front tomorrow, to prepare positions…he has to arrange fortifications…so you may be just in time for another act of the war."

"Do you really think so?"

"I don't know; I have no opinions; what is the use of guessing? It is either over or it is not. We shall know soon enough."

"They say Witte will be a national hero for having made peace."

"So much the worse for him. A national hero today is a national scapegoat tomorrow."

"But do you think you ought to have gone on with the war?"

"I think it would perhaps have been no worse – a choice of evils."

"In Russia everyone is keen about politics now; nobody cares about the war. They all say great things will happen: a new Constitution – Reforms – Liberty."

"When the cat's away, the mice talk."

"Who is the cat?"

"The troops, of course."

"Then you don't believe in reforms?"

"Words, words, words. Some day the peasants will take all the land; and as for the rest of the population, they will have to choose between King Log and King Stork. If they turn out King Log, whom they have now got, they will get King Stork; he will eat them. All my politics are to be found in half a dozen old fables...it is a pity the *intelligentsia* do not lay those to heart. The peasants have done so for centuries, and invented others of their own."

"Then you don't think there will be a revolution now?"

"No; and if there is, I don't think there will be any real reform; but there will be – there are already, as you know – what they call in the history books *quelques Jacqueries* going on all over the place...and they will certainly go on till the troops get home...and then all will depend on the troops. If they *all* mutiny, well, then, *ça y est*; if not, nothing...till the next row."

"Do you think, with the disturbances that are going on, one could safely live in Russia, in the country?"

"Certainly, if you are sensible, and come to an arrangement with the peasants. You would have to sell them at least two-thirds of the land. But why do you ask?"

"Because I have bought Susieki," said Miles.

Alyosha whistled, and then laughed.

"Bought Susieki! *Aida! Molodyets!* The whole estate?"

"No, that has been sold; but the house, the garden, the stables, about fifty acres of field, and the wood."

"Well, you have astonished me," said Alyosha. "We will talk about it later; we must go to Marya Ivanovna's… I have to see someone first. I will call for you at the hotel presently."

Later on, Alyosha called for Miles. They went to the same house which Miles had visited the first time he had been at Kharbin. Zhilkov was there, and the partridge. Somebody played the piano; somebody sang; *vindt* was played; tea and vodka were drunk; supper was eaten. An officer quarrelled with one of the officials, ostensibly about politics, really about Marya Ivanovna. She took little notice of Alyosha, less of Miles, although she greeted him civilly.

Miles got home at two in the morning.

CHAPTER XXX

A week later Miles arrived at Headquarters, at Gun-chu-ling. There he met the Press Censors – Diettrich was still there, but not Ivanov – some Russian journalists, and several other acquaintances. The foreign journalists had gone home.

He asked for news of Elena Ilyin. He was told that she was with a Red Cross detachment, somewhere between advanced Headquarters and the extreme right flank of the army.

Miles telegraphed to the battery, and asked them to send horses for him to the advanced Headquarters at Go-dzia-dan, where the Commander-in-Chief was living in a train.

Three days later he arrived at Go-dzia-dan, and stayed the night there with the Russian correspondents in their railway carriage. The next morning two Cossacks reported, with a horse to take him to the battery. The battery was billeted in a village in Mongolia, about ninety miles off.

Miles started early in the morning with the Cossacks; they halted for the midday meal at an encampment of the Red Cross, and there the first person he met was Elena.

"I thought you would come, some time," she said. "You stopped at Kharbin? You saw Alyosha?"

"Yes; he is going back to Verkhneudinsk next week."

There was a silence.

"I had a letter from Karl Zygmundovitch yesterday," Elena said a moment later. "He told me what you had done. Will you ever be able to live there?"

Miles blushed and stammered.

"I don't know; I think so. I suppose so... Karl Zygmundovitch is going to look after it for me. I think my aunt will like it."

"And are you going back to England soon?"

"Oh yes, soon. I want to say goodbye to the people who were so kind to me."

"Alyosha's sister was here," said Elena, "but she went back to Kharbin yesterday. You must come and have some food. You know everyone here."

Miles had luncheon with the Red Cross. They were discussing politics; their opinions were violent. They did not believe in the new Duma that had been promised by a recent decree.

After luncheon, Miles said he must go on at once; he had far to go.

Before starting, he said goodbye to Elena. She walked with him for a few moments under the trees, while the Cossacks were getting ready.

Miles wondered whether he could say anything that would hint that his hopes lay – or had lain – in one direction; and as he was thinking of this, Elena said to him: "You think Alyosha will go back to Verkhneudinsk?"

"Yes, I think he will."

"How was he looking?"

"Very well; just the same."

"Yes, that is it; he is always just the same... He will never change; the worst of it is, no more will I."

She laughed sadly. Miles knew, once and for all, that he could never speak; and that it could never be of any use if he did, however long he lived, even if Alyosha were to die. But he now felt it easy to say: "I had hoped to give Susieki to you both as a wedding present."

"Oh!" said Elena; "I knew you could not have bought it for yourself!"

She laughed again; but there were tears in her eyes.

"You are very good, Mihal Ivanytch," she said. "But don't think it is tragic – I mean, for us. It was always impossible from the first; it could never have come off... You see it was *really* impossible... He knew, and he knew that I knew... And yet... I sometimes think that if he had come to me when I arrived from Susieki and had said...well, if he had been different...who knows what might have happened – *wife or no wife*? As it was, I found him analysing, weighing, wondering, saying, 'Perhaps after all, no'...and then I realised Marya Ivanovna's power. For once in her life she has done a good deed, although she only did it from mischief, and to keep Alyosha...and perhaps in a way for the sake of his wife. She had a kind of sense of *solidarité*, and there is a kind of *crooked straightness* about her. I admire her. I do, really. I am thankful to you, and so is Alyosha. You have done him good. I wonder whether we shall meet again; perhaps you will stop here on your way home. I expect we shall still be here, but one never knows. So now, *dosvidania*, and thank you. You must get rid of Susieki somehow; it will be a white elephant. Some merchant will take it off your hands."

"It was to prevent that that I bought it," said Miles.

He kissed Elena Nikolayevna's hand.

"Goodbye," he said.

He rode away with the two Cossacks. Elena looked at him and smiled as he waved. Miles felt inclined to cry. He had never felt so sad before. Life seemed to be over for him. All the point and salt and colour of it seemed to have vanished.

He and his Cossacks rode along till moonrise, when they arrived at a big Chinese town, where they slept in the yard.

The next morning at dawn they started again, and halted for the midday meal in a village that already seemed half Mongolian. They ate hard rusks, black bread, and drank tea. They rode along bad roads, through pools of water, till in the afternoon they reached grassy steppes. The landscape was different. Miles' horse suddenly shied violently. They had met a man on a camel. This meant they were in Mongolia. They met more natives, riding sideways on ponies, and dressed in coats of jewel-like colours: cerulean, crimson, and orange.

At eight o'clock they arrived at a town; they still had to ride two miles further to the village where the battery was billeted.

There, in a house of the kind which Miles knew so well – one-storied, and built round a quadrangle, in which there were horses, dogs, and hens – Miles found his old friends, and all the circumstance of war. The clerks were still clicking on typewriters, placed on packing cases between guttering candles; the battery cook was carrying the food – *Boeuf Strogonoff* – in a pail, with a knowing air. In the room used for the Mess, the doctor, Gerard, and one of the Cossack officers, were discussing whether Dostoyevsky was or was not a great writer; at a wooden table someone was doing a Patience; others were lying on the *kang*. Someone was reading a Moscow newspaper a month old.

"Well," they all cried out in chorus, after they had greeted him and shaken hands, and shouted for food. "Is it peace? Are you bringing us peace or war? There was fighting at the outposts yesterday."

Miles was besieged with so many questions at the same time that he could answer none.

The village was near a wood, and a wide brown river. Next door to them, in a small house, a Chinese sage was preparing students for their examination at Peking to take a degree. He taught his pupils peripatetically, and intoned Chinese lyrics in a sing-song. He wore large round horn-rimmed spectacles. A little farther on the Cossacks had built themselves a *bania*, a steam bath.

Miles was tired after his long ride; he spent the next day resting. The weather was warm; they bathed in the river. They rode; they slept; they argued; they played Patience and *vingt-*

et-un. It was a dreamy life, pleasanter than it had ever been before. They were no longer haunted by the thought of a possible move at any moment in the day or night... There was no more thought of battle, wounds, shrapnel, *shimoze*, bullets.

Heated discussions raged on internal politics; wild hopes found expression. Some of the officers said there would now be a real Constitution; that the dawn of better things was breaking. Others were pessimistic. Every day some of them rode into the town to buy provisions; there they met Greeks trading in sponges, Navy Cut cigarettes, and cheap spurious wines.

One day Miles went to the town with one of the officers and a Chinese interpreter. At the corner of one of the streets, standing near a light tripod which supported a small board, they met a man dressed in a black silk robe, embroidered with silver moons. He wore a black and silver conical cap. The interpreter said he was a magician. He was telling fortunes with small slips of carved wood that looked like paper cutters.

Miles asked to have his fortune told. He gave a coin. The wizard shook his sticks in a wooden cup, uttered a long rigmarole, threw the sticks on to the board that was before him, and interpreted their coincidence. Miles asked what it meant. The interpreter said: "Magician he say you go home west-way, and you have obstacles. You get, one sun, two suns, message from home, letter, quick news. Bad news. You lose plenty money. Bad man he burn your house."

"And then?" asked Miles.

"Magician he say no can prophesy more than hundred days."

They went home, and Miles wondered.

There was no letter awaiting him when he got back. The next day was fine and hot. He forgot the gloomy fancies that the Chinese wizard's words had set buzzing in his head.

It was so hot that they all went to bathe in the river. That evening there was one of those pink sunsets and mauve twilights that Miles had learned to love so much – a large misty moon hanging over the delicate willow-trees and turning the water to silver. Miles walked home with Gérard and the doctor. The doctor was delighted to be able to talk Russian to Miles now; he poured out to him his hopes for the future. He was hopeful. That night some guests came to dine and sleep. The battery entertained them as well as they could with the material at their disposal; after supper they played cards.

The next day was colder; the autumn suddenly made itself felt. They moved into the town. The village was not fit for cold weather.

That evening a telegram came for Miles. it ran thus:

"Poor Saxby died suddenly. Heart. Please come
home at once. Urgent. Writing Moscow,
Consul."

Miles said goodbye to his friends. He started the next morning for Gun-chu-ling with some of the officers. They stopped at the town where he had spent the night on his way out; from there they went by a light field railway to Gun-chu-ling, and thence by train to Kharbin. Thus it was that Miles could not stop at the Red Cross detachment. He did not see Elena Ilyin again. At Kharbin he met Alyosha. Miles told him his news.

· "You will have to go home, and manage your business," said Alyosha. "Your leave is over; but it has been worth it. What will you do with Susieki?"

" I will give it to you, if you like," said Miles. "Or you could be my steward, if you like, and manage it for me."

As soon as he had said this, he felt he had made a mistake. Alyosha could, of course, not bear to live at Susieki, unless he lived there with Elena.

"It is very kind, but I couldn't live there. I must go back to Verkhneudinsk. You must sell it. You must get Karl

Zygmundovitch to sell it for you. He will cheat you, but no matter. Men – and especially you – are made to be cheated."

"I shall not sell it unless I am obliged to," said Miles. "I will come out next summer, and – " he stammered.

"I am obliged to go to Moscow," said Alyosha, "on a matter of business for my Aunt Kitty; so I will come as far as Moscow with you. We will go together to Susieki. I should like to see it once more, and to see it with you."

So two days later Miles and Alyosha started for Moscow.

Thanks to Alyosha, they had comfortable seats in the train. The journey was uneventful till they reached Irkutsk and beyond.

At Verkhneudinsk, Alyosha's wife came to meet him at the station. She was short, fair, and had light-blue sensible eyes. One could not call her pretty, but she was engaging; she had no pretence to any kind of elegance. But she reminded Miles of some of the pictures of the Empress Catharine. She wore a cheap astrakan jacket and an astrakan cap. There was nothing in the least common about her, and no sort of nonsense. She was as transparent as crystal.

The moment she kissed Alyosha on the platform, and shook hands with Miles, smiling, and saying she had heard a lot about him, Miles saw how impossible it would have been for Alyosha to leave her – out of the question. The train did not stop long at the station; they sat in the waiting-room and drank tea. Anna Ivanovna – that was her name – told them the local news.

When it was time for them to go, Anna Ivanovna shook hands warmly with Miles, and said with a friendly smile: "You must come and stay with us here when you come back. Of course you will come back."

Alyosha told her about Susieki. She laughed and said: "It is a good idea, only Mihal Ivanovitch will be lonely without some-one to look after him. We must find a nice Russian wife for him. A Russian wife is just what he needs. He might marry Olga Dimitrievna."

She kissed Alyosha and blessed him, and said goodbye to Miles.

Miles and Alyosha passed Irkutsk, crossed the Urals and the Volga, and arrived at the small town of Kuznetsk, where the train came to a stop owing to a strike which had broken out all over the country. They were held up at this small station for four days; on the fourth day they got a stage further. Finally, they arrived at Moscow late in the night on October 30th (October 17th, Old Style), the day on which Russia had been granted an ambiguous charter which altered the course of her history.

The town was dark when they arrived, the strike only just over, but the next morning the town was decorated with flags; but many people felt that the serious troubles were only just about to begin; there was little real gaiety, in spite of public manifestations. The "Marseillaise" was played at restaurants as well as the National Anthem.

Miles went to the Consulate, and there he found several letters from Aunt Fanny.

Saxby's illness had been sudden.

He had had a mild attack of pleurisy, and had thought nothing of it; it had turned to pneumonia; even then his wife had thought that with careful nursing he would soon get better. He had then had a heart attack, and had died twelve hours later.

This was not all. He had left the affairs of the old-standing house of Consterdine in a deplorable condition, owing to his conservative methods of handling the business. He had been too proud to admit that all was not well; he had actually, since Miles' absence, paid Miles' dividends out of his own pocket, and had seriously undermined his own private fortune and that of his children. Aunt Fanny had heard all this from the head clerk. Miles, she said, would have to take the business seriously in hand for his own sake, as well as for Saxby's children – she might have said, for herself also, but she did not.

Miles would have to come back at once; he realised he must now work hard for his living. He would have to sell the house at Madeira; even that would not fill the gap in his fortune, for there was Susieki, about which Aunt Fanny knew nothing as yet. Miles would need every penny he could scrape together.

He told Alyosha the news.

"I shall have to go home at once," he said; "but I can't go before I see Karl Zygmundovitch, and settle things with him, or at least make arrangements for the future."

They sent the steward a telegram, and started for Susieki that night.

When they got there, they were met at the station by Karl Zygmundovitch.

"I have bad news for you, Mihal Ivanytch," he said. "The house is burnt down. Last night there were some celebrations in the village – a wedding – everyone was out. Ivan was drunk, and so was his father. Somehow or other, the house caught fire, and it has been burnt to the ground. It was an accident. The people from the village did their best to put out the fire, but they were, of course, too late."

" Let us go and see it," said Miles.

He felt indifferent. One thing more or less, what did it matter now?

They drove to the house in the steward's carriage. Up past the pond and the lime trees, up the drive past the lilac bushes and the flower beds, which were still bright and gay with dishevelled asters and dahlias.

There was a charred remnant of smoking ruins; the creeper on the stone steps of the verandah was still intact.

"We saved what furniture and what things we could," said Karl Zygmundovitch.

Spread out on the grass there were oil paintings, books, pictures, an old harp, china, cutlery, an astronomical globe, a cup and ball, and various miscellaneous objects. Miles noticed the *Melodies of Thomas Moore*, for Harp and Pianoforte; some

bound volumes of *Punch, Le Journal de la Jeunesse*; some
French picture books telling the adventures of *M. Jabot* and *M.
Vieux Bois*, and a little old edition of Goethe. There, too, was a
straw hat that had hung in the hall, and that Elena had often
worn in the garden; and there, too, a malacca cane with a gold
band round it which she had told him that her Uncle Pierre had
bought in Paris.

"I am having all this stuff removed to my house," said Karl
Zygmundovitch; and at that moment two of the stablemen
came to fetch a fresh load of effects, which they began to pile
on to a cart.

"I have already sent down two loads," said Karl
Zygmundovitch.

"Of course a great many things were destroyed – most of the
china and cutlery – and a large portrait in the sitting-room of
Pyotr Ivanytch's father; but it is a wonder that so much
was saved."

"Let us go to the garden," said Alyosha. "We will leave Karl
Zygmundovitch to finish his business; we will come back
directly."

Miles and Alyosha walked down to the pond; they sat for a
moment under a large, faded lime tree in silence; they watched
the stagnant water, on which the yellow leaves were floating.
After a while they got up and walked through the wood; they
walked through the damp undergrowth till they could see the
river through the trees, which were ragged now, and crimson
and yellow. Here and there a fir tree showed up black against
the tattered foliage. It was a still autumn day. There was
moisture in the air, and the smell of burning weeds. They had
neither of them spoken a word until Alyosha said suddenly:
"That was a woodcock; did you see it? We used to shoot here
once upon a time."

"Do you think it was an accident?" asked Miles.

"The fire? Very likely; but the result is the same, if it was or if it wasn't. We must go back now, and talk business. It is here I used to walk with Elena. I am glad to have seen it once more."

They walked back to the house, and round it. The final cartload of effects was being sent off. There was nothing left.

"I am afraid the books have been damaged," said Karl Zygmundovitch. "The water from the fire engine did more damage than the fire. I will show you what we have saved at my house."

They walked to Karl Zygmundovitch's house, which was close by. There they inspected the property. Many pieces of furniture had been saved, although the upper storey had been completely destroyed.

"The men worked well," said Karl Zygmundovitch; "the fire engine arrived immediately; there was no difficulty about water, but Pyotr Ilyitch will be sad. We were just going to pack up and send him the things he wished to keep."

They had a heavy meal, and when it was over Alyosha said: "Now to talk business."

He and the steward started a long discussion, most of which was unintelligible to Miles...

Karl Zygmundovitch was instructed to get rid of the land on which the house stood, at the best possible price, as soon as possible... When everything was settled, Miles and Alyosha drove back to the station, and caught the afternoon train for Moscow, arriving there early the next morning.

Miles took a ticket for London. He started the same evening. Alyosha met him at the station.

"I have finished Aunt Kitty's business," said Alyosha. "I shall start the day after tomorrow for Verkhneudinsk; I shall not come back to Europe, or to European Russia, for a long time – perhaps never; but I daresay we may meet again – one never knows. You may come back to Russia quite soon, or even to the Far East."

"I don't think it is at all probable," said Miles.

"It was improbable your coming here at all."

"Yes," said Miles. "If I hadn't spilt some soda water, it would never have happened."

"Perhaps you will spill some more soda water on some other person."

"Will you go straight back to Verkhneudinsk?" asked Miles.

"Yes; I shall not go on to Kharbin; Marya Ivanovna and her husband have been transferred to Vladivostok."

"And your uncle and aunt – won't you ever see them?"

"Go to Nice? Or Paris? It will be difficult; I may meet them one summer – if they go to Germany or Switzerland – if I can get away for a holiday. It will depend on my business – although I am well off now. I have done well out of the war – quite well. I have made myself a position. I was highly commended."

Miles felt a lump in his throat as the time for saying goodbye to Alyosha drew near. They went into the buffet and ordered some vodka, and drank three final toasts: the first to each other, the second to the future, and the third to Elena Nikolayevna.

The first bell had rung; they walked to the railway carriage and stood outside it.

"If ever you should come to London," said Miles, "Consterdine & Co. will always find me in the City."

At that moment, Bloum and Elizaveta Ivanovna came rushing up. They had come to say goodbye to Miles. Miles had been to see them the day before, but they had not been at home. He had left a note, saying he was leaving the next day, and telling them his train.

Miles introduced Alyosha to the Bloums. They exchanged civilities.

"To think of Mihal Ivanovitch going now, just as it is beginning to be interesting here! And just as he is beginning to talk Russian so well!" said Elizaveta Ivanovna.

"I am afraid things may soon become too interesting," said Miles.

"No! no!" said Bloum cheerfully; "things are really getting worse. If only Witte would resign! The worse things are, the better; that is what I have always said."

"How is everybody?" asked Miles – "Wilson, Roberts, and your niece, and Vera Petrovna?"

"My Englishmen are very well," said Elizaveta Ivanovna – "but Vera Petrovna! Oh! alas! alas! Poor child! poor thing!" She wrung her hands.

"Why, what has happened to her?" asked Miles.

"Shot herself, poor child! Last Sunday. She quarrelled with her brother over the estate; she wanted to make over the land to her peasants; her brother refused. He is a hard man, an out-and-out reactionary. So she made a will, leaving her land to the peasants, all of it – and she shot herself near Chehov's monument on Sunday afternoon. Now they say the will must be annulled, because she committed suicide! Of course they will annul it! Liza is almost out of her mind on account of it all!"

"I am so sorry," said Miles.

The second bell rang.

"Well, we mustn't keep you," said Elizaveta Ivanovna, glancing at Alyosha. She and Bloum said goodbye, and she gave Miles her blessing. Elizaveta Ivanovna made the Sign of the Cross; she also gave him a little holy medal, and then left him alone with his friend.

Miles shook hands a last time with Alyosha. He got into the carriage, opened the window, and leant out.

"You don't regret the time you have spent here?" said Alyosha. "If you had stayed at home, your disasters would probably not have happened."

"It was well worth it," said Miles. "It was *all* worth it. Whatever happens, it will have been worth it."

Miles meant it, thinking, as he spoke, of his brief romance, so sweet while it lasted; so suddenly, so irretrievably shattered: a little casket of dreams he had burnt and buried under the birch trees at Susieki.

He would not now have had it otherwise, even if he could –
not for worlds.

"At any rate you have had leave," said Alyosha; "leave to live,
as Aunt Lizzy said in Paris."

"That's Shakespeare," said Miles. "You see, thanks to your
aunts, I've read Shakespeare:

> " 'If tinkers may have leave to live,
> And bear the sow-skin budget,
> Then my account I well may give,
> And in the stocks avouch it.' "

"*Les beaux esprits se rencontrent*," said Alyosha. "Well, you
escaped, like a schoolboy; played truant; went to the *École
Buissonnière* for the time. You may never have such a
chance again."

The third bell rang. It sounded like a knell to Miles. He knew
that his leave was over. He was going back to school.

"Goodbye, Alyosha," he said, "and thank you again for
everything. I suppose, if there is another war somewhere else,
you couldn't possibly go to it?"

The train began to move.

"Why not?" said Alyosha.

MAURICE BARING

'C'

Baring's homage to a decadent and carefree Edwardian age depicts a society as yet untainted by the traumas and complexities of twentieth-century living. With wit and subtlety a happy picture is drawn of family life, house parties in the country and a leisured existence clouded only by the rumblings of the Boer War. Against this spectacle Caryl Bramsley (the *C* of the title) is presented – a young man of terrific promise but scant achievement, whose tragic-comic tale offsets the privileged milieu.

CAT'S CRADLE

This sophisticated and intricate novel, based on true events, takes place in the late nineteenth century and begins with Henry Clifford, a man of taste and worldly philosophy, whose simple determination to do as he likes and live as he wishes is threatened when his daughter falls in love with an unsuitable man. With subtle twists and turns in a fascinating portrait of society, Maurice Baring conveys the moral that love is too strong to be overcome by mere mortals.

MAURICE BARING

THE COAT WITHOUT SEAM

The story of a miraculous relic, believed to be a piece of the seamless coat won by a soldier on Mount Golgotha after Jesus of Nazareth's crucifixion, captivates young Christopher Trevenen after his sister dies tragically and motivates the very core of his existence from then on, culminating in a profound and tragic realization.

DAPHNE ADEANE

Barrister Basil Wake and his arresting wife Hyacinth lead a well-appointed existence in the social whirl of London's early 1900s. For eight years Hyacinth has conducted a most discreet affair with Parliamentarian Michael Choyce, who seems to fit into the Wakes' lives so conveniently. But an invitation to attend a Private View and a startling portrait of the mysterious and beautiful Daphne Adeane signifies a change in this comfortable set-up.

MAURICE BARING

IN MY END IS MY BEGINNING

This historical novel tells the tragic story of Mary Queen of Scots, from her childhood until the beginning of her end, whose unwise marital and political actions provoked rebellion among Scottish nobles and forced her to flee to England, where she was beheaded as a Roman Catholic threat to the throne. The clash of opinion over whether Mary was a martyr or a murderess is perfectly represented by four eye-witnesses (The Four Maries – her ladies-in-waiting) who narrate this captivating story with distinctive conclusions.

THE PUPPET SHOW OF MEMORY

It was into the famous and powerful Baring family of merchant bankers that Maurice Baring was born in 1874, the seventh of eight children. A man of immense subtlety and style, Baring absorbed every drop of culture that his fortunate background showered upon him; in combination with his many natural talents and prolific writing this assured him a place in literary history.

In this classic autobiography, spanning a remarkable period of history, Maurice Baring shares the details of an inspirational childhood in nineteenth-century England and a varied adulthood all over the world, collecting new friends and remarkable experiences. It has been said that Baring's greatest talent was for discovering the best in people, that he had a genius for friendship, and in this superb book his erudition and perception are abundantly clear.

'A classic autobiography' *Dictionary of National Biography*

OTHER TITLES BY MAURICE BARING AVAILABLE DIRECT FROM HOUSE OF STRATUS

Quantity	£	$(US)	$(CAN)	€
'C'	8.99	16.50	24.95	16.50
CAT'S CRADLE	8.99	16.50	24.95	16.50
THE COAT WITHOUT SEAM	8.99	16.50	24.95	16.50
DAPHNE ADEANE	8.99	16.50	24.95	16.50
IN MY END IS MY BEGINNING	8.99	16.50	24.95	16.50
THE PUPPET SHOW OF MEMORY	8.99	16.50	24.95	16.50

ALL HOUSE OF STRATUS BOOKS ARE AVAILABLE FROM GOOD BOOKSHOPS OR DIRECT FROM THE PUBLISHER:

Internet: www.houseofstratus.com including author interviews, reviews, features.

Email: sales@houseofstratus.com please quote author, title, and credit card details.

Hotline: UK ONLY: 0800 169 1780, please quote author, title and credit card details.
INTERNATIONAL: +44 (0) 20 7494 6400, please quote author, title and credit card details.

Send to: House of Stratus Sales Department
24c Old Burlington Street
London
W1X 1RL
UK

Please allow for postage costs charged per order plus an amount per book as set out in the tables below:

	£(Sterling)	$(US)	$(CAN)	€(Euros)
Cost per order				
UK	1.50	2.25	3.50	2.50
Europe	3.00	4.50	6.75	5.00
North America	3.00	4.50	6.75	5.00
Rest of World	3.00	4.50	6.75	5.00
Additional cost per book				
UK	0.50	0.75	1.15	0.85
Europe	1.00	1.50	2.30	1.70
North America	2.00	3.00	4.60	3.40
Rest of World	2.50	3.75	5.75	4.25

PLEASE SEND CHEQUE, POSTAL ORDER (STERLING ONLY), EUROCHEQUE, OR INTERNATIONAL MONEY ORDER (PLEASE CIRCLE METHOD OF PAYMENT YOU WISH TO USE)
MAKE PAYABLE TO: STRATUS HOLDINGS plc

Cost of book(s): —————————— Example: 3 x books at £6.99 each: £20.97

Cost of order: —————————— Example: £2.00 (Delivery to UK address)

Additional cost per book: ————— Example: 3 x £0.50: £1.50

Order total including postage: ——— Example: £24.47

Please tick currency you wish to use and add total amount of order:

☐ £ (Sterling)   ☐ $ (US)   ☐ $ (CAN)   ☐ € (EUROS)

VISA, MASTERCARD, SWITCH, AMEX, SOLO, JCB:

☐☐☐☐☐☐☐☐☐☐☐☐☐☐☐☐☐☐☐☐

Issue number (Switch only):

☐☐☐

Start Date: **Expiry Date:**

☐☐ / ☐☐   ☐☐ / ☐☐

Signature: _____

NAME: _____

ADDRESS: _____

_____

POSTCODE: _____

Please allow 28 days for delivery.

Prices subject to change without notice.
Please tick box if you do not wish to receive any additional information. ☐

House of Stratus publishes many other titles in this genre; please check our website (**www.houseofstratus.com**) for more details.